MURDER FOR REVENGE

EDITED BY OTTO PENZLER

Delacorte ☰ Press

Published by
Delacorte Press
Bantam Doubleday Dell Publishing Group, Inc.
1540 Broadway
New York, New York 10036

"Like a Bone in the Throat" by Lawrence Block © 1998
by Lawrence Block
"Power Play" by Mary Higgins Clark © 1998 by Mary Higgins Clark
"Fatherhood" by Thomas H. Cook © 1998 by Thomas H. Cook
"West End" by Vicki Hendricks © 1998 by Vicki Hendricks
"Caveat Emptor" by Joan Hess © 1998 by Joan Hess
"Eradicum Homo Horribilus" by Judith Kelman © 1998
by Judith Kelman
"Dead Cat Bounce" by Eric Lustbader © 1998 by Eric Lustbader
"Angie's Delight" by Phillip Margolin © 1998 by Phillip Margolin
"Front Man" by David Morrell © 1998 by David Morrell
"Murder-Two" by Joyce Carol Oates © 1998 by The Ontario Review Press
"The Enemy" by Shel Silverstein © 1998 by Shel Silverstein
"Mr. Clubb and Mr. Cuff" by Peter Straub © 1998 by Peter Straub

Copyright © 1998 by Otto Penzler

Library of Congress Cataloging in Publication Data
Murder for revenge / edited by Otto Penzler.
p. cm.
Contents: Like a bone in the throat / Lawrence Block—Power play / Mary
Higgins Clark—Fatherhood / Thomas H. Cook—West end / Vicki Hendricks—
Caveat emptor / Joan Hess—Eradicum homo horribilus / Judith Kelman—Dead
cat bounce / Eric Lustbader—Angie's delight / Phillip Margolin—Front man /
David Morrell—Murder-two / Joyce Carol Oates—The enemy / Shel
Silverstein—Mr. Clubb and Mr. Cuff / Peter Straub.
ISBN 0-385-31715-8
1. Detective and mystery stories, American. I. Penzler, Otto.
PS648.D4M859 1998
813'.087208—dc21   97-35945
CIP

Book Design by Barbara Berger

Manufactured in the United States of America

Published simultaneously in Canada

April 1998

10 9 8 7 6 5 4 3 2 1
BVG

To Nat Sobel—
whose friendship, creativity, and loyalty
can never be repaid.

Contents
▼▼▼

Introduction

▼▼▼

BY OTTO PENZLER

Is there a more human emotion than revenge? In fact, does any other life-form known to us engage in revenge, or even consider it?

Animals kill other animals for food, or self-defense, or for power, for rank within the community. But for revenge? No.

Humans, on the other hand, have engaged in this activity through all of recorded history. There have been many motivations for seeking revenge—political and financial, for example—but it is unlikely that any desire for revenge has been more frequently dragged from the center of a person's soul than the anguish of lost love.

Whether that love is taken away by a decision of the beloved or surreptitiously stolen by a rival lover, or heinously and permanently erased by a murderer of that love object, the passion for revenge springs readily into the heart to avenge that greatest of all losses. Power and money can often be acquired anew, but a lost love is almost always gone forever, and the frustration of that stolen joy may easily suggest the notion of vengeance.

Now, it is common for good and gentle people to whisper calmly that such thoughts should be banished from the mind. What good, they ask, can come of it? Seeking vengeance cannot return the lost, stolen, diminished, or vanished object of desire.

True, of course, else animals would certainly engage in acts of vengeance to retrieve their slaughtered pups or chicks or whatever their dead and consumed offspring are called. Mates of those once beloved that have served as meals for their predators would surely find a way to avenge their grief if they instinctively knew it would serve a useful purpose. But that is a pragmatist's view of revenge and has no bearing on this matter.

As there are levels of all emotions, so there are levels of revenge and the desire—indeed, the *need*—for it. We are not concerned here with the hard foul on a basketball court that requires an even harder foul at the opposite end of the court. This book isn't about a petty slight that inspires an immediate response of an equally trivial nature.

No, here we are dealing with wrongs of such magnitude that the heart fills with bile and hatred until it overflows. Such venomous fury cannot be controlled and the only suitable response is the most extreme that a man or woman can deliver: murder, or perhaps more accurately, death, because it is possible that revenge is proper and necessary and the word *murder* hints strongly at wrongdoing.

The tricky part of being a single force of policeman, judge, jury, and executioner is the lack of checks and balances. There is no voice of reason, no softening influence of distance, no notion of charity. When the white-hot lava of hate spews out of the heart, the injured has no focus beyond revenge and is blind to any other consideration.

"Vengeance is mine; I will repay." Well, it's a pretty clear thought and it glows like the brightest neon on the brain of the avenger. There are some, of course, who recall that this was said (or at least quoted as having been said) by the Lord, not by an out-of-control, grief-consumed human being who may not be best able to plot the most appropriate course of action.

Murder for Revenge offers different points of view. Some stories suggest (well, no, actually they shout) that revenge inevitably doubles back to the vengeful, causing greater harm than the initial injury. Other authors illustrate the comfort and justice that can be derived from unleashing the tethered rage of the innocent victim. And some even suggest that there's something to be said for going either way, neither way being flawless; some might say this approach is kind of wimpy, but it's pretty much the way the world works, if you ask me.

But see for yourself the many nuances of revenge offered in this wonderful (I can say that because I didn't write it) book. Shel Silverstein's story/poem/tale/fable/whatever is not unlike John Dickson Carr's locked-room lecture, in which he offers more varieties of a solution to a complex problem than most people dare dream about. Peter Straub became so mesmerized with the endlessly delicious possibilities of revenge that his short story stretched into a memorable novella. Thomas H. Cook said he hadn't written a short story in such a long time that he didn't know if he could even do it again and, within fifteen minutes of nonstop eating, drinking, and talking, came up with the extraordinary little gem that awaits you. David Morrell said he had just finished a story that was based on a real-life figure, causing him such outrage that he had to write it as a piece of fiction to free himself from the anger that injustice instills in some.

However you feel about revenge, you will find a story in these pages that will support your view, and another that will make you blink and reconsider. It is a tribute to the strength of this visceral emotion that it has produced such powerful evocations of a fundamental human passion.

Otto Penzler

Lawrence Block

Rapidly becoming one of the most honored authors in America, Lawrence Block has accomplished a rare trifecta. He is equally admired by critics, readers, and his fellow mystery writers. Men like his work, women like his work, American readers like his work, readers around the world like his work. He writes tough hard-boiled novels about Matthew Scudder that have legions of fans. He writes comedic soft-boiled novels about Bernie Rhodenbarr that have legions of fans. Can the man do no wrong?

Well, no. Stephen King once called him the only worthy successor to John D. MacDonald, and Matt Scudder the only worthy successor to Travis McGee, which is pretty good company. Irritatingly, he is also a very fast writer, though he hates to admit it.

When he was very young (not really that long ago), he wrote a full-length novel starting on Friday night to meet a Monday deadline. He casually mentioned once that he was going to a retreat for a month to write his next novel. I asked how it was possible to write a book that fast. His friend Donald Westlake said the biggest problem was what he would do to occupy the last two weeks.

Block wrote one of the half-dozen best mystery short stories of the past decade, ''By the Dawn's Early Light,'' and the following suspense story is a worthy successor.

Like a Bone in the Throat

BY LAWRENCE BLOCK

Throughout the trial Paul Dandridge did the same thing every day. He wore a suit and tie, and he occupied a seat toward the front of the courtroom, and his eyes, time and time again, returned to the man who had killed his sister.

He was never called upon to testify. The facts were virtually undisputed, the evidence overwhelming. The defendant, William Charles Croydon, had abducted Dandridge's sister at knifepoint as she walked from the college library to her off-campus apartment. He had taken her to an isolated and rather primitive cabin in the woods, where he had subjected her to repeated sexual assaults over a period of three days, at the conclusion of which he had caused her death—by manual strangulation.

Croydon took the stand in his own defense. He was a handsome young man who'd spent his thirtieth birthday in a jail cell awaiting trial, and his preppy good looks had already brought him letters and photographs and even a few marriage proposals from women of all ages. (Paul Dandridge was twenty-seven at the time. His sister, Karen, had been twenty when she died. The trial ended just weeks before her twenty-first birthday.)

On the stand, William Croydon claimed that he had no recollection of choking the life out of Karen Dandridge, but allowed as how he had no choice but to believe he'd done it. According to his testimony, the young woman had willingly accompanied him to the remote cabin, and had been an enthusiastic sexual partner with a penchant for rough sex. She had also supplied some particularly strong marijuana with hallucinogenic properties and had insisted that he smoke it with her. At one point, after indulging heavily in the unfamiliar drug, he had lost consciousness and awakened later to find his partner beside him, dead.

His first thought, he'd told the court, was that someone had broken into the cabin while he was sleeping, had killed Karen, and might return to kill him. Accordingly he'd panicked and rushed out of there, abandoning Karen's corpse. Now, faced with all the evidence arrayed against him, he was compelled to believe he had somehow committed this awful crime, although he had no recollection of it whatsoever, and although it was utterly foreign to his nature.

The district attorney, prosecuting this case himself, tore Croydon apart on cross-examination. He cited the bite marks on the victim's breasts, the rope burns indicating prolonged restraint, the steps Croydon had taken in an attempt to conceal his presence in the cabin. "You must be right," Croydon would admit, with a shrug and a sad smile. "All I can say is that I don't remember any of it."

The jury was eleven to one for conviction right from the jump, but it took six hours to make it unanimous. *Mr. Foreman, have you reached a verdict? We have, Your Honor. On the sole count of the indictment, murder in the first degree, how do you find? We find the defendant, William Charles Croydon, guilty.*

One woman cried out. A couple of others sobbed. The DA

accepted congratulations. The defense attorney put an arm around his client. Paul Dandridge, his jaw set, looked at Croydon.

Their eyes met, and Paul Dandridge tried to read the expression in the killer's eyes. But he couldn't make it out.

Two weeks later, at the sentencing hearing, Paul Dandridge got to testify.

He talked about his sister, and what a wonderful person she had been. He spoke of the brilliance of her intellect, the gentleness of her spirit, the promise of her young life. He spoke of the effect of her death upon him. They had lost both parents, he told the court, and Karen was all the family he'd had in the world. And now she was gone. In order for his sister to rest in peace, and in order for him to get on with his own life, he urged that her murderer be sentenced to death.

Croydon's attorney argued that the case did not meet the criteria for the death penalty, that while his client possessed a criminal record he had never been charged with a crime remotely of this nature, and that the rough-sex-and-drugs defense carried a strong implication of mitigating circumstances. Even if the jury had rejected the defense, surely the defendant ought to be spared the ultimate penalty, and justice would be best served if he were sentenced to life in prison.

The DA pushed hard for the death penalty, contending that the rough-sex defense was the cynical last-ditch stand of a remorseless killer, and that the jury had rightly seen that it was wholly without merit. Although her killer might well have taken drugs, there was no forensic evidence to indicate that Karen Dandridge herself had been under the influence of anything other than a powerful and ruthless murderer. Karen Dandridge needed to be avenged, he maintained, and society needed to be assured that her killer would never, ever, be able to do it again.

Paul Dandridge was looking at Croydon when the judge pronounced the sentence, hoping to see something in those cold blue eyes. But as the words were spoken—*death by lethal injection*—there was nothing for Paul to see. Croydon closed his eyes.

When he opened them a moment later, there was no expression to be seen in them.

They made you fairly comfortable on Death Row. Which was just as well, because in this state you could sit there for a long time. A guy serving a life sentence could make parole and be out on the street in a lot less time than a guy on Death Row could run out of appeals. In that joint alone, there were four men with more than ten years apiece on Death Row, and one who was closing in on twenty.

One of the things they'd let Billy Croydon have was a typewriter. He'd never learned to type properly, the way they taught you in typing class, but he was writing enough these days so that he was getting pretty good at it, just using two fingers on each hand. He wrote letters to his lawyer, and he wrote letters to the women who wrote to him. It wasn't too hard to keep them writing, but the trick lay in getting them to do what he wanted. They wrote plenty of letters, but he wanted them to write really hot letters, describing in detail what they'd done with other guys in the past, and what they'd do if by some miracle they could be in his cell with him now.

They sent pictures, too, and some of them were good looking and some of them were not. "That's a great picture," he would write back, "but I wish I had one that showed more of your physical beauty." It turned out to be surprisingly easy to get most of them to send increasingly revealing pictures. Before long he had them buying Polaroid cameras with timers and posing in obedience to his elaborate instructions. They'd do anything, the bitches, and he was sure they got off on it too.

Today, though, he didn't feel like writing to any of them. He rolled a sheet of paper into the typewriter and looked at it, and the image that came to him was the grim face of that hard-ass brother of Karen Dandridge's. What was his name, anyway? Paul, wasn't it?

"Dear Paul," he typed, and frowned for a moment in concentration. Then he started typing again.

"Sitting here in this cell waiting for the day to come when they put a needle in my arm and flush me down God's own toilet, I found myself thinking about your testimony in court. I remember how you said your sister was a good-hearted girl who spent her short life bringing pleasure to everyone who knew her. According to your testimony, knowing this helped you rejoice in her life at the same time that it made her death so hard to take.

"Well, Paul, in the interest of helping you rejoice some more, I thought I'd tell you just how much pleasure your little sister brought to me. I've got to tell you that in all my life I never got more pleasure from anybody. My first look at Karen brought me pleasure, just watching her walk across campus, just looking at those jiggling tits and that tight little ass and imagining the fun I was going to have with them.

"Then when I had her tied up in the backseat of the car with her mouth taped shut, I have to say she went on being a real source of pleasure. Just looking at her in the rearview mirror was enjoyable, and from time to time I would stop the car and lean into the back to run my hands over her body. I don't think she liked it much, but I enjoyed it enough for the both of us.

"Tell me something, Paul. Did you ever fool around with Karen yourself? I bet you did. I can picture her when she was maybe eleven, twelve years old, with her little titties just beginning to bud out, and you'd have been seventeen or eighteen yourself, so how could you stay away from her? She's sleeping and you walk into her room and sit on the edge of her bed. . . ."

He went on, describing the scene he imagined, and it excited him more than the pictures or letters from the women. He stopped and thought about relieving his excitement but decided to wait. He finished the scene as he imagined it and went on:

"Paul, old buddy, if you didn't get any of that you were

missing a good thing. I can't tell you the pleasure I got out of your sweet little sister. Maybe I can give you some idea by describing our first time together." And he did, recalling it all to mind, savoring it in his memory, reliving it as he typed it out on the page.

"I suppose you know she was no virgin," he wrote, "but she was pretty new at it all the same. And then when I turned her facedown, well, I can tell you she'd never done *that* before. She didn't like it much either. I had the tape off her mouth and I swear I thought she'd wake the neighbors, even though there weren't any. I guess it hurt her some, Paul, but that was just an example of your darling sister sacrificing everything to give pleasure to others, just like you said. And it worked, because I had a hell of a good time."

God, this was great. It really brought it all back.

"Here's the thing," he wrote. "The more we did it, the better it got. You'd think I would have grown tired of her, but I didn't. I wanted to keep on having her over and over again forever, but at the same time I felt this urgent need to finish it, because I knew that would be the best part.

"And I wasn't disappointed, Paul, because the most pleasure your sister ever gave anybody was right at the very end. I was on top of her, buried in her to the hilt, and I had my hands wrapped around her neck. And the ultimate pleasure came with me squeezing and looking into her eyes and squeezing harder and harder and going on looking into those eyes all the while and watching the life go right out of them."

He was too excited now. He had to stop and relieve himself. Afterward he read the letter and got excited all over again. A great letter, better than anything he could get any of his bitches to write to him, but he couldn't send it, not in a million years.

Not that it wouldn't be a pleasure to rub the brother's nose in it. Without the bastard's testimony, he might have stood a good chance to beat the death sentence. With it, he was sunk.

Still, you never knew. Appeals would take a long time. Maybe he could do himself a little good here.

He rolled a fresh sheet of paper in the typewriter. "Dear Mr. Dandridge," he wrote. "I'm well aware that the last thing on earth you want to read is a letter from me. I know that in your place I would feel no different myself. But I cannot seem to stop myself from reaching out to you. Soon I'll be strapped down onto a gurney and given a lethal injection. That frightens me horribly, but I'd gladly die a thousand times over if only it would bring your sister back to life. I may not remember killing her, but I know I must have done it, and I would give anything to undo it. With all my heart, I wish she were alive today."

Well, that last part was true, he thought. He wished to God she were alive, and right there in that cell with him, so that he could do her all over again, start to finish.

He went on and finished the letter, making it nothing but an apology, accepting responsibility, expressing remorse. It wasn't a letter that sought anything, not even forgiveness, and it struck him as a good opening shot. Probably nothing would ever come of it, but you never knew.

After he'd sent it off, he took out the first letter he'd written and read it through, relishing the feelings that coursed through him and strengthened him. He'd keep this, maybe even add to it from time to time. It was really great the way it brought it all back.

Paul destroyed the first letter.

He opened it, unaware of its source, and was a sentence or two into it before he realized what he was reading. It was, incredibly, a letter from the man who had killed his sister.

He felt a chill. He wanted to stop reading but he couldn't stop reading. He forced himself to stay with it all the way to the end.

The nerve of the man. The unadulterated gall.

Expressing remorse. Saying how sorry he was. Not asking for anything, not trying to justify himself, not attempting to disavow responsibility.

But there had been no remorse in the blue eyes, and Paul didn't believe there was a particle of genuine remorse in the letter either. And what difference did it make if there was?

Karen was dead. Remorse wouldn't bring her back.

His lawyer had told him they had nothing to worry about, they were sure to get a stay of execution. The appeal process, always drawn out in capital cases, was in its early days. They'd get the stay in plenty of time, and the clock would start ticking all over again.

And it wasn't as though it got to the point where they were asking him what he wanted for a last meal. That happened sometimes; there was a guy three cells down who'd had his last meal twice already, but it didn't get that close for Billy Croydon. Two and a half weeks to go and the stay came through.

That was a relief, but at the same time he almost wished it had run out a little closer to the wire. Not for his benefit, but just to keep a couple of his correspondents on the edges of their chairs.

Two of them, actually. One was a fat girl who lived at home with her mother in Burns, Oregon, the other a sharp-jawed old maid employed as a corporate librarian in Philadelphia. Both had displayed a remarkable willingness to pose as he specified for their Polaroid cameras, doing interesting things and showing themselves in interesting ways. And, as the countdown had continued toward his date with death, both had proclaimed their willingness to join him in heaven.

No joy in that. In order for them to follow him to the grave, he'd have to be in it himself, wouldn't he? They could cop out and he'd never even know it.

Still, there was great power in knowing they'd even made the promise. And maybe there was something here he could work with.

He went to the typewriter. "My darling," he wrote. "The only thing that makes these last days bearable is the love we have for each other. Your pictures and letters sustain me, and the knowledge that we will be together in the next world draws much of the fear out of the abyss that yawns before me.

"Soon they will strap me down and fill my veins with poison, and I will awaken in the void. If only I could make that final journey knowing you would be waiting there for me! My angel, do you have the courage to make the trip ahead of me? Do you love me that much? I can't ask so great a sacrifice of you, and yet I am driven to ask it, because how dare I withhold from you something that is so important to me?"

He read it over, crossed out *sacrifice,* and penciled in *proof of love.* It wasn't quite right, and he'd have to work on it some more. Could either of the bitches possibly go for it? Could he possibly get them to do themselves for love?

And, even if they did, how would he know about it? Some hatchet-faced dame in Philly slashes her wrists in the bathtub, some fat girl hangs herself in Oregon, who's going to know to tell him so he can get off on it? *Darling, do it in front of a video cam, and have them send me the tape.* Be a kick, but it'd never happen.

Didn't Manson get his girls to cut *X*'s on their foreheads? Maybe he could get his to cut themselves a little, where it wouldn't show except in the Polaroids. Would they do it? Maybe, if he worded it right.

Meanwhile, he had other fish to fry.

"Dear Paul," he typed. "I've never called you anything but 'Mr. Dandridge,' but I've written you so many letters, some of them just in the privacy of my mind, that I'll permit myself this liberty. And for all I know you throw my letters away unread. If so, well, I'm still not sorry I've spent the time writing them. It's a great help to me to get my thoughts on paper in this manner.

"I suppose you already know that I got another stay of execution. I can imagine your exasperation at the news. Would it surprise you to know that my own reaction was much the same? I don't want to die, Paul, but I don't want to live like this, either, while lawyers scurry around just trying to postpone the inevitable. Better for both of us if they'd just killed me right away.

"Though I suppose I should be grateful for this chance to make my peace, with you and with myself. I can't bring myself to ask for your forgiveness, and I certainly can't summon up whatever is required for me to forgive myself, but perhaps that will come with time. They seem to be giving me plenty of time, even if they do persist in doling it out to me bit by bit. . . ."

When he found the letter, Paul Dandridge followed what had become standard practice for him. He set it aside while he opened and tended to the rest of his mail. Then he went into the kitchen and brewed himself a pot of coffee. He poured a cup and sat down with it and opened the letter from Croydon.

When the second letter came he'd read it through to the end, then crumpled it in his fist. He hadn't known whether to throw it in the garbage or burn it in the fireplace, and in the end he'd done neither. Instead he'd carefully unfolded it and smoothed out its creases and read it again before putting it away.

Since then he'd saved all the letters. It had been almost three years since sentence was pronounced on William Croydon, and longer than that since Karen had died at his hands. (Literally at his hands, he thought; the hands that typed the letter and folded it into its envelope had encircled Karen's neck and strangled her. The very hands.)

Now Croydon was thirty-three and Paul was thirty himself, and he had been receiving letters at the approximate rate of one every two months. This was the fifteenth, and it seemed to mark a new stage in their one-sided correspondence. Croydon had addressed him by his first name.

"Better for both of us if they'd just killed me right away." Ah, but they hadn't, had they? And they wouldn't either. It would drag on and on and on. A lawyer he'd consulted had told him it would not be unrealistic to expect another ten years of delay. For

God's sake, he'd be forty years old by the time the state got around to doing the job.

It occurred to him, not for the first time, that he and Croydon were fellow prisoners. He was not confined to a cell and not under a sentence of death, but it struck him that his life held only the illusion of freedom. He wouldn't really be free until Croydon's ordeal was over. Until then he was confined in a prison without walls, unable to get on with his life, unable to have a life, just marking time.

He went over to his desk, took out a sheet of letterhead, uncapped a pen. For a long moment he hesitated. Then he sighed gently and touched pen to paper.

"Dear Croydon," he wrote. "I don't know what to call you. I can't bear to address you by your first name or to call you 'Mr. Croydon.' Not that I ever expected to call you anything at all. I guess I thought you'd be dead by now. God knows I wished it. . . ."

Once he got started, it was surprisingly easy to find the words.

An answer from Dandridge.

Unbelievable.

If he had a shot, Paul Dandridge was it. The stays and the appeals would only carry you so far. The chance that any court along the way would grant him a reversal and a new trial was remote at best. His only real hope was a commutation of his death sentence to life imprisonment.

Not that he wanted to spend the rest of his life in prison. In a sense, you lived better on Death Row than if you were doing life in general prison population. But in another sense the difference between a life sentence and a death sentence was, well, the difference between life and death. If he got his sentence commuted to life, that meant the day would come when he made parole and hit the street. They might not come right out and say that, but that was what it would amount to, especially if he worked the system right.

And Paul Dandridge was the key to getting his sentence commuted.

He remembered how the prick had testified at the presentencing hearing. If any single thing had ensured the death sentence, it was Dandridge's testimony. And, if anything could swing a commutation of sentence for him, it was a change of heart on the part of Karen Dandridge's brother.

Worth a shot.

"Dear Paul," he typed. "I can't possibly tell you the sense of peace that came over me when I realized the letter I was holding was from you. . . ."

Paul Dandridge, seated at his desk, uncapped his pen and wrote the day's date at the top of a sheet of letterhead. He paused and looked at what he had written. It was, he realized, the fifth anniversary of his sister's death, and he hadn't been aware of that fact until he'd inscribed the date at the top of a letter to the man who'd killed her.

Another irony, he thought. They seemed to be infinite.

"Dear Billy," he wrote. "You'll appreciate this. It wasn't until I'd written the date on this letter that I realized its significance. It's been exactly five years since the day that changed both our lives forever."

He took a breath, considered his words. He wrote, "And I guess it's time to acknowledge formally something I've acknowledged in my heart some time ago. While I may never get over Karen's death, the bitter hatred that has burned in me for so long has finally cooled. And so I'd like to say that you have my forgiveness in full measure. And now I think it's time for you to forgive yourself. . . ."

● ● ●

It was hard to sit still.

That was something he'd had no real trouble doing since the first day the cell door closed with him inside. You had to be able to sit still to do time, and it was never hard for him. Even during the several occasions when he'd been a few weeks away from an execution date, he'd never been one to pace the floor or climb the walls.

But today was the hearing. Today the board was hearing testimony from three individuals. One was a psychiatrist who would supply some professional arguments for commuting his sentence from death to life. Another was his fourth-grade teacher, who would tell the board how rough he'd had it in childhood and what a good little boy he was underneath it all. He wondered where they'd dug her up, and how she could possibly remember him. He didn't remember her at all.

The third witness, and the only really important one, was Paul Dandridge. Not only was he supplying the only testimony likely to carry much weight, but it was he who had spent money to locate Croydon's fourth-grade teacher, he who had enlisted the services of the shrink.

His buddy, Paul. A crusader, moving heaven and earth to save Billy Croydon's life.

Just the way he'd planned it.

He paced, back and forth, back and forth, and then he stopped and retrieved from his locker the letter that had started it all. The first letter to Paul Dandridge, the one he'd had the sense not to send. How many times had he reread it over the years, bringing the whole thing back into focus?

". . . when I turned her facedown, well, I can tell you she'd never done *that* before." Jesus, no, she hadn't liked it at all. He read and remembered, warmed by the memory.

What did he have these days but his memories? The women who'd been writing him had long since given it up. Even the ones who'd sworn to follow him to death had lost interest during the endless round of stays and appeals. He still had the letters and pictures they'd sent, but the pictures were unappealing, only serving to remind him what a bunch of pigs they all were, and the letters were sheer fantasy with no underpinning of reality. They described, and none too vividly, events that had never happened and events that would never happen. The sense of power to compel them to write those letters and pose for their pictures had faded over time. Now they only bored him and left him faintly disgusted.

Of his own memories, only that of Karen Dandridge held any real flavor. The other two girls, the ones he'd done before Karen, were almost impossible to recall. They were brief encounters, impulsive, unplanned, and over almost before they'd begun. He'd surprised one in a lonely part of the park, just pulled her skirt up and her panties down and went at her, hauling off and smacking her with a rock a couple of times when she wouldn't keep quiet. That shut her up, and when he finished he found out why. She was dead. He'd evidently cracked her skull and killed her, and he'd been thrusting away at dead meat.

Hardly a memory to stir the blood ten years later. The second one wasn't much better either. He'd been about half drunk, and that had the effect of blurring the memory. He'd snapped her neck afterward, the little bitch, and he remembered that part, but he couldn't remember what it had felt like.

One good thing. Nobody ever found out about either of those two. If they had, he wouldn't have a prayer at today's hearing.

After the hearing, Paul managed to slip out before the press could catch up with him. Two days later, however, when the governor acted on the board's recommendation and commuted William Croydon's sentence to life imprisonment, one persistent reporter managed to get Paul in front of a video camera.

"For a long time I wanted vengeance," he admitted. "I honestly believed that I could only come to terms with the loss of my sister by seeing her killer put to death."

What changed that? the reporter wanted to know.

He stopped to consider his answer. "The dawning realization," he said, "that I could really only recover from Karen's death not by seeing Billy Croydon punished but by letting go of the need to punish. In the simplest terms, I had to forgive him."

And could he do that? Could he forgive the man who had brutally murdered his sister?

"Not overnight," he said. "It took time. I can't even swear I've forgiven him completely. But I've come far enough in the process to realize capital punishment is not only inhumane but pointless. Karen's death was wrong, but Billy Croydon's death would be another wrong, and two wrongs don't make a right. Now that his sentence has been lifted, I can get on with the process of complete forgiveness."

The reporter commented that it sounded as though Paul Dandridge had gone through some sort of religious conversion experience.

"I don't know about religion," Paul said, looking right at the camera. "I don't really consider myself a religious person. But something's happened, something transformational in nature, and I suppose you could call it spiritual."

With his sentence commuted, Billy Croydon drew a transfer to another penitentiary, where he was assigned a cell in general population. After years of waiting to die he was being given a chance to create a life for himself within the prison's walls. He had a job in the prison laundry, he had access to the library and exercise yard. He didn't have his freedom, but he had life.

On the sixteenth day of his new life, three hard-eyed lifers cornered him in the room where they stored the bed linen. He'd noticed one of the men earlier, had caught him staring at him a few times, looking at Croydon the way you'd look at a woman. He hadn't spotted the other two before, but they had the same look in their eyes as the one he recognized.

There wasn't a thing he could do.

They raped him, all three of them, and they weren't gentle about it either. He fought at first but their response to that was savage and prompt, and he gasped at the pain and quit his struggling. He tried to disassociate himself from what was being done to him, tried to take his mind away to some private place. That was a way old cons had of doing time, getting through the hours on end of vacant boredom. This time it didn't really work.

They left him doubled up on the floor, warned him against saying anything to the hacks, and drove the point home with a boot to the ribs.

He managed to get back to his cell, and the following day he put in a request for a transfer to B Block, where you were locked down twenty-three hours a day. He was used to that on Death Row, so he knew he could live with it.

So much for making a life inside the walls. What he had to do was get out.

He still had his typewriter. He sat down, flexed his fingers. One of the rapists had bent his little finger back the day before, and it still hurt, but it wasn't one that he used for typing. He took a breath and started in.

"Dear Paul . . ."

"Dear Billy,

"As always, it was good to hear from you. I write not with news but just in the hope that I can lighten your spirits and build your resolve for the long road ahead. Winning your freedom won't be an easy task, but it's my conviction that working together we can make it happen. . . .

"Yours, Paul."

"Dear Paul,

"Thanks for the books. I missed a lot, all those years when I never opened a book. It's funny—my life seems so much more spacious now, even though I'm spending all but one hour a day in a dreary little cell. But it's like that poem that starts, 'Stone walls do not a prison make / Nor iron bars a cage.' (I'd have to say, though, that the stone walls and iron bars around this place make a pretty solid prison.)

"I don't expect much from the parole board next month, but it's a start. . . ."

"Dear Billy,

"I was deeply saddened by the parole board's decision, although everything I'd heard had led me to expect nothing else. Even though you've been locked up more than enough time to be eligible, the thinking evidently holds that Death Row time somehow counts less than regular prison time, and that the board wants to see how you do as a prisoner serving a life sentence before letting you return to the outside world. I'm not sure I understand the logic there. . . .

"I'm glad you're taking it so well.

"Your friend, Paul."

"Dear Paul,

"Once again, thanks for the books. They're a healthy cut above what's available here. This joint prides itself in its library, but when you say 'Kierkegaard' to the prison librarian he looks at you funny, and you don't dare try him on Martin Buber.

"I shouldn't talk, because I'm having troubles of my own with both of those guys. I haven't got anybody else to bounce this off, so do you mind if I press you into service? Here's my take on Kierkegaard. . . .

"Well, that's the latest from the Jailhouse Philosopher, who is pleased to be

"Your friend, Billy."

"Dear Billy,

"Well, once again it's time for the annual appearance before parole board—or the annual circus, as you call it with plenty of justification. Last year we thought maybe the third time was the charm, and it turned out we were wrong, but maybe it'll be different this year. . . ."

"Dear Paul,

" 'Maybe it'll be different this time.' Isn't that what Charlie Brown tells himself before he tries to kick the football? And Lucy always snatches it away.

"Still, some of the deep thinkers I've been reading stress that hope is important even when it's unwarranted. And, although I'm a little scared to admit it, I have a good feeling this time.

"And if they never let me out, well, I've reached a point where I honestly don't mind. I've found an inner life here that's far superior to anything I had in my years as a free man. Between my books, my solitude, and my correspondence with you, I have a life I can live with. Of course I'm hoping for parole, but if they snatch the football away again, it ain't gonna kill me. . . ."

"Dear Billy,

". . . Just a thought, but maybe that's the line you should take with them. That you'd welcome parole, but you've made a life for yourself within the walls and you can stay there indefinitely if you have to.

"I don't know, maybe that's the wrong strategy altogether, but I think it might impress them. . . ."

"Dear Paul,

"Who knows what's likely to impress them? On the other hand, what have I got to lose?"

• • •

Billy Croydon sat at the end of the long conference table, speaking when spoken to, uttering his replies in a low voice, giving pro forma responses to the same questions they asked him every year. At the end they asked him, as usual, if there was anything he wanted to say.

Well, what the hell, he thought. What did he have to lose?

"I'm sure it won't surprise you," he began, "to hear that I've come before you in the hope of being granted early release. I've had hearings before, and when I was turned down it was devastating. Well, I may not be doing myself any good by saying this, but this time around it won't destroy me if you decide to deny me parole. Almost in spite of myself, I've made a life for myself within prison walls. I've found an inner life, a life of the spirit, that's superior to anything I had as a free man. . . ."

Were they buying it? Hard to tell. On the other hand, since it happened to be the truth, it didn't really matter whether they bought it or not.

He pushed on to the end. The chairman scanned the room, then looked at him and nodded shortly.

"Thank you, Mr. Croydon," he said. "I think that will be all for now."

"I think I speak for all of us," the chairman said, "when I say how much weight we attach to your appearance before this board. We're used to hearing the pleas of victims and their survivors, but almost invariably they come here to beseech us to deny parole. You're virtually unique, Mr. Dandridge, in appearing as the champion of the very man who . . ."

"Killed my sister," Paul said levelly.

"Yes. You've appeared before us on prior occasions, Mr. Dandridge, and while we were greatly impressed by your ability to forgive William Croydon and by the relationship you've forged with him, it seems to me that there's been a change in your own sentiments. Last year, I recall, while you pleaded on Mr. Croydon's behalf, we sensed that you did not wholeheartedly believe he was ready to be returned to society."

"Perhaps I had some hesitation."

"But this year . . ."

"Billy Croydon's a changed man. The process of change has been completed. I know that he's ready to get on with his life."

"There's no denying the power of your testimony, especially in light of its source." The chairman cleared his throat. "Thank you, Mr. Dandridge. I think that will be all for now."

"Well?" Paul said. "How do you feel?"

Billy considered the question. "Hard to say," he said. "Everything's a little unreal. Even being in a car. Last time I was in a moving vehicle was when I got my commutation and they transferred me from the other prison. It's not like Rip Van Winkle. I know what everything looks like from television, cars included. Tell the truth, I feel a little shaky."

"I guess that's to be expected."

"I suppose." He tugged his seat belt to tighten it. "You want to know how I feel, I feel vulnerable. All those years I was locked down twenty-three hours out of twenty-four. I knew what to expect, I knew I was safe. Now I'm a free man, and it scares the crap out of me."

"Look in the glove compartment," Paul said.

"Jesus, Johnnie Walker Black."

"I figured you might be feeling a little anxious. That ought to take the edge off."

"Yeah, Dutch courage," Billy said. "Why Dutch, do you happen to know? I've always wondered."

"No idea."

He weighed the bottle in his hand. "Been a long time," he said. "Haven't had a taste of anything since they locked me up."

"There was nothing available in prison?"

"Oh, there was stuff. The jungle juice cons made out of potatoes and raisins, and some good stuff that got smuggled in. But I wasn't in population, so I didn't have access. And anyway it seemed like more trouble than it was worth."

"Well, you're a free man now. Why don't you drink to it? I'm driving or I'd join you."

"Well . . ."

"Go ahead."

"Why not?" he said, and uncapped the bottle and held it to the light. "Pretty color, huh? Well, here's to freedom, huh?" He took a long drink, shuddered at the burn of the whiskey. "Kicks like a mule," he said.

"You're not used to it."

"I'm not." He put the cap on the bottle and had a little trouble screwing it back on. "Hitting me hard," he reported. "Like I was a little kid getting his first taste of it. Whew."

"You'll be all right."

"Spinning," Billy said, and slumped in his seat.

Paul glanced over at him, looked at him again a minute later. Then, after checking the mirror, he pulled the car off the road and braked to a stop.

Billy was conscious for a little while before he opened his eyes. He tried to get his bearings first. The last thing he remembered was a wave of dizziness after the slug of Scotch hit bottom. He was still sitting upright, but it didn't feel like a car seat, and he didn't sense any movement. No, he was in some sort of chair, and he seemed to be tied to it.

That didn't make any sense. A dream? He'd had lucid dreams before and knew how real they were, how you could be in them and wonder if you were dreaming and convince yourself you weren't. The way you broke the surface and got out of it was by opening your eyes. You had to force yourself, had to open your

real eyes and not just your eyes in the dream, but it could be done.
. . . There!

He was in a chair, in a room he'd never seen before, looking out a window at a view he'd never seen before. An open field, woods behind it.

He turned his head to the left and saw a wall paneled in knotty cedar. He turned to the right and saw Paul Dandridge, wearing boots and jeans and a plaid flannel shirt and sitting in an easy chair with a book. He said, "Hey!" and Paul lowered the book and looked at him.

"Ah," Paul said. "You're awake."

"What's going on?"

"What do you think?"

"There was something in the whiskey."

"There was indeed," Paul agreed. "You started to stir just as we made the turn off the state road. I gave you a booster shot with a hypodermic needle."

"I don't remember."

"You never felt it. I was afraid for a minute there that I'd given you too much. That would have been ironic, wouldn't you say? 'Death by lethal injection.' The sentence carried out finally after all these years, and you wouldn't have even known it happened."

He couldn't take it in. "Paul," he said, "for God's sake, what's it all about?"

"What's it about?" Paul considered his response. "It's about time."

"Time?"

"It's the last act of the drama."

"Where are we?"

"A cabin in the woods. Not *the* cabin. That would be ironic, wouldn't it?"

"What do you mean?"

"If I killed you in the same cabin where you killed Karen.

Ironic, but not really feasible. So this is a different cabin in different woods, but it will have to do."

"You're going to kill me?"

"Of course."

"For God's sake, why?"

"Because that's how it ends, Billy. That's the point of the whole game. That's how I planned it from the beginning."

"I can't believe this."

"Why is it so hard to believe? We conned each other, Billy. You pretended to repent and I pretended to believe you. You pretended to reform and I pretended to be on your side. Now we can both stop pretending."

Billy was silent for a moment. Then he said, "I was trying to con you at the beginning."

"No kidding."

"There was a point where it turned into something else, but it started out as a scam. It was the only way I could think of to stay alive. You saw through it?"

"Of course."

"But you pretended to go along with it. Why?"

"Is it that hard to figure out?"

"It doesn't make any sense. What do you gain by it? My death? If you wanted me dead all you had to do was tear up my letter. The state was all set to kill me."

"They'd have taken forever," Paul said bitterly. "Delay after delay, and always the possibility of a reversal and a retrial, always the possibility of a commutation of sentence."

"There wouldn't have been a reversal, and it took you working for me to get my sentence commuted. There would have been delays, but there'd already been a few of them before I got around to writing to you. It couldn't have lasted too many years longer, and it would have added up to a lot less than it has now, with all the time I spent serving life and waiting for the parole board to open the doors. If you'd just let it go, I'd be dead and buried by now."

"You'll be dead soon," Paul told him. "And buried. It won't be much longer. Your grave's already dug. I took care of that before I drove to the prison to pick you up."

"They'll come after you, Paul. When I don't show up for my initial appointment with my parole officer—"

"They'll get in touch, and I'll tell them we had a drink and shook hands and you went off on your own. It's not my fault if you decided to skip town and violate the terms of your parole."

He took a breath. He said, "Paul, don't do this."

"Why not?"

"Because I'm begging you. I don't want to die."

"Ah," Paul said. "*That's* why."

"What do you mean?"

"If I left it to the state," he said, "they'd have been killing a dead man. By the time the last appeal was denied and the last request for a stay of execution turned down, you'd have been resigned to the inevitable. They'd strap you to a gurney and give you a shot, and it would be just like going to sleep."

"That's what they say."

"But now you want to live. You adjusted to prison, you made a life for yourself in there, and then you finally made parole, icing on the cake, and now you genuinely want to live. You've really got a life now, Billy, and I'm going to take it away from you."

"You're serious about this."

"I've never been more serious about anything."

"You must have been planning this for years."

"From the very beginning."

"Jesus, it's the most thoroughly premeditated crime in the history of the world, isn't it? Nothing I can do about it either. You've got me tied tight and the chair won't tip over. Is there anything I can say that'll make you change your mind?"

"Of course not."

"That's what I thought." He sighed. "Get it over with."

"I don't think so."

"Huh?"

"This won't be what the state hands out," Paul Dandridge said. "A minute ago you were begging me to let you live. Before it's over you'll be begging me to kill you."

"You're going to torture me."

"That's the idea."

"In fact you've already started, haven't you? This is the mental part."

"Very perceptive of you, Billy."

"For all the good it does me. This is all because of what I did to your sister, isn't it?"

"Obviously."

"I didn't do it, you know. It was another Billy Croydon that killed her, and I can barely remember what he was like."

"That doesn't matter."

"Not to you, evidently, and you're the one calling the shots. I'm sure Kierkegaard had something useful to say about this sort of situation, but I'm damned if I can call it to mind. You knew I was conning you, huh? Right from the jump?"

"Of course."

"I thought it was a pretty good letter I wrote you."

"It was a masterpiece, Billy. But that didn't mean it wasn't easy to see through."

"So now you dish it out and I take it," Billy Croydon said, "until you get bored and end it, and I wind up in the grave you've already dug for me. And that's the end of it. I wonder if there's a way to turn it around."

"Not a chance."

"Oh, I know I'm not getting out of here alive, Paul, but there's more than one way of turning something around. Let's see now. You know, the letter you got wasn't the first one I wrote to you."

"So?"

"The past is always with you, isn't it? I'm not the same man as the guy who killed your sister, but he's still there inside somewhere. Just a question of calling him up."

"What's that supposed to mean?"

"Just talking to myself, I guess. I was starting to tell you about that first letter. I never sent it, you know, but I kept it. For the longest time I held on to it and read it whenever I wanted to relive the experience. Then it stopped working, or maybe I stopped wanting to call up the past, but whatever it was I quit reading it. I still held on to it, and then one day I realized I didn't want to own it anymore. So I tore it up and got rid of it."

"That's fascinating."

"But I read it so many times I bet I can bring it back word for word." His eyes locked with Paul Dandridge's, and his lips turned up in the slightest suggestion of a smile. He said, " 'Dear Paul, Sitting here in this cell waiting for the day to come when they put a needle in my arm and flush me down God's own toilet, I found myself thinking about your testimony in court. I remember how you said your sister was a good-hearted girl who spent her short life bringing pleasure to everyone who knew her. According to your testimony, knowing this helped you rejoice in her life at the same time that it made her death so hard to take.

" 'Well, Paul, in the interest of helping you rejoice some more, I thought I'd tell you just how much pleasure your little sister brought to me. I've got to tell you that in all my life I never got more pleasure from anybody. My first look at Karen brought me pleasure, just watching her walk across campus, just looking at those jiggling tits and that tight little ass and imagining the fun I was going to have with them.' "

"Stop it, Croydon!"

"You don't want to miss this, Paulie. 'Then when I had her tied up in the backseat of the car with her mouth taped shut, I have to say she went on being a real source of pleasure. Just looking at her in the rearview mirror was enjoyable, and from time to time I would stop the car and lean into the back to run my hands over her body. I don't think she liked it much, but I enjoyed it enough for the both of us.' "

"You're a son of a bitch."

"And you're an asshole. You should have let the state put me out of everybody's misery. Failing that, you should have let go of the hate and sent the new William Croydon off to rejoin society. There's a lot more to the letter, and I remember it perfectly." He tilted his head, resumed quoting from memory. " 'Tell me something, Paul. Did you ever fool around with Karen yourself? I bet you did. I can picture her when she was maybe eleven, twelve years old, with her little titties just beginning to bud out, and you'd have been seventeen or eighteen yourself, so how could you stay away from her? She's sleeping and you walk into her room and sit on the edge of her bed.' " He grinned. "I always liked that part. And there's lots more. You enjoying your revenge, Paulie? Is it as sweet as they say it is?"

Mary Higgins Clark

Mary Higgins Clark is a phenomenon, certainly, and one who has earned her status on the world's best-seller lists by dint of hard work. In the very best sense, she is the novelist-as-Everywoman, and her devoted readers identify not only with her imperiled heroines but with the author herself. The romantic suspense tradition, after all, is a great one, with roots stretching back to the delicious Gothic excesses of Ann Radcliffe and racing forward to the modern era as hearalded by Daphne du Maurier.

Clark's books and stories, however, are firmly contemporary. Shunning moats and manor houses, she reminds us time and again of the many sorts of courage women exemplify in the lives they lead today—as professionals, as wives, mothers, stalwart friends. Add sudden death to the mixture, along with villainy and betrayal, plus a surprise twist or two, and you have the ingredients for another best seller. It may look easy to pull this off, keeping fans hooked, turning pages into the small hours of the morning, but it's not. There have been, and are, many imitators, convinced that they can use the same ingredients to cook up their own best sellers, but they just can't match the priceless recipe.

Power Play
▼▼▼

BY MARY HIGGINS CLARK

So fair a brow to be so troubled, Henry thought as he looked across the table at Sunday. She had just returned from Washington and to his anxious eye seemed thoroughly exhausted. She'd changed into a caftan for dinner and her complexion seemed deadly pale against the shimmering blue-green silk. Her hair, the color of winter wheat, was loose around her neck and her eyes, usually so sparkling, were clouded and sleepy.

For the last weeks she'd fought her heart out to line up enough votes in Congress to pass a law guaranteeing both breakfast and lunch to needy schoolchildren. She'd succeeded but at the price of bruising exhaustion.

Henry well understood the feeling. During his eight years as president of the United States he'd often been thoroughly weary—not only in body but in spirit.

"You're not exactly famished, are you, love?" he asked tenderly. "Poor Yves is so proud of the Dover sole. You'd swear he'd caught it himself."

Sunday smiled and for a moment the fatigue was lifted from her expression. "Knowing Yves, he probably did exactly that." Then she said ruefully, "Oh, Henry, you know how it is. I've twisted so many arms that I don't think I have a friend left on Capitol Hill."

"You have one on Pennsylvania Avenue," Henry told her. "Des called me this afternoon."

Desmond Ogilvey, the current president of the United States, was Henry's successor in office.

Sunday looked at him, astonished. "What did he say? People in his own party were the ones who fought me the hardest."

"Not all his people," Henry corrected. "Des wanted that bill as much as you did. He loves it that you're the one who got it through. He said that he was reminded of what Ben-Gurion said about Golda Meir: 'She's the only man in my cabinet.' "

"That was very nice of Des."

"Yes, it was, but he also mentioned that you looked mighty tired the last time he saw you and I was happy to be able to tell him that we're off for a vacation. Just the two of us—no Secret Service. How does that sound?"

Sims, the butler for the Britland family for the past thirty-odd years, was pouring wine into Sunday's glass. Henry could see his conspiratorial nod of approval.

"Oh, Henry, I'd love that." Sunday sighed. "But how can you manage it? We can't go two feet without you being surrounded."

"After fourteen months of marriage, you still don't know everything about me, sweetheart." Henry was beginning to enjoy himself thoroughly. The last fourteen months were still a miracle to him. On his final night in the White House he'd given a reception for the incoming members of Congress, one of whom was Sunday. Thirty-one years old, a public defender, she'd won the seat of the incumbent congressman in Jersey City in a stunning upset.

Henry had flirted with her and had been both amused and chagrined when she reproached him. Then when she turned down his invitation to dine with him because she was taking her parents to dinner, he'd known that the beautiful young woman with the candid blue eyes was the one he'd been searching for. They were married six weeks later and he happily saw himself removed from *People* magazine's choice as the number-one eligible bachelor in the United States, having swept all categories: looks, intelligence, charm, humor, position, and wealth.

Now when Congress was in session, Henry spent most weekdays at Drumdoe, their country estate in New Jersey, writing his memoirs.

But not for the next several weeks, he thought. "Sims and I have it all planned," he announced triumphantly. "We will go in disguise and incognito. The passports are ready."

"Passports! Where are we going, for heaven's sake?"

"For heaven's sake, indeed. You are going to the Middle East. We will board a cruise ship in Bombay—"

"You mean Mumbai," Sunday interrupted. "The Indian government changed Bombay back to its original name. As former president I'm sure you must have heard that."

"Do be quiet, darling," Henry said with dignity. "Remember, a little knowledge is dangerous. Now if I may continue: We sail from Mumbai through the Indian Ocean, to the sea of Arabia, on to the Red Sea, and finally through the Mediterranean. Along the way we will stop at Jordan, Egypt, and Ahman, disembark in Piraeus, and fly home from there. How does that sound?"

"It sounds glorious, but just a few questions: Why go on a cruise ship when you own a yacht?" Sunday paused. "Oh. I see. The recognition factor?"

"Exactly. Which brings me to show you why it won't be a problem for us personally." Henry stood up. "Since you obviously are not going to eat another morsel, come along. You might enjoy having a look at your new persona."

Three days later Harry and Sandra Potter checked into the Taj Mahal Hotel in Mumbai, formerly Bombay. To the casual observer they seemed an ordinary couple, the kind who never received a second glance.

She had short dark hair and round tinted glasses. Her slacks suit, the sort favored by women whose mothers had grown up wearing sweater sets, was stodgy beige in color and rectangular in shape; it succeeded in adding twenty pounds to her appearance as well as crying out to be matched with the sensible oxfords she was also wearing.

Her husband, gray haired with a wispy Vandyke, obviously favored an equally conservative look. His poplin pants were topped with a somber brown jacket and heavily starched shirt. Even his brown-and-beige-striped bow tie managed to look prim. The panel of the old television show *What's My Line?* would have pegged him instantly as a teacher.

A courteous attendant led them to their room in the old section of the hotel overlooking the bay. As Henry had explained to Sunday, "I always had a suite when I stayed at the Taj but the rooms adjacent to the suites are very nice. My father and mother put the valet and personal maid in them, and we don't want to stand out."

They went up in the elevator to the sixth floor, then followed the attendant down a half flight to a corridor. Sunday heard Henry murmur "Uh-oh" under his breath as they turned the corner and saw four armed soldiers standing at attention outside one of the doors. A man in civilian clothes was striding up and down the corridor. His watchful glance settled on them, studied them intently, then dismissed them with a flicker of his eyelids.

"Must be someone very important staying here," Henry said

to the attendant. The slight Boston accent he had affected did not conceal the deference in his voice.

"A visiting government official," the attendant whispered, then looked flustered as though he had said too much. He led them to the door next to the guarded suite, opened it, and stepped aside to let them enter.

The luggage arrived as he was leaving. The instant they were alone, Henry covered the room in long strides and double-locked the door. "We've had our first acid test," he whispered. "That has to be Hasna Ibn Saata in there."

Sunday pulled off the black wig that was making her scalp vaguely itchy. Her blond hair tumbled on her shoulders. "Who is he and why the acid test?" She realized she was whispering.

Henry looked around and put a warning finger to his lips. He went over to the television, turned it on, and put his lips to her ear. "I don't think this room is bugged, but we might as well take precautions. Saata is the confidant and advisor of the sultan of Ahman, which is our first stop on the trip. The hidden city of the silver stone is a must-see.

"The sultan and I became close friends when we were at Harvard and he took me there almost twenty-five years ago. It has a rich history and its warren of hidden caves and secret passages played a major role in the ancient history of Ahman. That's the part of the country where I learned to ride a camel and got pretty good at speaking Arabic."

"Can you still speak it?"

"Not much opportunity to brush up, I'm afraid. I can understand it fine, but I'd have to make myself understood in pidgin Arabic now.

"While on those trips together," Henry continued, "Hasna would often come over to brief the sultan on internal affairs in Ahman. That plainclothesman was Hasna's chief of security, al Hez."

"He really looked us over," Sunday whispered back.

"I know he did, and I'm sure he didn't recognize us. He's

always been a cheeky sort, but he saved Hasna's life years ago and of course can do no harm as far as the sultan is concerned. I only wish we could stop in on Mac while we're in his kingdom."

"Mac?"

"That's the sultan's nickname. At Harvard he was crown prince, and we all knew that before too long he'd be one of the last absolute monarchs alive. His full name is Muhammad Abdul a Faisam, but he loved McDonald's burgers so much that one of the guys started calling him Mac. He got such a kick out of it that the name caught on. I doubt many people are using it now."

"Didn't he make a state visit when you were president?"

"Yes, he did. He brought his son, the present crown prince, and his eighteen-year-old daughter. Mac's exactly my age, forty-four, but he married young. His entire kingdom trembles at his glance, but that night his daughter took so long to get ready that they were half an hour late, which simply isn't done at a state dinner. When Mac apologized to me he said, "Henry, wasn't it Theodore Roosevelt who said that he could either run the country or run his daughter, Alice, but he couldn't do both?"

"Sounds like a nice guy."

"Nice but also formidable and very impressive. Like King Hussein and King Hassan, he's a direct descendant of Muhammad, which is an extremely honorable state in the Islamic religion. Our CIA guys tell us there are rumors of trouble brewing, but so far no real evidence. With huge oil revenues pouring into the country, that sort of thing is bound to happen. I have a feeling that my friend next door is going around getting support from the neighboring countries to make sure any rebels won't find outside support. Now wash your face and put your wig back on. The Potters are going for a walk before dinner."

Later, when they were settled for the night, Sunday whispered drowsily, "Henry, this is such fun, just being touristy and no one fussing over us. Mumbai is a marvelous city."

"Another time we'll see India properly. Now go to sleep. We board the *Bel-Mare* right after breakfast."

In the morning when they left their room to check out, the door of the next suite opened and a frail, elderly man came out, accompanied by the man Henry had identified as the chief security officer. Sunday tried to look nonchalant as she passed him, but then acknowledged his courteous nod. He was wearing traditional Arab dress and his fine, chiseled features were enhanced by the white burnoose that covered his head and neck.

I could imagine his face on a coin, she thought.

Henry did not comment until they were in a taxi on the way to the dock. "I was shocked to see Hasna look so frail," he said. "He's aged ten years since he was in Washington with Mac two years ago. Things must be worse in Ahman than our guys realize. The strong ties Mac has forged between his country and ours aren't popular with some of his neighbors." Then he shook his head. "Wait a minute. This is R and R for you, sweetheart. No political talk."

And that's like telling either one of us not to breathe, Sunday thought with amusement. She was enjoying herself thoroughly. Putting on the disguise and traveling without escorts made her feel as though for a very short time she and Henry could be as totally alone in a crowd as they were in their own suite at home.

And after a couple of weeks, we'll both be anxious to get back in harness, she realized, but for the moment Capitol Hill seemed very far away.

Jack Collins, Henry's senior Secret Service agent, had been aghast at the plan. "Mr. President, I absolutely have to tell you that it is dangerous, it is foolish, it is reckless." Then he'd stopped, afraid he'd overstepped himself.

Henry had clasped him on the shoulder. "And it's also necessary. Come on, Jack. You'll be glad to have two weeks off, admit it."

"Not like this, sir. Will we at least know your itinerary?"

"I'm afraid the President has insisted that I leave it here. It's in a sealed envelope in my desk, which will not be opened unless Sims doesn't hear from us regularly by either phone or fax."

Sunday smiled to herself, remembering the shocked expression on Jack Collins's face when he heard that arrangement.

The cab pulled up to the gangplank of the *Bel-Mare*. The ocean liner was on a world cruise and they were sailing on the segment from Mumbai to Piraeus.

Nothing in Henry's demeanor suggested that he was not entirely used to carrying his own tote bag and camera as they made their way up the gangplank with the hundred or so other passengers who were boarding the ship. However, when he saw their accommodations he looked dismayed. "Darling, there must be some mistake. I reserved a first-class cabin."

"This is a first-class cabin, sir," the steward said proudly.

When he was gone, Sunday said, "Henry, dear, it's not trick photography. It is the cabin you reserved. It's just that on ocean liners there's an economy of space. Three years ago I went through the Panama Canal with a couple of my college buddies. The three of us were in a cabin half this size."

"Amazing." Henry sighed. "Simply amazing. The room in the Taj Mahal suddenly seems gigantic." He frowned. "Why do I have a bad feeling about Hasna?" he asked. "I'm glad we're going to Ahman, and not just for sightseeing. I'm beginning to wonder if things aren't a lot worse there than we've been led to believe."

"Wouldn't the sultan have asked for help if he needed it?"

"The Muslim states are not very happy with the United States. He might not have thought it politic. On the other hand, Mac is a strong leader. He's put down uprisings before. Now, love, let's unpack and go on deck to watch the ship set sail. Then three days at sea to Ahman."

Hasna Ibn Saata had not survived for seventy-six years, fifty of them as a confidant to the late sultan and then to his son, the present monarch, without having a sixth sense that, like a security system, sounded an alarm when an intruder entered the premises.

But why now? he pondered as he rested in his suite at the Taj Mahal after his morning meeting with the representative of the prime minister of India. There was no intruder. The guards at his door were his personal force, trusted and caring. Al Hez had taken a bullet for him once. *He would do it again if need be,* Saata assured himself. *Even though he now heads our military, he still insists on personally accompanying me when I leave the country.*

Then why the growing certainty that danger was close? It was probably because the fruit juice that room service had delivered when he returned was not sitting well. Vague, smothering pains were beginning to cause discomfort in his chest.

Was that the sound of voices in the foyer?

Al Hez was alone there guarding the bolted door. Hasna got up slowly, then noiselessly moved across the room, taking care not to be in view of anyone in the foyer. Standing behind the partially open door, he listened intently.

Age had not diminished his acute hearing. As the meaning of al Hez's words sank in, Hasna Ibn Saata shook his head sadly. Al Hez was talking to Rasna, the head of the guards, outside the suite. *My trusted bodyguard, Rasna,* Hasna Ibn Saata thought. *My trusted aide, al Hez,* who had just said, "Stop worrying. You will be well rewarded. The juice should do its work soon. The old man will be dead in minutes."

Poison. Hasna Ibn Saata made his way back to the chair. His throat was closing. It was increasingly more difficult to breathe. No wonder the rebels were becoming so strong. Al Hez, who was privy to the innermost secrets of the palace, was one of them.

In the last moments of his life Hasna Ibn Saata's hand reached for the phone. He had to warn His Majesty. He pressed the button that would bring the operator on the line, then felt the phone being taken from his hand.

He looked up. Through darkening vision he could see al Hez bending over him, smiling.

"Why?" he whispered. But he knew. Al Hez's father had been hanged by the sultan's father, his innocence established after his death.

It was as though al Hez could read his mind. "My father wasn't innocent," he whispered, "but you were the one who had him arrested. If he had succeeded I would be sitting in the palace now. But my time has come. Die knowing that in a few days American tourists will be kidnaped and massacred in Ahman, supposedly by bands of rebellious Bedouins. The United States will welcome the restoration of order when the sultan is assassinated by those same people and I take control to save my country."

"No, no . . ." Hasna Ibn Saata felt his knees buckle. He managed to whisper, "Allah, save His Majesty," before his lifeless body sank to the carpet.

The first night aboard ship they dined alone at a window table. A full moon shone on the tranquil waters of the Arabian Sea. Sunday sipped wine, listened to the soft strains of the violinist in the background, and smiled at Henry. "The only thing that keeps this from being perfect is that this damn wig is beginning to feel like a helmet," she said.

"I must admit that seeing you in that wig and getup brings to mind the biblical reminder about hiding your light under a bushel," Henry commented, "but it is nice to be anonymous. Enjoying yourself?"

"You know I am. I saw that in the list of activities someone is lecturing on Ahman tomorrow morning, and I'd like to go."

"So would I," Henry said promptly. "The lecturer is also going to head our tour to the Silver Mountain in Ahman. I understand it's only six of us in the group because it's a pretty strenuous trip. An hour in the bus, then two hours on horseback through the mountains. I'm glad you learned to ride."

"How could I have not learned when one of your wedding

presents to me was a horse?" Sunday asked. "Before that my idea of riding was to go on a carousel."

The next morning at the lecture, Sunday observed Henry's barely concealed annoyance as the lecturer, Maja bin Sayyid, a native of Ahman, discussed his country. At first his remarks had been interesting; that ninety percent of Ahman was covered with rocky and sandy desert separated by ten-thousand-foot mountains from the lush and fertile coastal plains; that vast supplies of oil had been discovered fifteen years ago; that the present sultan had been responsible for sweeping social reforms such as compulsory school-ing for girls, hospitals and health centers, and foreign investment.

It was here that Sayyid drew Henry's wrath. "That does not mean our sultan is honored by all his people. Quite frankly, many of us are not pleased to be in America's hip pocket, as you might say. We feel the sultan's education at Harvard was not good for our way of life."

Henry stood up. "Can you be more specific?" he asked coldly.

The lecturer shrugged. "I am veering off my subject. I know only a small group are planning to take the arduous journey to the Silver Mountain, which is a pity. It is a breathtaking sight, a city of ornate buildings chiseled out of the rock in the secret valley seven thousand years ago and only rediscovered early in this century. So far, I am happy to say, it does not have a McDonald's."

"That McDonald's crack referred to the sultan's nickname didn't it?" Sunday asked Henry as they walked back to their room.

"It certainly did, and I'm surprised anyone from Ahman rep-resenting his country on this ship would have the gall to make such a statement," Henry said. "It says to me that affairs in Ahman may be approaching a crisis. I intend to get into conversation with that guide on the bus tomorrow. According to his credits he's a retired military officer. That's not the kind of insolence to the monarch you expect from an officer, retired or not."

When they reached the cabin, he locked the door. "Take off that wig," he suggested. "I miss the real you."

"Gladly," Sunday agreed. "But shouldn't you check in with Sims?"

"Good God, yes. I almost forgot. I certainly don't want him giving the White House a no-contact report on us."

One of the phones in Drumdoe was registered to Arthur Sims. It was the one Henry called now. Sims answered on the first ring.

"Harry Potter, here," Henry said.

"Oh, Mr. . . . Potter, good to hear your voice."

It was clear to Henry that Sims had almost called him Mr. President. "Just to let the family know we're having a grand time," he said heartily.

"Very quiet around here, sir. We miss you and Mrs. Potter."

"We'll keep in touch."

Sunday had been reading the abbreviated copy of the *International Herald Tribune* that had been slipped under their door. "Henry, look," she exclaimed.

They both stared at the picture of Hasna Ibn Saata. The caption under it read "Advisor to the sultan of Ahman dead of heart attack in Mumbai."

Together they skimmed the story. His body had been found by his security chief, General al Hez, and his longtime personal physician, Dr. Ayla Ramas.

"Ramas," Henry snapped. "I never heard of him. He's not Hasna's longtime personal physician."

He took the paper from Sunday. "I'm very glad to have the opportunity to try to get that guide to talk tomorrow. My gut instinct tells me that Mac may have serious trouble brewing. Hasna looked terribly frail. If he felt he had to go personally to India, it must have been a mighty important mission."

In his stateroom four decks down, Maja bin Sayyid was on

the phone to General al Hez, who had returned to Ahman with the body. As Henry had, he spoke as though in casual conversation. "Yes, sir," he said, "I am happy to report that I have found exactly the caliber of tourists we were seeking. Tomorrow I will escort a group of six to Silver Mountain. Four of them will interest you. The Camerons; Lloyd and Audrey. He is the retired chairman of Parker and Van Ness International Investments. She founded Audrey Cosmetics. Very well known to the media. They just gave five hundred million dollars to found a research hospital. They're quite elderly. Why they thought they could do the horseback part of the trip amazes me."

He smiled at the "Very good" he heard from his listener. "I also will be escorting Pamela and Muffie Andrews, who are the wife and daughter of Winston Andrews, the chairman of Andrews Communications.

"Quite right, sir. The media giant."

He listened again, then smiled. "I knew you'd be pleased. The other couple are Harry and Sandra Potter, a nondescript former high school teacher and his wife. But surely they may have a few influential friends in academic circles."

When bin Sayyid hung up, he began to go over the plan step by step. They would dock at nine tomorrow morning. A small motor coach would be awaiting them on the pier. They would drive slowly through the port city of Acqiom to allow the visitors to enjoy the ancient architecture and quaint streets.

In a way playing the role of a guide amused him. He knew he had been very foolish yesterday to show his contempt for the sultan. Today in his bus lecture he would praise His Majesty, pointing out the modern buildings, the handsome hotels, the better roads, the state-of-the-art schools—all of which had been built by the sultan with revenue from the oil fields.

When al Hez is president of Ahman I will take his place as general of the Army, Sayyid thought, envisioning the palace he would build with his share of the oil revenues.

Mentally he reviewed the plan. The tour bus would appear to

break down three kilometers from Silver Mountain. It would be surrounded by men on horseback who would subdue the six passengers. They would be held in one of the mountain caves two ranges away from Silver Mountain and ransom demands would be made.

Bin Sayyid smiled coldly. Winston Andrews controlled TV network and cable channels, newspapers, and radio stations around the world. When word was released that his wife and daughter were being held prisoner by a band of rogue Bedouins, the media would screech the story. Add to that the powerful business connections of the Camerons, which would raise vociferous protests for the illustrious couple.

From within Ahman the revolution would start. The sultan would be denounced as a corrupt leader, a despot who could not maintain law and order.

When the bodies are found, General al Hez will be welcomed by the world as a fearless warrior who avenged the deaths by finding and punishing the kidnapers and deposing the sultan, who will of course die attempting to escape.

A masterful plan, Sayyid thought. There was just one question. Was it worthwhile to bother with keeping the Potters alive at all? Wouldn't it be better to simply dispatch them at once? Mr. Potter annoyed him intensely.

Regretfully, he shook his head. No, better to let the outside world hope and pray for all the captives. Better to let the sultan promise a swift and safe end to the ordeal, as he surely would. Then when hopes were dashed, he would be blamed.

The next morning Sunday was sure she wasn't wrong. In the bus she could see contempt in the eyes of the guide when Henry asked him a question. But his answer was smooth enough.

"Oh, sir, you can understand. In any country there is a measure of political unrest. No matter how benevolent an absolute monarch may be, there are those who long to have a voice in their own governing. Your democracy has set an example, has it not?"

"He's too oily for me," Sunday whispered to Henry as the minibus drove slowly through the crowded streets of Acqiom.

"I agree," Henry murmured in her ear. "But never mind him. I used to explore Silver Mountain with Mac during summer vacations. We can go off by ourselves when we get there. I'll be your guide."

If we get there, Sunday thought ruefully as the minibus began to make coughing sounds. For the past two hours they'd been riding on a seemingly endless road through the desert. Except for occasional clusters of small flat-roofed stone houses, it seemed to be virtually uninhabited, the only company the trucks and tour buses that whizzed past them on the two-lane road.

Several times Henry had commented on the leisurely pace the driver had set. "It's not exactly the Amalfi coast, where the view is mind boggling," he said. "The ship sails at seven. At this rate we'll spend more time on the road than in one of the great wonders of antiquity."

It was clear that the seventeen-year-old daughter of Winston Andrews was in absolute agreement. "Mom, this is so boring," she commented a number of times, obviously not caring who heard her.

By the time the range that held the Silver Mountain loomed before them, there were no buses or trucks in either direction. The driver suddenly pulled off onto a road between two crevices. Almost hidden, it wound to the right. He stopped the minibus several hundred yards later.

The guide and he conferred, then Sayyid stood up. "Will everyone please leave the vehicle?" he asked courteously. "The driver must try to locate the trouble with the engine and feels it would be safer. He hopes it will not be too long."

As he rose Henry said, "I'm a fairly good mechanic. I'd be happy to help locate the trouble."

Sayyid looked at him dismissively. "The driver will not require assistance, Mr. Potter."

"Nevertheless he's going to get it if he doesn't locate the trouble soon," Henry said firmly when the passengers were gathered outside. They had all moved to stand in the shadow of an overhanging boulder, shielded from the now blazingly hot midday sun. The hood of the minibus was up. Both the driver and guide were bent over the engine.

"I don't know why Daddy made us take this trip," Muffie Andrews complained to her mother.

Pamela Andrews, stylishly thin with auburn hair, snapped, "Because he thought you might actually learn something about history and the way other people live."

Lloyd and Audrey Cameron, silver haired and both somewhat frail, came over to Henry. "I don't like either that driver or the guide, Mr. Potter," Lloyd Cameron said quietly. "Do you think there's any possibility that there's more to this than a faulty engine?"

Sunday looked at Henry and realized that that was exactly what he was thinking. His eyes were narrowed and his forehead creased. "There's something up," he agreed. "I want everyone to get back in the bus. I'm going to tell that pair that I'm an engineer and insist on helping them. But I want all of you inside the bus when I do it."

"But . . ." Sunday bit her lip on her protest. Henry had a black belt in karate. Even so, she found herself wishing that Jack Collins and the other guys in their Secret Service detail were around.

As Henry went to speak to the driver and guide, she took the lead in getting the others to slip quietly on the bus.

Muffie Andrews protested, "It'll be hot in there."

"You heard my husband. Get in," Sunday told her sharply.

She realized that Lloyd Cameron was perspiring heavily.

Reaching a hand under his arm, she helped him up. She noticed him wince in pain. "Are you all right?" she asked quickly.

"Nothing a nitroglycerin tablet won't help," Audrey Cameron said, the worry in her voice evident.

Outside Henry was arguing with the driver and guide. "How can you possibly tell what's wrong without turning the engine over?" From the corner of his eye he could see that everyone was on the bus. He knew the key was in the ignition. These two were stalling, but for what? Waiting for accomplices? How much would they get if their purpose was robbery? Enough, he realized. Both Pamela Andrews and Audrey Cameron were wearing valuable diamond rings. Lloyd Cameron had a Rolex watch similiar to the one he usually wore himself.

Then his blood froze. In Arabic the driver said to Sayyid, "Why wait to kill this one and his wife? Do it now."

In two steps Henry had leapt on the bus, and slammed and locked the door. He turned the key, raced the engine, and jerked into reverse. He saw Sayyid and the driver reach into their pockets. "Duck," he shouted. But before he could switch into drive, thundering hoofs signaled the arrival of a dozen armed men, attired in burnooses and robes, who surrounded the bus, their rifles pointing at the windows. Without being told, Henry stopped the bus and turned off the engine.

In New Jersey, Sims paced the library waiting and hoping for the phone listed in his name to ring. The call he expected was already hours late. His instructions were to open the sealed envelope with the travel itinerary and call the White House if a full twenty-four hours lapsed without phone contact.

Not twenty-four hours yet, Sims comforted himself. *I am sure all is well.*

The ringing of the phone was a symphony to his ears. With dignified haste he reached for it. "Mr. Potter, good morning."

He was crushed when he heard the familiar voice of Jack

Collins, the head Secret Service agent. Collins did not waste time. "Sims, I've got the willies sitting around doing nothing. Has Ranger been checking in on time?"

Sims's fears crystallized. Something had gone wrong. Collins had sensed it too. "I'm afraid Mr. . . . er, Potter is twelve hours behind schedule."

"Twelve hours!" Collins exploded. "Open the packet."

"We are under firm orders to wait a full twenty-four hours before we check the itinerary," Sims protested.

"I'm on my way," Collins said. "By the time I get there it'll be a full sixteen hours. I'll take responsibility for opening the envelope."

He had just reached Drumdoe when the regular NBC program was interrupted. "A breaking story," Tom Brokaw announced briskly. "Six American tourists have been kidnaped in Ahman. The victims are the wife and daughter of media mogul Winston Andrews; philanthropist Lloyd Cameron and his wife, Audrey, founder and CEO of the Audrey Cosmetics empire. Not much is known about the other two, Harry and Sandra Potter, a retired educator and his wife from Massachusetts. The minibus they were in disappeared on its way to Silver Mountain, the legendary city carved out of rock some seven thousand years ago and only discovered again in this century."

Brokaw warned, "The State Department has issued a travel warning urging Americans to stay away from Ahman, since it is obvious their safety cannot be guaranteed."

Jack Collins and Sims stared at each other.

"Give me the itinerary," Collins demanded. Ashen, Sims nodded and went to the center drawer of Henry's desk.

Collins ripped open the envelope, scanned it, groaned, then with flying fingers pressed the numbers on the phone that would connect him to the Oval Office.

● ● ●

Desmond Ogilvey sat at his desk, the presidential seal behind him, surrounded by his advisors. It had been an uncommonly pleasant day in late March and he'd been longing to play a fast eighteen holes of golf with the Speaker of the House, whom he'd just scathingly attacked in the media but who also was one of his best friends.

A lean, spare man who epitomized the stereotype of the academic he once had been, Des Ogilvey was a remarkably intelligent, shrewd statesman who never forgot that he'd been plucked from congressional obscurity by his predecessor and best friend, Henry Parker Britland, IV.

Instead of golf, the day had brought a major crisis, a new hot-potato hostage situation.

Hostage. The word sickened him. Lebanon . . . Iran . . . hijacked planes. Innocent victims, cries for retribution at home, fractured political alliances abroad, sounding board for revolutionists.

This time in Ahman; six Americans vanished on their way to Silver Mountain. The minibus they'd been riding in found one hundred miles to the north of their planned destination.

The kidnapers had chosen their targets well. The wife and daughter of Winston Andrews: he'd already been on the phone three times and was now in his private jet heading for Ahman. Lloyd and Audrey Cameron: they'd been at a state dinner only a month ago. If those people were not returned unscathed, all hell would break loose. Somebody in Ahman would be hung out to dry, and in this case Des was sure it would be the sultan. Mac, westernized, smart, our friend in the volatile Middle East, was vulnerable. His absolute monarchy had been a source of criticism no matter how many reforms he had instigated.

And of course there was another couple involved, a former high-school teacher from Massachusetts, some poor schmuck named Harry Potter and his wife. Probably saved money all their lives to take that upscale cruise.

The private phone rang. Only one person called on this one.

Henry. Just the person he wanted to talk to about this calamity. Henry was a big buddy of the sultan.

Ogilvey answered with his automatic greeting to Henry. "Mr. President," he said. Then listened. "Oh, my God!" he groaned.

His advisors and aides leapt to their feet. He waved them back, continued to listen to his caller, then finally snapped, "I'll call you back, Collins."

Hanging up, he said quietly, "Get me the sultan of Ahman."

"Right away, sir." His chief of staff reached for a nearby phone.

Ogilvey considered. "No. Wait. Hold it." He looked without pleasure at the anxious faces around him. "Get out, all of you. I need to think."

When he was alone, he folded his hands under his chin. The kidnapers didn't know who they had, but they'd been daring enough to select other highly visible targets. God knows what they would do if they were aware they were holding a former president of the United States and his congresswoman wife.

Some hostages were released when a ransom was paid. So far, the kidnapers had not made any demands. Maybe money was what they wanted. *There's only one thing I can do right now,* Desmond Ogilvey agonized. *Keep my mouth shut and trust Henry. He's gotten out of other tight spots.*

Henry had appeared to be drifting in and out of consciousness since the guide smashed a rifle butt on the side of his head before they were carried on horseback to this place. First their captors had forced the women to slip a long black *sharshaf,* the traditional Islamic garment, over their own clothing and veil their faces. Lloyd Cameron and the unconscious Henry had been dressed in long flowing robes, their heads covered with burnooses. To any observer they might have been a band of Bedouins traveling through the mountains. No one would have realized that the horsemen surrounding them had guns trained at their hearts.

The unconscious Henry had been thrown across the saddle of a horse. Sunday had been frantic until they finally arrived at their destination. Henry whispered that he wanted the captors to believe that he was badly injured.

But now she had to talk to him. "I think Lloyd Cameron is going into a full-fledged heart attack," she murmured as she held her face to his.

It was the second day of captivity. They were being kept in a network of caves in the mountain range behind Silver City.

Their captors had taken them into the shallow but well-hidden warren, finally settling in the next-to-the-last cave, barricading the narrow area between them and this final chamberlike area with rocks and sheets of tin. Only a space as wide as a small window had been left for food to be passed back and an observer to periodically check on them.

Muffie Andrews was asleep on her mother's shoulder as far to the back as possible. Even though it was cold she had yanked off the *sharshaf* and veil.

Lloyd Cameron was half lying, half sitting against the wall nearest to the hint of fresh air that came through the open space. His gasping breath was deep and irregular; Audrey Cameron had her arm around him. Even in the near darkness the agony of worry on her face was clearly visible.

Henry's finger touched her lips and Sunday realized he was trying to overhear what their captors were saying. Henry was a linguist, and she remembered that Arabic was one of the many languages he understood and spoke.

She could feel his body tense. Whatever he was hearing was upsetting him.

Henry strained to hear their captors. As the voices rose and fell, he sickened, realizing that they had no intention of seeking ransom. They were discussing that the first two hostages, the insignificant teacher and his wife, would be shot at ten o'clock tomorrow morning and their bodies dumped on the outskirts of the city.

The sultan, General al Hez at his side, would of course deplore the violence and beg that the lives of the other hostages be spared. The next morning when those four bodies were found, al Hez would declare a revolution against the corrupt regime that had rejected his demands for permission to wipe out the wandering tribes of murdering Bedouins and in the name of the people execute the sultan and his family as they try to escape.

We're all going to die, Henry thought helplessly. *There's no way out of here.*

"The girl . . . the young beauty . . . a shame to let her die. I could get ten thousand camels for her. . . ." It was the voice of their guide, bin Sayyid.

I wouldn't put it past him to put his hands on her, Henry thought.

"This place . . . this Shinona Cavern . . . will again be enshrined in history. . . ." It was the bus driver's deep, clipped tone.

Shinona Cavern . . . Henry thought. Shinona Cavern . . . *Mac brought me here the summer he showed me around Silver Mountain.* It was the place where the legend is that an ancient king took refuge against a palace plot. He was followed here but escaped through the secret passageway that goes underground to the temple in Silver Mountain. Mac showed me the way. I'm sure it's right here in this chamber.

The voices of their captors began to trail off. It was almost midnight. He sensed that soon they'd be checking on them one last time before morning. He lolled his head to the side as though still unconscious, then whispered, "Sunday, demand they throw blankets back here. Tell them you're afraid Lloyd Cameron will die before ransom can be paid."

It isn't in the plan for Cameron to die yet, he thought.

A moment later he heard Sunday's voice speaking fiercely. "Listen, bin Sayyid, I know you're still 'guiding' us, you creep.

Unless you want a dead hostage, you'll at least give us something
to cover Mr. Cameron."

Good girl, Henry thought, then held his breath.

He heard a short barking spat of laughter, then through slitted eyes watched as, a few minutes later, a rolled blanket was
pushed through the opening, followed by another one. Then a
third cover of sorts began to come into view to the accompani-
ment of a spattering of small rocks.

It worked, he thought exultantly. "Sunday, while they're still
watching, pull me back farther," he whispered, "as much away
from their direct view as possible. Then cover me and pass the
other blankets around."

It only took a few minutes before his goal was accomplished.
He sensed bin Sayyid was watching as Sunday tucked the blanket
around him, then handed out the others.

When she lay down beside him, her back to the opening,
shielding him from view, Sayyid snapped, "Sleep well. I don't want
to hear any more demands. Got that?"

Quickly Henry whispered instructions. Sunday nodded,
grabbed the soiled, scratchy blanket, shaped it to resemble a body,
and threw her arm over it. The Camerons, grateful for the bit of
warmth, were huddled together. They stared when he slid over to
them.

"I'm going for help," Henry whispered. "Hang on. Pretend
to stay asleep as long as possible."

Muffie Andrews had awakened. He put his lips against her
ear. "You've got to keep that *sharshaf* and veil on." He murmured
to Pamela Andrews, "If bin Sayyid tries to come near her, say she's
unwell."

They both understood what he meant. Pamela Andrews's
eyes widened in fear. "At least it isn't boring," Muffie tried to
joke.

Henry patted her shoulder.

For an instant he touched Sunday's hand, then began inching
on his stomach to the place at the side and back of this chamber

where, twenty-five years ago, he and the crown prince of Ahman had lifted the stone that led to a tunnel, hardly wider than a drain-pipe, that had saved a sultan's life twenty-five hundred years ago.

Three hours later, just outside Silver Mountain, the sleeping fourteen-year-old attendant of the camels used for picture-taking tourists stirred in his sleep. But he did not awaken as one of the camels was led from the enclosure by a man in a long robe and burnoose.

Henry, his robe torn and filthy, led the camel a safe distance before he ordered it to kneel. An instant later he was galloping to the capital city, a distance of at least four hours. He had to get in touch with Des. It was the only way.

In the cave, Sunday spent the night praying. Sometimes she heard Audrey Cameron murmuring to her husband. She thought she heard Muffie Andrews weeping. But, as a random touch of daylight started to trickle into the cavern, she thought: If he got through he might be in Acqiom now. Maybe help is already on the way.

It was nearly seven and the hot desert sun was rising high over the ancient city of Acqiom when Henry abandoned the ex-hausted camel and set into town on foot. Seven o'clock here, thir-teen hours difference. Des would be in the White House. But how to get to him? He'd have to try to steal a tourist's pocketbook in the market. Get a credit card. Make the call.

But the market was deserted. In the bay he could see two gleaming ocean liners. They probably had arrived during the night, but the tourists wouldn't be here until at least nine. He couldn't wait that long.

Despairingly he walked through the city in the direction of the palace. Built by Mac when he became monarch, it was a modern building with low, rounded rooftops and a pink-and-cream marble facade that reflected the brilliance of the sunrise. He could see that the palace was surrounded by guards.

Henry looked up at the windows that he knew were the private apartments of the monarch. He wanted to shout, "Mac!" the way he had when they were students in Cambridge. So near . . . But that traitor al Hez was in there too. At a hint of danger he'd step up his plan.

Henry turned. There was only one thing he could do. Would it work? Get to a hotel, get to a phone. He could not waste time. Sunday was going to be executed in less than two hours. When they realized he was missing, they might kill all the hostages.

The streets were still quiet, the shops still shuttered. In the direction of the bay, Henry could see the tip of a spire. Of course! The spire was part of the lavish new hotel they'd noticed on the minibus. "The sultan wished to promote tourism," Sayyid had announced, his voice dripping with sarcasm.

There's sure to be plenty of phones there. He had to get to one. But looking like this, they'd never let him in the door.

He loitered in the parking lot facing the entrance for fifteen minutes before he found his opportunity. The doorman stepped into the parking valet's booth to the side of the entrance. He did not see the tall man in a soiled robe and torn burnoose, his pasted Vandyke beard slipping from his chin, stride through the wide luggage door into the lobby, which, to Henry's dismay, was filled with media people. Pulling the loose end of the burnoose over his chin, Henry drifted through the crowd toward the corridor, where a sign indicated rest rooms and telephones.

He had almost cleared the lobby when an elevator door opened and Winston Andrews, accompanied by General al Hez, emerged.

Microphones were thrust at them; cameras popped, as Andrews, his face creased with fury and worry, announced, "I am going by helicopter to again stand by at the point where my wife and daughter disappeared. I am ready to pay any price to get them back. I have been heartened by the support of General al Hez, who has been candid about the problems of roving criminals in this country. He was personally responsible for rescuing a group of German tourists last year."

Al Hez stepped forward. "I am ashamed that this has happened in my country. It should not have happened. All our resources are scouring the countryside. I return to the palace to be with the sultan."

Why isn't Mac speaking for himself? Henry thought. That swine al Hez is setting up the revolt. Andrews won't blame him no matter what happens.

Accompanied by the general, Andrews strode through the lobby, angrily pushing away mikes that were raised before him. Any thought Henry had fleetingly entertained about trying to communicate with one of his associates disappeared. Sure, Andrews would believe him, but the slightest leak would be disaster. He didn't doubt that those thugs were in touch with events. They'd kill the captives and get away if they thought something had gone wrong.

"You look familiar, friend."

Henry turned, instinctively reaching to be sure the burnoose was covering the lower half of his face. It was Dan Rather, anchorman of CBS. His cameraman was behind him, the camera trained on Henry.

Henry frowned. "What do you want?" he barked in Arabic.

Rather looked uncertain. "Sorry."

Henry thought, *I can trust Dan,* but then became aware of curious eyes on them. No. Not here and now. Ignoring the famous broadcaster, he again headed for the corridor. A phone booth was empty. He picked up the receiver, pressed zero, and asked to be connected to an overseas operator. Finally one came on.

"A collect call." He gave the number registered to Sims at Drumdoe.

There was no answer.

Ten minutes later he tried again, this time giving the main number.

Again no answer. They'd given the rest of the household staff a holiday, but where was Sims?

Of course. He had opened the envelope. He had contacted Des. If Henry knew anything it was that Sims and Collins, with all the Secret Service guys, were on the way here now.

There was a line for the phone booth. Henry glanced out at a sea of angry faces. There was just one thing he could do. "Another number collect," he told the operator, then prayed. "Please God let him take the call."

It was seven-fifty. Sunday knew that for the last hour their captors had been looking in to see if they were awake. Now she was sure that unless they all began to stir, suspicion would be aroused. Had Henry gotten to Acqiom? Who had he contacted there? What had he overheard last night that so upset him?

No use thinking about it, she decided.

Clearly it was going to be a brilliantly sunny day. Light was filtering into this cavern far more than it had yesterday or the day before. The blanket that last night had been a reasonable facsimile of a man's body now seemed pathetic as a disguise.

Muffie Andrews seemed to understand the problem. She left her mother's side, their blanket in hand. "Mrs. Potter, maybe your husband would like our blanket too."

Together they threw it over the supposed form of Henry.

"Such caring," bin Sayyid's voice echoed hollowly from the opening. "Surely your husband would enjoy a last meal, Mrs. Potter."

Last meal, Sunday thought.

"And, Muffie," bin Sayyid continued. "You don't have to

wear the *sharshaf* or veil now. Why don't you take them off?" It was not a request.

Pamela Andrews stood up, thrusting Muffie at Sunday. "My daughter will remain suitably garbed. I must speak to you, Mr. Sayyid." She began to move forward when the faint sound of a vehicle approaching made Sayyid turn abruptly from the opening.

Desmond Ogilvey was about to leave his office with Patrick Blair, his chief of staff, to once again face the media, when one of his private phones rang. Probably his mother calling to offer suggestions on what to do in the crisis. He wasn't up to it.

Impatiently, he put his hand on the door of the Oval Office as the ringing continued to permeate the room. There was an urgency about it that was bothering him.

Reluctantly he nodded to Blair. "Tell my mother I'll call her back."

He watched impatiently as Blair's brief hello was followed by widened eyes. "Are you kidding?" the chief of staff demanded.

Some instinct made Ogilvey rush across the room.

"Sir, it's got to be a sick joke," Blair told him. "The operator wants to know if you'll accept a collect call from a Mr. Potter."

At eight-thirty, Henry waited impatiently, watching the side gate of the palace. Every passing second was agony. Had Des been able to get through to Mac or had the call been stopped inside the palace? If he did get through, had Mac believed that he could trust none of his Army brass, that his own life was in danger? And if he did understand, would he be able to get out of the palace unnoticed?

If Mac didn't show up . . . It was one of the few times in his life that Henry felt absolutely helpless. There was no alternate plan that could possibly work.

Sunday. The other hostages . . . Please, God . . . Henry realized he was praying. Time was so short. He needed a miracle.

And then he saw what he had been desperate to see. A service van stopped at the guard's station and was permitted to pass. It drove up the street, around the corner, and slowed.

The driver rolled down the tinted window. He was dressed in a coarse, dark robe, a flowing burnoose, and heavy dark glasses. But when he whipped the glasses off, nothing could conceal the aristocratic features of the sultan of Ahman.

Three minutes later, aware that time was racing against them, they drove back to the palace. This time the guard waited before opening the door.

"Insolent . . ." the sultan muttered.

Henry jammed his foot on his friend's instep. "Mac, wait!"

The gate opened. They drove through. In the service parking area the sultan ripped off the coarse robe, revealing a western business suit. "Let's go, Henry."

A few minutes later, in his magnificent private office, surrounded by officers of the division that was his personal guard, he sent for General al Hez. When the man arrived, confident and with self-satisfaction emanating from every pore, he was astonished to be surrounded by the soldiers.

"You and your entire staff are under arrest," the sultan told him. "You are a traitor to your country and your people. For the sake of your ancestors and descendants, the captives had better be safe."

Al Hez paled, then gasped as Henry stepped forward. "I know that you have ordered my wife executed in less than an hour. Call it off."

Now al Hez smiled. "I know what will happen to me, but it's already too late for her, Mr. Potter. I have given the final order to proceed. No more communication will be accepted as genuine."

• • •

The car or van that had arrived had distracted Sayyid. Nearly an hour had passed. What was going on? *If only I understood Arabic,* Sunday fretted. Cautiously she slipped up to the opening and stood next to it. Clearly some sort of preparations were being made, but for what? She could tell that Sayyid and the driver lapsed into English occasionally. Then she heard Sayyid say, "I can wait for the girl. It's only fifteen minutes more till ten o'clock. After we get rid of the Potter couple, we can do what we want. The old man is helpless and the other women terrified. At five of ten, tell them to pull open the barrier and drag the first two out."

Henry and the sultan were in the first of the armada of helicopters. They had just had their first glimpse of the mountain range where the prisoners were being held. "Almost there, Henry," the sultan promised.

"If only we had time to go through the tunnel." Henry's throat was closing with tension. It was two minutes of ten.

"We don't but Allah is with us. We will be there in time."

"They might panic and shoot all of them."

"They will know their only hope for mercy is if the hostages remain unharmed."

Henry looked back. Two dozen helicopters, each containing six armed men, enough to overpower the kidnapers but too many to surprise them. They'd already be poised to shoot Sunday.

They were over the cave. Henry looked down, then sickened as he realized there was barely room for one helicopter to land near it. In the important first moments the soldiers would be useless.

"Put it down," the sultan commanded the pilot. The descent was rapid. As the wheels touched the rocky surface, both men jumped out. There were only seconds left till ten o'clock.

"We can't wait," Henry snapped.

"I know it. Stay here," the sultan ordered the pilot and copilot. "It's too late for guns."

• • •

The captors had broken the barrier and were coming for her. Lloyd Cameron made a futile effort to stand. Audrey Cameron, Muffie, and Pamela Andrews were shrieking.

Sunday fought back. She stiffened her palm and cracked it on the throat of the first man who tried to grab her, then attempted to kick the second one. But then her arms were roughly yanked behind her back and Sayyid was in front of her.

"Get him," he ordered, nodding to the prone figure that was supposed to be Henry's body.

The yelp of surprise from the man who found himself holding an empty blanket and the realization that Henry was missing stunned Sayyid. He grabbed Sunday by the hair and yanked her face up to his. "Where is he? How did he escape?"

She did not answer. He yanked again and the black wig came off in his hand. Her blond shoulder-length hair tumbled out.

His look of astonishment was followed by a shriek from Audrey Cameron. In a trembling voice she cried, "I knew you seemed familiar. You're Sunday. Then that was the president."

The president. Of what? Sayyid stared at Sunday and realization dawned. He had had the former president of the United States under his control and didn't even know it. The game was over. But he could still have satisfaction. He'd always had his own contingency escape plan. In two hours he'd be over the border. But first . . .

His men, confused, and somewhat frightened, were staring at Sunday. Sayyid shoved her away.

"Take aim," he said.

They pointed their guns at Sunday.

"All of them," Sayyid snapped.

There was a roaring sound outside. A helicopter. Al Hez must have made his escape and come for him.

He lifted his hand. The men, now frightened and confused by the noise outside the cave, knew to fire when he dropped it.

He looked at Sunday. "For you I would have given twenty thousand camels."

"Stop!" The voice of majesty filled the chamber. Side by side Henry and the sultan stepped through the widened opening.

Awed, the kidnapers stared at their monarch.

"Mercy and exile will be given to those who put down their guns," the sultan said, his tone frightening in its absolute authority.

The clatter of rifles was followed by the deep, subservient bows of the outlaws.

"Majesty, your generosity . . ." Sayyid began.

As Henry reached for Sunday and running feet signaled the arrival of the royal troops, the sultan addressed Sayyid. "My generosity is not for you. You were not carrying a gun."

"So in some ways, the trip was quite successful, was it not, sir?" Sims asked as he presented Henry with a glass of champagne. After staying a night in the palace they were on their way home in Henry's private jet, which had flown Sims and the Secret Service detail to Ahman.

Sunday gasped. "How do you figure it was successful, Sims?"

"Well, from what I understand, madam, you weren't recognized for days. That must have been refreshing, only I do hope you won't try it again soon. It was quite distressing for us, oh my, yes."

Sunday thought of the moment when she'd been sure she was going to die. "Sims," she said, "you do have a way with words. It was quite distressing, oh my, yes!"

When Sims left, she said, "Henry, you had a few last words with the sultan. What did he want to tell you?"

"It was pretty interesting. When I sympathized with him about Hasna's death, he told me that one of al Hez's group at the Taj Mahal has confessed that Hasna was poisoned. But then we talked about the attempted revolution. Mac said that he's going to make some changes in government, set up ministers who represent the different areas of his country, give the people more of a voice in the government. He asked if I approved. Of course, I did. Then we both quoted an interesting proverb that we used to debate."

Sunday waited.

"No man is wise enough or good enough to be trusted with unlimited power," Henry said solemnly.

"I absolutely agree," Sunday said, "and not the least because if that weren't true in our country, I'd be out of a job."

Thomas H. Cook

If there have been more beautifully written books in the past three years than Thomas H. Cook's Mortal Memory, Breakheart Hill, *and* The Chatham School Affair, *I failed to read them. Although his early work was first rate—after all, he received Edgar Allan Poe Award nominations for* Sacrificial Ground *and* Blood Innocents, *as well as for a true crime book,* Blood Echoes, *his more recent, more mature novels are truly distinguished.*

It is always trite to say that a given work transcends its genre (as the Los Angeles Times *has said of Cook's work), because that is inevitably true of superior works of art. It remains, however, impossible not to say it of those books. They are mysteries, of course, in the sense that they contain crime and suspense and murder, but they are firstly poignant, elegant portraits of people and families that remain etched in the consciousness long after the covers have been closed.*

The following tale, conceived almost miraculously in the midst of a conversation, offers one of the most unexpected twists you are likely to experience—a surprise ending to end surprise endings.

Fatherhood

▼▼▼

BY THOMAS H. COOK

Watching them from a distance, the way she rocked backward and forward in her grief, her arms gathered around his lifeless body, I could feel nothing but a sense of icy satisfaction, relishing the fact that both of them had finally gotten what they deserved. Death for him. For her, perpetual mourning.

She'd worn a somber gown for the occasion, her face sunk deep inside a cavernous black hood. She stared down at him and ran her fingers through his blood-soaked hair, her features so hideously distorted by her misery it seemed impossible that she'd ever been young and beautiful, or ever felt delight in anything.

By then the years had so divided us and embittered me that I could no longer think of her as someone I'd once loved. But I *had* loved her, and there were times when, despite everything, I could still recall the single moment of intense happiness I'd had with her.

She'd been only a girl when we first met, the town beauty. Practically the only beautiful thing in the town at all, for it was a small, drab place set down in the middle of a desert waste. To find something beautiful in such a place was nearly miracle enough.

She was already being pursued by the local boys, of course. They were dazzled by her black hair and dark oval eyes, skin that gave off a striking olive glow. I yearned for her no less ardently than they, but I kept my distance.

Looking out my shop window, I would often see her as she swept down the street, heading toward the market, a large basket on her arm. Coming back, the basket now filled with fruit and vegetables, she'd sometimes stop to wipe a line of sweat from her forehead, her eyes glancing briefly toward the very window where I stood, watching her, and from which I always quickly retreated.

The fact is, she frightened me. I was afraid of the look that might come into her eyes if she saw me staring at her, their pity, perhaps even contempt, for a portly, middle-aged bachelor who worked in a dusty shop, lived alone in a single musty room, had no prospects for the future, and who had nothing to offer a vibrant young woman like herself.

And so I never expected to speak to her or approach her in any way. To the extent that she would ever know me, it seemed certain it would be as the anonymous figure she sometimes noticed as she made her way to the market, a person of no consequence or distinction, as flat and featureless in her mind as the old stones she trod upon. My fate would be to watch her silently forever, see her life unfold from behind my shop window, first as a young woman hastening to the market, then as a bride strolling arm-in-arm with her new husband, finally as a mother with children following be-hind her, her beauty deepening with the years, becoming fuller and richer while I kept my post at the window, growing old and sickly, a ghostly, gray-haired figure whose life had finally added up to nothing more than a long and fruitless longing.

Then it happened. One of those accidents that make a per-petual mystery of life, that bless the unworthy and doom the de-serving, and which give to all of nature the aspect of a flighty, cruel, and unloving queen.

One of my customers had tethered a horse to the post outside my shop. It was sleek and beautiful, and coming back from the market, the girl of my dreams stopped to admire it. First she patted its haunches. Then she moved up the twitching flanks to stroke its moist black muzzle. Finally, she fed it an ear of corn from the overflowing basket she'd placed at her feet.

"It is yours?" she asked me as I came out the door, my arms filled with the wood I used in my trade.

I stopped, astonished to see her staring at me, unable to believe that she'd actually addressed her question to me.

"No," I said. "It belongs to one of my customers."

She returned her attention to the horse, drawing her fingers down the side of its neck, twining her fingers in its long brown mane. "He must be very rich to have a horse like this." She looked at the wood still gathered in my arms. "What do you do for him?"

"Build things. Tables. Chairs. Whatever he wants."

She offered a quick smile, patted the horse a final time, then retrieved her basket from the street and sauntered slowly away, her brown arms swinging girlishly in the afternoon light, her whole manner so casual and lighthearted that only a sudden burst of air from my mouth made me realize that during the time I'd watched her stroll away from me, I had not released a breath.

I didn't talk to her again for almost three months, though I saw her in the street no less often than before. A young man sometimes joined her now, as beautifully tanned as she was, with curly black hair. He was tall and slender, and his step was firm, assured, the walk of a boy who had never wanted for anything, who'd inherited good looks and would inherit lots of money, the sort whose bright future is entirely assured. He would marry her, I knew, for he seemed to have the beauty and advantage that would inevitably attract her. For days I watched as they came and went from the market together, holding hands as young lovers do, while

I stood alone, shrunken and insubstantial, a husk the smallest breeze could send skittering down the dusty street.

Then, just as suddenly, the boy disappeared, and she was alone again. There were other changes too. Her walk struck me as less lively than it had been before, her head lowered slightly, as I had never seen it, her eyes cast toward the paving stones.

That anyone, even a spoiled, wealthy youth, might cast off such a girl as she seemed inconceivable to me. Instead, I imagined that he'd died or been sent away for some reason, that she had fallen under the veil of his loss, and might well be doomed to dwell within its shadows forever, a fate in one so young and beautiful that struck me as inestimably forlorn.

And so I acted, stationing myself on the little wooden bench outside my shop, waiting for her hour after hour, day after day, until she finally appeared again, her hair draped over her shoulders like shimmering black wings.

"Hello," I said.

She stopped and turned toward me. "Hello."

"I have something for you."

She looked at me quizzically, but did not draw back as I approached her.

"I made this for you," I said as I handed it to her.

It was a horse I'd carved from an olive branch.

"It's beautiful," she said, smiling quietly. "Thank you."

"You're welcome," I said and, like one who truly loves, asked nothing in return.

We met often after that. She sometimes came into my shop, and over time I taught her to build and mend, feel the textures and qualities of wood. She worked well with her hands, and I enjoyed my new role of craftsman and teacher. The real payment was in her presence, however—the tenderness in her voice, the light in her eyes, the smell of her hair—how it lingered long after she'd returned to her home on the other side of town.

Soon, we began to walk the streets together, then along the outskirts of the village. For a time she seemed happy, and it struck me that I had succeeded in lifting her out of the melancholy I had found her in.

Then, rather suddenly, it fell upon her once again. Her mood darkened and she grew more silent and inward. I could see that some old trouble had descended upon her, or some new one that I had not anticipated and which she felt it necessary to conceal. Finally, late one afternoon when we found ourselves on a hill outside the village, I put it to her bluntly.

"What's the matter?" I asked.

She shook her head, and gave no answer.

"You seem very worried," I added. "You're too young to have so much care."

She glanced away from me, let her eyes settle upon the far fields. The evening shade was falling. Soon it would be night.

"Some people are singled out to bear a certain burden," she said.

"All people feel singled out for the burdens they bear."

"But people who feel chosen. For some special suffering, I mean. Do you think they ever wonder why it was them, why it wasn't someone else?"

"They all do, I'm sure."

"What do you think your burden is?"

Never to be loved by you, I thought, then said, "I don't think I have one burden in particular." I shrugged. "Just to live. That's all."

She said nothing more on the subject. For a time, she was silent, but her eyes moved about restlessly. It was clear that much was going on in her mind.

At last she seemed to come to a conclusion, turned to me, and said, "Do you want to marry me?"

I felt the whole vast world close around my throat, so that I only stared at her silently until, at last, the word broke from me. "Yes." I should have stopped, but instead I began to stammer. "But I know that you could not possibly . . . that I'm not the one who can . . . that you must be . . ."

She pressed a single finger against my lips.

"Stop," she said. Then she let her body drift backward, pressing herself against the earth, her arms lifting toward me, open and outstretched and welcoming.

Any other man would have leapt at such an opportunity, but fear seized me and I couldn't move.

"What is it?" she asked.

"I'm afraid."

"Of what?"

"That I wouldn't be able to . . ."

I could see that she understood me, recognized the source of my disabling panic. There seemed no point in not stating it directly. "I'm a virgin," I told her.

She reached out and drew me down to her. "So am I," she said.

I didn't know how it was supposed to feel, but after a time she grew so warm and moist, my pleasure in her rising and deepening with each offer and acceptance, that I finally felt my whole body release itself to her, quaking and shivering as she gathered me more tightly into her arms. I had never known such happiness, nor ever would again, since to make love to the one you love is the greatest joy there is.

For a moment we lay together, she beneath me, breathing quietly, the side of her face pressed against mine.

"I love you," I told her, then lifted myself from her so that I could see her face.

She was not looking at me, nor even in my direction. Instead, her eyes were fixed on the sky that hung above us, the bright coin of the moon, the scattered stars, glistening with tears as she peered upward to where I knew her thoughts had flown. Away from me. Away. Away. Toward the one she truly loved and still longed for, the boy whose beauty was equal to her own, and for whom I could serve as nothing more than a base and unworthy substitute.

● ● ●

And yet I loved her, married her, then watched in growing astonishment as her belly grew day by day until our son was born.

Our son. So the townspeople called him. So she called him and I called him. But I knew that he was not mine. His skin had a different shade, his hair a different texture. He was tall and narrow at the waist, I was short and stocky. There could be no doubt that he was the fruit of other loins than mine. Not my child, at all, but rather the son of that handsome young boy she'd strolled the town streets with, and whose disappearance, whether by death or desertion, had left her so bereft and downcast that I'd tried to cheer her with a carved horse, walked the streets and byways with her, soothed and consoled her, sat with her on the far hillside, even made love to her there, and later married her, and in consequence of all that now found myself the parent and support of a child who was clearly not my own.

He was born barely six months after our night of love. Born weighty and full bodied and with a great mass of black hair, so that it could not be doubted that he had lived out the full term of his nurture.

From the first moment, she adored him, coddled him, made him the apple of her eye. She read to him and sang to him, and wiped his soiled face and feet and hindquarters. He was her "dear one," her "beloved," her "treasure."

But he was none of these things to me. Each time I saw him, I also saw his father, that lank and irresponsible youth who'd stolen my wife's love at so early an age that it could never be recaptured by her or reinvested in me. He had taken the love she might have better spent elsewhere, and in doing that, he had left both of us impoverished. I hated him, and I yearned for vengeance. But he had fled to parts unknown, and so I had no throat to squeeze, no flesh to cut. In his stead, I had only his son. And thus, I took out my revenge on a boy who, as the years passed, looked more and more like his youthful father, who had the same limber gait and airy disposition, a boy who had little use for my craft, took no interest in my business, preferring to linger in the town square, talking idly to the old men who gathered there, or while away the hours by reading books on the very hillside where I'd made love to his mother, and who, even as I'd released myself to her, had slept in the warm depths of her flesh.

I often thought of that. The fact that my "son" had been inside her that night, that my own seed had labored to reach a womb already hardened against them. Sometimes, lost in such dreadful speculations I would strike out at him, using my tongue like a knife, hurling glances toward him like balls of flame.

"Why do you hate him so?" my wife asked me time after time during those early years. "He wants to love you, but you won't let him."

My response was always the same, an icy silence, followed by a shrug.

And so the years passed, my mood growing colder and more sullen as I continued to live as a stranger in my own household. In the evening, I would sit by the fire and watch as a wife who had deceived me and a son who was not my son played games or read together, laughed at private jokes, and discussed subjects in which I had no interest and from whose content and significance I felt purposely excluded. Everything they did served only to heighten my solitary rage. The sound of their laughter was like a blade thrust into my ear, and when they huddled in conversation at the far corner of the room, their whispers came to me like the hissing of serpents.

During this time my wife and I had terrible rows. Once, as I tried to leave the room, she grabbed my arm and whirled me back around. "You're driving him from the house," she said. "He'll end up on the street if you don't stop it. Is that what you want?"

For once, I answered with the truth. "Yes, I do. I don't want him to live here anymore."

She looked at me, utterly shocked not only by what I'd said, but the spitefulness with which I'd said it. "Where do you expect him to live?"

I refused to retreat. "I don't care where he lives," I answered. "He's old enough to be on his own." There was a pause before I released the words I'd managed to choke back for years. "And if he can't take care of himself, then let his *real* father take care of him for a while."

With that, I watched as tears welled up in her eyes before she turned and fled the room.

But even after that, she didn't leave. Nor did her son. And so, in the end, I had to stay in the same house with them, live a life of silent, inner smoldering.

A year later he turned fifteen. He was nearly a foot taller than I was by then. He'd also gained something of a reputation as a scholar, a fact that pleased his mother as much as it disgusted me. For what was the use of all his learning if the central truth of his life remained unrevealed? What good all his command of philosophy and theology if he would never know who his father was, never know where he'd gotten his curly black hair and lean physique, nor even that keenness of mind which, given the fact that he thought me his natural father, must have struck him as the most inexplicable thing of all?

But for all our vast differences of mind and appearance, he never seemed to doubt that I truly was his father. He never asked about other relatives, nor about any matter pertaining to his origins or birth. When I called him to his chores, he answered, "Yes, Father," and when he asked my permission, it was always, "May I, Father?" do this or that. Indeed, he appeared to relish using the word. So much so, that I finally decided it was his way of mocking me, calling me "Father" at every opportunity for no other reason than to emphasize the point either that he knew I was not his father, or that he wished that I were not.

For fifteen years I had endured the insult he represented to me, my wife's deviousness, her false claim of virginity, the fact that I'd had to maintain a charade from the moment of his birth, claiming a paternity that neither I nor any of my neighbors for one moment believed to be genuine. It had not been easy, but I had borne it all. But with his final attempt to humiliate me by means of

this exaggerated show of filial obedience and devotion, this inces-
sant repetition of "Father, this" and "Father, that," he had finally
broken the back of my self-control.

And so I told him to get out, that he was no longer welcome
in my house, that no more meals would be provided, nor any bed
for him to sleep in, nor a fire to warm him, nor clothes for his back.

We stood together in the backyard, he watching me silently
while I told him all this. He'd grown a beard during the preceding
few weeks, his hair had fallen to his shoulders, and he'd taken to
going barefoot. "Yes, Father" was all he said when I finished.
Then he turned, walked back into the house, gathered a few personal items in a plain cloth knapsack, and headed down the street,
leaving only a brief note for his mother, its sneeringly ironic message clearly intended to render me one final injury, "Tell Father
that I love him, and that I always will."

I didn't see him again for eighteen years, though I knew that
my wife maintained contact, sometimes even making long treks to
visit whatever town he was passing through. She would return
quite exhausted, especially in the later years, when her hair was
gray and her once radiant skin had become so easily bruised that
the gentlest pressure left marks upon it.

I never asked about her trips, never asked a single question
about how her son was doing. Nor did I miss him in the least. And
yet, his absence never gave me the relief I'd expected. For it didn't
seem enough, my simply throwing him out of the house. I had
thought it might satisfy my need to get even with his father and my
wife for blighting my life, forcing me to live a transparent and
humiliating lie. But it hadn't.

Vengeance turned out to be a hungrier animal than I'd supposed. Nothing seemed to satisfy it. The more I thought of my
"son," the more I got news of his various travels and accomplishments, heard tales of the easy life he had, merely wandering about,

living off the bounty of others, the more I wanted to strike at him again, this time more brutally.

He had become quite well known by then, at least in the surrounding area. He'd organized a kind of traveling magic show, people said, and had invented an interesting patter to go along with his tricks. But when they went on to describe the things he said, it seemed to me that the "message" he offered was typical of the time. He was no different from the countless others who believed that they'd found the secret to fulfillment, and that their mission was to reveal that secret to the pathetic multitude.

I knew better, of course. I knew that the only happiness that is possible comes by accepting how little life has to offer. But knowing something and being able to live according to that knowledge are two different things. I knew that I'd been wronged, and that I had to accept it. But I could never put it behind me, never get over the feeling that someone had to pay for the lie my wife had told me, the false son whose very existence kept that lie whirling madly in my brain. I suppose that's why I went after him again. Just the fact that I couldn't live without revenge, couldn't live without exacting another, graver penalty.

It took me three years to bring him down, but in the end it was worth it.

She never knew that I was behind it. That for the preceding three years I'd silently waged my campaign against him, writing anonymous letters, warning various officials that he had to be watched, investigated, that he said violent things, urged people to violence, that he was the leader of a secret society pledged to destroy everything the rest of us held dear. By using bits of information gathered from my wife, I kept them informed about his every move so that agents could be sent to look and listen. He was arrogant and smug, and he had his real father's confidence that he could get away with anything. I knew it was just a matter of time before he'd say or do something for which he could be arrested.

I did all of that, but she never knew, never had the slightest hint that I was orchestrating his destruction. I realized just how fully I had deceived her only a few minutes after they'd finally peeled her away from his dead body and took it away to prepare it for burial. We were walking down the hill together, away from the place where they'd hung him, my wife muttering about how terrible it was, about how brutally the mob had taunted and reviled him. Such people could always be stirred up against someone like our son, she said, a "true visionary," as she called him, who'd never had a chance against them.

I answered her sharply. "He was a fraud," I said. "He didn't have the answer to anything."

She shook her head, stopped, and turned back toward the hill. It was not only the place where they'd executed him, but also the place where we'd first made love, an irony I'd found delicious as they'd led him to the execution site, his eyes wandering and disoriented, as if he'd never expected anything so terrible to happen to him, as if he were like his real father, wealthy and irresponsible, beyond the fate of ordinary men.

A wave of malicious bitterness swept over me. "He got what he deserved," I blurted out.

She seemed hardly to hear me, her eyes still fixed on the hill, as if the secret of his fate were written on its rocky slope. "No one told me it would be like this," she said. "That I would lose him in this way."

I grasped her arm and tugged her on down the hill. "A mother is never prepared for what happens to her child," I said. "You just have to accept it, that's all."

She nodded slowly, perhaps accepting it, then walked on down the hill with me. Once at home, she lay down on her bed. From the adjoining room, I could hear her weeping softly, but I had no more words for her, so I simply left her to her grief.

Night had begun to fall, but the storm that had swept through earlier that day had passed, leaving a clear blue twilight in its wake. I walked to the window and looked out. Far away, I could see the hill where he'd been brought low at last. It struck me that even in the last moments of his life, he'd tried to get at me just one more time. In my mind I could see him glaring down at me, goading me in exactly the way he had before I'd kicked him out of the house, emphasizing the word *Father* when he'd finally spoken to me. He'd known very well that this was the last time he'd ever talk to me. That's why he'd made such a production of it, staring right into my eyes, lifting his voice over the noise of the mob so that everybody would be sure to hear him. He'd been determined to demonstrate his defiance, his bitterness, the depth of his loathing for me. Even so, he'd been clever enough to pretend that it was the mob he cared about. But I knew that his whole purpose had been to humiliate me one last time by addressing me directly. "Father," he'd said in that hateful tone of his, "Father, forgive them, for they know not what they do."

Vicki Hendricks

When putting together an anthology with a theme, such as this one, sometimes a name leaps out that begs to be part of it.

I'd read an early copy of Miami Purity *by Vicki Hendricks and it made an impression. It is dark and sexy and violent—the ultimate female noir novel. When it came time to ask authors for a story, I thought,* Now, that Vicki Hendricks knows something about revenge! *She agreed to provide a story and it's a good one, laced with firsthand knowledge of the area and of boats. This story was written by the light of a kerosene lamp in the same location as the one described here.*

Until recently, the author lived on a sailboat in south Florida with two cats and two ferrets. I don't know if she ever had been involved with anyone like the fellow in this story, but if she had, you'd like to think that the real-life model came to a bad end.

 West End

BY VICKI HENDRICKS

Kyle switched hands on the tiller and gave Regina his used toothpick. She looked at the frayed end and flipped the pick into the Atlantic.

"Regina, you know we only have half a pack left. I wanted you to put that back in the galley to save for tomorrow."

"Sorry, Kyle, I thought it was finished. I can do without my share."

"There was one end left. Just ask if you're not sure. Always ask. Remember that."

He turned his head the other way and she saluted. He looked so distinguished with his graying hair curling from under his hat, but he never lightened up on her sailing education. They had been sailing the *Spring Fling* together for the last six years of their marriage. Kyle was a sailor above all else, even when the idea of owning a boat had just been a twinkle in his eye.

"Nice turn of the bilge," he'd said to her the first time they slept together, when she was just nineteen, nearly twenty years in the past. At the time she didn't know he was comparing the shape of her buttocks to the hull of a sailboat.

He turned back to face her. "Do me a favor. Go down in the cabin." He looked off to port.

"And do what?"

"Go down and I'll tell you when you get there."

She felt a retort like backwash in her throat but swallowed it. She turned to step down the companionway steps.

"Regina!"

"What?"

"Oh, I thought you were going to walk down forward instead of backward," he said.

"Don't you think I know anything?"

He didn't answer, was staring off into the horizon again.

"Okay. I'm waiting. Kyle?"

"Go into the forward starboard locker on the second shelf toward midships."

"And?"

"Get the little black leather case and find my fingernail clippers."

"Why didn't you just ask for the clippers? I know where you keep them."

No answer.

She didn't expect one. She took the clippers up and pressed them into his hand.

"Now take the tiller. Keep the compass on ninety degrees."

"Gotcha, Skipper."

Regina took the smooth varnished tiller and held it gently with two fingers as Kyle had shown her again and again. She shifted her eyes from the compass to the top of the mast to check the wind vane. They were sailing on a run, straight downwind, with the jib to port and the main to starboard. It was going to be tricky to keep the boat on course and the sails filled. She didn't want to jibe. Even in these light conditions, Kyle would have a fit. The Pearson forty-two-footer was their only child.

Kyle put his head down and began working on his nail.

Regina was sailing well, keeping the course, barely moving the tiller. She'd found the groove.

Kyle said he needed to go down to take off his foul-weather gear and get into some lighter clothes.

"Fine, honey," she said. "I've got it."

He stepped below and she filled herself with fresh salty air. She looked at the small islands in the distance, Carter Cays. They only had three miles to go until they could anchor for the night and make a nice conch chowder for dinner. Conch. Conch had become her favorite seafood. She remembered the conch fritters she'd had at the Star Bar in West End a few days before.

She thought of one of the locals, Rodney. She'd danced three times with him. Ooh, the sway of his young hips, the way he smoothed her hair behind her ear. He said he liked long blond hair. He was probably fifteen years younger than she was. Kyle was fifteen years older. That was balance, she thought. Just like the sails. If the sails are balanced, the slot is just right for maximum speed and stability. Sailing, that's what she should be thinking about.

The jib began to flutter. "Starboard!" Kyle said. He always caught the least sound, didn't even look up.

She'd already turned slightly to starboard, but as always, she jumped at his order and turned some more. It was too much. The wind caught the backside of the main and, before she could correct her course, banged the boom across to the other side. The noise sent lightning zinging through Regina's brain.

"Fuck. God damn, Regina. You trying to tear the rigging off the fucking boat? Can't I count on you to do anything for one second? Jesus Christ!"

She didn't answer. It was true, she'd let her mind wander and her hand follow. She needed practice. But maybe she didn't want any. She looked at the mast. Luckily no harm was done. Kyle went forward to inspect.

The long day became longer when Kyle felt it necessary to reanchor three times at Carter Cays. He refused to get an electric winch, being a purist in every sense. He refused anything to make sailing easier and only used the engine for docking, anchoring, and emergency. They'd sit for days if the wind died or tack for a week with the wind tight on the nose. He even anchored and picked up under sail, if possible.

Today, thank God, it wasn't possible in the small space between the island and the shoal. Kyle pulled in the anchor from the bow while Regina worked the tiller and throttle.

"Starboard, more, more!" Kyle screamed.

"Starboard!" She repeated his order as instructed. She had pushed the tiller immediately, but the boat never responded fast enough for Kyle to realize. Soon she'd gone too far.

"Port! Port!"

"Port!"

"Neutral! Neutral!"

"Neutral!" she yelled.

She went through it at every stop, every spring, when Kyle decided it was time for a couple relaxing months in the Bahamas. She loved the water and exploring the small islands and snorkeling across the shallows to find conch. She could swim with the exotic fish and nosy barracudas all day, but Kyle's anal attitude never ceased to make her nervous.

He dropped the main and told her to get the sail cover, although she was already bringing it up from below. She tied the cover over his neatly rolled sail, exactly as he had instructed her over the years, shifting and straightening it until it was perfect and she was dripping with sweat.

"Sit down," Kyle said when she'd finished. He was sipping a gin and tonic. He motioned her to the cockpit.

She thought of having a drink herself, but decided to wait

until after his lecture. Kyle wouldn't think she was attentive enough.

"Do you know why you jibed today?" he asked.

"Yes, I do," she answered.

"Then tell me."

She gave a long and tedious description of how she'd turned too far and the wind had gotten behind the sail, then waited through his repetition of everything she already knew. Her mind floated back to the Star Bar. She was caught up in a warm breeze of memory and feeling, swaying next to Rodney, although she had never touched him.

"I only tell you this and go over everything so carefully because I want you to be the best sailor you can be. Understand?"

"Yes, I do," she said.

He squeezed her shoulder and kissed her. "Now cook us one of your delicious dinners. And be careful not to use more than one paper towel. We only have three rolls left." Regina knew they could buy supplies on Green Turtle in a couple days, but no way would Kyle pay the double prices of the Bahamas.

She stepped down into the galley and started peeling the potatoes for conch chowder. Her mind went right back to the warm place inside itself, the dim, paneled interior of the Star Bar. The jukebox was playing and Rodney was touching her hair. It was the only detail she needed.

Kyle fell asleep early that night. Regina was grateful. He was as demanding a lover as a captain.

She sat on deck. She felt the anger begin to seethe in her stomach, hotter than the Tabasco sauce in the chowder. She wondered how many more times they would have to make this trip. She'd thought last year was the end. Kyle's epileptic seizures had recurred after years of no incidents.

"We could fly and rent a luxury suite at the Green Turtle Club," Regina had suggested. "Take it easy for a change."

"Over my dead body," Kyle had shouted. "I'm not going to sit in a hotel room and be waited on." The volume of his voice convinced her, although she'd never before noticed his opposition to being waited on.

Having built up his business, Kyle could afford to hire another computer engineer and cut his own working hours. The doctor put him on new medication, and Kyle had himself under control again. He insisted the sailing calmed him and made him forget the stress of work, the snarls of traffic, and his brother the alcoholic, who was always in need of money.

She knew Kyle would be up at first light, ready to put the outboard on the dinghy and head to the reef where they'd learned to find conch a few years ago. But she couldn't settle down and quench the singeing resentment in her throat. She stepped back down into the galley to get a toothpick. At least she could dislodge an annoying bit from between her teeth.

She opened the box and took one pick out. The box was nearly full. Kyle had lied in order to make her feel guilty. A smug feeling came over her. She shook half of the toothpicks into her hand, and put the box back. She went up on deck and looked at the moon, a silver pearl, and flung the toothpicks away, out into the water. She heard the lightest shower as they hit. It was too dark to see, but she imagined them headed away like a little flotilla toward freedom.

Kyle wouldn't be able to comment. There was still half a box left like he'd said.

After that she dozed right off, facing the sky on a seat cushion with a beach towel pulled over her. She was looking at the Pleiades, Kyle's favorite constellation, imagining Rodney's lips on her neck.

In the morning Regina awoke full of lightness and energy. She knew they'd be spending a lazy day exploring in the dinghy and snorkeling the shallows where she wouldn't have to concentrate. Her mind could go to the warm space she had created with Rodney. It didn't matter that she knew nothing about him, that he could be a married man or a paid gigolo.

When Kyle noted her feet were not in the right spot in the

dinghy, and when she was too slow getting the anchor up, and later when she pinned the wet clothes on the safety lines in the wrong direction for optimal drying, she didn't even care. She had freed her spirit. "I'm trying," she said to Kyle. She adopted his ideal for her, without mocking. "I want to be the best sailor I can be."

That evening she climbed to the point of the V-berth and took Kyle's penis into her mouth.

"Move a little toward starboard," Kyle said. That meant he wanted her to lie with her breasts on his right thigh. She pushed herself against him without stopping the movement of her head. She didn't think about what she was doing. It was just her usual routine, in a boat in the middle of nowhere with a husband who had all the answers and all the questions. She felt his stiffness tighten and knew he was coming. She automatically added her hand on his "tiller" and slipped her mouth off in the last second before she pumped him out. Then she held tight until he relaxed. It was how he had trained her. She grabbed a handful of Kleenex and swabbed his deck, as he liked to say.

"Umm. Thanks. Your turn tomorrow," Kyle said. In a couple seconds the snoring started.

Regina got up to throw away the tissues and lit one of the kerosene lamps in the galley. Kyle wouldn't want her draining the battery by turning on a light, even though the wind generator and solar panels always provided plenty of power. Conserve, conserve. Nothing is ever enough when you can't get more.

She sat naked on a bunk in the soft glow and closed her eyes against the burn of the kerosene fumes. She landed herself right into Rodney's household. It was a small concrete block place on the rocky beach of West End, with no giant TV screen, no pool or Jacuzzi, no dock for a Pearson, maybe a dog or even a child running around. Whose child? She was sitting next to Rodney on a crushed velvet sofa, feeling the breeze through the screen door, watching a pink sunset out the living room window.

It was ridiculous. What would she do in West End? There

certainly wasn't any work, even if Rodney was free and interested in her. She couldn't give up her secretary position at the community college. Rodney was only a fantasy, but she could enjoy the feeling.

She opened the locker where Kyle kept his nail clippers and unzipped the leather pouch. Up on deck she hurled the clippers as far as she could and heard a plunk as they hit the water and sank to the sandy turtle-grass bottom. They would corrode, no matter how sturdy the metal. For some reason it gave her pleasure.

The next day she woke up happy again. Kyle's complaints couldn't spoil her mood. Together they motored to shore in the dinghy and bought fresh conch from some Bahamians, who had brought hundreds in their power boat to clean them at the deserted dock. Regina looked at the brown arms and long, dark hair on the man who handed her the conchs. Each time she reached for a slippery, rubbery handful of mollusk, she felt the warmth of his hand.

She took her Joy bath that day in the dinghy, whipping her hair into froth with a few drops of the yellow liquid, then smearing a white sheen over her body. She was now an even brown from the last two days of having no necessity for clothes. She smoothed her slippery breasts and thought how beautiful she was.

Kyle didn't notice the missing clippers. That night she dumped a pair of his Sperry boat shoes with socks. He had two pairs anyway. The last night at Carter she filled a medium trash bag with his visor, Swiss Army knife, the last bottle of gin, his shaving lotion, favorite Jockey shorts, and a Tupperware container with hanks of lines, all neatly looped, that Kyle had been saving up for years. The sound of the package hitting the water gave Regina a peace she'd never known before. She didn't feel guilty. She was tidying up—less to make a mess. A place for everything and everything in its place. Kyle didn't need any of that stuff.

He had set the alarm for six, before first light, so they could make it to their next destination, Green Turtle Cay. There they would dock to fill up on fuel and water and socialize with other sailing couples.

Kyle complained he couldn't find his shaving lotion.

"I don't know, honey," Regina said. "Maybe you set the bottle on deck and it got knocked over."

"You know I always put everything back in its place." He looked for his other pair of boat shoes that morning also. Regina watched him search and wonder at himself. He put on his damp shoes.

It was a cloudy, gusty day, winds reaching over twenty-five knots, according to Kyle's calculations. He put three reefs in the main and hooked up the storm jib that was hardly bigger than a hanky. They were on a run like before, only faster. It was an exhilarating ride. Regina watched the clouds blow away in front of them as they flew. Kyle was quiet for once, maybe enjoying himself. Suddenly the sun came out full and hot on their backs and faces.

"Regina, get my visor from the locker above the chart table."

She went down and started rummaging, knowing it was gone. She noticed she was whistling as she stepped back on deck.

"I can't find it, honey. Did you put it back last time?"

"Yes, I certainly did. I don't understand it." He paused to think.

"Yes, dear."

"Regina, I'm going to give you the tiller for thirty seconds while I look. You just aren't seeing it." He put his finger under her chin to bring her head up. "Remember what we learned the last time—about handling the tiller on a run?"

She nodded and smiled. "I know exactly what to do," she said.

Kyle stepped down the companionway and she swung the tiller hard to port, bracing herself. The boom slammed across with a crack like lightning. She thought the whole mast was going to topple, but it held.

She heard the roar of Kyle's obscenity from below. She looked down and saw him flopped across the settee. His eyes were glazed and his face was comic with anger. She wondered if he'd hit his head.

"You jibed!" he yelled. "You fucking jibed again!"

Regina smiled. A lunatic grin strained at her cheeks. She held the tiller alee, then brought it back amidships, and trimmed the sheets for a broad reach.

"What are you doing?" Kyle screamed. "Trying for a knock-down?"

"I was thinking I might, but I hate to get everything wet. Remember the time you did it?"

Kyle's eyes widened and he started to choke.

"Regina, get me those pills. Please. The Dilantin—on the shelf by the binoculars. I can't get up."

Regina put her hands on her hips. "Please, you said? You've fallen and you can't get up?"

Regina trimmed the sails and tied the tiller so the *Spring Fling* would hove to. She reached the shelf inside the cabin without leaving the cockpit. "Here they are, sweetheart," she said. "What should I do now? See, Kyle, I'm asking—like you always tell me to do."

She heard a gurgle. He was lying flat on his back staring through the hatch at her.

She held up the pills. The bottle flipped from her hand and flew portside. She couldn't distinguish a splash, with the wind and slapping waves, but they were gone. "Oops. The pills are with your aftershave and your dry shoes."

She listened to the noises coming from his throat. She thought he was listening.

"I'd need to put on my snorkeling gear. I could also look for your nail clippers and favorite underwear—but I'm afraid they're long gone. Maybe you'd like to go in after them?"

Kyle started shaking violently, his arms and legs hyperextending, drool running down his neck. Regina went up to release the jib and pull it down.

She returned and glanced into the cabin to see Kyle's head

lolling on the back of the settee. His eyes were wide open. His body was slumped partly onto the sole.

She slipped down the companionway and felt the side of his neck for a pulse. There wasn't any; neither was there the sickening odor of his aftershave.

She turned on the VHF and picked up the mike. Channel sixteen came on automatically. She pressed the button and yelled hysterically. "Mayday! Mayday! This is the *Spring Fling*. Need assistance immediately." She let up on the button and waited. No response. She tried again. "Mayday! Mayday!"

This time she got an answer. It was a sailboat west of Carter, from where she had come. She told them in a frantic voice that the captain was unconscious and she was an inexperienced mate. They responded that they would keep trying for the Bahamian Air Rescue. She told them she'd get her position from the GPS. She thanked them, her voice shaking.

Regina turned the boat into the wind, went forward and dropped the main, then returned to the cockpit and started the engine in neutral. She got out the GPS, locked in the satellites, noted her position, and got the waypoint for Carter on the route to West End. She adjusted her compass course and pushed the throttle forward until she had 2,000 rpm's, as recommended. The engine was tuned perfectly, as Kyle always kept it. This was surely emergency use.

She knew the Rescue team would be there in no time to take Kyle's body. She was on her way to Rodney, taking her chance, a big one, leaving her wealthy, conservative life behind. But without Kyle, Rodney didn't matter so much. She didn't need to think of his hand on her hair or his living room glowing in the sunset.

She went back forward, rolled the sail, and secured the ties with square knots. She knew it wouldn't be neat enough for Kyle. She glanced down at his body, staring wide-eyed from the settee, silent for once. She hooked the GPS to the autopilot—no need for more steering practice—and went below. She pulled out the sail cover and tied it down one last time, over Kyle's dead body.

Stepping back on deck she saw that the Dilantin bottle had caught at the port gunwale and was rolling along the deck.

She opened the bottle and took one pill to Kyle. "Here, I found them. They weren't in their place." She peeled the sail cover from his face, opened his teeth, and put a tablet on his bloody tongue. She closed his jaw. A tear dropped from her eye to Kyle's cheek, but she felt no regret.

She took a beer from the fridge and went back to the cockpit and stretched out across a cushion. The engine soothed her with its loud rhythm. Regina relaxed, confident in her ability to safely make the two-day run to West End.

Joan Hess

It is not uncommon to encounter Joan Hess and immediately think she's mad at somebody about something. This is a formidable-looking woman who isn't about to take any nonsense, you bet. Of course, after a couple of seconds, it is entirely likely that she'll have a great smile on her face, and she's guaranteed to put one on anybody within earshot. She is, and there can be no argument about this, one of the funniest people on the planet.

The story that follows is not comic, but many of her novels are, and she has developed a large and appreciative readership. With more than twenty books to her credit in a relatively brief time, she has still managed to find the energy to join and be active in a large number of mystery organizations, including Sisters in Crime, Mystery Writers of America, American Crime Writers' League, and the Arkansas Mystery Writers Alliance; perhaps coincidentally, she lives in Arkansas.

Hess doesn't only write a lot of books, she writes good ones, as evidenced by her many awards, which include the American Mystery Award, an Agatha, and a McCavity.

Caveat Emptor

BY JOAN HESS

The first time she came walking across the street, I pegged her for a whiner. Her shoulders drooped like she thought she was carrying a goodly portion of the world's woes in a backpack, and from her expression, I could tell right off that she didn't think it was fair. I had news for her: nobody ever promised it would be. If it were, I'd have been playing pinochle beside a pool instead of watching soap operas while I ironed as the world turned.

She came onto the porch. "May I please use your phone?"

"Long distance?" I said cautiously.

"I need to call Mr. Wafford. He was supposed to have the utilities turned on by today, but nothing's on."

I took a closer look. She was at most in her late twenties, with short brown hair and a jaw about as square as I'd ever seen. Her eyes were sizzling with frustration, but her smile was friendly. Smiling back, I said, "You bought the house over there?"

"I'm Sarah Benston. I signed the papers last week, and Mr.

Wafford promised to arrange for the utilities to be on when we got here. It's after nine o'clock. My son and I have been on the road for fourteen hours, and there's no way we get by without water and electricity. I was hoping that he could still do something."

"You bring your son inside and let me give him a glass of juice," I said. "You can call Wafford if you want, but you're welcome to camp out over here. How old's your boy?"

"Cody's ten. I guess it's too late to call Mr. Wafford. He won't be able to do anything at this time of night."

I still wasn't sure what to make of her as she brought in a listless child, rolled out a sleeping bag for him in a corner, and kissed him good-night.

"So you bought the Sticklemann house?" I asked her as we sat down at the kitchen table.

She took a sip of coffee and nodded. "It seemed smart, even though my ex can't remember to send his child-support payments. I never finished my degree, so I decided to move back here and take classes. I was going to rent an apartment, but then Mr. Wafford explained how I could buy a house and build up equity. After the three or four years it'll take to graduate, I can sell the house and make a small profit. Cody's used to having a yard."

"How long since the divorce?" I asked.

"A year." Sarah put down her cup. "I know this is an imposition, Mrs. . . . ?"

"James, honey, but you call me Deanna. I know what you're going through. My daughter got divorced four years ago, and she had a real tough time before she threw up her hands and moved back in with me. Now she has a job, a good one, at an insurance office in town. She's dating a real polite boy she knew back in high school. Her daughter Amy's eight, so she's in bed. It's not a good idea having three generations of women in the same house, but we do what we got to do. You have a job, Sarah?"

"As a teacher's aide," she said with a shrug. "It's minimum wage, but the house payment's not much more than what I'd be paying in rent. Mr. Wafford is financing the sale privately, since I probably couldn't have qualified for a loan. Even if I had, I'd have been charged closing costs of more than three thousand dollars. This way, I only had to put down five percent, which left me enough to pay for the rental truck and the utility deposits."

"It'll work out," I said soothingly, although I had my doubts. My daughter had needed food stamps and welfare and everything else she could get until she'd found a job. I would have helped her out, but all I had were my monthly disability checks.

I made her a bed on the sofa, then sat and gazed out my bedroom window at the Sticklemann place, wondering just how much Jeremiah ("Call me 'Jem' ") Wafford had told this nice young woman.

Not nearly enough, I suspected.

I watched her from the porch the next day. I would have liked to help her haul in suitcases and furniture, but my back wasn't up to it. Her boy did what he could, trying to be the man of the family; finally, Perniski from up the road took pity on her and carried boxes, mattresses, bed frames, and mismatched chairs inside the house. All the same, she did most of the work, and I could see she had spirit.

Cody proved to be a mannersome child, and he ended up most weekday afternoons with Amy, watching movies on the television. Sarah tried to pay me for looking after him. I refused, saying that he was no trouble. He wasn't.

A month after she moved in, she came knocking on my front door. I could tell right off that she was upset, but I pretended not to notice and said, "You have time for coffee?"

"What's the deal with the water lines?" she said, close to sputtering with outrage. "The toilet backed up and flooded the bathroom. The plumber says that all the houses out here have substandard pipes from the nineteen fifties, and there's nothing he can do short of replacing everything from the house to the main sewer line. Where am I going to find a thousand dollars?"

I sat her down on the porch swing. "There are some things Wafford didn't tell you, honey. After he bought the house, he slapped fresh paint on it and put down new linoleum—but it's still an old house. Don't be surprised if the roof leaks when it rains. Mrs. Sticklemann had to put pots and pans in every room."

Sarah stared at me. "What can I do? I called Mr. Wafford, but he reminded me that he recommended I pay for an inspection. It would have cost three hundred dollars. All I could hear him talking about were the possibilities for flower beds and a vegetable garden, and how Cody could play in the creek."

"Don't let him do that," I said. "Clover Creek may sound charming, but it's downstream from a poultry plant. Some government men were out here last spring, trying to figure out why all the fish bellied up."

"Anything else I should know?" she asked grimly.

I hoped she wasn't the sort to blame the messenger. "There's been some trouble with the folks in the house up at the corner. A couple of months ago the cops raided it and arrested them for selling drugs. One's doing time in the state prison, but two of them are back. That's why I walk up to where the school bus lets the children off in the afternoons. I've warned Cody about them too."

"Thanks, Deanna. I'd better go check the mailbox. Maybe this is the year I win a million-dollar sweepstakes."

We didn't talk for a long while after this, but only because she was busy with her job and her late-afternoon classes. Cody always kept a watch for her out the window, and as soon as her car pulled into the driveway, he'd say good-bye and dart across the road to help her carry in groceries. She and my daughter were friendly enough, but they didn't really hit it off. Amy, on the other hand, was crazy about Cody; he returned her affection with the lofty sophistication of an older man.

Sarah continued having trouble with the house. When I asked Cody about an exterminator's van, he said the carpet in his bedroom had fleas and showed me welts on his legs. On another day, he told me that his mother had called Mr. Wafford and then banged down the receiver and apologized for using "naughty" words.

She had spirit all right, I thought. Too bad she hadn't had common sense as well when she signed the papers in Wafford's office. It wasn't hard to imagine how he'd conned her, though. He was a slick one behind his hearty laugh and grandfatherly face. He'd owned half the houses along the road at one time or another. Most of the folks who'd fallen for his "equity" pitch had discovered a whole new side to him when they fell behind on their payments. There was a reason why he drove a flashy Cadillac.

"You're not going to believe this," Sarah said one evening while we watched Amy and Cody play on a tire swing in the yard. "There are bats in the attic. I saw them streaming out from under an eave last night."

"You have mice in the garage, don't you? Bats are nothing more than mice with wings."

She shuddered. "I called Wafford, and he said the same thing, then gave me a lecture about how they eat insects. From the way he carried on, I thought I was expected to thank him for providing mosquito control. What if one gets downstairs?"

"Mrs. Sticklemann kept a tennis racket in the hall. I don't think she ever had to use it, though."

"That's comforting," she said dryly. "I was waiting for you to say she died of rabies."

"Nothing like that," I said, then stood up and raised my voice. "Amy, you need to get busy on your spelling words for the test on Friday. Go on in the house and get out your book."

Sarah gave me a look like she knew darn well I was tiptoeing around something, but she called to Cody and they left. I felt bad not telling her, but she had more than enough problems. Sometimes when you buy a lemon, you can squeeze it till your face turns blue, but you still can't make lemonade.

Later that evening when the telephone rang, I answered it without enthusiasm, expecting my daughter to give me some cockamamie story about how she had to work late.

"Deanna," Sarah said abruptly, "go into your living room. Don't turn on the light. There's a man out on the road, staring at my house. He's been there for at least half an hour. Should I call the police?"

"Hold on." I put down the receiver and did as she'd asked, then came back and picked it up. "I see him, honey. You say he's been there half an hour?"

"That's when I first noticed him. Could he be confused and think I'm our neighborhood drug dealer?"

"No," I said, "that's not his problem. You call the police if you want, Sarah, but I don't think it'll do much good."

"Do you know who he is?"

"Yes, I do. You come over tomorrow after you get home from work and I'll tell you about him. In the meantime, just ignore him. He'll go away before too long."

"Who is he?" she demanded. "How do you know he'll go away? What if he breaks into the house?"

"He won't come any closer than he already is," I said. "You and Cody are perfectly safe. I'll see you tomorrow."

I hung up and went back to the window. The figure was still there, all slouched over with his hands in his pockets, looking like a marble statue in the glow from the streetlight. I felt bad about making Sarah wait, but it was going to take a lot of time to explain it all in such a way that she wouldn't get too panicky.

"Damn that Jem Wafford," I said under my breath.

• • •

"Who is he?" Sarah demanded as soon as Cody and Amy ran around the corner of the house.

"Gerald Sticklemann," I said. "It's a long story. Are you sure you don't want coffee or a glass of iced tea?"

"Just tell me—okay?"

"Well, Gerald never was what you'd call normal. I knew the first time I laid eyes on him that there was something wrong. That was thirty years ago, when Hank and I bought this house. Gerald was close to the same age as my boys, but he never rode a bicycle or came over to play baseball in the summers. A little yellow bus came every day to take him to a special school for children that couldn't learn like they were supposed to. I made sure none of my children ever teased him, but there were some teenage boys up the road who used to call him ugly names and throw rocks at him when they rode their bicycles past the house."

"That doesn't explain why he was here last night."

"I'm getting to it," I said. "Mr. Sticklemann died not more than two years after we moved in, leaving his wife with a small income from a life insurance policy. She cleaned houses and made enough for her and Gerald to get by. There wasn't any question of him getting a proper job after he finished with that school. The only times I saw him were when he went walking down that path that leads down to the creek."

"This is all very touching, Deanna, but I need to fix dinner and get Cody started on his homework."

I held up my hands. "I'm just trying to make you understand about him. Over the years, families came and went, but the Sticklemanns stayed the same, like a soap opera without a plot. Eventually, she got too old to work and spent a lot of time with her vegetable garden. Wafford tried on occasion to convince her to sell him the house. I'd see him on the porch, his hat in his hands, grinning like a mule with a mouthful of briars, but I don't think he ever made it into the living room."

Sarah looked at her watch. "Will you please get to the point?"

"Mrs. Sticklemann died five years ago. Nobody knows exactly when because Gerald never said a word to anybody and kept doing what he always did, day in and day out. It was at least six weeks before one of her old friends came out to find out what was going on. I was in my yard when the woman came stumbling back outside, as bug-eyed and green as a bullfrog. I brought her over here so she could use my telephone, and while we waited for the police, she told me that Gerald had left his mother's body in her bed. It was in the late summer, and the flies and the stench were something awful."

"Did she die of natural causes?" Sarah asked in a tremulous voice.

"Oh, yes, there was never any question about that. The real question was what to do about Gerald. The only crime he'd committed was not notifying anybody when his mother died. He ended up in some sort of sheltered home with others of his kind. A distant cousin who was managing Gerald's affairs sold the house to Wafford. The problem is that Gerald slips out every now and then and comes back here, looking for his mother. He doesn't mean any harm."

Sarah stared at the house, her mouth so tight her lips were invisible. After a long moment, she said, "This is too much. Wafford not only forgot to tell me about the faulty plumbing, the fleas and bats, the rotten floorboards under the linoleum, the drug dealers up the street, the contaminated water in the—" She broke off and rubbed her face as though she could erase the sight of the house across the street. "I can't believe he didn't warn me about any of this! I don't have enough money to move to an apartment and put up two months' rent and a security deposit. It's all well and good for you to say this middle-aged child won't try to come into the house some night when we're asleep, but you can't be sure."

"As long as you lock your doors and windows before you go to bed, you and Cody will be all right," I said with more confidence than I felt.

Sarah swung around to look at me. "Wafford knew all about Gerald, didn't he? Doesn't his failure to tell me constitute fraud?"

"You'll have to ask a lawyer, but I wouldn't count on it. Wafford first sold the house to a nice young couple with a baby. They weren't any happier than you when they discovered all the problems, including Gerald. Wafford and the husband had such a heated argument in the driveway one afternoon that I almost called the police. Not long after that the couple packed up and left. The next day Wafford put a 'For Sale' sign in the yard. He was whistling."

Cody and Amy came running into the front yard with a bird's egg they'd found and we changed the subject.

"A policeman came to our house last night," Cody confided in me as he, Amy, and I walked back from the bus stop a week later.

"He did?" I murmured.

"He went into the kitchen with my mother. They talked for a long time, but I couldn't hear what they said."

"Did he arrest her?" asked Amy.

Cody made a face at her. "No, nitwit. They just talked, and then he left. My mother was mad, but she wouldn't tell me why."

I knew why, having seen Gerald at the edge of the road when I went into the front room to find my reading glasses. I'd considered calling Sarah to remind her to check the locks, but then I'd seen her in an upstairs window. Her face had been as pale as Gerald's.

I didn't say anything, and by the time we reached my house, Cody had forgotten about the policeman and was telling Amy about pirate ships. Sarah called an hour later and asked if I could give Cody supper.

"Glad to," I said. "You going to the library to study?"

"I have an appointment with Wafford. He wasn't happy about it, but I told him that if he wouldn't see me at his office at six o'clock, I'd go to his house and stand in the street until his neighbors started calling the police."

I let Amy and Cody eat in front of the TV set while they watched an old swashbuckler movie from the forties. It may have been considered gory in its time, but it wasn't nearly as violent as the Saturday-morning cartoons Amy watched religiously.

Sarah knocked on the door just as the movie ended. I sent the children to Amy's room, then set a cup of coffee on the table in front of her.

She ignored it. "I'm so mad that I can visualize myself buying a gun and shooting that man right between his beady eyes. Better yet, I could tar and feather him, then tie him to the back bumper and drag him through town. I don't suppose you have any tar out in the carport?"

"Sorry," I said, a little taken aback at the venomous edge in her voice.

"I wanted to slap the smirk right off his face. He kept calling me 'little lady' and 'sweetheart,' all the while assuring me that the house was a real bargain and he'd done me a favor by selling it to me at less than fair market value. I offered to let him buy it back at the same price, but he gave me a bunch of bull about his cash-flow problems. Well, I've got a cash-flow problem too—all my cash keeps flowing into that black hole across the street. There's a leak under the kitchen sink, and the door to the hall closet is so warped I can't get it open. Cody found a dead bat in the bathroom last weekend. On top of everything else, I've got to worry that Gerald may bust into the house in the middle of the night."

I patted her hand. "He never hurt anyone."

"There's always a first time, isn't there? The police won't do anything because Gerald isn't breaking the law. I talked to the county prosecutor this morning about a restraining order. He can't take action until Gerald makes explicit threats or starts waving a weapon. Or murders us in our beds. He'd be in big trouble then. Isn't that comforting?"

"Now, Sarah," I said, "Gerald's not going to do something like that. He's just confused and lonely."

"And I'm the proud owner of a house with rats in the basement and bats in the belfry." Her cheeks flushed, but she managed to get herself under control and added, "I'm not going to take it, Deanna. I've been pushed around all my life, first by my parents and then by an abusive jerk who used to hit me when his car wouldn't start on cold mornings."

"Maybe you and Cody could stay here until you can afford an apartment," I said. "I can sleep in Amy's room on a cot. It'll be crowded in the morning when we have to share the one bathroom, but—"

"No, thanks. This is my problem and I'm going to solve it. I'll think of something."

She gathered up Cody's coat and books, then called him. He appeared with a construction-paper eye-patch, a mustache drawn with a felt-tipped pen, and a piece of paper covered with pencil markings.

"I'm Long John Silver," he announced, "and I know where the buried treasure lies."

Something strange flashed across her face. "In the basement?" she said softly.

"No, down by the creek under a big tree. Tomorrow I'm going to dig it up and give you a chest filled with gold doubloons."

"Sounds good to me," she said, helping him on with his coat.

After they left, I settled Amy at the kitchen table with her geography workbook and a gnawed pencil. Most of the time I sat with her to make sure she didn't start doodling, but that evening I was too distracted to stay put.

When my daughter finally came home, I went into my bedroom and lay down, wondering just what Sarah might have in mind.

Jem Wafford should have been doing the same.

• • •

What she did a few nights later was so peculiar I almost went across the street to make sure she wasn't drunk. I was in the front room when I noticed Gerald was back. He was getting to be a familiar figure in his overcoat, his hands in his pockets, his bald head reminding me of a full moon. I glanced at the upstairs windows to see if Sarah was there, but the shades were drawn.

I stayed where I was, my fingers crossed in hopes she hadn't gone out and bought a gun. Gerald may have frightened her, but she'd have a hard time convincing a jury she'd shot him in self-defense.

I was beginning to feel relieved when her front porch light went on and she came outside. Her hands were blessedly empty, and she was dressed only in jeans and a thin T-shirt. I expected her to start cursing at Gerald, but she went down the steps and across the yard to join him. He retreated, but she kept smiling and talking like he was a neighbor from down the street. Pretty soon he stopped edging away from her and began to bobble his head. I couldn't see if he was saying anything in response—I'd have been surprised if he had—but Sarah didn't seem to notice. After a moment, she put her hand on his arm and led him toward her house. He moved reluctantly, but she kept her grip on him. Before long, they were inside and the front door was closed.

My heart was pounding so hard that I sat down in the rocking chair and forced myself to take a couple of slow breaths. I'd been the one swearing that Gerald wouldn't hurt anyone, but I had no way of knowing how his mother's death might have affected him deep down inside. Staring at the house was one thing; actually being inside it might set off all kinds of raw emotions.

I waited twenty minutes, then broke down and dialed Sarah's telephone number. I didn't know what I was going to do if she didn't answer, but she picked up the receiver.

"Is everything okay?" I asked, trying to keep the urgency out of my voice so Amy wouldn't get alarmed.

"Everything's fine, Deanna. Gerald and I are having a nice talk about when he and his mother lived here."

"I just thought I'd better . . ."

"I know," she said. "I'd do the same thing if the situation was reversed. I need to get back to my guest now. Don't worry about us."

All the same, I stayed by the window until I saw Gerald leave, and I made sure I got a good look at Sarah standing in the doorway. Rather than scared, she had a funny smile on her face. Smug.

"I saw you and your mother had company last night," I said to Cody the following afternoon after I'd softened him up with ice cream and cookies.

"Yeah," he said without enthusiasm. "She made me turn off the television and go upstairs, even though I already did my homework."

"So you didn't hear what they were saying?"

"No. May I please have some more ice cream?"

Amy snickered. "Pirates don't eat ice cream unless it's got blood and bones mixed in it."

"Says who?" he retorted, baring his teeth.

She obligingly squealed and ran out the back door, with Cody on her heels. My attempt to play private detective had flopped like a bad movie, I thought, as I set their bowls in the sink and turned on the water.

And I had a feeling I wouldn't do much better with Sarah.

Gerald appeared several times over the next few weeks, and each time Sarah went outside and escorted him into the house. Cody let drop one afternoon that Gerald had eaten supper with them the previous night and, for some reason that he wouldn't explain, solemnly swore that Gerald was descended from real pirates. Sarah smiled and waved when I saw her in her driveway, but she stopped coming over to have coffee before she fetched Cody. Some days I wanted to go across the street, grab her shoulders, and shake the truth out of her. I didn't do anything, though, except weasel what I could out of Cody while we walked home from the bus stop.

One afternoon while I was waiting for them, Jem Wafford's Cadillac swung around the corner and sped down the street. Years ago he'd given up trying to persuade me to sell, so he didn't bother to nod at me. As soon as Cody and Amy climbed off the bus, I hustled them to the house. Wafford was sitting in his car in Sarah's driveway. I told the children to make themselves peanut butter sandwiches, then crossed the street and waited until he climbed out.

"Mrs. James," he said, pretending he hadn't left me in a cloud of dust minutes earlier, "how are you doing? Your back any better these days?"

"My back is none of your business," I said. "Are you looking for Sarah? She usually doesn't get home till six o'clock."

He took out a handkerchief and wiped his neck. "I dropped by on the chance I'd catch her on her day off."

"She doesn't have a day off. She's a full-time student and puts in thirty hours a week at a preschool. Weekends, she studies and does housework."

"You've got to admire that kind of determination," he said, beaming at me like he and I were the proud parents of a prodigy. "A single woman with a child, struggling to put herself through school so she can—"

"What do you want, Wafford?" I said bluntly.

"Is she still having trouble with Gerald?"

"You'll have to ask her yourself."

Wafford leaned his bulk against the Cadillac and gazed up at the second-story windows. "What about you, Mrs. James? Have you talked to Gerald recently?"

My curiosity got the better of me, so instead of stomping off, I said, "Not that I recall. Why?"

"At his request, I stopped by the group home where he lives. We had a real interesting talk. I'm just wondering"—he tapped his temple—"how reliable he is."

"I couldn't say."

"He's been out here quite a bit, hasn't he?"

"What if he has?" I shot back.

"He told me that his mother was a miser, that she squirreled away a good deal of cash before she died." Wafford looked at me, his mouth curled in a smile but his eyes slitted like a snake's. "You ever get the idea she was putting away cash for a rainy day?"

Something was going on. I didn't know what, and if somebody'd offered me a million dollars, I couldn't have come up with the right answer.

"Maybe," I said cautiously. "She stayed to herself."

"Gerald seems to think she did," he said, "but he's not the most reliable witness, considering."

"Considering," I echoed. To this day I can't explain why I added, "But he's not the kind who tells tales. His imagination was never a strong point."

"No, it wouldn't be," Wafford said with a snicker. "Mr. Sticklemann's family owned all the land out this way once upon a time. They sold it off part and parcel over the years, most likely for cash. Folks like that didn't trust real-estate brokers and bankers."

"I don't suppose so," I said, still feeling like I had a role in a play. I could almost hear Sarah coaching me from the wings, but my script was too blurry to read. "Mrs. Sticklemann wasn't the kind to deal with bankers. She was real independent."

"That's what I was thinking." Wafford took another swipe at his neck, then stuffed his handkerchief in his pocket.

"She sure didn't squander any of it. She had that ancient Pontiac when she died, and heaven knows she never took a vacation or had repairs done to the house."

Just then Sarah drove up. I was waiting for her to snarl at

him, so I was a little bewildered when she asked me to watch Cody for a while longer and invited Wafford to go inside for iced tea.

Wafford's car was still in the driveway long after Cody'd gone home and Amy had eaten supper. I was reluctant to do any more than watch from behind the curtain in the front-room window, and that's what I was doing when Sarah came walking across the street for what turned out to be the last time.

I opened the front door as she came onto the porch. "Everything all right?" I demanded.

"Wafford has offered to buy back the house for what I have in it and more. We agreed that I'd move out tonight and collect my furniture later. I want to thank you for everything you've done, Deanna. I'll write once Cody, Gerald, and I have a new address."

"Gerald?"

"I've agreed to take him with us to be my resident baby-sitter and handyman. He did me a favor and I owe him big. I'll swing by the home and pick him up on my way out of town."

I was afraid to go into it any further. "What about your classes?"

"I'm not sure I want to be a teacher," she said with a wry grin. "I may decide to go into real estate. I've learned quite a bit over the last few months."

"What about Wafford?"

"He's inspecting the property to make sure it's in the same condition as it was when I bought it. He'll leave before too long."

She hugged me, then turned around and went home. Over the next hour, she and Cody loaded the car with suitcases and boxes. Wafford's Cadillac was in the shadows at the far end of the driveway, but he never emerged with an armload of anything. Not that he was the kind to help anybody.

Amy finally started nagging me to help her with her homework, so I abandoned my vigil and went into the kitchen. After she'd finished and gone to bed, I went back to the front room. Sarah's car was gone. Wafford's car was still there, and a light was on in the back of the house. I couldn't imagine what he was doing.

It was none of my business, so I made myself some popcorn and turned on a movie.

The next morning I noticed Wafford's car was gone too. I fixed pancakes, then listened to my daughter gripe about her boss before she gulped down a cup of coffee and shooed Amy out the door to drive her to school.

The ritual was familiar, but not comforting. Once I had the house to myself, I tidied up and started a load of laundry, but the window in the front room was a magnet. Why had Sarah befriended Gerald, of all people? Even odder, why had Wafford agreed to buy back the house? He'd always circled like a vulture, waiting to foreclose on hapless widows and families whose breadwinners had been fired or become disabled.

I hadn't received any great insights by three o'clock, when it was time to walk to the bus stop. I was almost there when Mr. Perniski came outside, dressed in his customary cardigan sweater and khaki pants.

"What's going on at the end of the road?" he said. "That young woman was acting mighty peculiar last night."

"Sarah?"

"You betcha. She pulled into the driveway over there"—he pointed at our neighborhood drug dealer's establishment—"and gave that one with the beard what looked like a key. Long about midnight, he went sneaking down the road toward her house. The last thing we need out here is another criminal. My grandson found a hypodermic needle in the ditch last summer. We have to—"

"Sarah and Cody moved out last night," I said, cutting him off. "Are you sure she gave him a key?"

"Hell, I ain't sure about nothing," Perniski muttered, then wandered away.

I thought about all this while I waited for the school bus, and I hadn't made much progress by the time Amy was occupied with a bag of cookies and old sitcoms on television. I finally slipped out and went across the street to what had been Sarah's house. The doors were locked, so all I could do was peer through windows at unoccupied rooms.

The police did not arrive for more than two days, and my instinctive response was to tell them nothing. After a moment, though, churchgoing woman that I am, I murmured something about the basement door, its shiny new bolt, and the possibility that Wafford's Cadillac was in a chop shop in the next county. As for Sarah Benston, I've never heard from her. I'm not real worried; as she said, she learned a lot about real estate during her brief stay across the street.

She can take care of herself.

Judith Kelman

Judith Kelman shares with her friend Mary Higgins Clark the ability to walk us gently to the edge of a well-manicured lawn where just beyond yawns a terrifying abyss. Her popular novels, which include Hush Little Darlings, The House on the Hill, *and* Fly Away Home, *are quite brilliant at turning seemingly secure suburban neighborhoods into bedroom communities for hell. It is not difficult to see how well earned is Kelman's success: she truly gets us where we live.*

Sometimes, however, writers just want to have fun. Here, in a story that positively drips gleeful venom, Kelman takes a new route through her usual territory. How does one imagine a fresh version of the familiar heroine-as-victim? Think high-school reunion and a moment, decades after the original adolescent humiliations, when justice is finally served . . . and found to be deliciously lethal.

Eradicum Homo Horribilus

▼▼▼

BY JUDITH KELMAN

Carlotta peered in her mailbox and froze. Twenty years had passed, but she recognized his handwriting at once: sharp hooks and vicious slashes; whimsical flourishes, meant to deceive.

Everything about the man was a nasty game of deceit, even his name. The return address read: "Chervil Lattimore, 14 Bismarck Circle, Rockville Centre, New York." *Chervil,* indeed, Carlotta huffed. She remembered elementary school, when he'd sometimes passed himself off as Basil. Later, for a time, he went by Sage. In high school, it was Lovage or Borage or Valerian. He claimed all variations on his real name, which was Herb.

Herbert Alton Lattimore IV. Thinking of the man made Carlotta furious. The nerve of him to invade her world after all this time! Wasn't it enough that he'd been the source of all her childhood misery? Wasn't it sufficient that he'd knocked her life off its intended course? What more could that hideous creature possibly want from her?

Carlotta considered several satisfying ways to dispense with this unthinkable intrusion. She could crumple the letter and toss it in the trash. She could burn it or tear it apart, as Herb had done to her. But, in the end, she yielded to the pull of curiosity. Surely, she would be consumed with questions if she didn't find out what the letter said. The last thing she could afford right now was a foolish distraction. Carlotta had to be in peak form for tomorrow's CPA exam.

In six attempts during the past five years, Carlotta had failed the Auditing section of the test. After the last time, Mr. Detuzzi from Human Resources had laid it on the line. If Carlotta flunked again, she would be dropped from all future consideration for an accounting position at the Carswell Communications Corporation, Inc., her sole place of employment since graduation.

Carlotta would be forced to spend the rest of her working days in the dreary bookkeeping department, where she had to endure the company of Martha Siwicki, the human hyena, and dumpy Irwin Draper, who mined his nose as if it held a mother lode of gold. As if the tedious job and her unseemly colleagues weren't bad enough, the bookkeeping office adjoined the company kitchen, so Carlotta's clothing, not to mention her hair, held the permanent stench of institutional gravy.

Carlotta had to get out. And this time, she was fully prepared to do so. She had enrolled in the Becker review course and studied several hours every day. To silence her strident inner doubts, she had entered into therapy with Dr. Friedrich Hume himself at Peoria's famed Hume Institute for Personal Enrichment. Nothing would stand in the way of her success, especially not some poisonous little *Herb*. She resolved to read the silly letter, toss it out, and be done with it.

Carlotta found her reading glasses on the desk beside a sepia wedding portrait of her parents, Rose and Sam. She cast a wistful glance at the young, loving pair. If only they were alive to see her now. For once, they would have reason to be proud of their only offspring. So what if she'd inherited her father's lackluster face and fireplug physique? Fiddle de dee that she tended to be a teensy bit high strung and hypersensitive like her mother. No biggie wiggy that she'd never married or had children or distinguished herself in any particular way. Carlotta Little was about to grab the gold ring, hit the heights, soar to the pinnacle: *accounting.*

She slashed the envelope and plucked out the lone vellum sheet. "My dearest Carlotta," the letter began. "I'm writing in the heartfelt hope that you can find some way to forgive me. No words can express how deeply sorry I am for the pain and distress I've surely caused you. These past few years cruel fate has forced me to reappraise my life and recognize what is truly important. Having known the agony of loss, I've come to treasure precious people such as you who have touched my life."

As she read, Carlotta's sod-colored eyes filled with tears. Herb's two-year-old son, conceived after years of excruciating infertility treatments, had drowned in the family pool during a valiant attempt to rescue his beloved Barney. The child's nanny was absorbed in a particularly compelling episode of *General Hospital* at the time.

Herb's wife, suicidal over the tragedy, had been committed to the Happy Hollows Sanitarium. Several months later, Giselle had appeared so improved, her doctor allowed her out on a day pass. She lunched with a friend, went shopping at Loehmann's, then hurled herself under the wheels of the four thirty-five express bus to Manhattan.

Carlotta shook her head in rueful empathy. Loehmann's could do that to a person.

Herb's horrendous misfortune did not stop there. His house had burned down, taking with it all precious mementos of his beloved wife and son. His family business, the venerable Lattimore Fidelity Fund, tottered at the brink of ruin following several years of lackluster performance. In a desperate effort to save the firm, Herb had taken a huge position in the EasySlim Corporation, manufacturers of a caplet designed to liquefy body fat, so it could be redistributed from, say, thighs to breasts. Unfortunately, the

FDA had banned the highly touted drug after tests found that it caused an alarming incidence of clinical consternation in laboratory rats.

Herb was undone. He developed psoriasis, a cranky colon, and a powerful thirst. In short order, he found himself addicted to cortisone creams, antiinflammatory pills, Jell-O brand pudding pops, and Jack Daniel's. Several months ago, he'd hit bottom and enrolled in a twelve-step program.

"It's difficult for me to believe that more than a year has passed since I buried my beautiful Giselle," Herb wrote. "I find myself mired in grief, unable to see past the dark clouds that engulf me. Still, my twelve-step sponsor insists that Giselle and little Herb would have wanted me to carry on, which I suppose is true.

"In that spirit, I've decided to invite a few special friends for a contemplative, healing retreat this coming Labor Day weekend. I'm asking everyone to bring one special thing to share. It could be a memory, a private thought, a poem—something from the *heart*.

"Please say you'll join us, Carlotta. Grant me this priceless opportunity to express my true feelings for you.

"Yours as ever, Chervil (Herb) Lattimore"

Carlotta's thoughts raced like a gerbil on a wheel. Why should she do anything for *Herb Lattimore* after all he'd put her through? How could she not after all he'd been through himself? Yes, no? Stay, go? She placed an emergency call to Dr. Hume at the Institute, but the psychiatrist was out of town for the weekend, and could not be reached. Dr. Romanowitz was covering, the receptionist said, but Carlotta declined to speak with him. It would take months to bring a new shrink up to speed.

Carlotta struggled to evict the matter from her mind, but she was unable to focus on anything else, including her studies. Lately, her practice test scores had been ranging in the high eighties to low nineties, but today, she managed a dismal forty-six on the dreaded Auditing section. The exercises she'd learned from Dr. Hume failed to silence the chorus of self-doubts singing in her head. *You shall not overcome, Carlotta. You are plain and dumb, Carlotta. Your time hasn't come—no wa-a-a-a-ay!*

The only brief distraction Carlotta found was with her plants. After dinner, she misted, swiped for mealybug, sprayed for white-fly, brushed off scale and mite, and sang her leafy charges' favorite tunes. The cacti were partial to "I've Got You Under My Skin." For the bromeliads, she crooned "Aloe, Dolly."

After her parents died, Carlotta had purchased a couple of plants to ease the gloom. To her delight, she found she had a natural flair for growing things. As her interest bloomed, she sub-scribed to gardening journals and joined horticultural societies. Soon, the house was awash with greenery and her mailbox brimmed with catalogs and correspondence from plant pals around the globe.

Even rare, exotic foliage flourished in Carlotta's care. Her reputation grew, and collectors began entrusting her with valuable seeds and hybrids. Her approach was simple. Plants, like people, thrived on consideration and respect. Carlotta took pains to learn each specimen's proper name and personal preferences. Every one was treated as a dear friend and honored guest in her home.

"Good afternoon, my darling *Phalaenopsis*," she crooned. "Tsk, tsk. Look at those overcrowded roots. Time to move to larger quarters, isn't it, my sweet little *Eupatorium rugosum*?"

Carlotta's plants could count on thoughtful, consistent care. No gimmicks; no games. From firsthand experience, she knew how damaging games could be and how they tended to grow out of hand. Herb had begun by joking about his name, and people were amused. Somehow, he'd concluded it was fine to make fun of others, to pervert their good names, impugn their characters, sub-ject them to soul-numbing, gut-wrenching, life-altering humilia-tions.

Carlotta flushed hot, recalling her first day as a second grader at the Wilson School. She was the new kid in Rockville Centre, having moved at midyear from the Flatbush section of Brooklyn. When a little boy approached her during morning recess, Carlotta was overjoyed. His name was Basil, he said, and he wanted to be her friend. First, he needed to use the lavatory. Then, he would save a seat for Carlotta in the lunchroom.

Standing on the cafeteria line, Carlotta could barely contain her excitement. She was going to be accepted in this terrifying new place. She would make lots of friends, perhaps achieve the holy grail of popularity. All was well.

After heaping her tray with macaroni and cheese and ambrosia salad and khaki-colored green beans and subsidized milk, Carlotta spotted Basil at a table in the rear. As promised, the seat beside him was empty. Carlotta hastened across the room, deposited her tray on the table, and sat.

She would never forget what happened next. She was steeped like a tea bag in warm, fetid slop. Carlotta shrieked and jumped from the chair, drawing all eyes. The mess ran down her legs, soaked her socks, and puddled in her shoes. The teacher in charge, loudmouth Mrs. Fargnioli, rushed over to investigate. "This little girl peed in her pants," she bellowed at the top of her pipe-organ lungs. "Call her parents. Call the office. Get a mop!"

Everyone pointed and laughed as Carlotta was led from the room. Her new skirt was plastered to her backside like a giant badge of shame. Her wet Mary Janes squeaked like frightened rodents. She was exiled to the nurse's office, where she waited until her mother arrived. Rose, red and sputtering, took her soggy daughter home. "Look what you've done to me, Carlotta. How am I going to hold my head up at canasta after this?"

Despite Carlotta's protestations of innocence, she was branded with the horrid nickname: Betsy Wetsy. No one believed her assertion that a boy named Basil had planted the offending substance on her chair. There was no Basil registered at the school. Herb Lattimore, whom she identified as the guilty party, was a model student with an unblemished good citizenship record. He, of all children, would never do such a thing. The principal had questioned Carlotta's grip on reality. Rose and Sam were advised to curtail their daughter's television viewing and restrict her to nonfiction books.

"Lord, no!" Carlotta shrieked. Absorbed in reverie, she had overwatered her prized helmet flower. Now, she hastened to empty the brimming saucer and aerate the sodden soil. "I'm *so* sorry, my darling *Aconitum napellus*. There, now, are you all right? Have I hurt you horribly? Can you ever forgive me?"

Suddenly, Carlotta saw the light. Forgiveness was the only proper course. Herb's transgressions were ancient history. As Dr. Hume so often advised, she needed to be rid of her anger toward that man. Carlotta had to put the past behind her, where it belonged. Accepting Herb's invitation would be a step toward that worthy end.

Carlotta had hoped the decision would bring her peace, but she was up all night, tossing and churning. She kept thinking of all the agony poor Herb had suffered. She was haunted by an image of little Herb, a towheaded angel floating facedown beside his purple dinosaur in the pool. She ached for the lovely Giselle, marked for eternity by tread marks from the White Plains express bus to Fifty-ninth Street.

Preparing for Herb's retreat loomed as a monumental task. Carlotta needed to lose five pounds and buy several new outfits. A change of hairdo was definitely in order, not to mention makeup consultation, color analysis, and perhaps an eye job. She had to arrange extra time off from work next Labor Day weekend, make travel plans, have her palm read, and hire a plant sitter. All night, she jotted notes to herself on the bedside pad she used to record her dreams for Dr. Hume. By morning, she had compiled a six-page list.

At the top was her most critical task: passing the CPA exam. Carlotta intended to face Herb and the others on equal footing, as an accountant. But the moment she opened the test booklet that morning, her hopes plummeted. She had trouble interpreting the questions. Basic facts eluded her. She kept checking to be sure she was in the proper room.

Back home, Carlotta groped with demons of despair. She wallowed for a while, weeping and moaning, until her leafy friends clamored for their evening care. She misted the plants with her special mixture of Evian, lime juice, and a bit of Smirnoff vodka. "There, there, my darling *Ficus benjamina*. Here you are, sweet *Dracaena marginata*, that should perk you right up."

Carlotta drank some of the mix and perked up a bit herself. Perhaps she had not done as poorly as she imagined on the exam. In any case, the official results would not be in for months. Why worry now about failing? She could jump off that bridge when she came to it.

Instead, she resolved to focus on the plans for her trip to Herb's retreat. Rockville Centre only had one hotel. Couldn't hurt to call now and reserve a room.

That impulse proved most fortunate. The reservations clerk informed Carlotta that the place was nearly booked for the holiday weekend. "We have two weddings and a family reunion scheduled. But I still have one nice single available with a fabulous view of the Toys R Us."

"Great. I'll take it," Carlotta said.

"Fine. Let me get a bit of information. Name?"

"Carlotta Little."

"Not the Carlotta Little who went to Southside High?"

The clerk identified herself as Toby Cornet, a redheaded puffball who had grunted beside Carlotta in remedial physical education.

"My, it has been an age," said Toby. "What brings you back to town after all these years?"

Knowing that Toby had not likely been invited, Carlotta hesitated to mention Herb Lattimore's retreat. Instead, she muttered something about a visit to console Herb after all the poor man's travail.

Toby whooped. "Drowned kid? Dead wife? Business on the skids? Who fed you such a bunch of horse plop?"

"It's not true?"

"No way. Herb Lattimore's never been married. He comes to the hotel two, three times a week for dinner, always with a different bimbo on his arm. They're all about twelve years old with huge gabongas and brains the size of chickpeas."

Carlotta bristled with disbelief. There was no baby son. No suicide. No house fire. No business reverses of any sort. The "healing" retreat was a phony. Herb was setting her up for another of his monstrous games.

"That guy is some practical joker." Toby chuckled. "Last Easter, he had two thousand baby chicks delivered to the hotel as a gag. But we showed him. Next day, we had two thousand painted eggs delivered to him. You've simply got to take a bullshitter like Herb by the horns. Beat him at his own game."

"Yes, Toby. I believe you're right."

"So, I guess you won't be needing that room after all."

"I most certainly will. Put it on my AmEx. Mark the room guaranteed."

Seething, Carlotta recalled every one of Herb Lattimore's slights and insults. She would never forget standing on the sidelines at the sixth-grade prom, aching in desolation as the others frugged to "At the Hop." Why didn't anyone want her? Wasn't there some way she could stand or smile or cock her head just so to attract one of the boys? *Dear Lord, send me someone. Anyone. Please!*

As if in answer, Herb had sauntered across the gym floor. "Hey, Carlotta. Want to dance?"

Flustered with delight, Carlotta took several moments to find her tongue. "Why, yes," she said at last. "That would be lovely."

Then, as she approached, Herb cringed and backed away. "You want to dance? Go find yourself a partner."

For years after that, Carlotta had avoided him. Then, when they were seniors in high school, Herb started calling the house. He'd charmed her parents as he did all adults. Rose and Sam could not understand Carlotta's refusal to go out with him. "Every night, you sit around like a bump on a log," Sam observed. "It's not like you're such a raving beauty, Carlotta. It's not like the boys are beating down your door."

"I'm not interested, Daddy. Okay?"

"But he seems like such a nice young man," Rose cajoled. "What do you have to lose?"

Eventually, they wore her down. Carlotta was pleasantly surprised on their first movie date, when Herb acted the perfect gentleman. The following month passed in a haze of romantic bliss: bowling, Skee Ball, Nathan's hot dogs, miniature golf. Perfection.

One magical night, they were alone in the Lattimores' rec room. The lights were dim, and Johnny Mathis's honeyed voice oozed from the hi fi: "Chances are . . ."

Herb asked Carlotta to wear his ring around her neck. He kissed her and confessed his undying love. When Carlotta admitted she felt the same, Herb implored her to express her affection in a physical way. He explained that he might suffer grave medical consequences if she did not. This would be their secret, he assured. A sacred trust.

Carlotta had believed him without reservation. For weeks, she hadn't the vaguest idea why people at school kept snickering and whispering as she passed. Then, after lunch one day, she went to the girls' room. Inside the door to the third stall, someone had scrawled the entire sordid story. Herb had pursued her on a ten-dollar bet. When Carlotta submitted to his advances, Herb's best friend, Googie Nathanson, had been hiding in the closet with a tape recorder. By now, virtually every student at Southside High had heard Carlotta in the throes of passion, shouting, "Hoooo, baby. Yes!"

The incident brought Carlotta to her emotional knees. She was unable to show her face at the high school. She missed several weeks of classes and nearly failed to graduate. Hiding at home, she became bitter and reclusive and terribly depressed. She found herself unable to trust men or much of anything. From then on, aside from her plants and the occasional Sara Lee chocolate swirl pound-cake, Carlotta's life held precious little pleasure.

But that was about to end. At long last, she knew how to beat Herb Lattimore at his own game.

Irwin Draper noticed the change immediately. When Carlotta strode into the bookkeeping office the following morning, dumpy Irwin popped his thumb from his nose like a champagne cork and frowned. "What's up, Carlotta? You look different."

"Why, nothing at all."

"Oh, yes, there is. You've changed. I can see it. You look—I don't know—taller somehow."

"Is that so, Irwin? Well, perhaps you're right. Perhaps I've grown." Irwin had certainly *not* grown, she noted smugly. The man was positively potbound.

"She can't *grow*, you big ninny." Martha Siwicki guffawed. "She's a middle-aged spinster, for Chrissakes."

Carlotta squinted at the brown spots on Martha's ham-sized hands. Definite sign of root rot. "Forgive me for being blunt, Martha, but you could benefit from less moisture and a hoe."

At their next session, Dr. Hume probed for the reasons behind her improved frame of mind. "Frankly, Carlotta, I'm surprised you're not upset about this latest development with Herb."

"I've told you, Dr. Hume. I can handle this."

"And I've told you, the only way to *handle* it is to be rid of the Herb issue, once and for all. You need to get done with him, Carlotta. You should have been rid of this long ago."

"I hear you, Dr. Hume, and I could not agree more."

"Why go to this so-called retreat, then? What can you possibly hope to gain?"

Carlotta smiled. "I think the better question is, What do I have to *lose*?"

The next months passed with striking calm. Nothing fazed Carlotta, not even the letter from the state board stating that she would have scored several points higher on the CPA exam had she decided to stay at home.

No biggie wiggy.

Her travel arrangements proceeded apace. She lost five

pounds and bought three striking new ensembles. She indulged in a complete makeover at Peoria's *Salon des Dames Frumpées*. A teenager down the block agreed to plant-sit during her absence.

Carlotta was a trifle nonplussed by Mr. Detuzzi's response to her request for extra time off around the Labor Day weekend. "Funny you should ask, Carlotta. Actually, I was going to suggest you take a nice long rest from your duties here at Carswell. You've got unemployment coming, plus you'll qualify for a nice pension in just a few short years. Ms. McGinness in outplacement will be happy to explain everything."

Fiddle de dee.

She had far more important issues to address. Uppermost in her mind was the special offering Herb had asked her to bring along to share. *Something from the heart*, he'd said. Carlotta's heart was full of things she'd love to share with Herbert Alton Lattimore IV. But one particular idea crept in and germinated. Carlotta compiled the necessary details from medical, horticultural, and culinary specialists. She consulted with the top criminal attorney in all of greater metropolitan Peoria. Everything she learned confirmed her belief that she'd hit on the perfect contribution.

Soon, Labor Day weekend was upon her. Carlotta primped and packed and bid adieu to her precious housemates. "Have a lovely weekend, my sweet *Cypripedium calceolus*," she said. "Don't cry for me, *Artemisia*."

A liveried chauffeur awaited Carlotta at the arrival gate at JFK. "Greetings, Ms. Little. I'm Hathaway. Mr. Lattimore asked me to drive you to the retreat."

He held forth a nosegay of sweetheart roses and baby's breath. "These are for you, ma'am. Compliments of Mr. Lattimore."

Carlotta recoiled in horror. "Murdered in their infancy, no less. Is there no depth to which that creature will not sink?"

"Excuse me, ma'am?"

"I most certainly will not," Carlotta huffed.

Herb's house was an imposing Tudor in the ultrarich Old

Canterbury section of town. Years ago, Carlotta would have been humbled by the opulent surroundings, but now she stood apart from such frivolities. Above them.

The Southside High School class of seventy-two elite was assembled among the priceless antiques in the living room. Julia and Apulia Venable, the cheerleading twins, looked terminally perky as ever. Wendy Whitley, prom queen emeritus, stood beside bull-necked Chip Savage, football captain turned shopping mall mogul. Googie Nathanson, sporting two extra chins and a mail-sack belly, stood puffing a fat Cuban cigar. There was pretty Pinky Goldhaven, willowy Raquel Morgenstern, pompous Myron Peltz, and—

"Hey, boys and girls, look who's here," Herb bellowed from across the room. "Carlotta, baby. Great to see you. Come give your old pal Chervil a great big smooch."

Carlotta stared him down. "So sorry to hear of all your troubles, Herb. I do hope you're feeling better than you look." For a specimen hybrid raised in prime hothouse conditions, he was in frightful shape.

Pinky Goldhaven tittered behind her palm. Googie Nathanson gesticulated with his stogie, spewing ash. "Have to say she got you that time, Herb. Looks like Carlotta's grown herself a backbone."

Herb sniffed. "Hey, I'm terrified. Really." He loped over, ferrying a full champagne flute, and draped his free arm across Carlotta's shoulders. "I've got a confession to make, kiddo. All that boo-hoo stuff in the letter I wrote was made up. I just wanted to be sure you'd come to our little reunion. Wouldn't be nearly as much fun without you."

"How resourceful, Herb. You wished me here, and here I am."

Herb eyed her quizzically. "You're not mad?"

"Certainly not. Why? Do I appear to be?"

"Hell, no. You appear to be zoned out. What are you on? Valium? 'Ludes?"

"It's called inner peace, Herb. Resolution. I believe you'll find me rather unflappable."

"You? Yeah, right." Pretending to stumble, Herb slopped his bubbly all over Carlotta's cream silk dress. "Oops. Hey, let me help you with that." He ducked into the kitchen and returned with a filthy sponge. Muddy blotches bloomed as he dabbed the wet spots. "Oh, my. Look what an awful mess. Not miffed, are you, O unflappable one?"

"About a little soil and moisture? Heavens no." Carlotta turned her back on him. "How are you, Pinky? Julia and Apulia, so lovely to see you girls again."

For the next three hours, Herb exhausted himself trying to light Carlotta's fuse. He served her Campari and soda in a dribble glass. He assailed her with shocks and rude noises and plastic vermin. When she needed to use the rest room, he directed her to a toilet rigged to back up with a menacing gurgle, then overflow in a rush of vile debris.

Slogging forth, Carlotta found Herb waiting in the hall. With a look of revulsion, he sniffed the air. "Nice aroma, honey. What's that you're wearing? *Eau de Poop?*"

"I can't say what it is, actually. But I'm so pleased you find it agreeable."

"Anything's better than the way you usually stink, Carlotta. Reminds me of that puke they used to serve Thursdays in middle school."

"How lovely that I bring back fond memories for you, Herb. Childhood was such a happy, carefree time, as I recall."

"Yeah? Then I bet you're going to love the little surprise I've planned for you." Herb squired her back to the living room. "Take a load off, Carlotta. Gather round, boys and ghouls. It's show time."

Carlotta checked the chair for booby traps and sat.

Holding his fist like a microphone, Herb boomed. "Our pest—I mean, guest—of honor has provided us all with so many laughs, I thought it only fitting that we offer her a special tribute tonight. Come with me now on this amusing jaunt down memory lane. Carlotta Little, *this* is your life.''

For the next hour, Carlotta sat through a wrenching rehash of every horrendous stunt Herb Lattimore had ever pulled at her expense. He began with the urine-soaked cafeteria chair in second grade. Next came the time he stole her training bra from the gym locker, and Carlotta saw it raised with the American flag during an all-school assembly. In eighth grade she was sentenced to a month of detentions after Herb scratched her initials in the fresh blacktop paving the schoolyard.

Some of his confessed mischief was news to Carlotta. She had not known that Herb was behind the premature eruption of her science-fair volcano or the mysterious disappearance of the thirty-page final paper on the life and times of Harry Houdini, over which she'd slaved for months. Because of the zero she received as a result, Carlotta had failed Social Studies and lost her coveted position as recording secretary of the Future Biographers of America.

"Last but not least, I'd like to present a recorded message from our special guest herself." Herb worked a remote, activating the sound system.

Carlotta's teenaged voice, ripe and husky, bellowed through the speakers. "That's it, Herb. Right there. Don't stop. Oh, my! Hoooo, baby. Yes!"

Everyone roared with laughter while the tape played on in a jeering, relentless loop. *"Hooo, baby. Yes! Hooobabyyeshoooooooooo-baaabeeeee Yesssssss!"*

Carlotta sat, unflinching, until the joke died of natural causes.

"Still not mad, Betsy Wetsy?" taunted Herb.

"Certainly not, Herb. In fact, I'm touched to think you'd go to all that trouble on my account."

"Hey, it's my pleasure. Honest," chortled Herb.

"Well, that's grand. Thankfully, I have something to give you in return. You asked that I bring something to share, something from the heart, and I have."

Carlotta plucked a small box from her purse. "For you, Herb. I made it myself."

"What is it? A bomb?"

"Don't be silly. Of course not. It's poison."

Frowning, Herb stepped away.

"Hey, what's up, Chervil? You scared?" Googie teased.

"Yeah, right. I'm sweating bullets." Herb swaggered toward Carlotta and took the box. He cut the yellow tape around it, slashing through the caution warnings. Inside was a single chocolate, marked with a skull and crossbones. "I've got to hand it to you, Carlotta. That's pretty cute."

"Oh, no, Herb." Carlotta's face was grave. "It is *not* cute at all. This is not a game, I assure you. And I'm warning you, in front of all these witnesses, that the chocolate in that box contains a highly lethal poison. One of the deadliest in the plant kingdom, in fact. I extracted it myself from the root of my *Aconitum napellus,* prize specimen of the family *Ranunculaceae.* Poor thing suffered some pain, I'm afraid. Actually, he's been acting a bit dejected since the surgery, but I'm told he'll enjoy a complete recovery."

"Sure, right. Whatever you say." Herb chuckled.

Carlotta's brow peaked in surprise. "Have you never heard of aconites? How surprising. I was certain you would have. They happen to be fellow herbs. Perennials such as yourself, in fact. Aconites are showy like you as well, Herb. And, like you, their venom has dire, disastrous effects."

Herb held the chocolate gingerly.

"Check it out: he's terrified." Googie guffawed.

"Shut your stupid trap," hissed Herb. "Let me get this straight, Carlotta. You're handing me this so-called poison chocolate and warning me not to eat it?"

"Definitely. Anyone foolish enough to ingest that would start to choke. He'd experience terrible restlessness, drooling, and nausea. Soon, his heartbeat would grow weak and irregular. He'd suffer dreadful chest pains, dizziness, prostration. There would be catastrophic damage to several major organs almost immediately.

By the time EMS arrived, it would be too late to reverse the effects. Death would be inevitable, but unfortunately, it could take hours for that sweet mercy. It's a rather excruciating way to go, I'm told." Carlotta had to smile at that, but she quickly reverted to a somber expression. "Sounds like the sort of end you'd only wish on your very worst enemy, Herb. Trust me."

Herb's gaze bounced nervously from the chocolate to Carlotta's face and back again. Beads of sweat erupted on his brow.

Googie slapped his chubby knee. "Look how she's got him going. Score one for Carlotta."

The others chimed in. "You should see the look on your face, Herb," said Raquel.

"Priceless," Wendy blurted. "You look like you're about to go pee-pee in your pants."

Herb's cheeks flamed. "Cut it out!"

"Buck up, there, Herb old man," chided Chip Savage. "It's only a game."

"No, it isn't," Carlotta insisted. "I'm telling you. This is perfectly serious."

"You've got him seriously scared. That's for sure." Googie flapped imaginary wings. "Kentucky fried chicken, Herb does chicken right."

"Don't call me that, Googie. I mean it."

Julia and Apulia took up the cry. "Chicken. Buck-buck-buckaw."

"Stop that, you two. I'm not kidding. And I'm *not* scared by some dumb joke." Herb's fingers quavered as he lifted the chocolate from the box.

"Don't do that, Herb. I'm warning you," said Carlotta.

"Carlotta's warning you," Googie taunted. "You better watch out."

"I'll eat the damned chocolate," Herb mewled. "I'll show you, Googie Nathanson. I'll show all of you." By shaky millimeters he moved the candy closer to his mouth.

"Wait just a darned minute," Carlotta demanded. "You've

heard me, Herb. All of you have heard me. Do you want your dear buddy to die, Googie? Is that what you're after?"

"You're really a scream, Carlotta," Googie said. "Go on, Herb. We dare you."

Carlotta puffed her disgust. "I simply cannot watch this. I'm leaving."

"Come on, Carlotta," Googie whined. "You can't go until he sucks down that *deadly* poison you brought. You'd be missing all the fun."

"Encouraging a dear friend to die is not my idea of fun, Googie."

The chocolate was five inches from Herb's mouth now. *Four.*

"Eat it, eat it," chorused the guests.

"Don't say I didn't warn you," Carlotta said.

Scrunching his eyes, Herb popped the chocolate in his mouth, chewed and quickly swallowed. A moment later, his eyes bugged and he made a harsh choking sound.

"Check him out," roared Googie. "That's priceless, Herb."

"You're too much, Herb. What a card," Myron whooped.

Carlotta sighed. "Poor Herb. Someone should call nine one one, not that they'll be able to do any good." She watched Herb clutch his throat and crumple to the floor. Then, she headed toward the foyer. "Au revoir, everyone. And to you, dear Herb: Good-bye."

An ebullient Carlotta misted and sprayed. "So sorry I'm late, my precious gloxinia. I do hope you weren't worried, darling *Cymbidium*. I'm afraid I simply lost track of the time."

The death of Herbert Alton Lattimore IV still commanded headlines. On her way home from the unemployment office, Carlotta had stopped to pick up the day's bounty of papers and magazines.

The coroner had closed the case this morning, deeming the incident a suicide. Oddly, Carlotta had not been called as a witness at the inquest, though she'd been fully prepared to tell the absolute, unadulterated truth. Several local friends had testified that Herb Lattimore was despondent in recent months. Googie Nathanson was quoted as saying, "He must have been even more depressed than I imagined. Why else would he do such a desperate, crazy thing?"

Why indeed? Carlotta mused. What could possibly drive a man to put his life on the line for some silly game? It was all too dreary and foolish to even consider.

She turned her full attention to her precious plants. Lovingly, she dusted the droopy leaves and parched blossoms of her ailing *Aconitum napellus.* The stem was lolling a bit as well. Carlotta propped it with a Popsicle stick and a bit of twine. "There now, sweetheart. I hope you aren't terribly, horribly angry with me for clipping your roots. You know I wouldn't have done such a thing if it weren't for a just and worthy cause."

Carlotta brushed aside a bit of soil and peered at the roots. Her heart soared. Things were healing just beautifully beneath the surface. All good things would follow in time.

Eric Lustbader

For many years, Eric Lustbader was identified on his dust jackets as Eric Van Lustbader, and the books were martial arts adventures that regularly found their way onto the best-seller lists. Having seen a Bruce Lee movie once, and years later a Chuck Norris movie, I viewed these martial arts productions as analogous to the wit they offered viewers—it was halfway there. However much "martial" there was on display, there was precious little "art."

Because I found no pleasure in the movies, I expected to find equally little to enchant me in books devoted to descriptions of the scenes I found so improbable on the screen.

Then I read a book by Marc Olden, which I liked. The author later recommended Eric Van Lustbader to me, and I learned that I'd been missing something after all. As time passed, however, Lustbader dropped the Van *and his novels became more mainstream crime novels set against a big canvas, much of it in the Far East, and they are a thrill a minute. Now, of course, I'm baffled that these thrilling adventure novels aren't made into movies. Preferably starring Steven Seagal or Sylvester Stallone or Bruce Willis or another of those bulked-up guys who can perform remarkable physical feats.*

The following story is nothing at all like those novels, it should be noted. Nor like the movies.

Dead Cat Bounce

▼▼▼

BY ERIC LUSTBADER

The night of my daughter's wedding, my husband, William VanDam, broke one of his inviolable rules.

"Persis," he said to me, "I've made a terrible mistake." He had never before admitted such a thing. To do so in his securities business would have meant immeasurable loss of reputation.

The best way to deal with this revelation, I decided, was to do nothing. Nothing spins so well as on its own momentum, I once heard him tell a junior partner. "Dear, why don't you take off your tux?" I said. I was sitting in my champagne silk charmeuse slip, at the dressing table in the truly hot hotel suite we had rented for the week. By *hot* I mean designer hot.

Observing Willie in the mirror, I could not help also seeing myself: black hair framing the pale oval face of a Madonna. "It's what, almost three-thirty in the morning?" I had removed my makeup as expertly as I had applied it hours ago, and was now massaging one of those botanical creams into the skin of my hands.

Because I was a concert pianist, I took extraordinary care of my hands. I confess my one abiding fear was that I would develop arthritis. I never went outside without donning butter-soft doeskin gloves, of which I had pairs in a virtual rainbow of colors. "You must be exhausted. I know I am. It was a truly glorious wedding, wasn't it?"

The air smelled of evening primrose as I stared at him in the mirror: a big man with a rough-hewn, handsome face. When we had first met, I had felt utterly transported by his commanding presence. He had given me shivers all over.

"I'm not in the least bit tired."

I could smell his sweat like a halo of rage. He never perspired like this in his office, not even during the excruciatingly complicated corporate mergers his securities firm brokered. It was the details that could kill you, as he had drummed into me time and again. Which was why people came to him: they knew he'd sew up every detail without reaching for the Zantac. He didn't miss one.

But he looked like he'd missed this one and now he was ready to tear his hair out.

"I may never sleep again. It's like ants crawling over my skin."

I swiveled around to face him. I heard the tone in his voice and was instantly warned. He had this wild streak—a volatile temper that had taken me quite some time to figure out. Often enough, he'd cruelly thrown back at me the fact that I was an orphan. *"Shape up or I'll abandon you as quickly as your mother did,"* he used to tell me when I disobeyed. He could always make me cry with that, even now.

I knew I needed to be calm. I rose, slipped off his black Armani tuxedo jacket, and hung it over a chair back. Then, leaning in so that my breasts pressed against his chest, I kissed him hard on the lips, the way he liked. "Come to bed now. Whatever's troubling you, can't it wait until morning?"

He leaned forward and slipped his left arm around my slender waist. But instead of embracing me fully, he slashed out with his right arm in a vicious arc, smashing my bottles of cream and lotion and nail polish to smithereens. Smears of colors ran down the mirror like blood.

"Does that answer your question?" His voice was acid; the fist he made trembled as nails dug into skin. My smooth surface had inflamed him all the more.

"Willie, for God's sake, calm down."

"If you've nothing else to contribute to the conversation, kindly keep quiet." He dropped his arm from around my waist. "Christ, what do you really know about the real world, Perse?" He was always lecturing about the real world, a place I apparently knew nothing about. "I took you out of the mess you had made of your life. I've kept you protected, safe from all the evil you were getting yourself into." He was quite correct in that. My parents had left me in a hospital, and seventeen years later, it was a hospital in which Willie had found me. If I looked at the insides of my wrists in the proper light I could still see the scars, straight as the razor blade that had caused them. By that time, I'd had it with evil. Every form of lowlife imaginable had gotten his claws into me. They were outsiders, and you might think so was I. But you'd be wrong. I wasn't even that. I was a parasite on the naked butt of an outsider. I have to admit, he had cause to despise what I'd been.

"Caroline is just like you, ignorant of life," he went on. "You can't expect me to do less for her."

"Is it Caro who's somehow upset you so?"

"In a manner of speaking. She just married that sonuvabitch Eddie."

My eyes opened wide.

"Oh, I know that look, Perse. You don't want to hear anything bad about him."

"He's Caroline's husband. Our son-in-law. Eddie's family now."

Now he seemed disgusted, impatient to turn away. But I held him to me with my sure and comforting artist's touch. "They love each other, Willie. I've rarely seen two people so crazy in love.

Think of how they danced while I played 'Rhapsody in Blue.'" I smiled, trying, in my way, to make him mimic me.

"That was Caroline's request," he said tightly. "Gershwin always moved her to tears. But what did *he* want?"

"The same, I'm sure. The look in their eyes while they danced—"

"He was looking at me, Perse. Because he knew."

I cocked my small, elegant head. I had been told many times that I looked like a ballet dancer, not a concert pianist. But ballet, what could I know of ballet in the filth of my former life? But music, oh, music was my sole escape. "Knew what?" The silence my husband generated was like a sound-damped engine. What remained unheard I felt. I gripped his powerful arms. "Willie, what could he know?"

"It started when Yates found Eddie had a license to carry a gun." Ross Yates was Willie's private investigator, one of Willie's major secrets from the outside world. Even Caroline didn't know of his existence, but I did. Of course, Willie had had Eddie investigated. "I asked him if he carried and he lied, said he didn't. And when I confronted him with Yates's report that showed the receipt for the nine-millimeter pistol he'd bought, he gave me another bullshit story that it had been stolen and he'd never replaced it."

"Was it bullshit?" I asked. "He seemed sincere."

"Sincere my ass. I'm the actor, here, Perse. How d'you think I make so much money? I know how to play a part. Just like our dear little Eddie-boy." Willie's mocking tone set my teeth on edge. "Yates showed up at the reception an hour ago to give me this." He broke away from me, slipped a set of folded papers out of the inside pocket of his tuxedo jacket.

"Let me see that." I reached for the papers, but Willie kept them out of my reach.

"No, Perse. I'll tell you as much as you need to know."

It was always this way with us. How can I be expected to learn about the real world if Willie keeps it out of sight?

For a moment I stared at the report, blue-white and ugly in

the lamplight of the gilt-and-cream-colored hotel suite. Then I turned and walked away from him.

I put on one of my favorite CDs: Eugene Ormandy's orchestral transcription of Bach's majestic Toccata and Fugue in D minor. I turned up the volume so he couldn't be heard over it. The chords burst in quiet thunder, filling the suite as if with purified air. Bach's great gift, it seemed to me, was bringing order out of chaos. Whenever I heard his music the emotions that had been tied in knots began to untangle.

Outside, it had begun to rain. Staring out the window at the spiked Manhattan skyline, I thought of the last few moments alone I'd had with Caro before we'd entered the chapel this evening.

"Are you sure this is what you want, darling?"

"Absolutely. God, I love him! Give me some credit, Mother. I'm as sure of Eddie as I am of anything." Caro, radiant in white, veiled like a vestal virgin, so like my younger self, so beautiful her heart-shaped face made me want to cry. *"I just want you and Daddy to be okay with this. I know you disapprove of Eddie."*

"Things will work themselves out, in time."

"Mom?"

"Um-hum." I was fiddling with her hair.

"I do love him so!"

Caro had tossed her head like a horse who's impatient for the race, and I thought, *Slow down, my darling, you have your whole life to live.* But of course things are so much clearer when you've a few years under your belt, and I was so determined that she shouldn't make the same mistakes I once did. That's a natural instinct in all mothers, isn't it?

The Bach toccata and fugue died in midmelody, and the silence of the present crashed in upon me. "Must we have this squalling late at night as well?" Willie said. He'd turned off the stereo. The artist's passion was something for which he had no understanding. Consequently, it was a threat to him, and his innate fear took the form of impatience. I recognized that and, for years, had forgiven him.

It seemed we must talk again. "How clearly I can recall the boys Caro brought home, one after the other," I said. I put my forehead against the thin pane of glass as if trying to melt through. "Abusive alcoholics, slack-jawed drug users with their greasy hair and their groping hands, grimy thrill-seekers with their tattooed scalps and their motorcycles." I felt so close to the rain, to being washed clean as a newborn kitten. "You know, it got to the point where I was sure she was doing it to torture us."

"Rubbing my face in the vileness of the world," Willie said.

"It was just as bad for me."

"Really?" He lifted an eyebrow. "But, Persis, my dear, you already had intimate knowledge of these vermin."

I smiled thinly at him. What else was there to do? Serenity was my watchword tonight.

"They made my skin crawl just looking at them," he went on, just as if he hadn't hurt me. "That junkie—"

"Yes. You were quite out of control that night."

"Whatever beating I gave him he deserved," he said. "Bringing drugs into my house."

"If the police hadn't come . . . You nearly killed him, Willie."

"And if I had, the world would have been a better place."

He believes it, I thought as I watched him make himself a drink. He always made himself a drink when he was working himself up to a difficult moment, either at home with me, or at the office with clients.

I continued to speak of Caro. "I doubt you know it, but I kept track of all her men friends. Because in some way each one was a reflection of her—or, at least, of what she was trying to do."

"And what was that?" Willie's tone was that of a professor who must put himself through the tedious task of listening to his students' fatuous theories before getting on with the real meat of the course.

How well I knew that tone of voice! He'd used it time and again since I'd been seventeen, when he'd begun to train me. And how I had needed training! Apart from breaking into the local high school at night to play the piano in the auditorium, I had no happy memories of my early years. Not surprising. Falling in with evil, I had no identity, no *self*. I had felt lost, a traveler in the midst of Grand Central Terminal with neither direction nor destination. That seemed long enough ago to be another lifetime.

"Caro had got the scissors out and was busy cutting the umbilical between child and parents," I said.

"You're wrong," Willie said angrily, as if all along he knew I would be. "She's saved that particular horror for tonight."

I stood without moving until Willie had to acknowledge my presence. It was a trick. *"The way to most effectively put the spotlight on yourself,"* he had drummed into me, *"is through understatement. In this case, stand perfectly still."* The first time I'd attempted it, at a party he'd taken me to, I'd seen how right he was.

When I had his attention, I took his old-fashioned glass away from him. "Oh, don't be so melodramatic, Willie." I kissed him several times, lightly as an arpeggio. "Face it. Eddie is different. He's the first real man her age she's cared about."

"Don't misunderstand me. I have no doubts about the depth of *her* feelings."

"Then take it from a woman," I said. "Eddie loves her."

"You've deduced this from what? Talking to Caroline, I suppose."

"And simple observation."

"Oh, yes. To be sure. He drives a Mercedes 500SL and wears made-for-measure clothes. The perfect man for our only child, isn't that what you think?" Willie had the impression that I coveted success as others prized diamonds or love. He was absolutely certain of this judgment because he had made me this way. It was his own image, but like most powerful men he didn't recognize it. Why had he done it? An enigma wrapped in a conundrum. Until you understood the man. What seemed on the surface perverse, was simply the basic instinct for self-preservation. He knew if he allowed me to fully surrender to my music he would come in a poor second. Willie had never come in second in his life, and he wasn't about to start with me.

"But you and Caroline are seeing what Eddie wants you to see." He slapped the papers of Yates's report so hard against his thigh that I jumped. "He's a monster. A fucking evil wind."

What did he want me to say? I knew, so I said just the opposite. "Willie, let her go. I promise she will not love you the less for loving Eddie. You're her daddy. My God, you make damn sure she still calls you that. You'll always be her daddy."

"You stupid cow, you still don't get it!" he shouted. Seeing the reaction in my white face, he forced his voice down. "This isn't about me. And, except in a minor way, it isn't even about her." He shook his fist. "If she stays married to him it'll end in tragedy, and Caroline will be irrevocably damaged. Maybe worse. She could wind up dead." Into the shocking silence, he said, "I should've seen it, but I didn't."

I looked down at the sheets of folded paper he still held out, and my eyes fluttered closed. "All right, go ahead," I whispered. "Tell me."

"This is the report of Yates's *second* investigation," Willie said.

Yates came only to the house, never to Willie's office. He arrived mostly late at night, at a ghostly hour, and always when Caroline had been out. But every once in a while he'd show up early in the morning, when the sky was still a pearlescent gray, yearning for the sun. At those times, I could hear his deep, raspy baritone as he reported to Willie in the study. Afterward, I would serve him coffee while Willie was upstairs getting ready to helicopter into Manhattan.

"First of all," Willie went on now, "Eddie's a goddamned fake. His last name's not Bennett. It's Bendarenski."

"So what? Many people shorten their names. I suppose he isn't an art dealer either."

"Oh, he imports artwork from all over and sells it here, just the way it seems," Willie said, as if he couldn't care less. "Only, some of the crates he gets contain more than paintings and sculpture."

I stared at him. "Like what?"

"Like drugs."

"Drugs?"

"Kilos of it," he said. "Cocaine, heroin, you name it, he sells—"

"Stop it!"

Willie seemed momentarily astonished by the force of my voice.

"This just isn't true. A mistake has been made. I know it!"

"Believe me, Ross Yates doesn't make mistakes."

I shook my head violently. "But we've met some of his clients. You know who they are—fabulously rich, famous—*everyone* knows them."

"Apparently, they don't know enough about them."

"Dear God!"

With a sob, I collapsed to my knees. My tears fell onto the strewn papers.

"I'm afraid there's more."

"No!" I cried. "I know more than I want to now!"

Willie knelt beside me, put his arm across my shoulders. "All right," he whispered. "How small you are, Perse. And how very female." It was this quality that had attracted him so powerfully when we had first met. *"You need to be protected,"* he had once told me long ago, *"from everyone who'll want a piece of you because of your talent."* He'd sucker-punched me, in an emotional manner of speaking. Because what he had meant was *"I can make you into anything I want."* And in the beginning he had been right. He could see that I was all too delighted to let him make the hard choices. Being an orphan had drained me, and falling into evil on the street had taken whatever had been left. It was as if he had lifted an insupportable weight off me. What had resulted was a folie à deux.

"Why?" I whispered. "Why didn't we know all this before the wedding?"

"It took all this time for Yates to get the goods." Willie kissed my temple. "It wasn't easy. Initially, he hit a stone wall; Eddie's clever, I'll give him that. But Ross is smart. That's why I hired him. It's Eddie's clients who made it so difficult for Yates to find out what he is. It's his clients who are protecting him. If he goes down, they'll follow. They can't afford to let that happen."

I turned to him. "What—what d'you mean?"

"I can't go to the police with this. Ross hasn't given me any proof that'll stand up with the DA."

"Meaning?" I knew a weak spot when I saw one. Willie had made certain of that.

He shrugged. "You don't know Ross. He sometimes uses methods that are . . . well, let's just say not open to the cops." There was that tone again, putting me in my proper place, protecting me from the world. "But it doesn't matter. Even if he had, he's assured me no one would listen. It's been hushed up."

"Oh, Willie—"

He picked me up tenderly and carried me across the threshold into the bedroom. He kissed my cheeks and damp forehead as he placed me into bed. How he adored me when I was utterly helpless. I could see him melt like ice cream in the sun.

"What about Caro?" I whispered up into his face. "What'll happen now?"

"Don't worry." He held my hand while he peered into my eyes. "I'll go talk to Eddie. He's venal. I'll make him an offer." A grim smile shone down on me. "The boy will recognize what's best for his own interests." He patted me. "Now go to sleep, Perse. I'll take care of everything. I promise. I've always been right, haven't I?"

I nodded. I watched him as he went into the bathroom, unfastening his silk braces. I heard him turn on the taps, then unzip his cosmetics kit bag.

When he came out, my eyes were closed and I made sure my breathing was slow and steady.

As soon as Willie left the suite, I jumped out of bed.

In the bathroom, I turned on the light and rummaged through his kit bag. It was oversized, custom made for him from stiff belting leather. I pushed aside shave cream, styptic pencil, dental floss. My fingertips found the hidden tab and I pulled. The zipper went right around the circumference of the bottom, revealing the pouch in which he kept his gun. Ever since he'd gotten the E-mail death threats a year ago, he'd obtained a permit and carried the .25-caliber Glock with him at all times.

I checked twice to make sure. The gun was gone. I hurried back into the bedroom.

Ask not for whom the bell tolls . . . I thought.

In the living room, one lamp was on. Within the halo of light it threw on the carpet, I could see the blue-white papers of Ross Yates's fateful report. I carefully gathered them up, placing the last page on top.

Ross Yates was nothing if not thorough. He'd discovered more than Willie had seen fit to tell me. Eddie had been previously married—to a woman both rich and young. She had died in a sailing incident. In heavy weather, the boom had caught her on the side of the head and she'd been pitched overboard. The Coast Guard had found no evidence of foul play, but the girl's sister had tried to keep Eddie from inheriting. It was her contention that he'd murdered his wife. Her efforts, it seemed, had come to nothing.

Now Eddie was married to Caroline.

I stared at the typewritten words. I could imagine what had gone through Willie's mind when he'd read this. All of his innate distrust of Eddie must have centered around this report. And God had hardened Pharaoh's heart.

I hurried back into the bedroom, pulled on leggings and a

clingy jersey top, slipped my feet into suede flats. I found that these simple acts left me breathless. I tried to calm myself with a mantra given to me by my yoga teacher, without success. I opened up a box in the closet, grabbed the black suede clutch bag that lay within, then, without a sound, I ran very quickly out of the hotel room.

Willie and I had secured for the newlyweds the presidential suite, a truly vast set of rooms that took up an entire corner of the hotel's penthouse floor. It was just for the wedding night. Late this afternoon, Caroline and Eddie would fly to Tortola, where he had a sailboat ready to take them through the Caribbean for two weeks.

I took the stairs. That made good sense, since I had insisted that Willie book the suite directly below.

The hallway carpeting was even thicker here on the top floor of the hotel. I went quickly and silently to the impressive double doors of the presidential suite. Glancing behind me down the empty corridor, I put my ear against the wooden door. I found that I was trembling.

Almost of its own accord, my slender shoulder pushed against the door. Unlocked and unlatched, it opened inward.

On the threshold, I paused. The slice of semidarkness beyond the door spilled over my feet, as if a grasping hand was pulling me inward. I felt as if I stood on the brink of another world, one that, even now when I confronted it, seemed inconceivable. I was re-minded of Ross Yates's description of scuba diving. *"The ocean is the great unknown,"* he had told me one morning over coffee. *"It's dark and it's cold and there are* things *down there—creatures we can't even imagine. But I can because I've seen them. That's why I get off on it."*

Holding my breath, I slipped my body sideways through the opening and plunged into the unknown. I stood absolutely still. I listened while the suite breathed. It was like the sound of a sick person on life support.

What came to me at length was a sob. It was a sound so stifled I swear I felt my heart constrict.

"Caro?"

With my musician's ear, tone was something I could identify in a heartbeat. I had recognized my daughter's voice.

"Caro!"

My daughter's voice was muffled by the bathroom door. "Caro, darling." A terrorized whimpering wrenched at my heart. "What are you doing in there, sweetheart? Please come out." That's when I saw the pale outline of the desk chair wedged under the doorknob.

"Get the hell away from there!"

I whirled, saw Willie standing in the open doorway to the master bedroom of the suite.

"I locked her in."

I moved to pull the chair away, but he grabbed my wrist.

"For her own protection, Perse. She would have tried to save him."

That was when I saw the gun in his hand. "What the hell have you done?"

"What had to be done." How can I say this right? He was trembling from head to foot. Not with fear, but with elation. "I've freed her." He meant Caro, of course. He was not wrong there.

"For God's sake, Perse. I have it all worked out. Why did you come up here? I told you I'd take care of everything. You were meant to sleep through it all."

I pulled away from him, and went into the bedroom. At first I saw very little. Willie or perhaps Caro had pulled the heavy drapes back so that the city's lights spangled the raindrops on the windowpanes, sending golden fingers into the darkness. I saw the huge bed with its rucked sheets. I walked slowly around the foot as if drawn by a magnet toward the far side. But then, death is the most powerful kind of magnet, isn't it?

"Perse, get out of there!" Willie had followed me into the bedroom. "Dammit, you'll fuck it all up!"

"Stay away from me." I was staring at the lumped shape twisted up in the bedding.

"Caroline didn't recognize me." Willie switched tactics, knowing he needed to placate me to get me the hell out of there now. "It's so dark in there, as far as she knows, a burglar broke into the room. I bundled her off to the bathroom before she saw my face." He raised a fist filled with Caro's jewelry and Eddie's Rolex watch and rings. "Shit, the less you know the better. What's done is done, but you being here—you're going to make it more difficult than it needs to be. Jesus, Perse, you know you're not strong enough to stand up to the cops. There'll be a thousand questions I'll have to answer."

The thing about the space around the lumped shape, I saw, was that it was dark as the blackest night. And shiny as an oil slick. The sickly-sweet smell of fresh blood stuck in my nostrils like tar. What I couldn't figure out was how he'd gotten the best of Eddie.

"Perse, have you been listening to me?" The urgency in Willie's voice had risen to fever pitch. "Time to—be careful! For Christ's sake, don't touch anything!"

But it was too late. I'd pulled back the bedcovers, and gasped. There was Eddie, lying on his back with the biggest hard-on I'd ever seen, or it would have been minutes ago when his heart was still pumping. *So this is how Willie did it,* I thought. For a moment, I felt sorry for Eddie. It must be damn hard to defend yourself when your brain's dulled by sex.

"What's happened here is already ancient history. Put it out of your head. Caroline can start her life over now. We'll get your fingerprints off the sheet and get the hell out of here."

He still doesn't get it, I thought. *But he will. This stupid cow will make sure of that.*

I reached into my purse and drew on a pair of gloves. Then I carefully unwrapped the heavy object from the butcher's paper. It smelled of machine oil, and a curious masculine scent almost as compelling as musk. My forefinger curled around the trigger. It felt oddly natural, like the ivory of keys beneath my fingertips. I turned and exhaled a long, slow breath. Then I squeezed the trigger of the 9mm gun.

The sound startled me, but Willie's body slamming back against the far wall did not. I watched him incuriously, sitting spread legged on the floor like an idiot child. Blood pumped out of his chest, and there was a stunned expression on his face that gave me a good measure of satisfaction. And why not? While it was true that for years I had forgiven him his fear of what made me happy and complete, this forgiveness had, without my knowing, turned to pity. As anyone who has lived a long life will tell you, it's a short step from pity to contempt. And, then, to hatred as pure as middle C. Still standing across the room, I carefully aimed at his head and squeezed off another shot. Bone and brains fountained outward with a great gout of blood. Like something on a movie screen, nothing more, I told myself.

Except for the stench.

I closed my mind to everything except what needed to be done. No need to hurry. This suite did not abut any others, and directly downstairs was my own suite. Nobody outside these rooms could have heard a thing.

I carefully rubbed the spot on the sheet I had touched with my bare fingers. Then I leaned over and placed the gun into Eddie's left hand. He was left handed, and this was his 9mm. I inserted his forefinger into the trigger guard and, pointing the 9mm toward Willie, I fired the gun so the paraffin test they'd be sure to do on Eddie would be positive.

Perfect.

To leave the bedroom I was required to step over the exsanguinating body of my husband. I was careful to avoid splotches of blood and gore soaking into the expensive carpet. I took the chair away from the bathroom door and opened it. Caro was huddled on the tiles, clearly in shock. What had Willie done to her? I wondered. Dark blotches had broken out on her forehead and left cheek, and had begun to swell. He had struck her to make the break-in seem more authentic. Of course Willie had had no intention of cutting a deal with Eddie. He'd gone up to the presidential suite to kill him. But then, I had known he would. It was only the eventual outcome that had been in doubt. *Men and their dangerously addictive toys,* I thought as I gently touched my daughter's shoulder.

Caro's eyes opened wide when she recognized me. She could hardly believe it.

"My darling . . ." I gathered my daughter to me, gently supported her against the sink as we embraced.

"Mom, what happened?" Caro's voice was that of a sleep-walker, high and thin with unnatural tension. "Someone broke in. I think—"

"Never you mind. That's a nightmare best forgotten." I filled a glass with water. From my bag I shook out a Valium and placed it on Caro's tongue. "Your mother's here now." I thought of what it was like to be orphaned, alone, in need of a sympathetic breast on which to rest one's weary head. "Swallow, precious. I'll take care of you."

Caro obediently washed the Valium down with water, and within five minutes I was able to walk her out of the suite, down the stairs, to the floor below. By the time I had tucked her into my own bed I was bathed in sweat.

I returned to the living room, and called the police. Then I placed Ross Yates's report on Eddie Bendarenski on the coffee table. It would be the first thing I'd show the police. That was key—the motive for the bad blood between Willie and Eddie.

Back in the bedroom, quiet as a mouse, I stripped off my gloves, inspected them for oil stains. I washed them, anyway, with leather cleaner, then folded them in half and placed them in the drawer with all the others. Already the specter of my husband, under whose thumb I had existed for so many years, was fading. He had led me out of the darkness into the light, without a thought that I might at some point examine the quality of that light. How could he possibly understand that the creature he had so painstakingly created had yearned only to be free? To do that he would have had to believe that I was an independent entity, who had grown far beyond the parameters he'd set for me. Sometime when he hadn't been looking, I had become a whole person, yearning to be a part of the real world. Willie could not conceive of such a thing.

How is that possible? He was living with me, after all. He saw me each day. But therein lies the answer. He saw what he wanted to see, and crushed beneath his heel any inkling that there might be more than what he himself had fashioned. He'd never had any intention of allowing me my freedom. My ignorance of the real world, as he put it, was what gave him his hold over me. And if I had been foolish enough to confess that I could not survive the prison of our marriage another moment, surely he would have laughed at my naïveté. And deliberately denied me what I wanted most—and now by my own hands had achieved.

I fixed myself a stiff drink. Slowly sipping it, I went to the stereo and put on the Bach, softly this time, because there was no longer any reason to turn up the volume.

Dawn brought the inevitable barrage of questions from the police. I was ready for them. I felt light as the air I breathed, and my elation made me want to shout. But of course I did not. It was Willie who had taught me how to act. I had fooled him, and I'd do the same with the police. No sweat.

I presented my frailness as an offering they might come upon of their own momentum. As ever, understatement. Tears came easily to me. Why not? I needed only to imagine the years of my indenture, or Caro in drugged sleep in the next room. I showed the handsome detective Caro's battered face, and assured him he could speak with her as soon as the doctor pronounced her recovered from shock. The potbellied detective was understanding and sympathetic even while he was double- and triple-checking my story. I admit I liked being treated with kid gloves which, I believed, was my due. He had heard me play Scriabin last year at Alice Tully Hall in Lincoln Center. He was somewhat awed, but he did his job nonetheless. I was almost as impressed with him as he was with me.

During a break in my statement, while he was bringing me coffee, I watched light as thin as a veil come into the early morning sky, and thought of something Ross Yates had told me about his work: *"Some people who don't know any better think I'm a piece of shit, rooting through the garbage. But you know what? They're just scared of me, because everyone's got secrets and I know how to get to them all. In this world, secrets are more valuable than gold."*

Eventually, it all blew over, like an evil wind. That was how Willie had described Eddie, but it also could be said of him. I had done everything perfectly. It was the considered opinion of the police that the two men had quarreled. The quarrel had escalated, and since both men were armed, the altercation had ended most tragically. Another example for the antigun lobby to use.

In the aftermath, I was reminded of something Willie had told me years ago. He'd come home in a particularly exultant mood, and I'd asked him why. *"Dead cat bounce,"* he had said, laughing. *"Don't look so appalled, Perse. It's a Wall Street term. You target a company that looks dead on its feet. The stock's hovering, say, between one and two because almost everyone's given up on it. Then somebody like me comes in and starts buying heavily. Word gets around, and the price moves a little, until the greedy people get wind of the price change. There must be a turnaround, they think. The company's going to be profitable again. So they buy—and others buy—in great quantity. Now the price shoots up to five, six, eight. That's when I sell, because this company's as dead as it was the day I bought the stock. The price collapses completely. That blip upward is called a dead cat bounce: the illusion of life."*

That's what my life had been up until the moment I killed Willie, I thought: an illusion.

My pride at outwitting the police was something Willie would have understood, even applauded. My elation at being free gave vent to rehearsals that left me breathless, swimming in another world. Willie had for so long denied me full entry to this world that I felt drunk after almost every practice session. In fact, I left the piano only to take care of Caro.

How she missed Eddie. How little she understood herself! But there'd be so much time now for self-revelation. For her, nights were the worst. She had terrible bouts of depression, despair, and uncontrollable weeping. At those times, she withdrew completely, and I was once again momentarily reminded of my younger self. I did not pity her, because I knew what hell Eddie would have made of her life. If he'd allowed her to live. But there could be no doubt that the house was stifling her and, itching to get back to performing, I took her to Venice as soon after the investigations were concluded as I dared.

Venice was my favorite city, a place that pierced me clear to my soul. My God, on this trip the sky was so blue! Caro complained of the smell, but to me the air was pungent with new life!

I played three nights at the Teatro della Fenice, the small but magnificent concert and opera house. Throughout my career, critics, while praising my impeccable technique, had now and again carped that my playing lacked true passion. These Venetian concerts were markedly different. For the first time, I lost myself completely in the music. Much to my astonishment, I made many in the audience weep. At the end, the packed house would not let me leave the stage, urging me back for encore upon encore. For these, I very shrewdly chose the nocturnes of Chopin, that most emotional of composers, and now the entire audience wept.

And it was here that Caroline, witness to the flowering of my soul, at last began to return to life. It was as if the complex mathematical patterns of Bach's music infused her with the innate orderliness of life, banishing the memory of the chaos that had so mercilessly overtaken her. It was as if the florid passion of Chopin had reawakened her heart so that she was reminded what it meant to love and be loved in return.

This metamorphosis, clearly apparent after the first concert, thrilled me to the tips of my fingers. I clutched her to me and kissed her repeatedly. And fell in love as if for the first time with the music of Bach and Chopin, with the people of Venice who fêted me in the cafés that lined the piazza outside the Fenice until dawnlight strayed like a striped cat through the cobbled streets.

The day after the last of the concerts dawned bright and clear. The sky was the color of the sea, and in between lay all of Venice, sun washed, ancient as time. Riding an unceasing wave of bliss, I hired a *motoscafo*—a private motor launch—which took us first to Burano, the island of fishermen, whose small row houses painted in lovely pastels looked like the set for *La Traviata*.

After a leisurely stroll along the narrow, crooked streets, we took the *motoscafo* farther into the great lagoon to the island of Torcello, where, centuries before, the original Venetians had made their home. I had booked a table for lunch in the flower-strewn garden at the Locanda Cipriani. There, we looked out over a thirteenth-century church whose cracked burnt-sienna facade oozed an aura that seemed barely Christian.

White, puffy clouds dotted the sky like the sailing vessels on the lagoon, and where the Venetian sunlight struck the trellises and vines, the flowers sang a rich and vibrant oratorio. When Caro excused herself to go inside, the man at the next table turned to me and asked in a deep, raspy baritone whether he could buy "the lady and her sister" a drink.

I couldn't help smiling. "Caroline's my daughter. We'd be delighted to accept the offer of a fellow American, but only if you join us for lunch. Are you alone?"

"As it happens, I am. Thank you," he said, as he came and sat opposite Caro's chair, at my left elbow.

"Are you here on business?" I asked.

"No, pleasure. You know, sightseeing, the usual." Under his breath, he said, "Right on time."

"What's the matter, Ross?" I said in the same hushed tone. "Didn't you think I'd make it?"

"After the way you put VanDam to sleep, I had no doubt," Ross Yates whispered. "But last night I dreamt you didn't come. Christ Almighty, this was the toughest month of my life. The longer I stayed away from you, the more I wanted you."

He was tall and rangy, like a cowboy, with windblown hair the color of flax. His face reminded me of a soldier's: tough, vigilant, competent. Seemingly not the kind of man to make such an admission. I very much liked that he had. That bastard Willie never would have opened up like that.

"You certainly know how to make a woman's head spin."

He laughed. "That isn't all I can make spin." His gray eyes appeared screwed into the bone of their sockets. They sparked with licentious memory. *When I say I'll do something,* they seemed to say, *it's as good as done.* "Those early mornings when VanDam was upstairs . . ." He chuckled. "I bet your kitchen table never saw that kind of action before or since. VanDam may have been a genius at business, but he sure was short on imagination. No way he ever made you sing like I do."

God, how right he was! And he laughed, seeing it in my eyes.

"It was my lucky day when I showed you the report on Eddie."

"And even luckier for both of us I made you sit on it until the wedding reception."

"You really do have a deliciously evil mind."

"Hush," I whispered. "Caro's coming back." I was flushed and excited and terrified all at once.

As he turned his most brilliant smile on Caroline, Ross said to me out of the corner of his mouth, "What a quick study you were, practicing with the gun you had me steal from Eddie. I told you everything would come out fine as long as you didn't jerk the trigger. You did just like I taught you: exhale and slowly squeeze it."

I was so pleased I put my hand on his thigh underneath the table.

Lunch at the Locanda was just as I had imagined it would be. Ross was gentle and funny with Caro, and she seemed to take an instant liking to him almost from the moment I introduced them. Good thing. He was going to be in our lives for a long time to come.

Still, Caro insisted on going out alone in the small hours of the night. I asked Ross to watch over her from a distance when she went, and prayed that time would heal her wounds.

Gradually, she grew calmer. Truth to tell, Ross was a good and comforting companion to us both.

"All my life," he told me one day in Venice, "I've settled for things. I was an Army brat, so I had to settle for making new friends almost every year. I didn't really want to be a PI, but I could never get my detective's shield in the NYPD; written tests were never my thing. The girl I fell in love with didn't love me, so I settled for someone I liked but didn't love. That lasted a half-dozen miserable years. Then, my luck changed." He smiled at me and my heart lifted. "I was hired by VanDam."

By the time we arrived in London it appeared that Caroline had returned to her old, sunny self. I was desperate to renew the sexual part of my affair with Ross, but with Caro around there never seemed to be a good time. Besides, as Ross pointed out, we'd be far better off in the long run if we waited awhile longer. He was right, but being discreet was playing havoc with my hormones. Killing Willie, being set free, had made me as randy as a rabbit.

My agent had booked a two-night engagement at the Royal Albert Hall. I was to play with the Royal Philharmonic, so there was a full week of rehearsals at the hall, more than was necessary for a solo recital. Also, there were egos other than mine to contend with. The conductor, a man whom I had always admired but had never before met, turned out to be a prima donna of the worst sort. Temper tantrums were not uncommon, and my own temper grew increasingly short. I'd work all day and then have difficulty sleeping at night. Ross was wonderful during this time. He sat in the dark, deserted theater with Caro until the tightness of my expression forced him to mount the stage and calm me down. He did this so many times that the musicians, generally a jealous lot, soon grew used to his presence on their exalted pulpit.

"Careful," he mouthed to me during a break late in the grueling rehearsals. "This man is a maximum boor, but he has the power to ruin you." Ross, a quick study if ever there was one, had already seen just how small and incestuous the world of classical music was. I appreciated his candor—and his concern, which was about 180 degrees from what Willie's reaction would have been. My late husband no doubt would have belted the maestro in the face, if he'd bothered to show up at all.

"I'll remember to love him as if he were my own brother." I looked up at the tiers of seats. "They don't look like holes, do they?" I drank from a bottle of Evian water Ross handed me. "The first time I came here, I couldn't help thinking of the Beatles' 'A Day in the Life.' I wonder if Lennon was tripping when he wrote the lyrics."

" 'I'd love to turn you ooon,' " Ross sang softly in a surprisingly good tenor voice.

I laughed and, draining the water, kissed him warmly on the cheek. "I'm so glad you're in my life."

I watched him climb down from the high stage and disappear into the darkness of the theater, where he took his seat beside Caro. The rehearsal carried on. But, gradually, I found that I was playing by memory alone. My mind seemed to be oddly detached from my body, elastic as gum, as distorted as if I was in a house of mirrors. Tripping like Lennon in the seventies.

My stomach turned abruptly queasy, and I stopped playing. My hands, arched and ready, hung suspended above the keyboard. They looked like spiders spinning a web, and I wanted to scream. I

missed my cue and, feeling like I was about to vomit, I lurched
drunkenly to my feet.

The bench upended behind me with a great clatter, and the
orchestra ceased to play.

"I . . . I . . ."

Somehow I became aware of Ross running down the center
aisle toward me while everyone on the stage was transfixed, unable
or unwilling to make a move or sound.

"I . . . I . . ."

Ross mounted the steep steps three at a time, and I tottered
toward him on legs I could no longer feel. He seemed to be standing at the edge, waiting for me. I was almost to his strong, welcoming arms when I lost all control of my body. I knew I was
going over the edge, and my arms began to flail. I made a desperate lunge for Ross's powerful shoulder, but it was too late. My
fingers grasped only air.

I fell, past all the thousand holes in Albert Hall.

I saw a quick flash of the maestro's face, distorted by shock.
Then I struck the floor with a numbing blow. A great roaring filled
my ears, drowning out even the thunder of the screams and shouts
of those all around me. It was the first chord of Bach's Toccata and
Fugue in D minor. It was the rush of my own blood.

I remembered that *toccata* came from the feminine past parti-
ciple of the Italian *toccare*, which meant "to touch." Bach's majestic chord touched me in the stunned release of my own breath.

In an instant, even that was gone.

"Welcome back." Ross, smiling faintly, stood over my hospital bed. "We thought we'd lost you."

"Mom!" On his left I could see Caro, her face a sea of worry.
"You're tougher than anyone believed. You came through."

I had a sudden urge to grab her and hold her tight, but I
couldn't move.

"You're paralyzed, Perse." Ross took a deep breath. "You broke your neck and your spine in four places."

Terror gripped me and, looking into Caro's sorrowful face, I was overcome by a desire to tell her how much I loved her. I opened my mouth, but no sound came out.

"I'm afraid your speech was affected too," Ross said. "Temporarily or permanently, the doctors don't know."

Ross must have seen all the blood drain from my face, because he asked Caro to fetch a doctor. Properly terrified, she fled. Then he did something really weird. He leaned over the bed, but instead of kissing me, he put his lips against my ear.

"You know what I thought about on those nighttime walks with Caroline?" he whispered. "Why settle for the mother when I can have it all? That's what I want. And, for once in my life, I'm going to get it. The way I see it, you're yesterday's news, someone else's history. VanDam made you over. Now I'll do the same with Caro. Face it, Perse. You're dangerous. I mean, you pulled the trigger on your own husband. How many women could do that, hmm? Not many, I imagine. It takes a cold, calculating mind; a certain cruelty. Lying next to you, who could sleep? I figure if you did it to him, one day, you could do it to me."

Why did his words fill me with so much dread? Because they expressed precisely the same pity and contempt I had harbored for Willie.

"By the way, if you haven't guessed by now, that was acid in your Evian." He meant LSD, of course. One of the drugs of my lost youth. "I thought maybe you'd kill yourself in the fall, but, no, like Caro said, you're too damn tough. So here you are." He pulled away for a moment to check my horrified expression. Then, to my dismay, he put his lips back against my ear and continued his horrific whispering.

"So I seduced her, and, hey, what d'you know, she was ripe for it. Like mother, like daughter." A little laugh, evil as sin. Sick with shock, I tried to turn my head away, but his hand held me fast. The smell of him, which only yesterday was intoxicating, now made me want to gag. "My God, what a juicy morsel she is!"

The doctor burst into the room and Ross stepped quickly back. The doctor, working on me, had his hands full. He couldn't see what I saw, and if he had, it would hardly mean a thing to him: Ross taking Caro's hand as she came back through the door. Ross kissing her shining hair, her red, curving lips, making me shiver so hard that the doctor became concerned all over again.

"I think you'd better leave now," he told them curtly. "She needs to rest."

No! I screamed in my mind. *Caro, don't leave me!* But, of course, what I meant was: *Don't leave with him! Don't believe his lies!* But it was too late. And now I realized that it had always been too late.

Tears in my eyes, I looked for Caro and Ross. But they were gone.

Phillip Margolin

Phillip Margolin has been compared by admiring reviewers to both Scott Turow and John Grisham—in other words, he is a writer capable of adding that chill edge of darkness to the hot legal thriller. Among his best-selling novels are The Burning Man, Gone but Not Forgotten, *and* After Dark. *As a criminal defense attorney himself, he's had more than his share of headline-grabbing murder cases and has argued before the Supreme Court. It is difficult to understand how he can keep topping himself—whether before a jury or his growing legion of fans—but so far he has managed never to disappoint.*

In this exquisite little tale, a relieved career criminal knows he has an alibi to die for—one that puts him far from the scene of the murder of which he is accused. There is no meticulously thought-out courtroom scene here, as the protagonist has figured out a better way to handle the situation.

Angie's Delight

BY PHILLIP MARGOLIN

Larry Hoffman was so nervous that he actually bounced in place while the guard unlocked the door that led from the jail into the contact visiting room. His future depended on the person who was waiting on the other side of the thick metal door. Would he see some wet-behind-the-ears, recent law-school grad, who would use his case for practice, or would he meet a wily old veteran who knew what it would take to save his ass? When you were down on your luck, the gods decided whether you lived or died. In Larry's case, the particular god in question was the clerk who assigned lawyers from the court-appointment list.

Larry heard a metallic snap, and the guard stepped back so his prisoner could enter the concrete-block room. Larry froze in the doorway for a moment. Then, a shudder passed through his undernourished five-nine frame, as he exhaled with relief. Seated at the circular table that took up most of the narrow room was a man in his forties attired in a gray three-piece suit that looked expensive. The man smiled confidently. His hair was sandy blond and a thick, well-groomed mustache covered his upper lip. When he stood, Larry could see that he was well over six feet tall and he was impressed by the lawyer's trim, athletic physique. The man in whose hands Larry's life rested looked relaxed, like someone who had been around the block, like someone who knew the ropes, like someone who would not be buffaloed by a belligerent DA or a prosecution-prone, defendant-eating judge.

"Mr. Hoffman," the lawyer said in a pleasant baritone, "I'm Noah Levine and I've been appointed to represent you."

Larry grasped the lawyer's hand, the way he would have gripped a log had he been cast into the sea without a life jacket. Levine's handshake was solid.

"Sit down, Mr. Hoffman," Levine said with an easy smile.

"Thanks for comin' over so fast. They told me I wouldn't see no one until this afternoon."

"You are charged with murder, Mr. Hoffman. There is no time to waste."

All right!! Larry thought gleefully, *I have me a tiger.*

"Larry . . . May I call you Larry?"

"Yeah. That's cool."

"Larry, before I talk to you about the facts of your case, I want to explain the attorney-client relationship. Have you ever been in jail before?"

"Oh, yeah. This is my, uh, let's see . . . the third time."

"And you've had a lawyer before?"

"Twice. They were both jerks. All they wanted me to do was plead guilty."

"Well, Larry, we aren't pleading to anything," Levine told him confidently. He wore steel-rimmed glasses. Behind the lenses were steely blue eyes. "We are going to take names and kick ass."

Larry grinned broadly. This guy was all right!

"Now, Larry, I don't know what your other lawyers told you, but with me, anything you say is confidential. If you tell me you killed fifty people and they're buried in your backyard, that stays between us."

"Hey, I didn't kill nobody."

"What I'm saying is, if you did, I could give a shit, because I'm your attorney, Larry, and my mission in life is to clear you of this accusation of murder."

"That accusation is false. I did not off the dude."

"I don't have any of the police reports, yet, but didn't the papers say that there were witnesses?"

"That was from the day before when I kicked O'Malley's ass."

"Yes. There was a fight."

"There wasn't no fight. I smacked the motherfucker around with a lead pipe to let him know I meant business. He never even threw a punch."

"And this was in front of witnesses?"

"Damn straight. It was a lesson. I wanted those other little shits to know what would happen if they tried to keep my money."

"What money was this?" Levine asked.

Larry paused. He looked a little nervous.

"This stays between us?"

"It would be unethical for me to tell anyone anything you tell me in confidence. If I were to tell even my wife, I could face disbarment."

Larry's head bobbed up and down. "Okay, then. The, uh, money . . . It was from selling my dope. Those motherfuckers are my dealers. Tyrone, Kaufman, and that fucker O'Malley. He was holding back. Tyrone, he told me. So, when they came over to pay me, I knew O'Malley would be short and I smacked him around to make my point."

"What exactly did you say would happen if he held back any more money?" Levine asked.

"I said I would kill his ass."

"That's what I was afraid of."

"But I didn't do it. Someone else wasted him."

"Do you have any idea who it was?"

"Nah. O'Malley was askin' for it. I'm not the only guy he pissed off."

"Unfortunately, you're the only person who threatened to kill him in front of witnesses. And it doesn't help that O'Malley was beaten to death by a blunt instrument."

Larry shrugged. "It wasn't me. That's all I can tell you."

"Well, Larry, we'll need to give the jury something more than your word. Do you have an alibi for the time of the murder?"

"When was it?"

"Saturday, between two and three in the morning."

"Saturday! Between two and three!" Larry repeated excitedly.

Levine nodded.

"Oh, man, I must be livin' right. I have a great alibi. . . ."

Suddenly, Larry paused. He ran his tongue across his lips.

"Uh, there might be a little problem."

"Yes?"

"What if my alibi involves something illegal?"

"That could present difficulties, but remember, you're charged with murder and you're facing a possible death sentence."

"Yeah, you're right. Besides, the bitch will never testify against me."

Levine looked interested. "Who are you talking about?"

"The bitch who was in the movie. Angie something. I don't remember her last name. She's some runaway I picked up at the bus station."

"I'm not following you."

"Okay. Look, selling dope ain't all I do. It's tough to make ends meet, so I got this other deal goin' with a couple of the independent video stores. Like, for special customers, I make these movies."

"What kind of movies?"

"Adult movies. Porno. I film 'em at my house, then I dupe 'em and sell 'em to these few guys. Sometimes, they're special order. You know, some guy has a fantasy, I do it for him on a video."

"What does this have to do with your alibi?"

"Okay. On Saturday, between one and three, I was doing this rape thing for this guy."

"A rape thing?"

"Yeah. He was real specific. He wanted a video. It had to be a redhead. She gets lured into the bedroom. Then, she gets beat up and tied to the bed. Then she gets raped and beat up some more. So, I go to the bus station. The girl's perfect. Young, big tits. The hair was a problem. She was brunette. But we dyed her hair.

"I told her I was a movie scout, which, I guess, was techni-cally true. I laid the thing out. She gets two hundred bucks for doing the movie. She was so fucking stupid. She bought the whole thing. She even believed it would all be acting and that she'd get paid."

Larry laughed and shook his head. "The bitch sure looked surprised the first time she got hit."

Levine looked upset for a second, but he composed himself.

"If you beat up this girl and raped her, what makes you think she'll testify for you?"

"That's the good part. We don't need her. See, I filmed this shit in my bedroom. I worked the camera part of the time and a guy named Rodney beat her up and raped her. Then, Rodney worked the camera."

"Well, this Rodney isn't going to admit he did that."

"Oh, I ain't countin' on Rodney. He's outta here, anyway. The guy's a drifter. I don't know where he's gone.

"No, the thing that's gonna save my ass is the TV. See, the TV was on all the time. It was next to the bed. You can see it in the video. And I'm in the picture too. This guy wanted two guys rapin' her, so I took my turn. And I did her second, which was between two and three in the morning. You can tell that by the show that's on the TV."

"Aren't you worried about being identified if the police see the video?" Levine asked.

"Nah. First, this bitch is long gone. We dumped her in a vacant lot and told her what we'd do to her if she ever went to the cops. She was so scared, she's probably in Alaska by now.

"Second, you can't tell from the movie if it's real or fake. I'd just say she was acting and no one could prove otherwise."

"How can I get ahold of the video?" Levine asked.

"It's still at my house. I was gonna dupe it and bring it to my people, but I was arrested for wasting O'Malley before I could do it."

"Is there only one copy?"

"Yeah."

"Then I better act fast. Tell me where it is and I'll have my investigator pick it up. I want to put it in my safe."

"Fuckin' A!" Larry shouted. "I got to say this. I was really scared I'd get another asshole for a lawyer, but you are really good."

Levine smiled modestly. "Why don't you wait to congratulate me until the charges are dropped. Now, where do I find the tape?"

"It's in my bedroom in the closet. There's a lot of tapes, so you're gonna have to look for it."

"How will the investigator know which one to take?"

"It's labeled *Angie's Delight*. I think it's up by the front on the top shelf."

Levine stood.

"You'll let me know if you get it, right?" Larry said.

"I don't want an innocent man sitting in jail for one second longer than is necessary. If we can pin down when the shows on the TV were aired and you're in the picture, you're home free."

Larry sprang to his feet when the guard told him his attorney was waiting to see him. It was four in the afternoon and he was thrilled that Levine was back so quickly. When the guard opened the door, Larry rushed into the room. He stopped dead, just as the door locked behind him.

"Who are you?" he asked the skinny young man in the ill-fitting brown suit. The man smiled nervously. He had short brown hair and thick tortoiseshell glasses. Larry noticed coffee stains on the frayed cuffs of his cheap white shirt.

"I'm Marty Long, your court-appointed counsel. I would have been over sooner, but you wouldn't believe my day," the young man said with an anxious chuckle. "First, I get stuck in Judge Lourde's courtroom. Then, just when I thought I could get in to see you, there was this emergency at the office. Anyway, I'm here now. So, let's get started."

"Wait a fucking second. Where's Levine?"

"Who?" Long said, looking up from the papers he was pulling out of a worn attaché case.

"My lawyer. Noah Levine. The guy was here this morning. He knew all about my case. He said he was court appointed."

Long looked confused. "We don't have a Noah Levine in the Public Defender's Office. I guess there could have been a screw-up." He laughed. "It happens all the time. I'd better check to make sure there aren't two lawyers working on this case. Actually, it would be a relief if you did have another lawyer. I'm swamped right now, and I was wondering how I was going to have time to do all the work on this, uh, it's a murder case, right?"

Larry stared openmouthed at the fidgeting lawyer. What a toad, he thought. Thank God, he had Levine on the case.

Tom Farrell helped ease his daughter into the front seat of the rental car. He had cranked the seat back so it was reclining. He hoped this would make it easier for Angie to sleep on the ride to the airport. They would take a five o'clock flight home to Nebraska.

As soon as she was settled in her seat, Farrell reached across and fastened Angie's seat belt. He avoided looking at her face. Whenever he saw the scars, the broken nose, and the bruises, it made him start to cry. He loved her so much, it broke his heart to think that something he might have done had caused her to run away. His pastor assured him it was the drugs that had destroyed Angie's childhood, but he wondered if he had driven her to them with the pressures he put on her to be perfect. The months she was gone had been hell for Tom and his wife. He vowed that they would never lose her again.

As soon as Angie's seat belt was fastened, Farrell sat back and started the car. He was driving out of the hospital parking lot when Angie said, "Daddy," in a voice so low he could barely hear her.

"What is it, sweetheart?"

"I'm suh . . . sorry."

Angie started to cry and Tom choked back his own tears.

"Don't apologize, princess. What happened is in the past. We're all starting over, as of today. Okay? I know some of this has been my fault and I'm going to change too."

The dam had broken when Angie saw Larry Hoffman's picture on the front page of the paper her father carried into her hospital room, along with the story of his arrest for murder. She had cried so hard during most of her account of the rape and beating that Farrell had a hard time understanding his daughter.

Farrell's original plan had been to kill Larry Hoffman in the contact room at the jail, then take whatever the justice system threw his way. It had been even easier than he'd hoped to gain Hoffman's confidence. By posing as his court-appointed defender, he could make certain that the slimebag was guilty of the things Angie had tearfully told him he had done to her before he ended Hoffman's sorry life. Farrell's plan had changed when Larry told him the significance of the videotape for his alibi.

"I love you and Mom, so much," Angie said.

"We love you too. Now, try to nap. We'll be home by tonight. Mom will be waiting at the airport."

"Get me home soon, Daddy. I don't want to be here any-more."

"I will sweetheart. I just have one stop to make."

Angie closed her eyes and Farrell headed toward the airport. On the way, he passed the landfill on the edge of town where he had stopped before going to the hospital. As they sped by, he glanced quickly at the mountain of garbage under which he had buried the false ID he had used to gain entrance to the jail and the videotape he had viewed once to make certain he was doing the right thing.

David Morrell

David Morrell is the award-winning author of First
Blood, *the 1972 novel in which Rambo first appeared. A
former professor of American literature, he has written
numerous best-selling thrillers including* The Brother-
hood of the Rose *(the basis for a highly rated NBC
miniseries),* The Fifth Profession, Desperate Measures,
and Extreme Denial. *His books have been translated
into twenty-two languages.*

    *The story that follows is based on a real-life situa-
tion. Morrell's inspiration to become a writer was Stir-
ling Silliphant, whose work for* Route 66 *and* Naked City
*made him one of the most acclaimed television writers of
all time. Over the years, Morrell and Silliphant became
friends, and one evening Silliphant confided that the TV
networks were less interested in his work now that he
was in his late sixties. His abilities hadn't diminished
and his work ethic remained in place, but the young
executives who run the television industry decided that
he couldn't speak to the demographically desirable
younger audience. Fed up with Hollywood, Silliphant
had a Beverly Hills garage sale and moved to Bangkok,
where he wrote what he wanted to and died of prostate
cancer at the age of seventy-eight. Morrell dedicated this
story to him.*

Front Man

▼▼▼

BY DAVID MORRELL

"Tell me that again," I said. "He must have been joking."

"Mort, you know what it's like at the networks these days."
My agent sighed. "Cost cutting. Layoffs. Executives so young they
think *L.A. Law* is nostalgia. He wasn't joking. He's willing to take
a meeting with you, but he's barely seen your work, and he wants a
list of your credits."

"All *two hundred and ninety* of them? Steve, I like to think
I'm not vain, but how can this guy be in charge of series development and not know what I've written?"

This conversation was on the phone. Midweek, midafternoon. I'd been revising computer printouts of what I'd written in
the morning, but frustration at what Steve had told me made me
press my pencil down so hard I broke its tip. Standing from my
desk, I clutched the phone tighter.

Steve hesitated before he replied. "No argument. You and I
know how much you contributed to television. You and Rod

Serling and Paddy Chayefsky practically invented TV drama. But that was then. This executive just started his job three months ago. He's only twenty-eight, for Christ's sake. He's been clawing his way to network power since he graduated from business school. He doesn't actually *watch* television. He's too damned busy to watch it, except for current in-house projects. What he does is program, check the ratings, and read the trades. If you'd won your Emmys for something this season, he might be impressed. But *The Sidewalks of New York*? That's something they show on Nickelodeon cable reruns, a company he doesn't work for, so what does he care?"

I stared out my study window. From my home on top of the Hollywood Hills, I had a view of rushing traffic on smoggy Sunset Boulevard, of Spago, Tower Records, and Château Marmont. But at the moment, I saw none of them, indignation blinding me.

"Steve, am I nuts, or are the scripts I sent you good?"

"Don't put yourself down. They're better than good. They don't only grab me. They're fucking smart. I *believe* them, and I can't say that for . . ." He named a current hit series about a female detective that made him a fortune in commissions but was two-thirds tits and ass and one-third car chases.

"So what's the real problem?" I asked, unable to suppress the stridency in my voice. "Why can't I get any work?"

"The truth?"

"Since when did I tolerate lies?"

"You won't get pissed off?"

"I *will* get pissed off if—"

"All right already. The truth is, it doesn't matter how well you write. The fact is, you're too old. The networks think you're out of touch with their demographics."

"Out of—"

"You promised you wouldn't get pissed off."

"But after I shifted from television, I won an Oscar for *The Dead of Noon*."

"Twenty years ago. To the networks, that's like the Dark

Ages. You know the axiom—What have you done for us lately?
The fact is, Mort, for the past two years, you've been out of town,
out of the country, out of the goddamn *industry.*"

My tear ducts ached. My hurried breathing made me dizzy.
"I had a good reason. The most important reason."

"Absolutely," Steve said. "In your place, I'd have done the
same. And your friends respect that reason. But the movers and
shakers, the new regime that doesn't give a shit about tradition,
they think you died or retired, if they give you a moment's thought
at all. *Then* isn't *now.* To them, last week's ratings are ancient
history. What's next? they want to know. What's new? they keep
asking. What they really mean is, What's *young?*"

"That sucks."

"Of course. But young viewers are loose with their dough,
my friend, and advertisers pay the bills. So the bottom line is, the
networks feel unless you're under thirty-five or, better yet, under
thirty, you can't communicate with their target audience. It's an
uphill grind for writers like you, of a certain age, no matter your
talent."

"Swell." My knuckles ached as I squeezed the phone. "So
what do I do? Throw my word processor out the window, and
collect on my Writers Guild pension?"

"It's not as bad as that. But bear in mind, your pension is the
highest any Guild member ever accumulated."

"But if I retire, I'll die like—"

"No, what I'm saying is be patient with this network kid. He
needs a little educating. Politely, you understand. Just pitch your
idea, look confident and dependable, show him your credits. He'll
come around. It's not as if you haven't been down this path before."

"When I was in my twenties."

"There you go. You identify with this kid already. You're in
his mind."

My voice dropped. "When's the meeting?"

"Friday. His office. I pulled in some favors to get you in so soon. Four P.M. I'll be at my house in Malibu. Call me when you're through."

"Steve . . ."

"Yeah, Mort?"

"Thanks for sticking with me."

"Hey, it's an honor. To me, you're a legend."

"What I need to be is a *working* legend."

"I've done what I can. Now it's up to you."

"Sure." I set down the phone, discovered I still had my broken pencil in one hand, dropped it, and massaged the aching knuckles of my other hand.

The reason I'd left L.A. two years ago, at the age of sixty-eight, was that my dear wife—

—Doris—

—my best friend—

—my cleverest editor—

—my exclusive lover—

—had been diagnosed as having a rare form of leukemia.

As her strength had waned, as her body had gradually failed to obey her splendid mind, I'd disrupted my workaholic's habit of writing every day and acted as her constant attendant. We'd traveled to every major cancer research center in the United States. We'd gone to specialists in Europe. We'd stayed in Europe because their hospice system is humane about pain-relieving drugs. We'd gotten as far as Sweden.

Where Doris had died.

And now, struggling with grief, I'd returned to my career. What other meaning did I have? It was either kill myself or write. So I wrote. And wrote. Even faster than in my prime, when I'd contributed every episode in the four-year run of *The Sidewalks of New York*.

And now a network yuppie bastard with the cultural memory of a four-year-old had asked for my credits. Before I gulped a stiff shot of Scotch, I vowed I'd show this town that *this* old fuck still had more juice than when I'd first started.

• • •

Century City. Every week, you see those monoliths of power behind the credits on this season's hit lawyer show, but I remembered, bitterly nostalgic, when the land those skyscrapers stood upon had been the back lot for 20th Century–Fox.

I parked my leased Audi on the second level of an underground ramp and took an elevator to the seventeenth floor of one of the buildings. The network's reception room was wide and lofty, with lots of leather couches where actors, writers, and producers made hurried phone calls to agents and assistants while they waited to be admitted to the Holy of Holies.

I stopped before a young, attractive woman at a desk. Thin. No bra. Presumably she wanted to be an actress and was biding her time, waiting for the right connections. She finished talking to one of three phones and studied me, her boredom tempered by the fear that, if she wasn't respectful, she might lose a chance to make an important contact.

I'm not bad looking. Although seventy, I keep in shape. Sure, my hair's receding. I have wrinkles around my eyes. But my family's genes are spectacular. I look ten years younger than I am, especially when I'm tanned, as I was after recent daily half-hour laps in my swimming pool.

My voice has the resonance of Ed McMahon. "Mort Davidson to see Arthur Lewis. I've got a four o'clock appointment."

The would-be-actress receptionist scanned a list. "Of course. You're expected. Unfortunately, Mr. Lewis has been detained. If you'll please wait over there." She pointed toward a couch and picked up a Judith Krantz novel. Evidently she'd decided that I couldn't promote her career.

So I waited.

And waited.

An hour later, the receptionist gestured for me to come over. Miracle of miracles, Arthur Lewis was ready to see me.

● ● ●

He wore an Armani linen suit, fashionably wrinkled. No tie. Gucci loafers. No socks. His skin was the color of bronze. His thick, curly black hair had a calculated, windblown look. Photographs of his blond wife and infant daughter stood on his glass-topped desk. His wife seemed even younger and thinner than he was. Posters of various current hit series hung on the wall. A tennis racket was propped in a corner.

"It's an honor to meet you. I'm a fan of everything you've done," he lied.

I made an appropriate humble comment.

His next remark contradicted what he'd just said. "Did you bring a list of your credits?"

I gave him a folder and sat on a leather chair across from him while he flipped through the pages. His expression communicated a mixture of boredom and stoic endurance.

Finally his eyebrows narrowed. "Impressive. I might add, astonishing. Really, it's hard to imagine anyone writing this much."

"Well, I've been in the business quite a while."

"Yes. You certainly have."

I couldn't tell if he referred to my age or my numerous credits. "There used to be a joke," I said.

"Oh?" His eyes were expressionless.

" 'How can Mort Davidson be so prolific?' This was back in the early sixties. The answer was 'He uses an electric typewriter.' "

"Very amusing," he said as if I'd farted.

"These days, of course, I use a word processor."

"Of course." He folded his hands on the desk and sat straighter. "So. Your agent said you had an idea that might appeal to us."

"That's right."

The phone rang.

"Excuse me a moment." He picked up the phone. Obviously, if he'd been genuinely interested in my pitch, he'd have instructed his secretary that he didn't want any calls.

An actor named Sid was important enough for Arthur Lewis to gush with compliments. And by all means, Sid shouldn't worry about the rewrites that would make his character more "with it" in today's generation. The writer in charge of the project was under orders to deliver the changes by Monday morning. If he didn't, that writer would never again work on something called *The Good-time Guys*. Sid was a helluva talent, Arthur Lewis assured him. Next week's episode would get a 35 ratings share at least. Arthur chuckled at a joke, set down the phone, and narrowed his eyebrows again. "So your idea that you think we might like." He glanced at his Rolex.

"It's about an at-risk youth center, a place where troubled kids can go and get away from their screwed-up families, the gangs, and the drug dealers on the streets. There's a center in the Valley that I see as our model—an old Victorian house that has several additions. Each week, we'd deal with a special problem— teenage pregnancy, substance abuse, runaways—but mostly this would be a series about emotions, about people, the kids, but also the staff, a wide range of interesting, committed professionals, an elderly administrator, a female social worker, a Hispanic who used to be in the gangs, a priest, whatever mix works. I call it—"

The phone rang again.

"Just a second," Arthur Lewis said.

Another grin. A producer this time. A series about a college sorority next to a fraternity, *Crazy 4 U,* had just become this season's new hit. Arthur Lewis was giving its cast and executives a party at Le Dôme tomorrow evening. Yes, he guaranteed. Ten cases of Dom Pérignon would arrive at the producer's home before the party. And beluga caviar? Enough for an after-party power party? No problem. And yes, Arthur Lewis was having the same frustrations as the producer. It was mighty damned hard to find a preschool for gifted children.

He set down the phone. His face turned to stone. "So that's your idea?"

"Drama, significance, emotion, action, and realism."

"But what's the hook?"

I shook my head in astonishment.

"Why would anyone want to watch it?" Arthur Lewis asked.

"To feel what it's like to help kids in trouble, to *understand* those kids."

"Didn't you have a stroke a while ago?"

"What?"

"I believe in honesty, so I'll be direct. You put in your time. You paid your dues. So why don't you back away gracefully?"

"I *didn't* have a stroke."

"Then why did I hear—?"

"My wife had cancer. She died. . . ." I caught my breath. "Six months ago."

"I see. I'm sorry. I mean that sincerely. But television isn't the same as when you created"—he checked my list of credits—"*The Sidewalks of New York*. A definite classic. One of my absolute personal favorites. But times have changed. The industry's a lot more competitive. The pressure's unbelievable. A series creator has to act as one of the producers, to oversee the product, to guarantee consistency. I'm talking thirteen hours a day minimum, and ideally the creator ought to contribute something to every script."

"That's what I did on *The Sidewalks of New York*."

"Oh?" Arthur Lewis looked blank. "I guess I didn't notice that in your credits." He straightened. "But my point's the same. Television's a pressure cooker. A game for people with energy."

"Did I need a wheelchair when I came in here?"

"You've lost me."

"Energy's not my problem. I'm full to bursting with the need to work. What matters is, What do you think of my idea?"

"It's—"

The phone rang.

Arthur Lewis looked relieved. "Let me get back to you."

"Of course. I know you're busy. Thanks for your time."

"Hey, *any*time. I'm always here and ready for new ideas." Again he checked his Rolex.

The phone kept ringing.

"Take care," he said.

"You too."

I took my list of credits off his desk.

The last thing I heard when I left was "No, that old fuck's wrong for the part. He's losing his hair. A wig? Get real. The audience can tell the difference. For God's sake, a hairpiece is death in the ratings."

Steve had said to phone him when the meeting was over. But I felt so upset I decided to hell with phoning him and drove up the Pacific Coast Highway toward his place in Malibu. Traffic was terrible—rush hour, Friday evening. For once, though, it had an advantage. After an hour, my anger began to abate enough for me to realize that I wouldn't accomplish much by showing up unexpectedly in a fit at Steve's. He'd been loyal. He didn't need my aggravation. As he'd told me, "I've done what I can. Now it's up to you." But there wasn't much I *could* do if my age and not my talent was how I was judged. Certainly that wasn't Steve's fault.

So I stopped at something called the Pacific Coast Diner and took the advice of a bumper sticker on a car I'd been stuck behind—CHILL OUT. Maybe a few drinks and a meditative dinner would calm me down. The restaurant had umbrella-topped tables on a balcony that looked toward the ocean. I had to wait a half hour, but a Scotch and soda made the time go quickly, and the crimson reflection of the setting sun on the ocean was spectacular.

Or would have been if I'd been paying attention. The truth was, I couldn't stop being upset. I had another Scotch and soda, ordered poached salmon, tried to enjoy my meal, and suddenly couldn't swallow, suddenly felt about as lonely as I'd felt since Doris had died. *Maybe the network executives are right*, I thought.

Maybe I am *too old. Maybe* I don't *know how to relate to a young audience. Maybe it's time I packed it in.*

"Mort Davidson," a voice said.

"Excuse me?" I blinked, distracted from my thoughts.

My waiter was holding the credit card I'd given him. "Mort Davidson." He looked at the name on the card, then at me. "The screenwriter?"

I spared him a bitter "Used to be" and nodded with what I hoped was a pleasant manner.

"Wow." He was tall and thin with sandy hair and a glowing tan. His blue eyes glinted. He had the sort of chiseled, handsome face that made me think he was yet another would-be actor. He looked to be about twenty-three. "When I saw your name, I thought, *'No, it couldn't be. Who knows how many Mort Davidsons there are? The odds against this being . . .'* But it *is* you. The screenwriter."

"Guilty," I managed to joke.

"I bet I've seen everything you ever wrote. I must have watched *The Dead of Noon* twenty-five times. I really learned a lot."

"Oh?" I was puzzled. What would my screenplay have taught him about acting?

"About structure. About pace. About not being afraid to let the characters talk. That's what's wrong with movies today. The characters don't have anything important to say."

At once it hit me. He wasn't a would-be actor.

"I'm a writer," he said. "Or trying to be. I mean, I've still got a lot to learn. That I'm working here proves what I mean." The glint went out of his eyes. "I still haven't sold anything." His enthusiasm was forced. "But, hey, nothing important is easy. I'll just keep writing until I crack the market. The boss is . . . I'd better not keep chattering at you. He doesn't like it. For sure, you've got better things to do than listen to me. I just wanted to say how much I like your work, Mr. Davidson. I'll bring your credit card right back. It's a pleasure to meet you."

As he left, it struck me that the speed with which he talked suggested not only energy but insecurity. For all his good looks, he felt like a loser.

Or maybe I was just transferring my own emotions onto him. This much was definite—getting a compliment was a hell of a lot better than a sharp stick in the eye or the meeting I'd endured.

When he came back with my credit card, I signed the bill and gave him a generous tip.

"Thanks, Mr. Davidson."

"Hang in there. You've got one important thing on your side."

"What's that?"

"You're young. You've got plenty of time to make it."

"Unless . . ."

I wondered what he meant.

"Unless I don't have what it takes."

"Well, the best advice I can give you is never doubt yourself."

As I left the restaurant and passed beneath hissing arc lamps toward my car, I couldn't ignore the irony. The waiter had youth but doubted his ability. I had confidence in my ability but was penalized because of my age. Despite the roar of traffic on the Pacific Coast Highway, I heard waves on the beach.

And that's when the notion came to me. A practical joke of sorts, like stories you hear about frustrated writers submitting Oscar-winning screenplays, *Casablanca,* for example, but the writers change the title and the characters' names. The notes they get back from producers as much as say that the screenplays are the lousiest junk the producers ever read. So then the writers tell the trade papers what they've done, the point being that they're trying to prove it doesn't matter *how* good a writer you are if you don't have connections.

Why not? I thought. It would be worth seeing the look on those bastards' faces.

• • •

"What's your name?"

"Ric Potter."

"Short for Richard?"

"No. For Eric."

I nodded. Breaking-the-ice conversation. "The reason I came back is I have something I want to discuss with you, a way that might help your career."

His eyes brightened.

At once, they darkened, as if he thought I might be trying to pick him up.

"Strictly business," I said. "Here's my card. If you want to talk about writing and how to make some money, give me a call."

His suspicion persisted, but his curiosity was stronger. "What time?"

"Eleven tomorrow?"

"Fine."

"Come over. Bring some of your scripts."

That was important. I had to find out if he could write or if he was fooling himself. My scheme wouldn't work unless he had a basic feel for the business. So the next morning, when he arrived exactly on time at my home in the hills above West Hollywood, we swapped: I let him see a script I'd just finished while I sat by the pool and read one of his. I finished around one o'clock. "Hungry?"

"Starved. Your script is wonderful," Ric said. "I can't get over the pace. The sense of reality. It didn't feel like a story."

"Thanks." I took some tuna salad and Perrier from the refrigerator. "Whole-wheat bread and kosher dills okay? Or maybe you'd rather go to a restaurant."

"After working in one every night?" Ric laughed.

But I could tell that he was marking time, that he was frustrated and anxious to know what I thought of his script. I remem-

bered how I had felt at his age, the insecurity when someone
important was reading my work. I got to the point.

"I like your story," I said.

He exhaled.

"But I don't think it's executed properly."

His cheek muscles tensed.

"Given what they're paying A-list actors these days, you have
to get the main character on screen as quickly as possible. *Your*
main character doesn't show up until page fifteen."

He sounded embarrassed. "I couldn't figure out a way to—"

"And the romantic element is so familiar it's tiresome. A
shower scene comes from a washed-up imagination."

That was tough, I knew, but I waited to see how he'd take it.
If he turned out to be the sensitive type, I wasn't going to get
anywhere.

"Yeah. Okay. Maybe I did rely on a lot of other movies I'd
seen."

His response encouraged me. "The humorous elements
don't work. I don't think comedy is your thing."

He squinted.

"The ending has no focus," I continued. "Was your main
character right or not? Simply leaving the dilemma up in the air is
going to piss off your audience."

He studied me. "You said you liked the story."

"Right. I did."

"Then why do I feel like I'm on the *Titanic*?"

"Because you've got a lot of craft to learn, and it's going to
take you quite a while to master it. If you ever do. There aren't any
guarantees. The average Guild member earns less than six thousand dollars a year. Writing screenplays is one of the most competitive enterprises in the world. But I think I can help you."

". . . Why?"

"Excuse me?"

"We met just last night. I was your waiter, for God's sake.
Now suddenly I'm in your house, having lunch with you, and

you're saying you want to help me. It can't be because of the force of my personality. You want something."

"Yes, but not what you're thinking. I told you last night—this is strictly business. Sit down and eat while I tell you how we can both make some money."

"This is Ric Potter," I said. We were at a reception in one of those mansions in the hills near the Hollywood Bowl. Sunset. A string quartet. Champagne. Plenty of movers and shakers. "Fox is very hot on one of his scripts. I think it'll go for a million."

The man to whom I'd introduced Ric was an executive at Warners. He couldn't have been over thirty. "Oh?"

"Yeah, it's got a youth angle."

"Oh?" The executive looked Ric up and down, confused, never having heard of him, at the same time worried because he didn't want to be out of the loop, fearing he *ought* to have heard of him.

"If I sound a little proud," I said, "it's because I discovered him. I found him last May when I was giving a talk to a young screenwriters' workshop at the American Film Institute. Ric convinced me to look at some things and . . . I'm glad I did. My *agent's* glad I did." I chuckled.

The executive tried to look amused, although he hated like hell to pay writers significant money. For his part, Ric tried to look modest but unbelievably talented, young, young, young, and hot, hot, hot.

"Well, don't let Fox tie you up," the executive told Ric. "Have your agent send me something."

"I'll do that, Mr. Ballard. Thanks," Ric said.

"Do I look old enough to be a 'mister'? Call me Ed."

We made the rounds. While all the executives considered me too old to be relevant to their sixteen-to-twenty-five audience, they still had reverence for what they thought of as an institution. Sure, they wouldn't buy anything from me, but they were more than happy to talk to me. After all, it didn't cost them any money, and it made them feel like they were part of a community.

By the time I was through introducing Ric, my rumors about him had been accepted as fact. Various executives from various studios considered themselves in competition with executives from other studios for the services of this hot new young writer who was getting a million dollars a script.

Ric had driven with me to the reception. On the way back, he kept shaking his head in amazement. "And that's the secret? I just needed the right guy to give me introductions? To be anointed as a successor?"

"Not quite. Don't let their chumminess fool you. They only care if you can deliver."

"Well, tomorrow I'll send them one of my scripts."

"No," I said. "Remember our agreement. Not one of your scripts. One of *mine*. By Eric Potter."

So there it was. The deal Ric and I had made was that I'd give him ten percent of whatever my scripts earned in exchange for his being my front man. For his part, he'd have to take calls and go to meetings and behave as if he'd actually written the scripts. Along the way, we'd inevitably talk about the intent and technique of the scripts, thus providing Ric with writing lessons. All in all, not a bad deal for him.

Except that he had insisted on *fifteen* percent.

"Hey, I can't go to meetings if I'm working three to eleven at the restaurant," he'd said. "Fifteen percent. And I'll need an advance. You'll have to pay me what I'm earning at the restaurant so I can be free for the meetings."

I wrote him a check for a thousand dollars.

The phone rang, interrupting the climactic speech of the script I was writing. Instead of picking up the receiver, I let my answering machine take it, but I answered anyhow when I heard my agent talking about Ric.

"What about him, Steve?"

"Ballard over at Warners likes the script you had me send him. He wants a few changes, but basically he's happy enough to offer seven hundred and fifty thousand."

"Ask for a million."

"I'll ask for nothing."

"I don't understand. Is this a new negotiating tactic?"

"You told me not to bother reading the script, just to do the kid a favor and send it over to Warners because Ballard asked for it. As you pointed out, I'm too busy to do any reading anyhow. But I made a copy of the script, and for the hell of it, last night I looked it over. Mort, what are you trying to pull? Ric Potter didn't write that script. *You* did. Under a different title, you showed it to me a year ago."

I didn't respond.

"Mort?"

"I'm making a point. The only thing wrong with my scripts is an industry bias against age. Pretend somebody young wrote them, and all of a sudden they're wonderful."

"Mort, I won't be a part of this."

"Why not?"

"It's misrepresentation. I'd be jeopardizing my credibility as an agent. You know how the clause in the contract reads—the writer guarantees that the script is solely his or her own work. If somebody else was involved, the studio wants to know about it—to protect itself against a plagiarism suit."

"But if you tell Ballard I wrote that script, he won't buy it."

"You're being paranoid, Mort."

"Facing facts and being practical. Don't screw this up."

"I told you, I won't go along with it."

"Then if you won't make the deal, I'll get somebody else who will."

A long pause. "Do you know what you're saying?"

"Ric Potter and I need a new agent."

I'll say this for Steve—even though he was furious about my leaving him, he finally swore, for old times' sake, at my insistence, that he wouldn't tell anybody what I was doing. He was loyal to the end. It broke my heart to leave him. The new agent I selected knew squat about the arrangement I had with Ric. She believed what I told her—that Ric and I were friends and by coincidence we'd decided simultaneously to get new representation. I could have chosen one of those superhuge agencies like CAA, but I've always been uncomfortable when I'm part of a mob and, in this case especially, it seemed to me that small and intimate were essential. The fewer people who knew my business, the better.

The Linda Carpenter Agency was located in a stone cottage just past the gates to the old Hollywoodland subdivision. Years ago, the "land" part of that subdivision's sign collapsed. The "Hollywood" part remained, and you see that sign all the time in film clips about Los Angeles. It's a distance up past houses in the hills. Nonetheless, from outside Linda Carpenter's stone cottage, you feel that the sign's looming over you.

I parked my Audi and got out with Ric. He was wearing sneakers, jeans, and a blue cotton pullover. At my insistence. I wanted his outfit to be self-consciously informal and youthful in contrast with my own mature, conservative slacks and sport coat. When we entered the office, Linda—who's thirty, with short red hair, and loves to look at gorgeous young men—sat straighter when I introduced Ric. His biceps bulged at the sleeves of his pullover. I was reminded again of how much—with his sandy hair, blue eyes, and glowing tan—he looked like an actor.

Linda took a moment before she reluctantly shifted her attention away from him, as if suddenly realizing that I was in the room. "Good to see you again, Mort. But you didn't have to come all this way. I could have met you for lunch at Le Dôme."

"A courtesy visit. I wanted to save you the long drive, not to mention the bill."

I said it as if I was joking. The rule is that agents always pick up the check when they're at a restaurant with clients.

Linda's smile was winning. Her red hair seemed brighter. "Anytime. I'm still surprised that you left Steve." She tactfully didn't ask what the problem had been. "I promise I'll work hard for you."

"I know you will," I said. "But I don't think you'll have to work hard for my friend here. Ric already has some interest in a script of his over at Warners."

"Oh?" Linda raised her elegant eyebrows. "Who's the executive?"

"Ballard."

"My, my." She frowned slightly. "And Steve isn't involved in this? Your ties are completely severed?"

"Completely. If you want, call him to make sure."

"That won't be necessary."

But I found out later that Linda did phone Steve, and he backed up what I'd said. Also he refused to discuss why we'd separated.

"I have a hunch the script can go for big dollars," I continued.

"How big is big?"

"A million."

Linda's eyes widened. "That certainly isn't small."

"Ballard heard there's a buzz about Ric. Ballard thinks that Ric might be a young Joe Eszterhas." The reference was to the screenwriter of *Basic Instinct,* who had become a phenomenon for writing sensation-based scripts on speculation and intriguing so many producers that he'd manipulated them into a bidding war and collected megabucks. "I have a suspicion that Ballard would like to make a preemptive bid and shut out the competition."

"Mort, you sound more like an agent than a writer."

"It's just a hunch."

"And Steve doesn't want a piece of this?"

I shook my head no.

Linda frowned harder.

But her frown dissolved the moment she turned again toward Ric and took another look at his perfect chin. "Did you bring a copy of the script?"

"Sure." Ric grinned with becoming modesty, the way I'd taught him. "Right here."

Linda took it and flipped to the end to make sure it wasn't longer than 115 pages—a shootable size. "What's it about?"

Ric gave the pitch that I'd taught him—the high concept first, then the target audience, the type of actor he had in mind, and ways the budget could be kept in check. The same as when we'd clocked it at my house, he took four minutes.

Linda listened with growing fascination. She turned to me. "Have you been coaching him?"

"Not much. Ric's a natural."

"He must be to act this polished."

"And he's young," I said.

"You don't need to remind me."

"And Ballard *certainly* doesn't need reminding," I said.

"Ric," Linda said, "from here on in, whatever you do, don't get writer's block. I'm going to make you the highest paid new kid in town."

Ric beamed.

"And, Mort," Linda said, "I think you're awfully generous to help your friend through the ropes like this."

"Well"—I shrugged—"isn't that what friends are for?"

I had joked with Linda that our trip to her office was a courtesy visit—to save her a long drive and the cost of buying us lunch at an expensive restaurant. That was partly true. But I also wanted to see how Ric made his pitch about the script. If he got nerves and screwed up, I didn't want it to be in Le Dôme, where producers at neighboring tables might see him get flustered. We were trying out the show on the road, so to speak, before we brought it to town. And I had to agree with Linda—Ric had done just fine.

I told him so, as we drove along Sunset Boulevard. "I won't always be there to back you up. In fact, it'll be rare that I am. We have to keep training you so you give the impression there's very little about writing or the business you don't understand. Most of getting along with studio executives is making them have confidence in you."

"You really think I impressed her?"

"It was obvious."

Ric thought about it, peering out the window, nodding. "Yeah."

So we went back to my home in the hills above West Hollywood, and I ran him through more variations of questions he might get asked—where he'd gotten the idea, what actors would be good in the roles, who he thought could direct the material, that sort of thing. At the start of a project, producers pay a lot of attention to a screenwriter, and they promise to keep consulting him the way they're consulting him now. It's all guff, of course. As soon as a director and a name actor are attached to a project, the producers suddenly get amnesia about the original screenwriter. But at the start, he's king, and I wanted Ric to be ready to answer any kind of question about the screenplay so he could be convincing that he'd actually written it.

Ric was a fast study. At eight, when I couldn't think of any more questions he might have to answer, we took a drive to dinner at a fish place near the Santa Monica pier. Afterward, we strolled to the end of the pier and watched the sunset.

"So this is what it's all about," Ric said.

"I'm not sure what you mean."

"The action. I can feel the action."

"Don't get fooled by Linda's optimism. Nothing might come of this."

Ric shook his head. "I'm close."

"I've got some pages I want to do tomorrow, but if you'll come around at four with your own new pages, I'll go over them for you. I'm curious to see how you're revising that script you showed me."

Ric kept staring out at the sunset and didn't answer for quite a while. "Yeah, my script."

As things turned out, I didn't get much work done the next day. I had just managed to solve a problem in a scene that was running too long when my phone rang. That was around ten o'clock, and rather than be interrupted, I let my answering machine take it. But when I heard Ric's excited voice, I picked up the phone.

"Slow down," I said. "Take it easy. What are you so worked up about?"

"They want the script!"

I wasn't prepared. "Warners?"

"Can you believe that this is happening so fast?"

"Ballard's actually taking it? How did you find this out?"

"Linda just phoned me!"

"Linda?" I frowned. "But why didn't Linda . . . ?" I was about to say, "Why didn't Linda phone *me*?" Then I realized my mistake. There wasn't any reason for Linda to phone me, except maybe to tell me the good news about my friend. But she definitely had to phone Ric. After all, he was supposedly the author of the screenplay.

Ric kept talking excitedly. "Linda says Ballard wants to have lunch with me."

"Great." The truth is, I was vaguely jealous. "When?"

"Today."

I was stunned. Any executive with power was always booked

several weeks in advance. For Ballard to decide to have lunch with Ric this soon, he would have had to cancel lunch with someone else. It definitely wouldn't have been the other way around. No one cancels lunch with Ballard.

"Amazing," I said.

"Apparently he's got big plans for me. By the way, he likes the script as is. No changes. At least, for now. Linda says when they sign a director, the director always asks for changes."

"Linda's right," I said. "And then the director'll insist that the changes aren't good enough and ask to bring in a friend to do the rewrite."

"No fucking way," Ric said.

"A screenwriter doesn't have any clout against a director. You've still got a lot to learn about industry politics. School isn't finished yet."

"Sure." Ric hurried on. "Linda got Ballard up to a million and a quarter for the script!"

For a moment, I had trouble breathing.

"Great." And this time I meant it.

Ric phoned again in thirty minutes. He was nervous about the meeting and needed reassurance.

Ric phoned thirty minutes after that, saying that he didn't feel comfortable going to a power lunch in the sneakers, jeans, and pullover that I had told him were necessary for the role he was playing.

"You have to," I said. "You've got to look like you don't belong to the Establishment or whatever the hell it is they call it these days. If you look like every other writer trying to make an impression, Ballard will *treat* you like every other writer. We're selling nonconformity. We're selling youth."

"I still say I'd feel more comfortable in a jacket by . . ." Ric mentioned the name of the latest trendy designer.

"Even assuming that's a good idea, which it isn't, how on

earth are you going to pay for it? A jacket by that designer costs fifteen hundred dollars.''

"I'll use my credit card," Ric said.

"But a month from now, you'll still have to pay the bill. You know the whopping interest rates those credit card companies charge.''

"Hey, I can afford it. I just made a million and a quarter bucks.''

"No, Ric. You're getting confused.''

"All right, I know Linda has to take her ten percent commission.''

"You're still confused. *You* don't get the bulk of that money. *I* do. What *you* get is fifteen percent of it.''

"That's still a lot of cash. Almost two hundred thousand dollars.''

"But remember, you probably won't get it for at least six months.''

"What?"

"On a spec script, they don't simply agree to buy it and hand you a check. The fine points on the negotiation have to be completed. Then the contracts have to be drawn up and reviewed and amended. Then their business office drags its feet, issuing the check. I once waited a year to get paid for a spec script.''

"But I can't wait that long. I've got . . .''

"Yes?''

"Responsibilities. Look, Mort, I have to go. I need to get ready for this meeting.''

"And I need to get back to my pages.''

"With all this excitement, you mean you're actually writing today?''

"*Every* day.''

"No shit.''

● ● ●

But I was too preoccupied to get much work done.

Ric finally phoned around five. "Lunch was fabulous."

I hadn't expected to feel so relieved. "Ballard didn't ask you any tricky questions? He's still convinced you wrote the script?"

"Not only that. He says I'm just the talent he's been looking for. A fresh imagination. Someone in tune with today's generation. He asked me to do a last-minute rewrite on an action picture he's starting next week."

"The Warlords?"

"That's the one."

"I've been hearing bad things about it," I said.

"Well, you won't hear anything bad anymore."

"Wait a . . . Are you telling me you accepted the job?"

"Damned right."

"Without talking to me about it first?" I straightened in shock. "What in God's name did you think you were doing?"

"Why would I need to talk to you? You're not my agent. Ballard called Linda from our table at the restaurant. The two of them settled the deal while I was sitting there. Man, when things happen, they happen. All those years of trying, and now, wham, pow, all of a sudden I'm there. And the best part is, since I'm a writer for hire on this job, they have to pay some of the money the minute I sit down to work, even if the contracts aren't ready."

"That's correct," I said. "On work for hire, you have to get paid on a schedule. The Writers Guild insists on that. You're learning fast. But, Ric, before you accepted the job, don't you think it would have been smart to read the script first—to see if it *can* be fixed?"

"How bad can it be?" Ric chuckled.

"You'd be surprised."

"It doesn't matter *how* bad. The fee's a hundred thousand dollars. I need the money."

"For *what?* You don't live expensively. You can afford to be patient and take jobs that build a career."

"Hey, I'll tell you what I can afford. Are you using that portable phone in your office?"

"Yes. But I don't see why that matters."

"Take a look out your front window."

Frowning, I left my office, went through the TV room and the living room, and peered past the blossoming rhododendron outside my front window. I scanned the curving driveway, then focused on the gate.

Ric was wearing a designer linen jacket, sitting in a red Ferrari, using a car phone, waving to me when he saw me at the window. "Like it?" he asked over the phone.

"For God's sake." I broke the connection, set down the phone, and stalked out the front door.

"Like it?" Ric repeated when I reached the gate. He gestured toward his jacket and the car.

"You didn't have time to . . . Where'd you get . . . ?"

"This morning, after Linda phoned about the offer from Ballard, I ordered the car over the phone. Picked it up after my meeting with Ballard. Nifty, huh?"

"But you don't have any assets. You mean they just let you drive the car off the lot?"

"Bought it on credit. I made Linda sign as the guarantor."

"You made Linda . . ." I couldn't believe what I was hearing. "Damn it, Ric, why don't you let me finish coaching you before you run off and . . . After I taught you about screenplay technique and industry politics, I wanted to explain to you how to handle your money."

"Hey, what's to teach? Money's for spending."

"Not in *this* business. You've got to put something away for when you have bad years."

"Well, I'm certainly not having any trouble earning money so far."

"What happened today is a fluke! This is the first script I've sold in longer than I care to think about. There aren't any guarantees."

"Then it's a good thing I came along, huh?" Ric grinned.

"Before you accepted the rewrite job, you should have asked me if I wanted to do it."

"But you're not involved in this. Why should I divide the money with you? *I'm* going to do it."

"In that case, you should have asked yourself another question."

"What?"

"Whether you've got the *ability* to do it."

Ric flushed with anger. "Of course, I've got the ability. You've read my stuff. All I needed was a break."

I didn't hear from Ric for three days. That was fine by me. I'd accomplished what I'd intended. I'd proven that a script with my name on it had less chance of being bought than the same script with a youngster's name on it. And to tell the truth, Ric's lack of discipline was annoying me. But after the third day, I confess I got curious. What was he up to?

He called at nine in the evening. "How's it going?"

"Fine," I said. "I had a good day's work."

"Yeah, that's what I'm calling about. Work."

"Oh?"

"I haven't been in touch lately because of this rewrite on *The Warlords.*"

I waited.

"I had a meeting with the director," Ric said. "Then I had a meeting with the star." He mentioned the name of the biggest action hero in the business. He hesitated. "I was wondering. Would you look at the material I've got?"

"You can't be serious. After the way you talked to me about it? You all but told me to get lost."

"I didn't mean to be rude. Honestly. This is all new to me, Mort. Come on, give me a break. As you keep reminding me, I don't have the experience you do. I'm young."

I had to hand it to him. He'd not only apologized. He'd used the right excuse.

"Mort?"

At first I didn't want to be bothered. I had my own work to think about, and *The Warlords* would probably be so bad that it would contaminate my mind.

But then my curiosity got the better of me. I couldn't help wondering what Ric would do to improve junk.

"Mort?"

"When do you want me to look at what you've done?"

"How about right now?"

"Now? It's after nine. It'll take you an hour to get here and—"

"I'm already here."

"What?"

"I'm on my car phone. Outside your gate again."

Ric sat across from me in my living room. I couldn't help noticing that his tan was darker, that he was wearing a different designer jacket, a more expensive one. Then I glanced at the title page on the script he'd handed me.

THE WARLORDS
Revisions by Eric Potter

I flipped through the pages. All of them were typed on white paper. That bothered me. Ric's inexperience was showing again. On last-minute rewrites, it's always helpful to submit changed pages on different-colored paper. That way, the producer and director can save time and not have to read the entire script to find the changes.

"These are the notes the director gave me," Ric said. He

handed me some crudely typed pages. "And these"—Ric handed me pages with scribbling on them—"are what the star gave me. It's a little hard to decipher them."

"More than a little. Jesus." I squinted at the scribbling and got a headache. "I'd better put on my glasses." They helped a little. I read what the director wanted. I switched to what the star wanted.

"These are the notes the producer gave me," Ric said.

I thanked God that they were neatly typed and studied them as well. Finally I leaned back and took off my glasses.

"Well?"

I sighed. "Typical. As near as I can tell, these three people are each talking about a different movie. The director wants more action and less characterization. The star has decided to be serious—he wants more characterization and less action. The producer wants it funny and less expensive. If they're not careful, this movie will have multiple personalities."

Ric looked at me anxiously.

"Okay," I said, feeling tired. "Get a beer from the refrigerator and watch television or something while I go through this. It would help if I knew where you'd made changes. Next time you're in a situation like this, identify your work with colored paper."

Ric frowned.

"What's the matter?" I asked.

"The changes."

"So? What about them?"

"Well, I haven't started to make them."

"You haven't . . . ? But on this title page, it says, 'Revisions by Eric Potter.' "

Ric looked sheepish. "The title page is as far as I got."

"Sweet Jesus. When are these revisions due?"

"Ballard gave me a week."

"And for the first three days of that week, you didn't work on the changes? What have you been doing?"

Ric glanced away.

Again I noticed that his tan was darker. "Don't tell me you've just been sitting in the sun?"

"Not exactly."

"Then *what* exactly?"

"I've been thinking about how to improve the script."

I was so agitated I had to stand. "You don't *think* about changes. You *make* changes. How much did you say you were being paid? A hundred thousand dollars?"

Ric nodded, uncomfortable.

"And the Writers Guild insists that on work for hire you get a portion of the money as soon as you start."

"Fifty thousand." Ric squirmed. "Linda got the check by messenger the day after I made the deal with Ballard."

"What a mess."

Ric lowered his head, more uncomfortable.

"If you don't hand in new pages four days from now, Ballard will want his money back."

"I know," Ric said, then added, "but I can't."

"What?"

"I already spent the money. A deposit on a condo up in Malibu."

I was stunned.

"And the money isn't the worst of it," I said. "Your reputation. *That's* worse. Ballard gave you an incredible break. He decided to take a chance on the bright new kid in town. He allowed you to jump over all the shit. But if you don't deliver, he'll be furious. He'll spread the word all over town that you're not dependable. You won't be hot anymore. We won't be able to sell another script as easily as we did this one."

"Look, I'm sorry, Mort. I know I bragged to you that I could do the job on my own. I was wrong. I don't have the experience. I admit it. I'm out of my depth."

"Even on a piece of shit like this."

Ric glanced down, then up. "I was wondering . . . Could you give me a hand?"

My mouth hung open in astonishment.

Before I could tell him no damned way, Ric quickly added, "It would really help both of us."

"How do you figure that?"

"You just said it yourself. If I don't deliver, Ballard will spread the word. No producer will trust me. You won't be able to sell another script through me."

My forehead began to throb. He was right, of course. If I wanted to keep selling scripts, if I wanted to see them produced, I needed him. I finally had to admit that, secretly, I had never intended the deception with Ric to be a one-time-only arrangement.

I swallowed and finally said, "All right."

"Thank you."

"But I won't clean up your messes for nothing."

"Of course not. The same arrangement as before. All I get out of this is fifteen percent."

"By rights, you shouldn't get anything."

"Hey, without me, Ballard wouldn't have offered the job."

"Since you already spent the first half of the payment, how do I get that money?"

Ric made an effort to think of a solution. "We'll have to wait until the money comes through on the spec script we sold. I'll give you the money out of the two hundred thousand that's owed to me."

"But you owe the Ferrari dealer a bundle. Otherwise Linda's responsible for your debt."

"I'll take care of it." Ric gestured impatiently. "I'll take care of all of it. What's important now is that you make the changes on *The Warlords*. Ballard has to pay the remaining fifty thousand dollars when I hand in the pages. That money's yours."

"Fine."

The script for *The Warlords* was even worse than I had feared. How do you change bad junk into good junk? In the process, how do you please a director, a star, and a producer who ask for widely different things? One of the rules I've learned over the years is that what people say they want isn't always what they mean. Sometimes it's a matter of interpretation. And after I endured reading the script for *The Warlords,* I thought I had that interpretation.

The director said he wanted more action and less characterization. In my opinion, the script already had more than enough action. The trouble was that some of the action sequences were redundant, and others weren't paced effectively. The biggest stunts occurred two thirds of the way into the story. The last third had stunts that suffered by comparison. So the trick here was to do some pruning and restructuring—to take the good stunts from the end and put them in the middle, to build on them and put the great stunts at the end, all the while struggling to retain the already feeble logic of the story.

The star said he wanted less action and more characterization. As far as I could tell, what he really wanted was to be sympathetic, to make the audience like the character he was playing. So I softened him a little, threw in some jokes, had him wait for an old lady to cross a street before he blew away the bad guys, basic things like that. Since his character was more like a robot than a human being, any vaguely human thing he did would make him sympathetic.

The producer said he wanted more humor and a less expensive budget. Well, by making the hero sympathetic, I added the jokes the producer wanted. By restructuring the sequence of stunts, I managed to eliminate some of the weaker ones, thus giving the star his request for less action and the producer his request for holding down the budget, since the preponderance of action scenes had been what inflated the budget in the first place.

I explained this to Ric as I made notes. "They'll all be happy."

"Amazing," Ric said.

"Thanks."

"No, what I mean is, the ideas you came up with, *I* could have thought of them."

"Oh?" My voice hardened. "Then why didn't you?"

"Because, well, they seem so obvious."

"*After* I thought of them. Good ideas always seem obvious in retrospect. The real job is putting them on paper. I'm going to have to work like crazy to get this job done in four days. And then there's a further problem. I have to teach you how to pitch these changes to Ballard, so he'll be convinced you're the one who wrote them."

"You can count on me," Ric said.

"I want you to . . ." Suddenly I found myself yawning and looked at my watch. "Three A.M.? I'm not used to staying up this late. I'd better get some sleep if I'm going to get this rewrite done in four days."

"I'm a night person myself," Ric said.

"Well, come back tomorrow at four in the afternoon. I'll take a break and start teaching you what to say to Ballard."

Ric didn't show up, of course. When I phoned his apartment, I got his answering machine. I couldn't get in touch with him the next day, or the day after that.

But the day the changes were due, he certainly showed up. He phoned again from his car outside the gate, and when I let him in, he was so eager to see the pages that he barely said hello to me.

"Where the hell have you been?"

"Mexico."

"What?"

"With all this stress, I needed to get away."

"What have you done to put you under stress? *I'm* the one who's been doing all the work."

Instead of responding, Ric sat on my living-room sofa and quickly leafed through the pages. I noticed he was wearing yet another designer jacket. His tan was even darker.

"Yeah," he said. "This is good." He quickly came to his feet. "I'd better get to the studio."

"But I haven't coached you about what to say to Ballard."

Ric stopped at the door. "Mort, I've been thinking. If this partnership is going to work, we need to give each other more space. You take care of the writing. Let me worry about what to say in meetings. Ballard likes me. I know how to handle him. Trust me."

And Ric was gone.

I waited to hear about what happened at the meeting. No phone call. When I finally broke down and phoned *him,* an electronic-sounding voice told me that his number was no longer in service. It took me a moment to figure out that he must have moved to the condo in Malibu. So I phoned Linda to get the new number, and she awkwardly told me that Ric had ordered her to keep it a secret.

"Even from me?"

"Especially from you. Did you guys have an argument or something?"

"No."

"Well, he made it sound as if you had. He kept complaining about how you were always telling him what to do."

"Of all the . . ." I almost told Linda the truth—that Ric hadn't written the script she had sold but rather *I* had. Then I realized that she'd be conscience-bound to tell the studio. The deception would make the studio feel chilly about the script. They would reread it with a new perspective, prejudiced by knowing the true identity of the author. The deal would fall through. I'd lose the biggest fee I'd ever been promised.

So I mumbled something about intending to talk with him and straighten out the problem. Then I hung up and cursed.

● ● ●

After I didn't hear from Ric for a week, it became obvious that Linda would long ago have forwarded to him the check for the rewrite on *The Warlords*. He'd had ample time to send me my money. He didn't intend to pay me.

That made me furious, partly because he'd betrayed me, partly because I didn't like being made to feel naive, and partly because I'm a professional. To me, it's a matter of honor that I get paid for what I write. Ric had violated one of my most basic rules.

My arrangement with him was finished. When I read about him in *Daily Variety* and *Hollywood Reporter*—about how Ballard was delighted with the rewrite and predicting that the script he had bought from Ric would be next year's smash hit, not to mention that Ric would win an Oscar for it—I was apoplectic. Ric was compared to Robert Towne and William Goldman, with the advantage that he was young and had a powerful understanding of today's generation. Ric had been hired for a half-million dollars to do another rewrite. Ric had promised that he would soon deliver another original script, for which he hinted that his agent would demand an enormous price. "Quality is always worth the cost," Ballard said.

I wanted to vomit.

As I knew he would have to, Ric eventually came to see me. Again the car phone at the gate. Three weeks later. After dark. A night person, after all.

I made a pretense of reluctance, feigned being moved by his whining, let him in and offered a beer. Even in the muted lights of my living room, he had the most perfect tan I had ever seen. His clothes were even more expensive and trendy. I hated him.

"You didn't send me my money for the rewrite on *The Warlords*."

"I'm sorry about that," Ric said. "That's part of the reason I'm here."

"To pay me?"

"To explain. My condo at Malibu. The owners demanded more money as a down payment. I couldn't give up the place. It's too fabulous. So I had to . . . Well, I knew you'd understand."

"But I don't."

"Mort, listen to me. I promise—as soon as the money comes through on the script we sold, I'll pay you everything I owe."

"You went to fifteen percent of the fee, to fifty percent, to one hundred percent. Do you think I work for nothing?"

"Mort, I can appreciate your feelings. But I was in a bind."

"You *still* are. I've been reading about you in the trade papers. You're getting a half million for a rewrite on another script, and you're also promising a new original script. How are you going to manage all that?"

"Well, I tried to do it on my own. I handed Ballard the script I showed you when we first met."

"Jesus, no."

"He didn't like it."

"What a surprise."

"I had to cover my tracks and tell him it was something I'd been fooling with but that I realized it needed a lot of work. I told him I agreed with his opinion. From now on, I intended to stick to the tried and true—the sort of thing I'd sold him."

I shook my head.

"I guess you were right," Ric said. "Good ideas seem obvious after somebody's thought of them. But maybe I don't have what it takes to come up with them. I've been acting like a jerk."

"I couldn't agree more."

"So what do you say?" Ric offered his hand. "Let's let bygones be bygones. I screwed up, but I've learned from my mistake. I'm willing to give our partnership another try if you are."

I stared at his hand.

Suddenly beads of sweat burst out onto his brow. He lifted his hand and wiped the sweat.

"What's the matter?"

"Hot in here."

"Not really. Actually I thought it was getting chilly."

"Feels stuffy."

"The beer I gave you. Maybe you drank it too fast."

"Maybe."

"You know, *I've* been thinking," I said.

The beer was drugged, of course. After the nausea wore off, giddiness set in, as it was supposed to. The drug, which I'd learned about years ago when I was working on a TV crime series, left its victim open to suggestion. It took me only ten minutes to convince him it was a great idea to do what I wanted. As I instructed, Ric giddily phoned Linda and told her that he was feeling stressed out and intended to go back down to Mexico. He told her he suddenly felt trapped by materialism. He needed a spiritual retreat. He might be away for as long as six months.

Linda was shocked. Listening to the speaker phone, I heard her demand to know how Ric intended to fulfill the contracts he'd signed. She said his voice was slurred and accused him of being drunk or high on something.

I picked up the phone, switched off the speaker, and interrupted to tell Linda that Ric was calling from my house and that we'd made up our differences, that he'd been pouring out his soul to me. He was drunk, yes, but what he had told her was no different than what he had told *me* when he was sober. He was leaving for Mexico tonight and might not be back for quite a while. How was he going to fulfill his contracts? No problem. Just because he was going on a retreat in Mexico, that didn't mean he wouldn't be writing. Honest work was what he thrived on. It was food for his soul.

By then, Ric was almost asleep. After I hung up, I roused him, made him sign two documents that I'd prepared, then made him tell me where he was living in Malibu. I put him in his car, drove over to his place, packed a couple of his suitcases, crammed them into the car, and set out for Mexico.

We got there shortly after dawn. He was somewhat conscious when we crossed the border, enough to be able to answer a few questions and to keep the Mexican immigration officer from becoming suspicious. After that, I drugged him again.

I drove until midafternoon, took a back road into the desert, gave him a final lethal amount of the drug, and dumped his body into a sinkhole. I drove back to Tijuana, left Ric's suitcases minus identification in an alley, left his Ferrari minus identification in another alley, the key in the ignition, and caught a bus back to Los Angeles. I was confident that neither the suitcases nor the car would ever be reported. I was also confident that by the time Ric's body was discovered, if ever, it would be in such bad shape that the Mexican authorities, with limited resources, wouldn't be able to identify it. Ric had once told me that he hadn't spoken to his parents in five years, so I knew *they* wouldn't wonder why he wasn't in touch with them. As far as his friends went, well, he didn't have any. He'd ditched them when he came into money. They wouldn't miss him.

For an old guy, I'm resilient. I'd kept up my energy, driven all night and most of the day. I finally got some sleep on the bus. Not shabby, although toward the end I felt as if something had broken in me and I doubt I'll ever be able to put in that much effort again. But I had to, you see. Ric was going to keep hounding me, enticing me, using me. And I was going to be too desperate to tell him to get lost. Because I knew that no matter how well I wrote, I would never be able to sell a script under my own name again.

When I first started as a writer, the money and the ego didn't matter to me as much as the need to work, to tell stories, to teach and delight, as the Latin poet Horace said. But when the money started coming in, I began to depend on it. And I grew to love the action of being with powerful people, of having a reputation for being able to deliver quality work with amazing speed. Ego. That's why I hated Ric the most. Because producers stroked his ego over scripts that I had written.

But not anymore. Ric was gone, and his agent had heard him say that he was going, and I had a document, with his signature on it, saying that he was going to mail in his scripts through me, that I was his mentor and that he wanted me to go to script meetings on his behalf. The document also gave me his power of attorney, with permission to oversee his income while he was away.

And that should have been the end of it. Linda was puzzled but went along. After all, she'd heard Ric on the phone. Ballard was even more puzzled, but he was also enormously pleased with the spec script that I pulled out of a drawer and sent in with Ric's name on it. As far as Ballard was concerned, if Ric wanted to be eccentric, that was fine as long as Ric kept delivering. Really, his speed and the quality of his work were amazing.

So in a way I got what I wanted—the action and the pleasure of selling my work. But there's a problem. When I sit down to do rewrites, when I type "Revisions by Eric Potter," I suddenly find myself gazing out the window, wanting to sit in the sun. At the same time, I find that I can't sleep. Like Ric, I've become a night person.

I've sold the spec scripts that I wrote over the years and kept in a drawer. All I had to do was change the titles. Nobody remembered reading the original stories. But I couldn't seem to do the rewrites, and now that I've run out of old scripts, now that I'm faced with writing something new . . .

For the first time in my life, I've got writer's block. All I have to do is think of the title page and the words *by Eric Potter,* and my imagination freezes. It's agony. All my life, every day, I've been a writer. For thirty-five years of married life, except for the last two when Doris got sick, I wrote every day. I sacrificed everything to my craft. I didn't have children because I thought it would interfere with my schedule. Nothing was more important than putting words on a page. Now I sit at my desk, stare at my word processor, and . . .

Mary had a little . . .

I can't bear this anymore.

I need rest.

The quick brown fox jumped over . . .

I need to forget about Ric.

Now is the time for all good men to . . .

Joyce Carol Oates

The high imaginative powers of Joyce Carol Oates are by now seen as a virtual force of nature: like waves, her fiction comes ever on, beating up against our fragile defenses and sucking us into the very heart of its intensity. She began her career in 1963 with the novel By the North Gate; *since then she's published scores of books, none less sharply observed or intricately textured than the next. Under the pseudonym Rosamond Smith, she produces some of the most compelling psychological suspense stories of our time.*

It is, of course, always an honor to be able to present a new work from her, particularly when it relates to a theme as suited to her hypnotic talents as revenge.

Trust Ms. Oates to spiral around the issues of guilt and motive, keeping us once again off balance and attempting, futilely, to hold our own against the onslaught of her diabolic inventiveness. "Murder-Two" quite intentionally echoes the headlines we wince to read these days, but the character of its subtle surprises is unique to this author.

Murder-Two

BY JOYCE CAROL OATES

1.

This, he swore.

He'd returned to the town house on East End Avenue after eleven P.M. and found the front door unlocked and, inside, his mother lying in a pool of squid ink on the hardwood floor at the foot of the stairs. She'd apparently fallen down the steep length of the stairs and broken her neck, judging from her twisted upper body. She'd also been bludgeoned to death, the back of her skull caved in, with one of her own golf clubs, a two-iron, but he hadn't seemed to see that, immediately.

Squid ink?—well, the blood had looked black in the dim foyer light. It was a trick his eyes played on his brain sometimes when he'd been studying too hard, getting too little sleep. An *optic tic*. Meaning you see something clearly, but it registers surreally in the brain as something else. Like in your neurological programming there's an occasional bleep.

In Derek Peck, Jr.'s, case, confronted with the crumpled,

lifeless body of his mother, this was an obvious symptom of trauma. Shock, the visceral numbness that blocks immediate grief—the unsayable, the unknowable. He'd last seen his mother, in that same buttercup-yellow quilted satin robe that had given her the look of an upright, bulky Easter toy, early that morning, before he'd left for school. He'd been away all day. And this abrupt, weird transition—from differential calculus to the body on the floor, from the anxiety-driven jokes of his Math Club friends (a hard core of them were meeting late, weekdays, preparing for upcoming SAT exams) to the profound and terrible silence of the town house that had seemed to him, even as he'd pushed open the mysteriously unlocked front door, a hostile silence, a silence that vibrated with dread.

He crouched over the body, staring in disbelief. "Mother? *Mother!*"

As if it was he, Derek, who'd done something bad, he the one to be punished.

He couldn't catch his breath. Hyperventilating! His heart beating so wildly he almost fainted. Too confused to think, *Maybe they're still here, upstairs?* for in his dazed state he seemed to lack even an animal's instinct for self-preservation.

Yes, and he felt to blame, somehow. Hadn't she instilled in him a reflex of guilt? If something was wrong in the household, it could probably be traced back to *him*. From the age of thirteen (when his father, Derek senior, had divorced his mother, Lucille, same as divorcing *him*), he'd been expected by his mother to behave like a second adult in the household, growing tall, lank, and anxious as if to accommodate that expectation, and his sand-colored body hair sprouting, and a fevered grimness about the eyes. Fifty-three percent of Derek's classmates, girls and boys, at the Mayhew Academy, were from "families of divorce," and most agreed that the worst of it is you have to learn to behave like an adult yet at the same time a lesser adult, one deprived of his or her full civil rights. That wasn't easy even for stoic streetwise Derek Peck with an IQ of, what was it?—158, at age fifteen. (He was seventeen now.) So his precarious adolescent sense of himself was seriously askew: not just his *body image* (his mother had allowed him to become overweight as a small child; they say that remains with you forever, irremediably imprinted in the earliest brain cells), but more crucially his *social identity*. For one minute she'd be treating him like an infant, calling him her baby, her baby-boy, and the next minute she was hurt, reproachful, accusing him of failing, like his father, to uphold his *moral responsibility* to her.

This *moral responsibility* was a backpack loaded with rocks. He could feel it, first fucking thing in the morning, exerting gravity even before he swung his legs out of bed.

Crouched over her now, badly trembling, shaking as in a cold wind, whispering, "Mommy?—can't you wake up? Mom-*my*, don't be—" balking at the word *dead* for it would hurt and incense Lucille like the word *old*, not that she'd been a vain or frivolous or self-conscious woman for Lucille Peck was anything but, a woman of dignity it was said of her admiringly by women who would not have wished to be her and by men who would not have wished to be married to her. *Mommy, don't be old!* Derek would never have murmured aloud, of course. Though possibly to himself frequently this past year or so seeing her wan, big-boned and brave face in harsh frontal sunshine when they happened to descend the front steps together in the morning, or at that eerie position in the kitchen where the overhead inset lights converged in such a way as to cruelly shadow her face downward, bruising the eye sockets and the soft fleshy tucks in her cheeks. Two summers ago when he'd been away for six weeks at Lake Placid and she'd driven to Kennedy to pick him up, so eager to see him again, and he'd stared appalled at the harsh lines bracketing her mouth like a pike's, and her smile too happy and what he felt was pity, and this, too, made him feel guilty. *You don't pity your own mother, asshole.*

If he'd come home immediately after school. By four P.M. Instead of a quick call from his friend Andy across the park, guilty mumbled excuse left on the answering tape, *Mother? I'm sorry guess I won't make dinner tonight, okay?—Math Club—study group—calculus—don't wait up for me, please.* How relieved he'd been, midway in his message she hadn't picked up the phone.

Had she been alive, when he'd called? Or already . . . dead?

Last time you saw your mother alive, Derek? they'd ask and he'd have to invent for he hadn't seen her, exactly. No eye contact.

And what had he *said*? A rushed schoolday morning, a Thursday. Nothing special about it. No premonition! Cold and windy and winter-glaring and he'd been restless to get out of the house, snatched a Diet Coke from the refrigerator so freezing his teeth ached. A blurred reproachful look of Mother in the kitchen billowing in her buttercup-yellow quilted robe as he'd backed off smiling *'Bye, Mom*!

Sure she'd been hurt, her only son avoiding her. She'd been a lonely woman even in her pride. Even with her activities that meant so much to her: Women's Art League, East Side Planned Parenthood Volunteers, HealthStyle Fitness Center, tennis and golf in East Hampton in the summer, subscription tickets to Lincoln Center. And her friends: most of them divorced middle-aged women, mothers like herself with high-school or college-age kids. Lucille *was* lonely; how was that his fault?—as if, his senior year in prep school, he'd become a fanatic about grades, obsessed with early admission to Harvard, Yale, Brown, Berkeley, just to avoid his mother at that raw, unmediated time of day that was breakfast.

But, God, how he'd loved her! He had. Planning to make it up to her for sure, SAT scores in the highest percentile he'd take her to the Stanhope for the champagne brunch then across the street to the museum for a mother-son Sunday excursion of a kind they hadn't had in years.

How still she was lying. He didn't dare touch her. His breathing was short, ragged. The squid-inky black beneath her twisted head had seeped and coagulated into the cracks of the floor. Her left arm was flung out in an attitude of exasperated appeal, the sleeve stained with red, her hand lying palm-up and the fingers curled like angry talons. He might have noted that her Movado watch was missing, her rings gone except Grandma's antique opal with the fluted gold setting—the thief, or thieves, hadn't been able to yank it off her swollen finger? He might have noted that her eyes were rolled up asymmetrically in her head, the right iris nearly vanished and the left leering like a drunken cres-cent-moon. He might have noted that the back of her skull was smashed soft and pulpy as a melon but there are some things about your mother out of tact and delicacy you don't acknowledge see-ing. *Mother's hair, though*—it was her only remaining good feature, she'd said. A pale silvery-brown, slightly coarse, a natural color like Wheaties. The mothers of his classmates all hoped to be youthful and glamorous with bleached or dyed hair but not Lucille Peck, she wasn't the type. You expected her cheeks to be ruddy without makeup and on her good days they were.

By this time of night Lucille's hair should have been dry from her shower of so many hours ago Derek vaguely recalled she'd had, the upstairs bathroom filled with steam. The mirrors. Shortness of breath! Tickets for some concert or ballet that night at Lincoln Center?—Lucille and a woman friend. But Derek didn't know about that. Or if he'd known he'd forgotten. Like about the golf club, the two-iron. Which closet? Upstairs, or down? The drawers of Lucille's bedroom bureau ransacked, *his* new Macintosh carried from his desk, then dropped onto the floor by the doorway as if—what? They'd changed their minds about bothering with it. Look-ing for quick cash, for drugs. That's the motive!

What's Booger up to, now? What's going down with Booger, you hear?

He touched her—at last. Groping for that big artery in the throat—cateroid?—car*toid*? Should have been pulsing but wasn't. And her skin clammy-cool. His hand leapt back as if he'd been burnt.

Jesus fucking Christ, was it possible—Lucille was *dead*?

And *he'd* be to blame?

That Booger, man! One wild dude.

His nostrils flared, his eyes leaked tears. He was in a state of panic, had to get help. It was time! But he wouldn't have noticed the time, would he?—11:48 P.M. His watch was a sleek black-faced Omega he'd bought with his own cash, but he wouldn't be conscious of the time exactly. By now he'd have dialed 911. Except thinking, confused, the phone was ripped out? (*Was* the phone ripped out?) Or one of them, his mother's killers, waiting in the darkened kitchen by the phone? Waiting to kill *him*?

He panicked, he freaked. Running back to the front door stumbling and shouting into the street where a taxi was slowing to let out an elderly couple, neighbors from the adjoining brownstone and they and the driver stared at this chalk-faced grief-stricken boy in an unbuttoned duffel coat, barehead running into the street screaming, "Help us! Help us! Somebody's killed my mother!"

2.

EAST SIDE WOMAN KILLED
ROBBERY BELIEVED MOTIVE

In a late edition of Friday's *New York Times,* the golf club–bludgeoning death of Lucille Peck, whom Marina Dyer had known as Lucy Siddons, was prominently featured on the front page of the Metro section. Marina's quick eye, skimming the page, fastened at once upon the face (middle aged, fleshy, yet unmistakable) of her old Finch classmate.

"Lucy! *No.*"

You understood that this must be a *death photo*: the positioning on the page, upper center; the celebration of a private individual of no evident civic or cultural significance, or beauty. For *Times* readers the news value lay in the victim's address, close by the mayor's residence. The subtext being *Even here, among the sequestered wealthy, such a brutal fate is possible.*

In a state of shock, though with professional interest, for Marina Dyer was a criminal defense attorney, Marina read the article, continued on an inner page and disappointing in its brevity. It was so familiar as to resemble a ballad. *One of us* (Caucasian, middle aged, law abiding, unarmed) surprised and savagely murdered in the very sanctity of her home; an instrument of class privilege, a golf club, snatched up by the killer as the murder weapon. The intruder or intruders, police said, were probably looking for quick cash, drug money. It was a careless, crude, cruel crime; a "senseless" crime; one of a number of unsolved break-ins on the East Side since last September, though it was the first to involve murder. The teenaged son of Lucille Peck had returned home to find the front door unlocked and his mother dead, at about eleven P.M., at which time she'd been dead approximately five hours. Neighbors spoke of having heard no unusual sounds from the Peck residence, but several did speak of "suspicious" strangers in the neighborhood. Police were "investigating."

Poor Lucy!

Marina noted that her former classmate was forty-four years old, a year (most likely, part of a year) older than Marina; that she'd been divorced since 1991 from Derek Peck, an insurance executive now living in Boston; that she was survived by just the one child, Derek Peck, Jr., a sister, and two brothers. What an end for Lucy Siddons, who shone in Marina's memory as if beaming with life: unstoppable Lucy, indefatigable Lucy, good-hearted Lucy: Lucy, who was twice president of the Finch class of 1970, and a dedicated alumna: Lucy, whom all the girls had admired, if not adored: Lucy, who'd been so kind to shy stammering wall-eyed Marina Dyer.

Though they'd both been living in Manhattan all these years, Marina in a town house of her own on West Seventy-sixth Street, very near Central Park, it had been five years since she'd seen Lucy, at their twentieth class reunion; even longer since the two had spoken together at length, earnestly. Or maybe they never had.

The son did it, Marina thought, folding up the newspaper. It wasn't an altogether serious thought but one that suited her professional skepticism.

3.

Boogerman! Fucking fan-tas-tic.

Where'd he come from?—the hot molten core of the Universe. At the instant of the Big Bang. Before which there was *nothing* and after which there would be *everything:* cosmic cum. For all sentient beings derive from a single source and that source long vanished, extinct.

The more you contemplated of origins the less you knew. He'd studied Wittgenstein—*Whereof one cannot speak, thereof one must be silent.* (A photocopied handout for Communication Arts class, the instructor a cool youngish guy with a Princeton Ph.D.) Yet he believed he could recall the circumstances of his birth. In 1978, in Barbados where his parents were vacationing, one week in late December. He was premature by five weeks and lucky to be alive, and though Barbados was an accident yet seventeen years later he saw in his dreams a cobalt-blue sky, rows of royal palms shedding their bark like scales, shriek-bright-feathered tropical birds; a fat white moon drooping in the sky like his mother's big belly, sharks' dorsal fins cresting the waves like the Death Raiders video game he'd been hooked on in junior high. Wild hurricane-nights kept him from sleeping a normal sleep. Din of voices as of drowning souls crashing on a beach.

He was into Metallica, Urge Overkill, Soul Asylum. His heroes were heavy-metal punks who'd never made it to the Top Ten or if they did fell right back again. He admired losers who killed themselves ODing like dying's a joke, one final FUCK YOU! to the world. But he was innocent of doing what they'd claimed he'd done to his mother, for God's sake. Absolutely unbelieving fucking fantastic, *he, Derek Peck, Jr.,* had been arrested and would be tried for a crime perpetrated upon his own mother he'd loved! perpetrated by animals (he could guess the color of their skin) who would've smashed his skull in, too, like cracking an egg, if he'd walked in that door five hours earlier.

4.

She wasn't prepared to fall in love, wasn't the type to fall in love with any client, yet here is what happened: just seeing him, his strange tawny-yearning eyes lifting to her face, *Help me! save me!*— that was it.

Derek Peck, Jr., was a Botticelli angel partly erased and crudely painted over by Eric Fischl. His thick stiffly moussed un-washed hair lifted in two flaring symmetrical wings that framed his elegantly bony, long-jawed face. His limbs were monkey-long and twitchy. His shoulders were narrow and high, his chest perceptibly concave. He might have been fourteen, or twenty-five. He was of a generation as distant from Marina Dyer's as another species. He wore a T-shirt stamped SOUL ASYLUM beneath a rumpled Armani jacket of the color of steel filings, and pinstriped Ralph Lauren fleece trousers stained at the crotch, and size-twelve Nikes. Mad blue veins thrummed at his temples. He was a preppy cokehead who'd managed until now to stay out of trouble, Marina had been warned by Derek Peck, Sr.'s, attorney, who'd arranged, through Marina's discreet urging, for her to interview for the boy's counsel: a probable psychopath-matricide who not only claimed complete innocence but seemed actually to believe it. He gave off a complex odor of the ripely organic and the chemical. His skin appeared heated, of the color and texture of singed oatmeal. His nostrils were rimmed in red like nascent fire and his eyes were a pale acety-lene yellow-green, flammable. You would not want to bring a match too close to those eyes, still less would you want to look too deeply into those eyes.

When Marina Dyer was introduced by Derek Peck, the boy stared at her hungrily. Yet he didn't get to his feet like the other men in the room. He leaned forward in his chair, the tendons standing out in his neck and the strain of *seeing, thinking,* visible in his young face. His handshake was fumbling at first, then suddenly strong, assured as an adult man's, hurtful. Unsmiling, the boy shook hair out of his eyes like a horse rearing its beautiful brute head, and a painful sensation ran through Marina Dyer like an electric shock. She had not experienced such a sensation in a long time.

In her soft contralto voice that gave nothing away, Marina said, "Derek, *hi*."

It was in the 1980s, in an era of celebrity-scandal trials, that Marina Dyer made her reputation as a "brilliant" criminal defense lawyer; by being in fact brilliant, and by working very hard, and by playing against type. There was the audacity of drama in her positioning of herself in a male-dominated courtroom. There was the startling fact of her physical size: she was a "petite" size five, self-effacing, shy seeming, a woman easy to overlook, though it would not be to your advantage to overlook her. She was meticulously and unglamorously groomed in a way to suggest a lofty indifference to fashion, an air of timelessness. She wore her sparrow-colored hair in a French twist, ballerina style; her favored suits were Chanels in subdued harvest colors and soft dark cashmere wools, the jackets giving some bulk to her narrow frame, the skirts always primly to midcalf. Her shoes, handbags, briefcases, were of exquisite Italian leather, expensive but understated. When an item began to show signs of wear, Marina replaced it with an identical item from the same Madison Avenue shop. Her slightly askew left eye, which some in fact had found charming, she'd long ago had corrected with surgery. Her eyes were now direct, sharply focused. A perpetually moist, shiny dark-brown, with a look of fanaticism at times, but an exclusively professional fanaticism, a fanaticism in the service of her clients, whom she defended with a legendary fervor. A small woman, Marina acquired size and authority in public arenas. In a courtroom, her normally reedy, indistinct voice acquired volume, timbre. Her passion seemed to be aroused in direct proportion to the challenge of presenting a client as "not guilty" to reasonable jurors, and there were times (her admiring fellow professionals joked about this) that her plain, ascetic face shone with the luminosity of Bernini's St. Teresa in her ecstasy. Her clients were martyrs, their prosecutors persecutors. There was a spiritual urgency to Marina Dyer's cases impossible for jurors to explain afterward, when their verdicts were sometimes questioned. *You would have had to be there, to hear her, to know.*

Marina's first highly publicized case was her successful defense of a U.S. congressman from Manhattan who'd been charged with criminal extortion and witness tampering; her second was the successful, if controversial, defense of a black performance artist charged with rape and assault of a druggie-fan who'd come uninvited to his suite at the Four Seasons. There had been a prominent, photogenic Wall Street trader charged with embezzlement, fraud, obstruction of justice; there had been a woman journalist charged with attempted murder in the shooting-wounding of a married lover; there had been lesser-known but still meritorious cases, rich with challenge. Marina's clients were not invariably acquitted but their sentences, given their probable guilt, were considered lenient. Sometimes they spent no time in prison at all, only in halfway houses; they paid fines, did community service. Even as Marina Dyer shunned publicity, she reaped it. After each victory, her fees rose. Yet she was not avaricious, nor even apparently ambitious. Her life was her work, and her work her life. Of course, she'd been dealt a few defeats, in her early career when she'd sometimes defended innocent or quasi-innocent people, for modest fees. With the innocent you risk emotions, breakdown, stammering at crucial moments on the witness stand. You risk the eruption of rage, despair. With accomplished liars, you know you can depend upon a performance. Psychopaths are best: they lie fluently, but they believe.

Marina's initial interview with Derek Peck, Jr., lasted for several hours and was intense, exhausting. If she took him on, this would be her first murder trial; this seventeen-year-old boy her first accused murderer. And what a brutal murder: matricide. Never had she spoken with, in such intimate quarters, a client like Derek Peck. Never had she gazed into, for long wordless moments, any eyes like his. The vehemence with which he stated his innocence was compelling. The fury that his innocence should be doubted was mesmerizing. *Had* this boy killed, in such a way?—"transgressed"?—violated the law, which was Marina Dyer's very life, as if it were of no more consequence than a paper bag to be crumpled in the hand and tossed away? The back of Lucille Peck's head had literally been smashed in by an estimated twenty or more blows of the golf club. Inside her bathrobe, her soft naked-flaccid body had been pummeled, bruised, bloodied; her genitals furiously lacerated. An unspeakable crime, a crime in violation of taboo. A tabloid crime, thrilling even at second or third hand.

In her new Chanel suit of such a purplish-plum wool it appeared black as a nun's habit, in her crisp chignon that gave to her profile an Avedon-lupine sharpness, Marina Dyer gazed upon the boy who was Lucy Siddons's son. It excited her more than she would have wished to acknowledge. Thinking, I *am unassailable,* I *am untouched.* It was the perfect revenge.

Lucy Siddons. My best friend, I'd loved her. Leaving a birthday card and a red silk square scarf in her locker, and it was days before she remembered to thank me though it was a warm thank-you, a big-toothed genuine smile. Lucy Siddons who was so popular, so at ease and emulated among the snobbish girls at Finch. Despite a blemished skin, buck teeth, hefty thighs, and waddling-duck walk for which she was teased, so lovingly teased. The secret was, Lucy had *personality.* That mysterious X-factor which, if you lack it, you can never acquire it. If you have to ponder it, it's out of your reach forever. And Lucy was *good, good hearted.* A practicing Christian from a wealthy Manhattan Episcopal family famed for their good works. Waving to Marina Dyer to come sit with her and her friends in the cafeteria, while her friends sat stonily smiling; choosing scrawny Marina Dyer for her basketball team in gym class, while the others groaned. But Lucy was good, so good.

Charity and pity for the despised girls of Finch spilled like coins from her pockets.

Did I love Lucy Siddons those three years of my life, yes I loved Lucy Siddons like no one since. But it was a pure, chaste love. A wholly one-sided love.

5.

His bail had been set at $350,000, the bond paid by his distraught father. Since the recent Republican election-sweep it appeared that capital punishment would soon be reinstated in New York State, but at the present time there was no murder-one charge, only murder-two for even the most brutal and/or premeditated crimes. Like the murder of Lucille Peck, about which there was, regrettably, so much local publicity in newspapers, magazines, on television and radio, Marina Dyer began to doubt her client could receive a fair trial in the New York City area. Derek was hurt, incredulous: "Look, why would *I* kill her, *I* was the one who loved her!" he whined in a childish voice, lighting up another cigarette out of his mashed pack of Camels. *"—I was the only fucking one who loved her in the fucking universe!"* Each time Derek met with Marina he made this declaration, or a variant. His eyes flamed with tears of indignation, moral outrage. Strangers had entered his house and killed his mother and *he* was being blamed! Could you believe it! His life and his father's life torn up, disrupted like a tornado had blown through! Derek wept angrily, opening himself to Marina as if he'd slashed his breastbone to expose his raging palpitating heart.

Profound and terrible moments that left Marina shaken for hours afterward.

Marina noted, though, that Derek never spoke of Lucille Peck as *my mother* or *Mother* but only as *her, she.* When she'd happened to mention to him that she'd known Lucille, years ago in school, the boy hadn't seemed to hear. He'd been frowning, scratching at his neck. Marina repeated gently, "Lucille was an outstanding presence at Finch. A dear friend." But still Derek hadn't seemed to hear.

Lucy Siddons's son, who bore virtually no resemblance to her. His glaring eyes, the angular face, hard-chiseled mouth. Sexuality reeked about him like unwashed hair, soiled T-shirt, and jeans. Nor did Derek resemble Derek Peck, Sr., so far as Marina could see.

In the Finch yearbook for 1970 there were numerous photos of Lucy Siddons and the other popular girls of the class, the activities beneath their smiling faces extensive, impressive; beneath Marina Dyer's single picture, the caption was brief. She'd been an honors student, of course, but she had not been a popular girl no matter her effort. Consoling herself, *I am biding my time. I can wait.*

And so it turned out to be, as in a fairy tale of rewards and punishments.

Rapidly and vacantly Derek Peck recited his story, his "alibi," as he'd recited it to the authorities numerous times. His voice resembled one simulated by computer. Specific times, addresses; names of friends who would "swear to it, I was with them every minute"; the precise route he'd taken by taxi, through Central Park, on his way back to East End Avenue; the shock of discovering *the body* at the foot of the stairs just off the foyer. Marina listened, fascinated. She did not want to think that this was a tale invented in a cocaine high, indelibly imprinted in the boy's reptile-brain. Unshakable. It failed to accommodate embarrassing details, enumerated in the investigating detectives' report: Derek's socks speckled with Lucille Peck's blood tossed down a laundry chute, wadded underwear on Derek's bathroom floor still damp at midnight from a shower he claimed to have taken at seven A.M. but had more plausibly taken at seven P.M. before applying gel to his hair and dressing in punk-Gap style for a manic evening downtown with certain of his heavy-metal friends. And the smears of Lucille Peck's blood on the very tiles of Derek's shower stall he hadn't noticed, hadn't wiped off. And the telephone call on Lucille's answering tape explaining he wouldn't be home for dinner he claimed to have made at about four P.M. but had very possibly made as late as ten P.M., from a SoHo club.

These contradictions, and others, infuriated Derek rather than troubled him, as if they represented glitches in the fabric of the universe for which he could hardly be held responsible. He had a child's conviction that all things must yield to his wish, his insistence. *What he truly believed, how could it not be so?* Of course, as Marina Dyer argued, it *was* possible that the true killer of Lucille Peck had deliberately stained Derek's socks with blood, and tossed them down the laundry chute to incriminate him; the killer, or killers, had taken time to shower in Derek's shower and left Derek's own wet, wadded underwear behind. And there was no absolute, unshakable proof that the answering tape always recorded calls in the precise chronological order in which they came in, not one hundred percent of the time, how could that be proven? (There were five calls on Lucille's answering tape for the day of her death, scattered throughout the day; Derek's was the last.)

The assistant district attorney who was prosecuting the case charged that Derek Peck, Jr.'s, motive for killing his mother was a simple one: money. His $500 monthly allowance hadn't been enough to cover his expenses, evidently. Mrs. Peck had canceled her son's Visa account in January, after he'd run up a bill of over $6,000; relatives reported "tension" between mother and son; certain of Derek's classmates said there were rumors he was in debt to drug dealers and terrified of being murdered. And Derek had wanted a Jeep Wrangler for his eighteenth birthday, he'd told friends. By killing his mother he might expect to inherit as much as $4 million and there was a $100,000 life-insurance policy naming him beneficiary, there was the handsome four-story East End town house worth as much as $2.5 million, there was a property in East Hampton, there were valuable possessions. In the five days between Lucille Peck's death and Derek's arrest he'd run up over $2,000 in bills—he'd gone on a manic buying spree, subsequently attributed to grief. Derek was hardly the model preppy student he claimed to be either: he'd been expelled from the Mayhew Academy for two weeks in January for "disruptive behavior," and it was generally known that he and another boy had cheated on a battery of IQ exams in ninth grade. He was currently failing all his subjects except a course in Postmodernist Aesthetics, in which films and comics of Superman, Batman, Dracula, and *Star Trek* were meticulously deconstructed under the tutelage of a Princeton-trained instructor. There was a Math Club whose meetings Derek had attended sporadically, but he hadn't been there the evening of his mother's death.

Why would his classmates lie about him?—Derek was aggrieved, wounded. His closest friend, Andy, turning against him!

Marina had to admire her young client's response to the detectives' damning report: he simply denied it. His hot-flamed eyes brimmed with tears of innocence, disbelief. The prosecution was the enemy, and the enemy's case was just something they'd thrown together, to blame an unsolved murder on him because he was a kid, and vulnerable. So he was into heavy metal, and he'd experimented with a few drugs, like everyone he knew, for God's sake. *He had not murdered his mother, and he didn't know who had.*

Marina tried to be detached, objective. She was certain that no one, including Derek himself, knew of her feelings for him. Her behavior was unfailingly professional, and would be. Yet she thought of him constantly, obsessively; he'd become the emotional center of her life, as if she were somehow pregnant with him, his anguished, angry spirit inside her. *Help me! save me!* She'd forgotten the subtle, circuitous ways in which she'd brought her name to the attention of Derek Peck, Sr.'s, attorney and began to think that Derek junior had himself chosen her. Very likely, Lucille had spoken of her to him: her old classmate and close friend Marina Dyer, now a prominent defense attorney. And perhaps he'd seen her photograph somewhere. It was more than coincidence, after all. She knew!

She filed her motions, she interviewed Lucille Peck's relatives, neighbors, friends; she began to assemble a voluminous case, with the aid of two assistants; she basked in the excitement of the upcoming trial, through which she would lead, like a warrior-woman, like Joan of Arc, her beleaguered client. They would be dissected in the press, they would be martyred. Yet they would triumph, she was sure.

Was Derek guilty? And if guilty, of what? If truly he could not recall his actions, was *he* guilty? Marina thought, *If I put him on the witness stand, if he presents himself to the court as he presents himself to me . . . how could the jury deny him?*

It was five weeks, six weeks, now ten weeks after the death of Lucille Peck and already the death, like all deaths, was rapidly receding. A late-summer date had been set for the trial to begin and it hovered at the horizon teasing, tantalizing, as the opening night of a play already in rehearsal. Marina had of course entered a plea of not guilty on behalf of her client, who had refused to consider any other option. Since he was innocent, he *could not* plead guilty to a lesser charge—first-degree, or second-degree, manslaughter, for instance. In Manhattan criminal law circles it was believed that going to trial with this case was, for Marina Dyer, an egregious error, but Marina refused to discuss any other alternative; she was as adamant as her client, she would enter into no negotiations. Her primary defense would be a systematic refutation of the prosecution's case, a denial seriatim of the "evidence"; passionate reiterations of Derek Peck's absolute innocence, in which, on the witness stand, he would be the star performer; a charge of police bungling and incompetence in failing to find the true killer, or killers, who had broken into other homes on the East Side; a hope of enlisting the jurors' sympathy. For Marina had learned long ago how the sympathy of jurors is a deep, deep well. You would not want to call these average Americans fools exactly, but they were strangely, almost magically, impressionable; at times, susceptible as children. They were, or would like to be, "good" people; decent, generous, forgiving, kind; not "condemning," "cruel." They looked, especially in Manhattan, where the reputation of the police was clouded, for reasons not to convict, and a good defense lawyer provides those reasons. Especially they would not want to convict, of a charge of second-degree murder, a young, attractive, and now motherless boy like Derek Peck, Jr.

Jurors are easily confused, and it was Marina Dyer's genius to confuse them to her advantage. For the wanting to be *good*, in defiance of justice, is one of mankind's greatest weaknesses.

6.

"Hey: you don't believe me, do you?"

He'd paused in his compulsive pacing of her office, a cigarette burning in his fingers. He eyed her suspiciously.

Marina looked up startled to see Derek hovering rather close beside her desk, giving off his hot citrus-acetylene smell. She'd been taking notes even as a tape recorder played. "Derek, it doesn't matter what I believe. As your attorney, I speak for you. Your best legal—"

Derek said pettishly, "No! You have to believe me—*I didn't kill her.*"

It was an awkward moment, a moment of exquisite tension in which there were numerous narrative possibilities. Marina Dyer and the son of her old, now deceased, friend Lucy Siddons shut away in Marina's office on a late, thundery-dark afternoon; only a revolving tape cassette bearing witness. Marina had reason to know that the boy was drinking, these long days before his trial; he was living in the town house, with his father, free on bail but not "free." He'd allowed her to know that he was clean of all drugs, absolutely. He was following her advice, her instructions. But did she believe him?

Marina said, again carefully, meeting the boy's glaring gaze, "Of course I believe you, Derek," as if it was the most natural thing in the world, and he naive to have doubted. "Now, please sit down, and let's continue. You were telling me about your parents' divorce. . . ."

" 'Cause if you don't believe me," Derek said, pushing out

his lower lip so it showed fleshy red as a skinned tomato, "—I'll find a fucking lawyer who *does*."

"Yes, but I do. Now sit down, please."

"You *do*? You *believe*—?"

"Derek, what have I been saying! Now, sit down."

The boy loomed above her, staring. For an instant, his expression showed fear. Then he groped his way backward, to his chair. His young, corroded face was flushed and he gazed at her, greeny-tawny eyes, with yearning, adoration.

Don't touch me! Marina murmured in her sleep, cresting with emotion. *I couldn't bear it.*

Marina Dyer. Strangers stared at her in public places. Whispered together, pointing her out. Her name and now her face had become media sanctioned, iconic. In restaurants, in hotel lobbies, at professional gatherings. At the New York City Ballet, for instance, which Marina attended with a friend . . . for it had been a performance of this ballet troupe Lucille Peck had been scheduled to attend the night of her death. *Is that woman the lawyer? the one who . . . ? that boy who killed his mother with the golf club . . . Peck?*

They were becoming famous together.

His street name, his name in the downtown clubs, Fez, Duke's, Mandible, was "Booger." He'd been pissed at first, then decided it was affection not mockery. A pretty white uptown boy, had to pay his dues. Had to buy respect, authority. It was a tough crowd, took a fucking lot to impress them—money, and more than money. A certain attitude. Laughing at him, *Oh, you Boogerman!— one wild dude.* But now they *were* impressed. *Whacked his old lady? No shit! That Booger, man! One wild dude.*

Never dreamt of *it*. Nor of Mother, who was gone from the house as if traveling. Except not calling home, not checking on him. No more disappointing Mother.

Never dreamt of any kind of violence, that wasn't his thing. He believed in *passive-ism*. There was the great Indian leader, a saint. *Gandy*. Taught the ethic of *passive-ism*, triumphed over the racist-British enemies. Except the movie was too long.

Didn't sleep at night but weird times during the day. At night watching TV, playing the computer, "Myst" his favorite he could lose himself in for hours. Avoided violent games, his stomach still queasy. Avoided calculus, even the thought of it: the betrayal. For he hadn't graduated, class of ninety-five moving on without him, fuckers. His friends were never home when he called. Even girls who'd been crazy for him, never home. Never returned his calls. *Him, Derek Peck! Boooogerman*. It was like a microchip had been inserted in his brain, he had these pathological reactions. Not being able to sleep for, say, forty-eight hours. Then crashing, dead. Then waking how many hours later dry-mouthed and heart-hammering, lying sideways on his churned-up bed, his head over the edge and Doc Martens combat boots on his feet, he's kicking like crazy like somebody or something has hold of his ankles and he's gripping with both hands an invisible rod, or baseball bat, or club—swinging it in his sleep, and his muscles twitched and spasmed and veins swelled in his head close to bursting. *Swinging swinging swinging!*—and in his pants, in his Calvin Klein briefs, he'd *come*.

When he went out he wore dark, very dark, glasses even at night. His long hair tied back rat-tail style and a Mets cap, reversed, on his head. He'd be getting his hair cut for the trial but just not yet, wasn't that like . . . giving in, surrendering . . . ? In the neighborhood pizzeria, in a place on Second Avenue he'd ducked into alone, signing napkins for some giggling girls, once a father and son about eight years old, another time two old women in their forties, fifties, staring like he was Son of Sam, sure okay! signing *Derek Peck, Jr.,* and dating it. His signature an extravagant red-ink scrawl. *Thank you!* and he knows they're watching him walk away, thrilled. Their one contact with fame.

His old man and especially his lady-lawyer would give him hell if they knew, but they didn't need to know everything. He was free on fucking bail, wasn't he?

7.

In the aftermath of a love affair in her early thirties, the last such affair of her life, Marina Dyer had taken a strenuous "ecological" field trip to the Galápagos Islands; one of those desperate trips we take at crucial times in our lives, reasoning that the experience will cauterize the emotional wound, make of its very misery something trivial, negligible. The trip was indeed strenuous, and cauterizing. There in the infamous Galápagos, in the vast Pacific Ocean due west of Ecuador and a mere ten miles south of the Equator, Marina had come to certain life-conclusions. She'd decided not to kill herself, for one thing. For why kill one*self,* when nature is so very eager to do it for you, and to gobble you up? The islands were rockbound, storm lashed, barren. Inhabited by reptiles, giant tortoises. There was little vegetation. Shrieking seabirds like damned souls except it was not possible to believe in "souls" here. *In no world but a fallen one could such lands exist,* Herman Melville had written of the Galápagos he'd called also the Enchanted Isles.

When she returned from her week's trip to hell, as she fondly spoke of it, Marina Dyer was observed to devote herself more passionately than ever, more single-mindedly than ever, to her profession. Practicing law would be her life, and she meant to make of her life a quantifiable and unmistakable success. What of "life" that was not consumed by law would be inconsequential. The law was only a game, of course: it had very little to do with justice, or morality; "right" or "wrong"; "common" sense. But the law was the only game in which she, Marina Dyer, could be a serious player. The only game in which, now and then, Marina Dyer might win.

There was Marina's brother-in-law who had never liked her but, until now, had been cordial, respectful. Staring at her as if he'd never seen her before. "How the hell can you defend that vicious little punk? How do you justify yourself, morally? He killed his *mother*, for God's sake!" Marina felt the shock of this unexpected assault as if she'd been struck in the face. Others in the room, including her sister, looked on, appalled. Marina said carefully, trying to control her voice, "But, Ben, you don't believe that only the obviously 'innocent' deserve legal counsel, do you?" It was an answer she had made numerous times, to such a question; the answer all lawyers make, reasonably, convincingly.

"Of course not. But people like you go too far."

" 'Too far'? 'People like me'—?"

"You know what I mean. Don't play dumb."

"But I don't. I don't know what you mean."

Her brother-in-law was by nature a courteous man, however strong his opinions. Yet how rudely he turned away from Marina, with a dismissive gesture. Marina called after him, stricken, "Ben, I don't know what you mean. Derek *is* innocent, I'm sure. The case against him is only circumstantial. The media . . ." Her pleading voice trailed off, he'd walked out of the room. Never had she been so deeply hurt, confused. Her own brother-in-law!

The bigot. Self-righteous bastard. *Never* would Marina consent to see the man again.

Marina?—don't cry.

They don't mean it, Marina. Don't feel bad, please!

Hiding in the locker-room lavatory after the humiliation of gym class. How many times. Even Lucy, one of the team captains, didn't want her: that was obvious. Marina Dyer and the other last-choices, a fat girl or two, myopic girls, uncoordinated clumsy asthmatic girls laughingly divided between the red team and the gold. *Then, the nightmare of the game itself.* Trying to avoid being struck by thundering hooves, crashing bodies. Yells, piercing laughter. Swinging flailing arms, muscular thighs. How hard the gleaming floor when you fell! The giant girls (Lucy Siddons among them glaring, fierce) ran over her if she didn't step aside, she had no existence for them. Marina, made by the gym teacher, so absurdly, a "guard." *You must play, Marina. You must try. Don't be silly. It's only a game. These are all just games. Get out there with your team!* But if the ball was thrown directly at her it would strike her chest and ricochet out of her hands and into the hands of another. If the ball sailed toward her head she was incapable of ducking but stood stupidly helpless, paralyzed. Her glasses flying. Her scream a child's scream, laughable. It was all laughable. Yet it was her life.

Lucy, good-hearted repentant Lucy, sought her out where she hid in a locked toilet stall, sobbing in fury, a bloodstained tissue pressed against her nose. *Marina?—don't cry. They don't mean it, they like you, come on back, what's wrong?* Good-hearted Lucy Siddons she'd hated the most.

8.

On the afternoon of the Friday before the Monday that would be the start of his trial, Derek Peck, Jr., broke down in Marina Dyer's office.

Marina had known something was wrong, the boy reeked of alcohol. He'd come with his father, but had told his father to wait outside; he insisted that Marina's assistant leave the room.

He began to cry, and to babble. To Marina's astonishment he fell hard onto his knees on her burgundy carpet, began banging his forehead against the glass-topped edge of her desk. He laughed, he wept. Saying in an anguished choking voice how sorry he was he'd forgotten his mother's last birthday he hadn't known would be her last and how hurt she'd been like he'd forgotten just to spite her and that wasn't true, Jesus he loved her! the only person in the fucking universe who loved her! And then at Thanksgiving this wild scene, she'd quarreled with the relatives so it was just her and him for Thanksgiving she insisted upon preparing a full Thanksgiving dinner for just two people and he said it was crazy but she insisted, no stopping her when her mind was made up and he'd known there would be trouble, that morning in the kitchen she'd started drinking early and he was up in his room smoking dope and his Walkman plugged in knowing there was no escape. And it wasn't even a turkey she roasted for the two of them, you needed at least a twenty-pound turkey otherwise the meat dried out she said so she bought two ducks, yes *two dead ducks* from this game shop on Lexington and Sixty-sixth and that might've been okay except she was drinking red wine and laughing kind of hysterical talking on the phone preparing this fancy stuffing she made every year, wild rice and mushrooms, olives, and also baked yams, plum sauce, corn bread, and chocolate-tapioca pudding that was supposed to be one of his favorite desserts from when he was little that just the smell of it made him feel like puking. *He* stayed out of it upstairs until finally she called him around four P.M. and he came down knowing it was going to be a true bummer but not knowing how bad, she was swaying-drunk and her eyes smeared and they were eating in the dining room with the chandelier lit, all the fancy Irish linens and Grandma's old china and silver and she insisted *he* carve the ducks, he tried to get out of it but couldn't and Jesus! what happens!—he pushes the knife in the duck breast and there's actual blood squirting out of it!—and a big sticky clot of blood inside so he dropped the knife and ran out of the room gagging, it'd just completely freaked him in the midst of being stoned he couldn't take it running out into the street and almost hit by a car and her screaming after him *Derek come back! Derek come back don't leave me!* but he split from that scene and didn't come back for a day and a half. And ever after that she was drinking more and saying weird things to him like he was her baby, she'd felt him kick and shudder in her belly, under her heart, she'd talk to him inside her belly for months before he was born she'd lie down on the bed and stroke him, his head, through her skin and they'd talk together she said, it was the closest she'd ever been with any living creature and he was embarrassed not knowing what to say except *he* didn't remember, it was so long ago, and she'd say yes oh yes in your heart you remember in your heart you're still my baby boy *you do remember* and he was getting pissed saying *fuck it, no: he didn't remember* any of it. And there was only one way to stop her from loving him he began to understand, but he hadn't wanted to, he'd asked could he transfer to school in Boston or somewhere living with his dad but she went crazy, *no no no* he wasn't going, she'd never allow it, she tried to hold him, hug and kiss him so he had to lock his door and barricade it practically and she'd be waiting for him half-naked just coming out of her bathroom pretending she'd been taking a shower and clutching at him and that night finally he must've freaked, something snapped in his head and he went for the two-iron, she hadn't had time even to scream it happened so fast and merciful, him running up behind her so she didn't see him exactly—"It was the only way to stop her loving me."

Marina stared at the boy's aggrieved, tearstained face. Mucus leaked alarmingly from his nose. What had he said? He had said . . . *what?*

Yet even now a part of Marina's mind remained detached, calculating. She was shocked by Derek's confession, but was she *surprised?* A lawyer is never surprised.

She said, quickly, "Your mother Lucille was a strong, domineering woman. I know, I knew her. As a girl, twenty-five years ago, she'd rush into a room and all the oxygen was sucked up. She'd rush into a room and it was like a wind had blown out all the windows!" Marina hardly knew what she was saying, only that words tumbled from her; radiance played about her face like a flame. "Lucille was a smothering presence in your life. She wasn't a normal mother. What you've told me only confirms what I'd suspected. I've seen other victims of psychic incest—I know! She hypnotized you, you were fighting for your life. It was your own life you were defending." Derek remained kneeling on the carpet, staring vacantly at Marina. Tight little beads of blood had formed on his reddened forehead, his snaky-greasy hair dropped into his eyes. All his energy was spent. He looked to Marina now, like an animal who hears, not words from his mistress, but sounds; the consolation of certain cadences, rhythms. Marina was saying, urgently, "That night, you lost control. Whatever happened, Derek, it wasn't you. *You are the victim.* She drove you to it! Your father, too, abrogated his responsibility to you—left you with *her,* alone with *her,* at the age of thirteen. Thirteen! That's what you've been denying all these months. That's the secret you haven't acknowledged. You had no thoughts of your own, did you? For years? Your thoughts were *hers,* in *her* voice." Derek nodded mutely. Marina had taken a tissue from the burnished-leather box on her desk and tenderly dabbed at his face. He lifted his face to her, shutting his eyes. As if this sudden closeness, this intimacy, was not new to them but somehow familiar. Marina saw the boy in the courtroom, her Derek: transformed: his face fresh scrubbed and his hair neatly cut, gleaming with health; his head uplifted, without guile or subterfuge. *It was the only way to stop her loving me.* He wore a navy-blue blazer bearing the elegant understated monogram of the Mayhew Academy. A white shirt, blue-striped tie. His hands clasped together in an attitude of Buddhistic calm. A boy, immature for his age. Emotional, susceptible. *Not guilty by reason of temporary insanity.* It was a transcendent vision and Marina knew she would realize it and that all who gazed upon Derek Peck, Jr., and heard him testify would realize it.

Derek leaned against Marina, who crouched over him, he'd hidden his wet, hot face against her legs as she held him, comforted him. What a rank animal heat quivered from him, what animal terror, urgency. He was sobbing, babbling incoherently, "—save me? Don't let them hurt me? Can I have immunity, if I confess? If I say what happened, if I tell the truth—"

Marina embraced him, her fingers at the nape of his neck. She said, "Of course I'll save you, Derek. That's why you came to me."

Shel Silverstein

The phrase Renaissance Man *tends to get a bit over-worked these days, but apply it to Shel Silverstein and it practically begins to seem inadequate. Not only has he produced with seeming ease country music hits and popular songs, but he's been equally successful at turning his hand to poetry, short stories, plays, and children's books. Moreover, his whimsically hip fables, beloved by readers of all ages, have made him a stalwart of the best-seller lists.* A Light in the Attic, *most remarkably, showed the kind of staying power on the* New York Times *chart—two years, to be precise—that most of the biggest names (John Grisham, Stephen King, and Michael Crichton) have never equaled for their own block-busters.*

And there's still more: his unmistakable illustrative style is another crucial element to his appeal. Just as no writer sounds *like Shel, no other artist's vision is as delightfully, sophisticatedly cockeyed.*

One can only marvel that he makes the time to respond so generously to his friends' requests. In the following work, let's be glad he did. Drawing on his characteristic passion for list making, he shows how the deed is not just in the wish but in the sublimation.

The Enemy

BY SHEL SILVERSTEIN

A man had an enemy
Whom he loathed, hated, and despised beyond words
And so he plotted and planned his revenge
Every morning he would wake and make lists
And every afternoon he would add to them
And every evening he would sit with his shoes off
And have a nice cup of tea
While he honed and polished them
And, oh, his dreams, his richly vengeful dreams
Of shooting him
And watching him die quickly—ha ha
Or poisoning him
And watching him die slow—ooh
And hearing him beg—ho-ho-ho
Or crushing him
Under a cement steamroller—squish-splish

Or knifing him
And seeing his blood spatter—mmm-mmm
Or bludgeoning him
And seeing his brains scatter—oh, yes—oh, yes
Or snapping his neck—crrrack
Or tearing out his heart—rrrip
Or puncturing him to death
With a very small pin—he-he-he
Or impaling him
On a jagged, rusted, feces-encrusted iron fence—yeow
Or setting him on fire
And hearing him sizzle—sssss
Or injecting him with rare and excruciating diseases—oh,
     yeah
Or imprisoning him in a sewer—starving him
Until he ate raw sewage
Until his stomach exploded—ka-boom
Or electrocuting him
And seeing him jump—jerk—sparkle—ahhh, beautiful
Or cutting his throat
With a butter knife—yuck—a *dull* one—yuck-yuck
Or disembowling him—oh
With a garden trowel—oh-oh—a dirty one—oh-oh-oh—a
     dirty rusty one—ahhh
Or dropping him from a plane—whoosh
Into a sea of vomit—splat—glub-glub
Or amputating his body an inch at a time
Starting from his toes up—hey-hey
Or a centimeter at a time
From his head down—yep, yep, yep
Or a millimeter at a time
From his fingertips in—wheee
Or sewing a hungry rat up
Inside his belly—uh-huh
Or choking him to death with a giant slimy boa constrictor

Until his neck squished to putty
And his face turned purple—and his eyes popped out
And his bodily fluids squirted, gushed and geysered
From every orifice
He began matching the deed to the day of the week
Sunday—stabbing
Monday—mauling
Tuesday—throttling
Wednesday—whipping
Thursday—tarantula
Could a live tarantula fit into a man's ear?
Would a transplanted shark fetus grow
Inside a human being?
And what about pinching?
Can one be pinched to death?
Prodded? Poked? Scratched?
These were possibilities worth considering
And *tickled*—to watch him expire while
That mouth laughed uncontrollably—ha ha ha
But the eyes—the eyes wouldn't be laughing—oh, no, no
On special occasions he thought of skinning him—alive
Then rolling his body—not gently—in rock salt and honey
Then suspending him—by a barbed-wire rope
Over an anthill under a hive of killer bees
With a sex-crazed syphilitic gorilla sodomizing him—ha ha
And if he moved forward a giant crocodile
Would snap his head off
And if he lay flat the ants would gnaw him
And if he raised up he would hit the hive
And the bees—the angry bees—would get him
And if he stayed still, the panting drooling gorilla
Would love him to pieces
And if he screamed he would wake the hungry hibernating
    Kodiak bear
Who slept fitfully at his feet—ha ha ha

Oh, what thoughts he had.
And time went by
And then one pleasant evening
While he luxuriated in thought
Of dipping his enemy into a bathtub of piranhas
Slowly—first the toes—then the feet . . . then
Watching that face twisted in a—
The face . . . the face . . . he didn't remember the face
And when he tried to recall
What his enemy had done
He couldn't remember that either
He had grown old
Old in plotting, old in dreaming, old in list making
Soon he might forget that there was an enemy at all
There was the terrifying possibility
That *he* might die before the other did
And his enemy would go unpunished
Or *worse*—the enemy might die first—
Of natural causes
Depriving him of his sweet revenge
He must act now
But how?
No time for the exquisite pleasure of slow starvation
He had no access to exotic poisons
Ants and bees were . . . unpredictable
And how do you train a gorilla
For something like that?
Stabbing? Choking? Amputations?
They needed an expert hand
And he was experienced in thought—not execution
A bullet . . . the *bullet* was it
Too quick? Yes, but after all
It was the intensity of the agony, rather than the duration
And—the horror—in those beady little eyes
The realization—ha ha

He bought a gun
He went to the house of his enemy
At least he remembered the address
He peered in the window
There he was—older and feeble
But as vile and despicable as ever
Even more vile and despicable in his decay
He leveled the gun
In a moment it would be all over
Flash—bang—plop—all over
The years of scheming and plotting
The endless plans—the endless lists
Flash—bang—scream—plop
He took aim between those red rheumy eyes
And then the thought struck him
The gun—was it loaded?
What if it misfired?
And what if he only wounded him
His hand was not that steady
Let him off with just the pain of a *wound*?
And be apprehended by the law?
Or miss him completely—
And, be apprehended by *him*
Find himself in *his* power
What horrible retribution that insidious
Mind might extract
No—not the gun—
A stupid choice—conceived in haste—big mistake
He dropped the gun and hurried home
He sat down in his chair
Until his heart stopped pounding
He leaned back
He closed his eyes
He thought about the rats
They wouldn't be that hard to come by

And yes, he was none too strong
But the other looked even weaker
Choking and stabbing were not out of the question
And what about garotte?
Feeding him broken glass?—or metal filings?
Or . . . or breaking his bones
All of them—one at a time—every tiny little
Bone of the foot—one at a time—
Or—hey—sewing the tip of his penis
Into his abdomen—yes—and then forcing
Him to drink gallons of Bloody Mary mix—mixed with lye
He got up and got his list
He danced into the kitchen
He made himself a nice cup of tea
He brought it back to his chair
And settled back down
Bludgeoning!—he hadn't thought of that before
Watching the pieces of that diseased brain—fly like. . . .
    Like confetti—ha ha ha ha ha ha
Bludgeoning—yes.
He put it under *B.*

Peter Straub

The suave trickster instincts of Peter Straub have never before been displayed quite as they are found here. From the quaintly comic yet undeniably sinister entrance of the titular pair to the scenes of extreme unpleasantness that follow, the author (renowned for such extravaganzas of the macabre as Ghost Story *and* Floating Dragon*) takes his elegant time scaring us out of our wits.*

The good news is that restraint *does figure as a definite factor in the ghastly delicacy of Mr. Straub's overall effect; the bad news, as I perhaps don't need to tell you, is that* restraint *is a word with more than one meaning.*

Still, it is clear that a great deal of fun went into the composition of "Mr. Clubb and Mr. Cuff." And that's news as good as it gets. Whether he's delving into the past in novels such as Koko, Mystery, *or, most recently,* The Hellfire Club, *or scraping the edge of our psyches in the present, Peter Straub is a writer we love to see enjoy himself. Even—and especially—at the expense of our own peace of mind.*

Mr. Clubb and Mr. Cuff

BY PETER STRAUB

1

I never intended to go astray, nor did I know what that meant. My journey began in an isolated hamlet notable for the piety of its inhabitants, and when I vowed to escape New Covenant I assumed that the values instilled within me there would forever be my guide. And so, with a depth of paradox I still only begin to comprehend, they have been. My journey, so triumphant, also so excruciating, is both *from* my native village and *of* it. For all its splendor, my life has been that of a child of New Covenant.

When in my limousine I scanned *The Wall Street Journal,* when in the private elevator I ascended to the rosewood-paneled office with harbor views, when in the partners' dining room I ordered squab on a mesclun bed from a prison-rescued waiter known to me alone as Charlie-Charlie, also when I navigated for my clients the complex waters of financial planning, above all when before her seduction by my enemy Graham Leeson I returned homeward to luxuriate in the attentions of my stunning Marguerite, when transported within the embraces of my wife, even then I carried within the frame houses dropped like afterthoughts down the streets of New Covenant, the stiff faces and suspicious eyes, the stony cordialities before and after services in the grim great Temple—the blank storefronts along Harmony Street—tattooed within me was the ugly, enigmatic beauty of my birthplace. Therefore I believe that when I strayed, and stray I did, make no mistake, it was but to come home, for I claim that the two strange gentlemen who beckoned me into error were the night of its night, the dust of its dust. In the period of my life's greatest turmoil—the month of my exposure to Mr. Clubb and Mr. Cuff, "Private Detectives Extraordinaire," as their business card described them—in the midst of the uproar I felt that I saw *the contradictory dimensions of* . . .

of . . .

I felt I saw . . . had seen, had at least glimpsed . . . what a wiser man might call . . . try to imagine the sheer difficulty of actually writing these words . . . the Meaning of Tragedy. You smirk, I don't blame you, in your place I'd do the same, but I assure you I saw *something.*

I must sketch in the few details necessary to understand my story. A day's walk from New York State's Canadian border, New Covenant was (and still is, still is) a town of just under a thousand inhabitants united by the puritanical Protestantism of the Church of the New Covenant, whose founders had broken away from the even more puritanical Saints of the Covenant. (The Saints had proscribed sexual congress in the hope of hastening the Second Coming.) The village flourished during the end of the nineteenth century, and settled into its permanent form around 1920.

To wit: Temple Square, where the Temple of the New Covenant and its bell tower, flanked left and right by the Youth Bible Study Center and the Combined Boys and Girls Elementary and

Middle School, dominate a modest greensward. Southerly stand the shop fronts of Harmony Street, the bank, also the modest placards indicating the locations of New Covenant's doctor, lawyer, and dentist; south of Harmony Street lie the two streets of frame houses sheltering the town's clerks and artisans, beyond these the farms of the rural faithful, beyond the farmland deep forest. North of Temple Square is Scripture Street, two blocks lined with the residences of the reverend and his Board of Brethren, the aforementioned doctor, dentist, and lawyer, the president and vice-president of the bank, also the families of some few wealthy converts devoted to Temple affairs. North of Scripture Street are more farms, then the resumption of the great forest in which our village described a sort of clearing.

My father was New Covenant's lawyer, and to Scripture Street was I born. Sundays I spent in the Youth Bible Study Center, weekdays in the Combined Boys and Girls Elementary and Middle School. New Covenant was my world, its people all I knew of the world. Three fourths of all mankind consisted of gaunt, bony, blond-haired individuals with chiseled features and blazing blue eyes, the men six feet or taller in height, the women some inches shorter—the remaining fourth being the Racketts, Mudges, and Blunts, our farm families, who after generations of intermarriage had coalesced into a tribe of squat, black-haired, gap-toothed, moon-faced males and females seldom taller than five feet four or five inches. Until I went to college I thought that all people were divided into the races of town and barn, fair and dark, the spotless and the mud spattered, the reverential and the sly.

Though Racketts, Mudges, and Blunts attended our school and worshiped in our Temple, though they were at least as prosperous as we in town save the converts in their mansions, we knew them tainted with an essential inferiority. Rather than intelligent they seemed *crafty*, rather than spiritual, *animal*. Both in classrooms and Temple, they sat together, watchful as dogs compelled for the nonce to be "good," now and again tilting their heads to pass a whispered comment. Despite Sunday baths and Sunday clothes, they bore an unerasable odor redolent of the barnyard. Their public self-effacement seemed to mask a peasant amusement, and when they separated into their wagons and other vehicles, they could be heard to share a peasant laughter.

I found this mysterious race unsettling, in fact profoundly annoying. At some level they frightened me—I found them compelling. Oppressed from my earliest days by life in New Covenant, I felt an inadmissible fascination for this secretive brood. Despite their inferiority, I wished to know what they knew. Locked deep within their shabbiness and shame I sensed the presence of a freedom I did not understand but found *thrilling*.

Because town never socialized with barn, our contacts were restricted to places of education, worship, and commerce. It would have been as unthinkable for me to take a seat beside Delbert Mudge or Charlie-Charlie Rackett in our fourth-grade classroom as for Delbert or Charlie-Charlie to invite me for an overnight in their farmhouse bedrooms. Did Delbert and Charlie-Charlie actually have bedrooms, where they slept alone in their own beds? I recall mornings when the atmosphere about Delbert and Charlie-Charlie suggested nights spent in close proximity to the pigpen, others when their worn dungarees exuded a freshness redolent of sunshine, wildflowers, and raspberries.

During recess an inviolable border separated the townies at the northern end of our play area from the barnies at the southern. Our play, superficially similar, demonstrated our essential differences, for we could not cast off the unconscious stiffness resulting from constant adult measurement of our spiritual worthiness. In contrast, the barnies did not play at playing but actually *played,* plunging back and forth across the grass, chortling over victories, grinning as they muttered what must have been jokes. (We were not adept at jokes.) When school closed at end of day, I tracked the homebound progress of Delbert, Charlie-Charlie, and clan with envious eyes and a divided heart.

Why should they have seemed in possession of a liberty I desired? After graduation from Middle School, we townies pro-

gressed to Shady Glen's Consolidated High, there to monitor ourselves and our fellows while encountering the temptations of the
wider world, in some cases then advancing into colleges and uni-
versities. Having concluded their educations with the seventh
grade's long division and *Hiawatha* recitations, the barnies one
and all returned to their barns. Some few, some very few, of *us,*
among whom I had determined early on to be numbered, left for
good, thereafter to be celebrated, denounced, or mourned. One of
us, Caleb Thurlow, violated every standard of caste and morality by
marrying Munna Blunt and vanishing into barnie-world. A dis-
graced, disinherited pariah during my childhood, Thurlow's increasingly pronounced stoop and decreasing teeth terrifyingly
mutated him into a blond, wasted barnie-parody on his furtive
annual Christmas appearances at Temple. One of *them,* one only,
my old classmate Charlie-Charlie Rackett, escaped his ordained
destiny in our twentieth year by liberating a plow horse and
Webley-Vickers pistol from the family farm to commit serial armed
robbery upon Shady Glen's George Washington Inn, Town Square
Feed & Grain, and Allsorts Emporium. Every witness to his crimes
recognized what, if not who, he was, and Charlie-Charlie was apprehended while boarding the Albany train in the next village west.
During the course of my own journey from and of New Covenant,
I tracked Charlie-Charlie's gloomy progress through the way stations of the penal system until at last I could secure his release at a
parole hearing with the offer of a respectable job in the financial
planning industry.

I had by then established myself as absolute monarch of three
floors in a Wall Street monolith. With my two junior partners, I
enjoyed the services of a fleet of paralegals, interns, analysts, investigators, and secretaries. I had chosen these partners carefully, for
as well as the usual expertise, skill, and dedication, I required
other, less conventional qualities.

I had sniffed out intelligent but unimaginative men of some
slight moral laziness; capable of cutting corners when they thought
no one would notice; controlled drinkers and secret drug-takers:

juniors with reason to be grateful for their positions. I wanted no *zealousness*. My employees were to be steadfastly incurious and able enough to handle their clients satisfactorily, at least with my paternal assistance.

My growing prominence had attracted the famous, the established, the notorious. Film stars and athletes, civic leaders, corporate pashas, and heirs to longstanding family fortunes regularly visited our offices, as did a number of conspicuously well-tailored gentlemen who had accumulated their wealth in a more colorful fashion. To these clients I suggested financial stratagems responsive to their labyrinthine needs. I had not schemed for their business. It simply *came to me*, willy-nilly, as our Temple held that salvation came to the elect. One May morning, a cryptic fellow in a pinstriped suit appeared in my office to pose a series of delicate questions. As soon as he opened his mouth, the cryptic fellow summoned irresistibly from memory a dour, squinting member of the Board of Brethren of New Covenant's Temple. I *knew* this man, and instantly I found the tone most acceptable to him. Tone is all to such people. After our interview he directed others of his kind to my office, and by December my business had tripled. Individually and universally these gentlemen pungently reminded me of the village I had long ago escaped, and I cherished my suspicious buccaneers even as I celebrated the distance between my moral life and theirs. While sheltering these self-justifying figures within elaborate trusts, while legitimizing subterranean floods of cash, I immersed myself within a familiar atmosphere of pious denial. Rebuking home, I *was* home.

Life had not yet taught me that revenge inexorably exacts its own revenge.

My researches eventually resulted in the hiring of the two junior partners known privately to me as Gilligan and the Captain. The first, a short, trim fellow with a comedian's rubber face and disheveled hair, brilliant with mutual funds but an ignoramus at estate planning, each morning worked so quietly as to become invisible. To Gilligan I had referred many of our actors and musicians, and those whose schedules permitted them to attend meetings before the lunch hour met their soft-spoken advisor in a dimly lighted office with curtained windows. After lunch, Gilligan tended toward the vibrant, the effusive, the extrovert. Red faced and sweating, he loosened his tie, turned on a powerful sound system, and ushered emaciated musicians with haystack hair into the atmosphere of a backstage party. Morning Gilligan spoke in whispers; Afternoon Gilligan batted our secretaries' shoulders as he bounced officeward down the corridors. I snapped him up as soon as one of my competitors let him go, and he proved a perfect complement to the Captain. Tall, plump, silver haired, this gentleman had come to me from a specialist in estates and trusts discomfited by his tendency to become pugnacious when outraged by a client's foul language, improper dress, or other offenses against good taste. Our tycoons and inheritors of family fortunes were in no danger of arousing the Captain's ire, and I myself handled the unshaven film stars' and heavy metallists' estate planning. Neither Gilligan nor the Captain had any contact with the cryptic gentlemen. Our office was an organism balanced in all its parts. Should any mutinous notions occur to my partners, my spy the devoted Charlie-Charlie Rackett, to them Charles the Perfect Waiter, every noon silently monitored their every utterance while replenishing Gilligan's wineglass. My marriage of two years seemed blissfully happy, my reputation and bank account flourished alike, and I anticipated perhaps another decade of labor followed by luxurious retirement. I could not have been less prepared for the disaster to come.

Mine, as disasters do, began at home. I admit my contribution to the difficulties. While immersed in the demands of my profession, I had married a beautiful woman twenty years my junior. It was my understanding that Marguerite had knowingly entered into a contract under which she enjoyed the fruits of income and social position while postponing a deeper marital communication until I cashed in and quit the game, at which point she and I could travel at will, occupying grand hotel suites and staterooms while acquiring every adornment which struck her eye. How could an arrangement so harmonious have failed to satisfy her? Even now I feel the old rancor. Marguerite had come into our office as a faded singer who wished to invest the remaining proceeds from a five- or six-year-old "hit," and after an initial consultation Morning Gilligan whispered her down the corridor for my customary lecture on estate tax, trusts, so forth and so on—in her case, due to the modesty of the funds in question, mere show. (Since during their preliminary discussion she had casually employed the Anglo-Saxon monosyllable for excrement, Gilligan dared not subject her to the Captain.) He escorted her into my chambers, and I glanced up with the customary show of interest. You may imagine a thick bolt of lightning slicing through a double-glazed office window, sizzling across the width of a polished teak desk, and striking me in the heart.

Already I was lost. Thirty minutes later I violated my most sacred edict by inviting a female client to a dinner date. She accepted, damn her. Six months later, Marguerite and I were married, damn us both. I had attained everything for which I had abandoned New Covenant, and for twenty-three months I inhabited the paradise of fools.

I need say only that the usual dreary signals, matters like unexplained absences, mysterious telephone calls abruptly terminated upon my appearance, and visitations of a melancholic, distracted *daemon*, forced me to set one of our investigators on Marguerite's trail, resulting in the discovery that my wife had been two-backed-beasting it with my sole professional equal, the slick, the smooth Graham Leeson, to whom I, swollen with uxorious pride a year after our wedding day, had introduced her during a function at the Waldorf-Astoria Hotel. I know what happened. I don't need a map. Exactly as I had decided to win her at our first meeting, Graham Leeson vowed to steal Marguerite from me the instant he set his handsome blue eyes on her between the fifty-thousand-dollar tables on the Starlight Roof.

My enemy enjoyed a number of natural advantages. Older

than she by but ten years to my twenty, at six-four three inches taller than I, this reptile had been blessed with a misleadingly winning Irish countenance and a full head of crinkly red-blond hair. (In contrast, my white tonsure accentuated the severity of the all-too-Cromwellian townie face.) I assumed her immune to such obvious charms, and I was wrong. I thought Marguerite could not fail to see the meagerness of Leeson's inner life, and I was wrong again. I suppose he exploited the inevitable temporary isolation of any spouse to a man in my position. He must have played upon her grudges, spoken to her secret vanities. Cynically, I am sure, he encouraged the illusion that she was an "artist." He flattered, he very likely wheedled. By every shabby means at his disposal he had overwhelmed her, most crucially by screwing her brains out three times a week in a corporate suite at a Park Avenue hotel.

After I had examined the photographs and other records arrayed before me by the investigator, an attack of nausea brought my dizzied head to the edge of my desk; then rage stiffened my backbone and induced a moment of hysterical blindness. My marriage was dead, my wife a repulsive stranger. Vision returned a second or two later. The checkbook floated from the desk drawer, the Waterman pen glided into position between thumb and forefinger, and while a shadow's efficient hand inscribed a check for ten thousand dollars, a disembodied voice informed the hapless investigator that the only service required of him henceforth would be eternal silence.

For perhaps an hour I sat alone in my office, postponing appointments and refusing telephone calls. In the moments when I had tried to envision my rival, what came to mind was some surly drummer or guitarist from her past, easily intimidated and readily bought off. In such a case, I should have inclined toward mercy. Had Marguerite offered a sufficiently self-abasing apology, I would have slashed her clothing allowance in half, restricted her public appearances to the two or three most crucial charity events of the year and perhaps as many dinners at my side in the restaurants where one is "seen," and ensured that the resultant mood of sackcloth and ashes prohibited any reversion to bad behavior by intermittent use of another investigator.

No question of mercy, now. Staring at the photographs of my life's former partner entangled with the man I detested most in the world, I shuddered with a combination of horror, despair, loathing, and—appallingly—an urgent spasm of sexual arousal. I unbuttoned my trousers, groaned in ecstatic torment, and helplessly ejaculated over the images on my desk. When I had recovered, weak-kneed and trembling I wiped away the evidence, fell into my chair, and picked up the telephone to request Charlie-Charlie Rackett's immediate presence in my office.

The cryptic gentlemen, experts in the nuances of retribution, might seem more obvious sources of assistance, but I could not afford obligations in that direction. Nor did I wish to expose my humiliation to clients for whom the issue of respect was all important. Devoted Charlie-Charlie's years in the jug had given him an extensive acquaintanceship among the dubious and irregular, and I had from time to time commandeered the services of one or another of his fellow yardbirds. My old companion sidled around my door and posted himself before me, all dignity on the outside, all curiosity within.

"I have been dealt a horrendous blow, Charlie-Charlie," I said, "and as soon as possible I wish to see one or two of the best."

Charlie-Charlie glanced at the folders. "You want serious people," he said, speaking in code. "Right?"

"I must have men who can be serious when seriousness is necessary," I said, replying in the same code.

While my lone surviving link to New Covenant struggled to understand this directive, it came to me that Charlie-Charlie had now become my only true confidant, and I bit down on an upwelling of fury. I realized that I had clamped shut my eyes, and opened them upon an uneasy Charlie-Charlie.

"You're sure," he said.

"Find them," I said, and, to restore some semblance of our conventional atmosphere asked, "The boys still okay?"

Telling me that the juniors remained content, he said, "Fat and happy. I'll find what you want, but it'll take a couple of days."

I nodded, and he was gone.

For the remainder of the day I turned in an inadequate impersonation of the executive who usually sat behind my desk and, after putting off the moment as long as reasonably possible, buried the awful files in a bottom drawer and returned to the town house I had purchased for my bride-to-be and which, I remembered with an unhappy pang, she had once in an uncharacteristic moment of cuteness called "our town home."

Since I had been too preoccupied to telephone wife, cook, or butler with the information that I would be late at the office, when I walked into our dining room the table had been laid with our china and silver, flowers arranged in the centerpiece, and in what I took to be a new dress, Marguerite glanced mildly up from her end of the table and murmured a greeting. Scarcely able to meet her eyes, I bent to bestow the usual homecoming kiss with a mixture of feeling more painful than I previously would have imagined myself capable. Some despicable portion of my being responded to her beauty with the old husbandly appreciation even as I went cold with the loathing I could not permit myself to show. I hated Marguerite for her treachery, her beauty for its falsity, myself for my susceptibility to what I knew was treacherous and false. Clumsily, my lips brushed the edge of an azure eye, and it came to me that she may well have been with Leeson while the investigator was displaying the images of her degradation. Through me coursed an involuntary tremor of revulsion with, strange to say, as its center a molten erotic core. Part of my extraordinary pain was the sense that I, too, had been contaminated: a layer of illusion had been peeled away, revealing monstrous blind groping slugs and maggots.

Having heard voices, Mr. Moncrieff, the butler I had employed upon the abrupt decision of the duke of Denbigh to cast off worldly ways and enter an order of Anglican monks, came through from the kitchen and awaited orders. His bland, courteous manner suggested, as usual, that he was making the best of having been shipwrecked on an island populated by illiterate savages. Marguerite said that she had been worried when I had not returned home at the customary time.

"I'm fine," I said. "No, I'm not fine. I feel unwell. Distinctly unwell. Grave difficulties at the office." With that I managed to make my way up the table to my chair, along the way signaling to Mr. Moncrieff that the Lord of the Savages wished him to bring in the predinner martini and then immediately begin serving whatever the cook had prepared. I took my seat at the head of the table, and Mr. Moncrieff removed the floral centerpiece to the sideboard. Marguerite regarded me with the appearance of probing concern. This was false, false, false. Unable to meet her eyes, I raised mine to the row of Canalettos along the wall, then the intricacies of the plaster molding above the paintings, at last to the chandelier depending from the central rosette on the ceiling. More had changed than my relationship with my wife. The molding, the blossoming chandelier, even Canaletto's Venice resounded with a cold, selfish lovelessness.

Marguerite remarked that I seemed agitated.

"No, I am not," I said. The butler placed the ice-cold drink before me, and I snatched up the glass and drained half its contents. "Yes, I am agitated, terribly," I said. "The difficulties at the office are more far reaching than I intimated." I polished off the martini and tasted only glycerine. "It is a matter of betrayal and treachery, made all the more wounding by the closeness of my relationship with the traitor."

I lowered my eyes to measure the effect of this thrust to the vitals of the traitor in question. She was looking back at me with a flawless imitation of wifely concern. For a moment I doubted her unfaithfulness. Then the memory of the photographs in my bottom drawer once again brought crawling into view the slugs and maggots. "I am sickened unto rage," I said, "and my rage demands vengeance. Can you understand this?"

Mr. Moncrieff carried into the dining room the tureens or

serving dishes containing whatever it was we were to eat that night, and my wife and I honored the silence which had become conventional during the presentation of our evening meal. When we were alone again, she nodded in affirmation.

I said, "I am grateful, for I value your opinions. I should like you to help me reach a difficult decision."

She thanked me in the simplest of terms.

"Consider this puzzle," I said. "Famously, vengeance is the Lord's, and therefore it is often imagined that vengeance exacted by anyone other is immoral. Yet if vengeance is the Lord's, then a mortal being who seeks it on his own behalf has engaged in a form of worship, even an alternate version of prayer. Many good Christians regularly pray for the establishment of justice, and what lies behind an act of vengeance but a desire for justice? God tells us that eternal torment awaits the wicked. He also demonstrates a pronounced affection for those who prove unwilling to let Him do all the work."

Marguerite expressed the opinion that justice was a fine thing indeed, and that a man such as myself would always labor in its behalf. She fell silent and regarded me with what on any night previous I would have seen as tender concern. Though I had not yet so informed her, she declared, the Benedict Arnold must have been one of my juniors, for no other employee could injure me so greatly. Which was the traitor?

"As yet I do not know," I said. "But once again I must be grateful for your grasp of my concerns. Soon I will put into position the bear traps which will result in the fiend's exposure. Unfortunately, my dear, this task will demand all of my energy over at least the next several days. Until the task is accomplished, it will be necessary for me to camp out in the ———— Hotel." I named the site of her assignations with Graham Leeson.

A subtle, momentary darkening of the eyes, her first genuine response of the evening, froze my heart as I set the bear trap into place. "I know, the ————'s vulgarity deepens with every passing week, but Gilligan's apartment is but a few doors north, the Captain's one block south. Once my investigators have installed their electronic devices, I shall be privy to every secret they possess. Might you not enjoy spending several days at Green Chimneys? The servants have the month off, but you might enjoy the solitude there more than you would being alone in town."

Green Chimneys, our country estate on a bluff above the Hudson River, lay two hours away. Marguerite's delight in the house had inspired me to construct on the grounds a fully equipped recording studio, where she typically spent days on end, trying out new "songs."

Charmingly, she thanked me for my consideration and said that she would enjoy a few days in seclusion at Green Chimneys. After I had exposed the traitor, I was to telephone her with the summons home. Accommodating on the surface, vile beneath, these words brought an anticipatory tinge of pleasure to her face, a delicate heightening of her beauty I would have, very likely *had*, misconstrued on earlier occasions. Any appetite I might have had disappeared before a visitation of nausea, and I announced myself exhausted. Marguerite intensified my discomfort by calling me her poor darling. I staggered to my bedroom, locked the door, threw off my clothes, and dropped into bed to endure a sleepless night.

I would never see my wife again.

2

Sometime after first light I had attained an uneasy slumber; finding it impossible to will myself out of bed on awakening, I relapsed into the same restless sleep. By the time I appeared within the dining room, Mr. Moncrieff, as well chilled as a good Chardonnay, informed me that madame had departed for the country some twenty minutes before. Despite the hour, did sir wish to breakfast? I consulted, trepidatiously, my wristwatch. It was ten-thirty: my unvarying practice was to arise at five-thirty, breakfast soon after, and arrive in my office well before seven. I rushed downstairs and, as soon as I slid into the backseat of the limousine, forbade awkward queries by pressing the button to raise the window between the driver and myself.

No such mechanism could shield me from Mrs. Rampage, my secretary, who thrust her head around the door a moment after I had expressed my desire for a hearty breakfast of poached eggs, bacon, and whole-wheat toast from the executive dining room. All calls and appointments were to be postponed or otherwise put off until the completion of my repast. Mrs. Rampage had informed me that two men without appointments had been awaiting my arrival since eight A.M. and asked if I would consent to see them immediately. I told her not to be absurd. The door to the outer world swung to admit her beseeching head. "Please," she said. "I don't know who they are, but they're *frightening* everybody."

This remark clarified all. Earlier than anticipated, Charlie-Charlie Rackett had deputized two men capable of seriousness when seriousness was called for. "I beg your pardon," I said. "Send them in."

Mrs. Rampage withdrew to lead into my sanctum two stout, stocky, short, dark-haired men. My spirits had taken wing the moment I beheld these fellows shouldering through the door, and I rose smiling to my feet. My secretary muttered an introduction, baffled as much by my cordiality as by her ignorance of my visitors' names.

"It is quite all right," I said. "All is in order, all is in train." New Covenant had just walked in.

Barnie-slyness, barnie-freedom, shone from their great round gap-toothed faces: in precisely the manner I remembered, these two suggested mocking peasant violence scantily disguised by an equally mocking impersonation of convention. Small wonder that they had intimidated Mrs. Rampage and her underlings, for their nearest exposure to a like phenomenon had been with our musicians, and when offstage they were pale, emaciated fellows of little physical vitality. Clothed in black suits, white shirts, and black neckties, holding their black derbies by their brims and turning their gappy smiles back and forth between Mrs. Rampage and myself, these barnies had evidently been loose in the world for some time. They were perfect for my task. *You will be irritated by their country manners, you will be annoyed by their native insubordination,* I told myself, *but you will never find men more suitable, so grant them what latitude they need.* I directed Mrs. Rampage to cancel all telephone calls and appointments for the next hour.

The door closed, and we were alone. Each of the black-suited darlings snapped a business card from his right jacket pocket and extended it to me with a twirl of the fingers. One card read:

MR. CLUBB AND MR. CUFF
Private Detectives Extraordinaire
Mr. Clubb

and the other:

MR. CLUBB AND MR. CUFF
Private Detectives Extraordinaire
Mr. Cuff

I inserted the cards into a pocket and expressed my delight at making their acquaintance.

"Becoming aware of your situation," said Mr. Clubb, "we preferred to report as quickly as we could."

"Entirely commendable," I said. "Will you gentlemen please sit down?"

"We prefer to stand," said Mr. Clubb.

"I trust you will not object if I again take my chair," I said, and did so. "To be honest, I am reluctant to describe the whole of my problem. It is a personal matter, therefore painful."

"It is a domestic matter," said Mr. Cuff.

I stared at him. He stared back with the sly imperturbability of his kind.

"Mr. Cuff," I said, "you have made a reasonable and, as it

happens, an accurate supposition, but in the future you will please refrain from speculation."

"Pardon my plain way of speaking, sir, but I was not speculating," he said. "Marital disturbances are domestic by nature."

"All too domestic, one might say," put in Mr. Clubb. "In the sense of pertaining to the home. As we have so often observed, you find your greatest pain right smack-dab in the living room, as it were."

"Which is a somewhat politer fashion of naming another room altogether." Mr. Cuff appeared to suppress a surge of barnie-glee.

Alarmingly, Charlie-Charlie had passed along altogether too much information, especially since the information in question should not have been in his possession. For an awful moment I imagined that the dismissed investigator had spoken to Charlie-Charlie. The man may have broadcast my disgrace to every person encountered on his final journey out of my office, inside the public elevator, thereafter even to the shoeshine "boys" and cup-rattling vermin lining the streets. It occurred to me that I might be forced to have the man silenced. Symmetry would then demand the silencing of valuable Charlie-Charlie. The inevitable next step would resemble a full-scale massacre.

My faith in Charlie-Charlie banished these fantasies by suggesting an alternate scenario and enabled me to endure the next utterance.

Mr. Clubb said, "Which in plainer terms would be to say the bedroom."

After speaking to my faithful spy, the Private Detectives Extraordinaire had taken the initiative by acting as if *already employed* and following Marguerite to her afternoon assignation at the —— Hotel. Here, already, was the insubordination I had foreseen, but instead of the expected annoyance I felt a thoroughgoing gratitude for the two men leaning slightly toward me, their animal senses alert to every nuance of my response. That they had come to my office armed with the essential secret absolved me from embarrassing explanations; blessedly, the hideous photographs would remain concealed in the bottom drawer.

"Gentlemen," I said, "I applaud your initiative."

They stood at ease. "Then we have an understanding," said Mr. Clubb. "At various times, various matters come to our attention. At these times we prefer to conduct ourselves according to the wishes of our employer, regardless of difficulty."

"Agreed," I said. "However, from this point forward I must insist—"

A rap at the door cut short my admonition. Mrs. Rampage brought in a coffeepot and cup, a plate beneath a silver cover, a rack with four slices of toast, two jam pots, silverware, a linen napkin, and a glass of water, and came to a halt some five or six feet short of the barnies. A sinfully arousing smell of butter and bacon emanated from the tray. Mrs. Rampage deliberated between placing my breakfast on the table to her left or venturing into proximity to my guests by bringing the tray to my desk. I gestured her forward, and she tacked wide to port and homed in on the desk. "All is in order, all is in train," I said. She nodded and backed out—literally walked backwards until she reached the door, groped for the knob, and vanished.

I removed the cover from the plate containing two poached eggs in a cup-sized bowl, four crisp rashers of bacon, and a mound of home-fried potatoes all the more welcome for being a surprise gift from our chef.

"And now, fellows, with your leave I shall—"

For the second time my sentence was cut off in midflow. A thick barnie-hand closed upon the handle of the coffeepot and proceeded to fill the cup. Mr. Clubb transported my coffee to his lips, smacked appreciatively at the taste, then took up a toast slice and plunged it like a dagger into my eggcup, releasing a thick yellow suppuration. He crunched the dripping toast between his teeth.

At that moment, when mere annoyance passed into dumb-founded ire, I might have sent them packing despite my earlier resolution, for Mr. Clubb's violation of my breakfast was as good as an announcement that he and his partner respected none of the conventional boundaries and would indulge in boorish, even disgusting behavior. I very nearly did send them packing, and both of them knew it. They awaited my reaction, whatever it should be. Then I understood that I was being tested, and half of my insight was that ordering them off would be a failure of imagination. I had asked Charlie-Charlie to send me serious men, not Boy Scouts, and in the rape of my breakfast were depths and dimensions of seriousness I had never suspected. In that instant of comprehension, I believe, I virtually knew all that was to come, down to the last detail, and gave a silent assent. My next insight was that the moment when I might have dismissed these fellows with a conviction of perfect rectitude had just passed, and with the sense of opening myself to unpredictable adventures I turned to Mr. Cuff. He lifted a rasher from my plate, folded it within a slice of toast, and displayed the result.

"Here are our methods in action," he said. "We prefer not to go hungry while you gorge yourself, speaking freely, for the one reason that all of this stuff represents what you ate every morning when you were a kid." Leaving me to digest this shapeless utterance, he bit into his impromptu sandwich and sent golden-brown crumbs showering to the carpet.

"For as the important, abstemious man you are now," said Mr. Clubb, "what do you eat in the mornings?"

"Toast and coffee," I said. "That's about it."

"But in childhood?"

"Eggs," I said. "Scrambled or fried, mainly. And bacon. Home fries too." Every fatty, cholesterol-crammed ounce of which, I forbore to add, had been delivered by barnie-hands directly from barnie-farms. I looked at the rigid bacon, the glistening potatoes, the mess in the eggcup. My stomach lurched.

"We prefer," Mr. Clubb said, "that you follow your true preferences instead of muddying mind and stomach by gobbling this crap in search of an inner peace which never existed in the first place, if you can be honest with yourself." He leaned over the desk and picked up the plate. His partner snatched a second piece of bacon and wrapped it within a second slice of toast. Mr. Clubb began working on the eggs, and Mr. Cuff grabbed a handful of home-fried potatoes. Mr. Clubb dropped the empty eggcup, finished his coffee, refilled the cup, and handed it to Mr. Cuff, who had just finished licking the residue of fried potato from his free hand.

I removed the third slice of toast from the rack. Forking home fries into his mouth, Mr. Clubb winked at me. I bit into the toast and considered the two little pots of jam, greengage, I think, and rosehip. Mr. Clubb waggled a finger. I contented myself with the last of the toast. After a while I drank from the glass of water. All in all I felt reasonably satisfied and, but for the deprivation of my customary cup of coffee, content with my decision. I glanced in some irritation at Mr. Cuff. He drained his cup, then tilted into it the third and final measure from the pot and offered it to me. "Thank you," I said. Mr. Cuff picked up the pot of greengage jam and sucked out its contents, loudly. Mr. Clubb did the same with the rosehip. They sent their tongues into the corners of the jam pots and cleaned out whatever adhered to the sides. Mr. Cuff burped. Overlappingly, Mr. Clubb burped.

"Now, that is what I call by the name of breakfast, Mr. Clubb," said Mr. Cuff. "Are we in agreement?"

"Deeply," said Mr. Clubb. "That is what I call by the name of breakfast now, what I have called by the name of breakfast in the past, and what I shall continue to call by that sweet name on every morning in the future." He turned to me and took his time, sucking first one tooth, then another. "Our morning meal, sir, consists of that simple fare with which we begin the day, except when in all good faith we wind up sitting in a waiting room with our stomachs growling because our future client has chosen to skulk in late for work." He inhaled. "Which was for the same exact reason which brought him to our attention in the first place and for which we went without in order to offer him our assistance. Which is, begging your pardon, sir, the other reason for which you ordered a breakfast you would ordinarily rather starve than eat, and all I ask before we get down to the business at hand is that you might begin to entertain the possibility that simple men like ourselves might possibly understand a thing or two."

"I see that you are faithful fellows," I began.

"Faithful as dogs," broke in Mr. Clubb.

"And that you understand my position," I continued.

"Down to its smallest particulars," he interrupted again. "We are on a long journey."

"And so it follows," I pressed on, "that you must also understand that no further initiatives may be taken without my express consent."

These last words seemed to raise a disturbing echo, of what I could not say, but an echo nonetheless, and my ultimatum failed to achieve the desired effect. Mr. Clubb smiled and said, "We intend to follow your inmost desires with the faithfulness, as I have said, of trusted dogs, for one of our sacred duties is that of bringing these to fulfillment, as evidenced, begging your pardon, sir, in the matter of the breakfast our actions spared you from gobbling up and sickening yourself with. Before you protest, sir, please let me put to you the question of you how you think you would be feeling right now if you had eaten that greasy stuff all by yourself?"

The straightforward truth announced itself and demanded utterance. "Poisoned," I said. After a second's pause, I added, "Disgusted."

"Yes, for you are a better man than you know. Imagine the situation. Allow yourself to picture what would have transpired had Mr. Cuff and myself not acted on your behalf. As your heart throbbed and your veins groaned, you would have taken in that while you were stuffing yourself the two of us stood hungry before you. You would have remembered that good woman informing you that we had patiently awaited your arrival since eight this morning, and at that point, sir, you would have experienced a self-disgust which would forever have tainted our relationship. From that point forth, sir, you would have been incapable of receiving the full benefits of our services."

I stared at the twinkling barnie. "Are you saying that if I had eaten my breakfast you would have refused to work for me?"

"You did eat your breakfast. The rest was ours."

This statement was so literally true that I burst into laughter and said, "Then I must thank you for saving me from myself. Now that you may accept employment, please inform me of the rates for your services."

"We have no rates," said Mr. Clubb.

"We prefer to leave compensation to the client," said Mr. Cuff.

This was crafty even by barnie-standards, but I knew a countermove. "What is the greatest sum you have ever been awarded for a single job?"

"Six hundred thousand dollars," said Mr. Clubb.

"And the smallest?"

"Nothing, zero, *nada*, zilch," said the same gentleman.

"And your feelings as to the disparity?"

"None," said Mr. Clubb. "What we are given is the correct amount. When the time comes, you shall know the sum to the penny."

To myself I said, *So I shall, and it shall be nothing;* to them, "We must devise a method by which I may pass along suggestions as I monitor your ongoing progress. Our future consultations should take place in anonymous public places on the order of street corners, public parks, diners, and the like. I must never be seen in your office."

"You must not, you could not," said Mr. Clubb. "We would prefer to install ourselves here within the privacy and seclusion of your own beautiful office."

"Here?" He had once again succeeded in dumbfounding me.

"Our installation within the client's work space proves so advantageous as to overcome all initial objections," said Mr. Cuff.

"And in this case, sir, we would occupy but the single corner behind me where the table stands against the window. We would come and go by means of your private elevator, exercise our natural functions in your private bathroom, and have our simple meals sent in from your kitchen. You would suffer no interference or awkwardness in the course of your business. So we prefer to do our job here, where we can do it best."

"You prefer to move in with me," I said, giving equal weight to every word.

"Prefer it to declining the offer of our help, thereby forcing you, sir, to seek the aid of less reliable individuals."

Several factors, first among them being the combination of delay, difficulty, and risk involved in finding replacements for the pair before me, led me to give further thought to this absurdity. Charlie-Charlie, a fellow of wide acquaintance among society's shadow-side, had sent me his best. Any others would be inferior. It was true that Mr. Clubb and Mr. Cuff could enter and leave my office unseen, granting us a greater degree of security possible in diners and public parks. There remained an insuperable problem.

"All you say may be true, but my partners and clients alike enter this office daily. How do I explain the presence of two strangers?"

"That is easily done, Mr. Cuff, is it not?" said Mr. Clubb.

"Indeed it is," said his partner. "Our experience has given us two infallible and complementary methods. The first of these is the installation of a screen to shield us from the view of those who visit this office."

I said, "You intend to hide behind a screen."

"During those periods when it is necessary for us to be on-site."

"Are you and Mr. Clubb capable of perfect silence? Do you never shuffle your feet, do you never cough?"

"You could justify our presence within these sacrosanct confines by the single manner most calculated to draw over Mr. Clubb and myself a blanket of respectable, anonymous impersonality."

"You wish to be introduced as my lawyers?" I asked.

"I invite you to consider a word," said Mr. Cuff. "Hold it steadily in your mind. Remark the inviolability which distinguishes those it identifies, measure its effect upon those who hear it. The word of which I speak, sir, is this: *consultant.*"

I opened my mouth to object and found I could not.

Every profession occasionally must draw upon the resources of impartial experts—consultants. Every institution of every kind has known the visitations of persons answerable only to the top and given access to all departments—consultants. Consultants are *supposed* to be invisible. Again I opened my mouth, this time to say, "Gentlemen, we are in business." I picked up my telephone and asked Mrs. Rampage to order immediate delivery from Bloomingdale's of an ornamental screen and then to remove the breakfast tray.

Eyes agleam with approval, Mr. Clubb and Mr. Cuff stepped forward to shake my hand.

"We are in business," said Mr. Clubb.

"Which is by way of saying," said Mr. Cuff, "jointly dedicated to a sacred purpose."

Mrs. Rampage entered, circled to the side of my desk, and gave my visitors a glance of deep-dyed wariness. Mr. Clubb and Mr. Cuff clasped their hands before them and looked heavenward. "About the screen," she said. "Bloomingdale's wants to know if you would prefer one six feet high in a black and red Chinese pattern or one ten feet high, Art Deco, in ochres, teals, and taupes."

My barnies nodded together at the heavens. "The latter, please, Mrs. Rampage," I said. "Have it delivered this afternoon, regardless of cost, and place it beside the table for the use of these gentlemen, Mr. Clubb and Mr. Cuff, highly regarded consultants to the financial industry. That table shall be their command post."

"Consultants," she said. "Oh."

The barnies dipped their heads. Much relaxed, Mrs. Rampage asked if I expected great changes in the future.

"We shall see," I said. "I wish you to extend every cooperation to these gentlemen. I need not remind you, I know, that
change is the first law of life."

She disappeared, no doubt on a beeline for her telephone.

Mr. Clubb stretched his arms above his head. "The preliminaries are out of the way, and we can move to the job at hand. You,
sir, have been most *exceedingly,* most *grievously* wronged. Do I
overstate?"

"You do not," I said.

"Would I overstate to assert that you have been injured, that
you have suffered a devastating wound?"

"No, you would not," I responded, with some heat.

Mr. Clubb settled a broad haunch upon the surface of my
desk. His face had taken on a grave, sweet serenity. "You seek
redress. Redress, sir, is a *correction,* but it is nothing more. You
imagine that it restores a lost balance, but it does nothing of the
kind. A crack has appeared on the earth's surface, causing wide-
spread loss of life. From all sides are heard the cries of the
wounded and dying. It is as though the earth itself has suffered an
injury akin to yours, is it not?"

He had expressed a feeling I had not known to be mine until
that moment, and my voice trembled as I said, "It is exactly."

"Exactly," he said. "For that reason I said *correction* rather
than *restoration.* Restoration is never possible. Change is the first
law of life."

"Yes, of course," I said, trying to get down to brass tacks.

Mr. Clubb hitched his buttock more comprehensively onto
the desk. "What will happen will indeed happen, but we prefer our
clients to acknowledge from the first that, apart from human
desires being a deep and messy business, outcomes are full of surprises. If you choose to repay one disaster with an equal and opposite disaster, we would reply, in our country fashion, there's a calf
that won't suck milk."

I said, "I know I can't pay my wife back in kind, how
could I?"

"Once we begin," he said, "we cannot undo our actions."

"Why should I want them undone?" I asked.

Mr. Clubb drew up his legs and sat cross-legged before me. Mr. Cuff placed a meaty hand on my shoulder. "I suppose there is no dispute," said Mr. Clubb, "that the injury you seek to redress is the adulterous behavior of your spouse."

Mr. Cuff's hand tightened on my shoulder.

"You wish that my partner and myself punish your spouse."

"I didn't hire you to read her bedtime stories," I said.

Mr. Cuff twice smacked my shoulder, painfully, in what I took to be approval.

"Are we assuming that her punishment is to be of a physical nature?" asked Mr. Clubb. His partner gave my shoulder another all-too-hearty squeeze.

"What other kind is there?" I asked, pulling away from Mr. Cuff's hand.

The hand closed on me again, and Mr. Clubb said, "Punishment of a mental or psychological nature. We could, for example, torment her with mysterious telephone calls and anonymous letters. We could use any of a hundred devices to make it impossible for her to sleep. Threatening incidents could be staged so often as to put her in a permanent state of terror."

"I want physical punishment," I said.

"That is our constant preference," he said. "Results are swifter and more conclusive when physical punishment is used. But again, we have a wide spectrum from which to choose. Are we looking for mild physical pain, real suffering, or something in between, on the order of, say, broken arms or legs?"

I thought of the change in Marguerite's eyes when I named the ———— Hotel. "Real suffering."

Another bone-crunching blow to my shoulder from Mr. Cuff and a wide, gappy smile from Mr. Clubb greeted this remark. "You, sir, are our favorite type of client," said Mr. Clubb. "A fellow who knows what he wants and is unafraid to put it into words. This suffering, now, did you wish it in brief or extended form?"

"Extended," I said. "I must say that I appreciate your thoughtfulness in consulting with me like this. I was not quite sure what I wanted of you when first I requested your services, but you have helped me become perfectly clear about it."

"That is our function," he said. "Now, sir. The extended form of real suffering permits two different conclusions, gradual cessation or termination. Which is your preference?"

I opened my mouth and closed it. I opened it again and stared at the ceiling. Did I want these men to murder my wife? No. Yes. No. Yes, but only after making sure that the unfaithful trollop understood exactly why she had to die. No, surely an extended term of excruciating torture would restore the world to proper balance. Yet I wanted the witch dead. But then I would be order-ing these barnies to kill her. "At the moment I cannot make that decision," I said. Irresistibly, my eyes found the bottom drawer containing the file of obscene photographs. "I'll let you know my decision after we have begun."

Mr. Cuff dropped his hand, and Mr. Clubb nodded with exaggerated, perhaps ironic, slowness. "And what of your rival, the seducer, sir? Do we have any wishes in regard to that gentleman, sir?"

The way these fellows could sharpen one's thinking was truly remarkable. "I most certainly do," I said. "What she gets, he gets. Fair is fair."

"Indeed, sir," said Mr. Clubb, "and, if you will permit me, sir, only fair is fair. And fairness demands that before we go any deeper into the particulars of the case we must examine the evi-dence as presented to yourself, and when I speak of fairness, sir, I refer to fairness particularly to yourself, for only the evidence seen by your own eyes can permit us to view this matter through them."

Again, I looked helplessly down at the bottom drawer. "That

will not be necessary. You will find my wife at our country estate, Green . . ."

My voice trailed off as Mr. Cuff's hand ground into my shoulder while he bent down and opened the drawer.

"Begging to differ," said Mr. Clubb, "but we are now and again in a better position than the client to determine what is necessary. Remember, sir, that while shame unshared is toxic to the soul, shame shared is the beginning of health. Besides, it only hurts for a little while."

Mr. Cuff drew the file from the drawer.

"My partner will concur that your inmost wish is that we examine the evidence," said Mr. Clubb. "Else you would not have signaled its location. We would prefer to have your explicit command to do so, but in the absence of explicit, implicit serves just about as well."

I gave an impatient, ambiguous wave of the hand, a gesture they cheerfully misunderstood.

"Then all is . . . how do you put it, sir? 'All is . . .' "

"All is in order, all is in train," I muttered.

"Just so. We have ever found it beneficial to establish a common language with our clients, in order to conduct ourselves within terms enhanced by their constant usage in the dialogue between us." He took the file from Mr. Cuff's hands. "We shall examine the contents of this folder at the table across the room. After the examination has been completed, my partner and I shall deliberate. And then, sir, we shall return for further instructions."

They strolled across the office and took adjoining chairs on the near side of the table, presenting me with two identical, wide, black-clothed backs. Their hats went to either side, the file between them. Attempting unsuccessfully to look away, I lifted my receiver and asked my secretary who, if anyone, had called in the interim and what appointments had been made for the morning.

Mr. Clubb opened the folder and leaned forward to inspect the topmost photograph.

My secretary informed me that Marguerite had telephoned

from the road with an inquiry concerning my health. Mr. Clubb's back and shoulders trembled with what I assumed was the shock of disgust. One of the scions was due at two P.M., and at four a cryptic gentleman would arrive. By their works shall ye know them, and Mrs. Rampage proved herself a diligent soul by asking if I wished her to place a call to Green Chimneys at three o'clock. Mr. Clubb thrust a photograph in front of Mr. Cuff. "I think not," I said. "Anything else?" She told me that Gilligan had expressed a desire to see me privately—meaning, without the Captain—sometime during the morning. A murmur came from the table. "Gilligan can wait," I said, and the murmur, expressive, I had thought, of dismay and sympathy, rose in volume and revealed itself as amusement.

They were chuckling—even chortling!

I replaced the telephone and said, "Gentlemen, please, your laughter is insupportable." The potential effect of this remark was undone by its being lost within a surge of coarse laughter. I believe that something else was at that moment lost . . . some dimension of my soul . . . an element akin to pride . . . akin to dignity . . . but whether the loss was for good or ill, then I could not say. For some time, in fact an impossibly lengthy time, they found cause for laughter in the wretched photographs. My occasional attempts to silence them went unheard as they passed the dread photographs back and forth, discarding some instantly and to others returning for a second, even a third, even a fourth and fifth, perusal.

And then at last the barnies reared back, uttered a few nostalgic chirrups of laughter, and returned the photographs to the folder. They were still twitching with remembered laughter, still flicking happy tears from their eyes, as they sauntered grinning back across the office and tossed the file onto my desk. "Ah, me, sir, a delightful experience," said Mr. Clubb. "Nature in all her lusty romantic splendor, one might say. Remarkably stimulating, I could add. Correct, sir?"

"I hadn't expected you fellows to be stimulated to mirth," I grumbled, ramming the foul thing into the drawer and out of view.

"Laughter is merely a portion of the stimulation to which I refer," he said. "Unless my sense of smell has led me astray, a thing I fancy it has yet to do, you could not but feel another sort of arousal altogether before these pictures, am I right?"

I refused to respond to this sally but feared that I felt the blood rising to my cheeks. Here they were again, the slugs and maggots.

"We are all brothers under the skin," said Mr. Clubb. "Remember my words. Shame unshared poisons the soul. And besides, it only hurts for a little while."

Now I could not respond. What was the "it" which hurt only for a little while—the pain of cuckoldry, the mystery of my shameful response to the photographs, or the horror of the barnies knowing what I had done?

"You will find it helpful, sir, to repeat after me: *It only hurts for a little while.*"

"It only hurts for a little while," I said, and the naive phrase reminded me that they were only barnies after all.

"Spoken like a child," Mr. Clubb most annoyingly said, "in, as it were, the tones and accents of purest innocence," and then righted matters by asking where Marguerite might be found. Had I not mentioned a country place named Green . . . ?

"Green Chimneys," I said, shaking off the unpleasant impression which the preceding few seconds had made upon me. "You will find it at the end of ——— Lane, turning off ——— Street just north of the town of ———. The four green chimneys easily visible above the hedge along ——— Lane are your landmark, though as it is the only building in sight you can hardly mistake it for another. My wife left our place in the city just after ten this morning, so she should be getting there"—I looked at my watch—"in thirty to forty-five minutes. She will unlock the front gate, but she will not relock it once she has passed through, for she never does. The woman does not have the self-preservation of a sparrow. Once she has entered the estate, she will travel up the drive and open the door of the garage with an electronic device. This door, I assure you, will remain open, and the door she will take into the house will not be locked."

"But there are maids and cooks and laundresses and boot-boys and suchlike to consider," said Mr. Cuff. "Plus a majordomo to conduct the entire orchestra and go around rattling the doors to make sure they're locked. Unless all of these parties are to be absent on account of the annual holiday."

"The servants have the month off," I said.

"A most suggestive consideration," said Mr. Clubb. "You possess a devilish clever mind, sir."

"Perhaps," I said, grateful for the restoration of the proper balance. "Marguerite will have stopped along the way for groceries and other essentials, so she will first carry the bags into the kitchen, which is the first room to the right off the corridor from the garage. Then I suppose she will take the staircase up to her bedroom and air it out." I took pen and paper from my topmost drawer and sketched the layout of the house as I spoke. "She may go around to the library, the morning room, and the drawing room, opening the shutters and a few windows. Somewhere during this process, she is likely to use the telephone. After that, she will leave the house by the rear entrance and take the path along the top of the bluff to a long, low building which looks like this."

I drew in the well-known outlines of the studio in its nest of trees on the bluff above the Hudson. "It is a recording studio I had built for her convenience. She may well plan to spend the entire afternoon inside it, and you will know if she is there by the lights." Then I could see Marguerite smiling to herself as she fitted her key into the lock on the studio door, see her let herself in and reach automatically for the light switch, and a wave of emotion rendered me speechless.

Mr. Clubb rescued me by asking, "It is your feeling, sir, that when the lady stops to use the telephone she will be placing a call to that energetic gentleman?"

"Yes, of course," I said, only barely refraining from adding *you dolt*. "She will seize the earliest opportunity to inform him of their good fortune."

He nodded with the extravagant caution I was startled to recognize from my own dealings with backward clients. "Let us pause to see all round the matter, sir. Will the lady wish to leave a suspicious entry in your telephone records? Isn't it more likely that the person she telephones will be you, sir? The call to the athletic gentleman will already have been placed, according to my way of seeing things, either from the roadside or the telephone in the grocery where you have her stop to pick up her essentials."

Though disliking these references to Leeson's physical condition, I admitted that he might have a point.

"So, in that case, sir, and I know that a mind as quick as yours has already overtaken mine, you would want to express yourself with the utmost cordiality when the missus calls again, so as not to tip your hand in even the slightest way. But that, I'm sure, goes without saying, after all you have been through, sir."

Without bothering to acknowledge this, I said, "Shouldn't you fellows really be leaving? No sense in wasting time, after all."

"Precisely why we shall wait here until the end of the day," said Mr. Clubb. "In cases of this unhappy sort, we find it more effective to deal with both parties at once, acting in concert when they are in prime condition to be taken by surprise. The gentleman is liable to leave his place of work at the end of the day, which implies to me that he is unlikely to appear at your lovely country place at any time before seven this evening, or, which is more likely, eight. At this time of the year, there is still enough light at nine o'clock to enable us to conceal our vehicle on the grounds, enter the house, and begin our business. At eleven o'clock, sir, we shall call with our initial report and request additional instructions."

I asked the fellow if he meant to idle away the entire afternoon in my office while I conducted my business.

"Mr. Cuff and I are never idle, sir. While you conduct your

business, we will be doing the same, laying out our plans, refining our strategies, choosing our methods and the order of their use."

"Oh, all right," I said, "but I trust you'll be quiet about it."

At that moment, Mrs. Rampage buzzed to say that Gilligan was before her, requesting to see me immediately, proof that bush telegraph is a more efficient means of spreading information than any newspaper. I told her to send him in, and a second later the Morning Gilligan, pale of face, dark hair tousled but not as yet completely wild, came treading softly toward my desk. He pretended to be surprised that I had visitors and pantomimed an apology which incorporated the suggestion that he depart and return later. "No, no," I said, "I am delighted to see you, for this gives me the opportunity to introduce you to our new consultants, who will be working closely with me for a time."

Gilligan swallowed, glanced at me with the deepest suspicion, and extended his hand as I made the introductions. "I regret that I am unfamiliar with your work, gentlemen," he said. "Might I ask the name of your firm? Is it Locust, Bleaney, Burns, or Charter, Carter, Maxton, and Coltrane?"

By naming the two most prominent consultancies in our industry, Gilligan was assessing the thinness of the ice beneath his feet: LBB specialized in investments, CCM & C in estates and trusts. If my visitors worked for the former, he would suspect that a guillotine hung above his neck; if the latter, the Captain was liable for the chop. "Neither," I said. "Mr. Clubb and Mr. Cuff are the directors of their own concern, which covers every aspect of the trade with such tactful professionalism that it is known to but the few for whom they will consent to work."

"Excellent," Gilligan whispered, gazing in some puzzlement at the map and floor plan atop my desk. "Tip-top."

"When their findings are given to me, they shall be given to all. In the meantime, I would prefer that you say as little as possible about the matter. Though change is a law of life, we wish to avoid unnecessary alarm."

"You know that you can depend on my silence," said Morning Gilligan, and it was true, I did know that. I also knew that his alter ego, Afternoon Gilligan, would babble the news to everyone who had not already heard it from Mrs. Rampage. By six P.M., our entire industry would be pondering the information that I had called in a consultancy team of such rarefied accomplishments *that they chose to remain unknown but to the very few*. None of my colleagues could dare admit to an ignorance of Clubb & Cuff, and my reputation, already great, would increase exponentially.

To distract him from the floor plan of Green Chimneys and the rough map of my estate, I said, "I assume some business brought you here, Gilligan."

"Oh! Yes—yes—of course," he said, and with a trace of embarrassment brought to my attention the pretext for his being there, the ominous plunge in value of an overseas fund in which we had advised one of his musicians to invest. Should we recommend selling the fund before more money was lost, or was it wisest to hold on? Only a minute was required to decide that the musician should retain his share of the fund until next quarter, when we anticipated a general improvement, but both Gilligan and I were aware that this recommendation could easily have been handled by telephone, and soon he was moving toward the door, smiling at the barnies in a pathetic display of false confidence.

The telephone rang a moment after the detectives had returned to the table. Mr. Clubb said, "Your wife, sir. Remember: the utmost cordiality." Here was false confidence, I thought, of an entirely different sort. I picked up the receiver to hear Mrs. Rampage tell me that my wife was on the line.

What followed was a banal conversation of the utmost *duplicity*. Marguerite pretended that my sudden departure from the dinner table and my late arrival at the office had caused her to fear for my health. I pretended that all was well, apart from a slight indigestion. Had the drive up been peaceful? Yes, the highways had been surprisingly empty. How was the house? A little musty, but otherwise fine. She had never quite realized, she said, how very large Green Chimneys was until she walked around in it, knowing she was going to be there alone. Had she been out to the studio? No, but she was looking forward to getting a lot of work done over the next three or four days and thought she would be working every night, as well. (Implicit in this remark was the information that I should be unable to reach her, the studio being without a telephone.) After a moment of awkward silence, she said, "I suppose it is too early for you to have identified your traitor." It was, I said, but the process would begin that evening. "I'm so sorry you have to go through this," she said. "I know how painful the discovery was for you, and I can only begin to imagine how angry you must be, but I hope you will be merciful. No amount of punishment can undo the damage, and if you try to exact retribution you will only injure yourself. The man is going to lose his job and his reputation. Isn't that punishment enough?" After a few meaningless pleasantries the conversation had clearly come to an end, although we still had yet to say good-bye. Then an odd thing happened to me. I nearly said, *Lock all the doors and windows tonight and let no one in.* I nearly said, *You are in grave danger and must come home.* With these words rising in my throat, I looked across the room at Mr. Clubb and Mr. Cuff, and Mr. Clubb winked at me. I heard myself bidding Marguerite farewell, and then heard her hang up her telephone.

"Well done, sir," said Mr. Clubb. "To aid Mr. Cuff and myself in the preparation of our inventory, can you tell us if you keep certain staples at Green Chimneys?"

"Staples?" I said, thinking he was referring to foodstuffs.

"Rope?" he asked. "Tools, especially pliers, hammers, and screwdrivers? A good saw? A variety of knives? Are there by any chance firearms?"

"No firearms," I said. "I believe all the other items you mention can be found in the house."

"Rope and tool chest in the basement, knives in the kitchen?"

"Yes," I said, "precisely." I had not ordered these barnies to murder my wife, I reminded myself; I had drawn back from that

precipice. By the time I went into the executive dining room for
my luncheon, I felt sufficiently restored to give Charlie-Charlie
that ancient symbol of approval, the thumbs-up sign.

3

When I returned to my office the screen had been set in
place, shielding from view the detectives in their preparations but
in no way muffling the rumble of comments and laughter they
brought to the task. "Gentlemen," I said in a voice loud enough
to be heard behind the screen—a most unsuitable affair decorated
with a pattern of alternating ocean liners, martini glasses, champagne bottles, and cigarettes—"you must modulate your voices, as
I have business to conduct here as well as you." There came a
somewhat softer rumble of acquiescence. I took my seat to dis-
cover my bottom desk drawer pulled out, the folder absent. Another roar of laughter jerked me once again to my feet.

I came around the side of the screen and stopped short. The
table lay concealed beneath drifts and mounds of yellow legal paper covered with lists of words and drawings of stick figures in
varying stages of dismemberment. Strewn through the yellow
pages were the photographs, loosely divided into those in which
either Marguerite or Graham Leeson provided the principal focus.
Crude genitalia had been drawn, without reference to either
party's actual gender, over and atop both of them. Aghast, I leaned
over and began gathering up the defaced photographs. "I must
insist . . ." I said. "I really must insist, you know. . . ."

Mr. Clubb immobilized my wrist with one hand and extracted the photographs with the other. "We prefer to work in our
time-honored fashion," he said. "Our methods may be unusual,
but they are ours. But before you take up the afternoon's occupa-
tions, sir, can you tell us if items on the handcuff order might be
found in the house?"

"No," I said. Mr. Cuff pulled a yellow page before him and wrote *handcuffs*.

"Chains?" asked Mr. Clubb.

"No chains," I said, and Mr. Cuff added *chains* to his list.

"That is all for the moment," said Mr. Clubb, and released me.

I took a step backwards and massaged my wrist, which stung as if from rope burn. "You speak of your methods," I said, "and I understand that you have them. But what can be the purpose of defacing my photographs in this grotesque fashion?"

"Sir," said Mr. Clubb in a stern, teacherly voice, "where you speak of defacing, we use the term *enhancement*. Enhancement is a tool we find vital to the method known by the name of Visualization."

I retired defeated to my desk. At five minutes before two, Mrs. Rampage informed me that the Captain and his scion, a thirty-year-old inheritor of a great family fortune named Mr. Chester Montfort d'M——, awaited my pleasure. Putting Mrs. Rampage on hold, I called out, "Please do give me absolute quiet, now. A client is on his way in."

First to appear was the Captain, his tall, rotund form as alert as a pointer's in a grouse field as he led in the taller, inexpressibly languid figure of Mr. Chester Montfort d'M——, a person marked in every inch of his being by great ease, humor, and stupidity. The Captain froze to gape horrified at the screen, but Montfort d'M—— continued round him to shake my hand and say, "Have to tell you, I like that thingamabob over there immensely. Reminds me of a similar thingamabob at the Beeswax Club a few years ago, whole flocks of girls used to come tumbling out. Don't suppose we're in for any unicycles and trumpets today, eh?"

The combination of the raffish screen and our client's unbridled memories brought a dangerous flush to the Captain's face, and I hastened to explain the presence of top-level consultants who preferred to pitch tent on-site, as it were, hence the installation of a screen, all the above in the service of, well, *service,* an all-important quality we . . .

"By Kitchener's mustache," said the Captain. "I remember the Beeswax Club. Don't suppose I'll ever forget the night Little Billy Pegleg jumped up and . . ." The color darkened on his cheeks, and he closed his mouth.

From behind the screen, I heard Mr. Clubb say, "Visualize *this.*" Mr. Cuff chuckled.

The Captain recovered himself and turned his sternest glare upon me. "Superb idea, consultants. A white-glove inspection tightens up any ship." His veiled glance toward the screen indicated that he had known of the presence of our "consultants" but, unlike Gilligan, had restrained himself from thrusting into my office until given legitimate reason. "That being the case, is it still quite proper that these people remain while we discuss Mr. Montfort d'M——'s confidential affairs?"

"Quite proper, I assure you," I said. "The consultants and I prefer to work in an atmosphere of complete cooperation. Indeed, this arrangement is a condition of their accepting our firm as their client."

"Indeed," said the Captain.

"Top of the tree, are they?" said Mr. Montfort d'M——. "Expect no less of you fellows. Fearful competence. *Terrifying* competence."

Mr. Cuff's voice could be heard saying, "Okay, visualize *this.*" Mr. Clubb uttered a high-pitched giggle.

"Enjoy their work," said Mr. Montfort d'M——.

"Shall we?" I gestured to their chairs. As a young man whose assets equaled four or five billion dollars (depending on the condition of the stock market, the value of real estate in half a dozen cities around the world, global warming, forest fires, and the like) our client was a catnip to the ladies, three of whom he had previously married and divorced after siring a child upon each, resulting in a great interlocking complexity of trusts, agreements, and contracts, all of which had to be reexamined on the occasion of his forthcoming wedding to a fourth young woman, named like her predecessors after a semiprecious stone. Due to the perspicacity of the Captain and myself, each new nuptial altered the terms of those previous so as to maintain our client's liability at an unvarying level. Our computers had enabled us to generate the documents well before his arrival, and all Mr. Montfort d'M—— had to do was listen to the revised terms and sign the papers, a task which generally induced a slumberous state except for those moments when a prized asset was in transition.

"Hold on, boys," he said ten minutes into our explanations, "you mean Opal has to give the racehorses to Garnet, and in return she gets the teak plantation from Turquoise, who turns around and gives Opal the ski resort in Aspen? Opal is crazy about those horses, and Turquoise just built a house."

I explained that his second wife could easily afford the purchase of a new stable with the income from the plantation, and his third would keep her new house. He bent to the task of scratching his signature on the form. A roar of laughter erupted behind the screen. The Captain glanced sideways in displeasure, and our client looked at me, blinking. "Now to the secondary trusts," I said. "As you will recall, three years ago—"

My words were cut short by the appearance of a chuckling Mr. Clubb clamping an unlighted cigar in his mouth, a legal pad in his hand, as he came toward us. The Captain and Mr. Montfort d'M—— goggled at him, and Mr. Clubb nodded. "Begging your pardon, sir, but some queries cannot wait. Pickax, sir? Dental floss? Awl?"

"No, yes, no," I said, and then introduced him to the other two men. The Captain appeared stunned, Mr. Montfort d'M—— cheerfully puzzled.

"We would prefer the existence of an attic," said Mr. Clubb.

"An attic exists," I said.

"I must admit my confusion," said the Captain. "Why is a consultant asking about awls and attics? What is dental floss to a consultant?"

"For the nonce, Captain," I said, "these gentlemen and I must communicate in a form of cipher or code, of which these are examples, but soon—"

"Plug your blowhole, Captain," broke in Mr. Clubb. "At the moment you are as useful as wind in an outhouse, always hoping you will excuse my simple way of expressing myself."

Sputtering, the Captain rose to his feet, his face rosier by far than during his involuntary reminiscence of what Little Billy Pegleg had done one night at the Beeswax Club.

"Steady on," I said, fearful of the heights of choler to which indignation could bring my portly, white-haired, but still powerful junior.

"Not on your life," bellowed the Captain. "I cannot brook . . . cannot tolerate . . . If this ill-mannered dwarf imagines excuse is possible after . . ." He raised a fist. Mr. Clubb said, "Pish tosh," and placed a hand on the nape of the Captain's neck. Instantly, the Captain's eyes rolled up, the color drained from his face, and he dropped like a sack into his chair.

"Hole in one," marveled Mr. Montfort d'M——. "World class. Old boy isn't dead, is he?"

The Captain exhaled uncertainly and licked his lips.

"With my apologies for the unpleasantness," said Mr. Clubb, "I have only two more queries at this juncture. Might we locate bedding in the aforesaid attic, and have you an implement such as a match or a lighter?"

"There are several old mattresses and bedframes in the attic," I said, "but as to matches, surely you do not . . ."

Understanding the request better than I, Mr. Montfort d'M—— extended a golden lighter and applied an inch of flame to the tip of Mr. Clubb's cigar. "Didn't think that part was code," he said. "Rules have changed? Smoking allowed?"

"From time to time during the workday my colleague and I prefer to smoke," said Mr. Clubb, expelling a reeking miasma across the desk. I had always found tobacco nauseating in its every form, and in all parts of our building smoking had, of course, long been prohibited.

"Three cheers, my man, plus three more after that," said Mr. Montfort d'M——, extracting a ridged case from an inside pocket, an absurdly phallic cigar from the case. "I prefer to smoke, too, you know, especially during these deadly conferences about who gets the pincushions and who gets the snuffboxes. Believe I'll join you in a corona." He submitted the object to a circumcision, *snick-snick,* and to my horror set it alight. "Ashtray?" I dumped paper clips from a crystal oyster shell and slid it toward him. "Mr. Clubb, is it?, Mr. Clubb, you are a fellow of wonderful accomplishments, still can't get over that marvelous whopbopaloobop on the Captain, and I'd like to ask if we could get together some evening, cigars-and-cognac kind of thing."

"We prefer to undertake one matter at a time," said Mr. Clubb. Mr. Cuff appeared beside the screen. He, too, was lighting up eight or nine inches of brown rope. "However, we welcome your appreciation and would be delighted to swap tales of derring-do at a later date."

"Very, very cool," said Mr. Montfort d'M——, "especially if you could teach me how to do the whopbopaloobop."

"This is a world full of hidden knowledge," Mr. Clubb said. "My partner and I have chosen as our sacred task the transmission of that knowledge."

"Amen," said Mr. Cuff.

Mr. Clubb bowed to my awed client and sauntered off. The Captain shook himself, rubbed his eyes, and took in the client's cigar. "My goodness," he said. "I believe . . . I can't imagine . . . heavens, is smoking permitted again? What a blessing." With that, he fumbled a cigarette from his shirt pocket, accepted a light from Mr. Montfort d'M——, and sucked in the fumes. Until that moment I had not known that the Captain was an addict of nicotine.

For the remainder of the hour a coiling layer of smoke like a low-lying cloud established itself beneath the ceiling and increased in density as it grew toward the floor while we extracted Mr. Montfort d'M——'s careless signature on the transfers and assignments. Now and again the Captain displaced one of a perpetual chain of cigarettes from his mouth to remark upon the peculiar pain in his neck. Finally I was able to send client and junior partner on their way with those words of final benediction, "All is in order, all is in train," freeing me at last to stride about my office flapping a copy of *Institutional Investor* at the cloud, a remedy our fixed windows made more symbolic than actual. The barnies further defeated the effort by wafting ceaseless billows of cigar effluvia over the screen, but as they seemed to be conducting their business in a conventionally businesslike manner I made no objection and retired in defeat to my desk for the preparations necessitated by the arrival in an hour of my next client, Mr. Arthur "This Building Is Condemned" C——, the most cryptic of all the cryptic gentlemen.

So deeply was I immersed in these preparations that only a polite cough and the supplication of "Begging your pardon, sir," brought to my awareness the presence of Mr. Clubb and Mr. Cuff before my desk. "What is it now?" I asked.

"We are, sir, in need of creature comforts," said Mr. Clubb. "Long hours of work have left us exceeding dry in the region of the mouth and throat, and the pressing sensation of thirst has made it impossible for us to maintain the concentration required to do our best."

"Meaning a drink would be greatly appreciated, sir," said Mr. Cuff.

"Of course, of course," I said. "You should have spoken earlier. I'll have Mrs. Rampage bring in a couple of bottles of water. We have San Pellegrino and Evian. Which would you prefer?"

With a smile almost menacing in its intensity, Mr. Cuff said, "We prefer drinks when we drink. *Drink* drinks, if you take my meaning."

"For the sake of the refreshment found in them," said Mr.

Clubb, ignoring my obvious dismay. "I speak of refreshment in its every aspect, from relief to the parched tongue, taste to the ready palate, warmth to the inner man, and to the highest of refreshments, that of the mind and soul. We prefer bottles of gin and bourbon, and while any decent gargle would be gratefully received, we have, like all men who partake of grape and grain, our favorite tipples. Mr. Cuff is partial to J. W. Dant bourbon, and I enjoy a glass of Bombay gin. A bucket of ice would not go amiss, and I could say the same for a case of ice-cold Old Bohemia beer. As a chaser."

"You consider it a good idea to consume alcohol before embarking on"—I sought for the correct phrase—"a mission so delicate?"

"We consider it an essential prelude. Alcohol inspires the mind and awakens the imagination. A fool dulls both by overindulgence, but up to that point, which is a highly individual matter, there is only enhancement. Through history, alcohol has been known for its sacred properties, and the both of us know during the sacrament of Holy Communion, priests and reverends happily serve as bartenders, passing out free drinks to all comers, children included."

"Besides that," I said after a pause, "I suppose you would prefer not to be compelled to quit my employment after we have made such strides together."

"We are on a great journey," he said.

I placed the order with Mrs. Rampage, and fifteen minutes later into my domain entered two ill-dressed youths laden with the requested liquors and a metal bucket in which the necks of beer bottles protruded from a bed of ice. I tipped the louts a dollar apiece, which they accepted with boorish lack of grace. Mrs. Rampage took in this activity with none of the revulsion for the polluted air and spirituous liquids I had anticipated.

The louts slouched away through the door she held open for them; the chuckling barnies disappeared from view with their refreshments; and, after fixing me for a moment of silence, her eyes alight with an expression I had never before observed in them, Mrs. Rampage ventured the amazing opinion that the recent relaxation of formalities should prove beneficial to the firm as a whole and added that, were Mr. Clubb and Mr. Cuff responsible for the reformation, they had already justified their reputation and would assuredly enhance my own.

"You believe so," I said, noting with momentarily delayed satisfaction that the effects of Afternoon Gilligan's indiscretions had already begun to declare themselves.

Employing the tactful verbal formula for *I wish to speak exactly half my mind and no more,* Mrs. Rampage said, "May I be frank, sir?"

"I depend on you to do no less," I said.

Her carriage and face at that moment became what I can only describe as girlish—years seemed to drop away from her. "I don't want to say too much, sir, and I hope you know how much everyone understands what a privilege it is to be a part of this firm." Like the Captain, but more attractively, she blushed. "Honest, I really mean that. Everybody knows that we're one of the two or three companies best at what we do."

"Thank you," I said.

"That's why I feel I can talk like this," said my ever-less-recognizable Mrs. Rampage. "Until today, everybody thought if they acted like themselves, the way they really were, you'd fire them right away. Because, and maybe I shouldn't say this, maybe I'm way out of line, sir, but it's because you always seem, well, so proper you could never forgive a person for not being as dignified as you are. Like the Captain is a heavy smoker and everybody knows it's not supposed to be permitted in this building, but a lot of companies here let their top people smoke in their offices as long as they're discreet because it shows they appreciate those people, and that's nice because it shows if you get to the top you can be appreciated, too, but here the Captain has to go all the way to the elevator and stand outside with the file clerks if he wants a cigarette. And in every other company I know the partners and important clients sometimes have a drink together and nobody thinks they're committing a terrible sin. You're a religious man, sir, we look up to you so much, but I think you're going to find that people will respect you even more once it gets out that you loosened the rules a little bit." She gave me a look in which I read that she feared having spoken too freely. "I just wanted to say that I think you're doing the right thing, sir."

What she was saying, of course, was that I was widely regarded as pompous, remote, and out of touch. "I had not known that my employees regarded me as a religious man," I said.

"Oh, we all do," she said with almost touching earnestness. "Because of the hymns."

"The hymns?"

"The ones you hum to yourself when you're working."

"Do I, indeed? Which ones?"

" 'Jesus Loves Me,' 'The Old Rugged Cross,' 'Abide With Me,' and 'Amazing Grace,' mostly. Sometimes 'Onward, Christian Soldiers.' "

Here, with a vengeance, were Temple Square and Scripture Street! Here was the Youth Bible Study Center, where the child-me had hours on end sung these same hymns during our Sunday school sessions! I did not know what to make of the new knowledge that I hummed them to myself at my desk, but it was some consolation that this unconscious habit had at least partially humanized me to my staff.

"You didn't know you did that? Oh, sir, that's so *cute*!"

Sounds of merriment from the far side of the office rescued Mrs. Rampage from the fear that this time she had truly overstepped the bounds, and she made a rapid exit. I stared after her for a moment, at first unsure how deeply I ought regret a situation in which my secretary found it possible to describe myself and my habits as *cute*, then resolving that it probably was, or eventually would be, all for the best. "All is in order, all is in train," I said to myself. "It only hurts for a little while." With that, I took my seat once more to continue delving into the elaborations of Mr. "This Building Is Condemned" C——'s financial life.

Another clink of bottle against glass and ripple of laughter brought with them the long-delayed recognition that this particular client would never consent to the presence of unknown "consultants." Unless the barnies could be removed for at least an hour, I should face the immediate loss of a substantial portion of my business.

"Fellows," I cried, "come up here now. We must address a most serious problem."

Glasses in hand, cigars nestled into the corners of their mouths, Mr. Clubb and Mr. Cuff sauntered into view. Once I had explained the issue in the most general terms, the detectives readily agreed to absent themselves for the required period. Where might they install themselves? "My bathroom," I said. "It has a small library attached, with a desk, a work table, leather chairs and sofa, a billiard table, a large-screen cable television set, and a bar. Since you have not yet had your luncheon, you may wish to order whatever you like from the kitchen."

Five minutes later, bottles, glasses, hats, and mounds of paper arranged on the bathroom table, the bucket of beer beside it, I exited through the concealed door to the right of my desk as Mr. Clubb ordered up from my doubtless astounded chef a meal of chicken wings, french fries, onion rings, and T-bone steaks, medium well. With plenty of time to spare, I immersed myself again in details, only to be brought up short by the recognition that I was humming, none too quietly, that most innocent of hymns, "Jesus Loves Me." And then, precisely at the appointed hour, Mrs. Rampage informed me of the arrival of my client and his associates, and I bade her bring them through.

A sly, slow-moving whale encased in an exquisite double-breasted black pinstripe, Mr. "This Building Is Condemned" C—— advanced into my office with his customary hauteur and offered me the customary nod of the head while his three "associates" formed a human breakwater in the center of the room. Regal

to the core, he affected not to notice Mrs. Rampage sliding a black
leather chair out of the middle distance and around the side of the
desk until it was in position, at which point he sat himself in it
without looking down. Then he inclined his slablike head and
raised a small, pallid hand. One of the "associates" promptly
moved to open the door for Mrs. Rampage's departure. At this
signal, I sat down, and the two remaining henchmen separated
themselves by a distance of perhaps eight feet. The third closed the
door and stationed himself by his general's right shoulder. These
formalities completed, my client shifted his close-set obsidian eyes
to mine and said, "You well?"

"Very well, thank you," I replied according to ancient formula. "And you?"

"Good," he said. "But things could still be better." This,
too, followed long-established formula, but his next words were a
startling deviation. He took in the stationary cloud and the corpse
of Montfort d'M——'s cigar rising like a monolith from the reef of
cigarette butts in the crystal shell, and, with the first genuine smile
I had ever seen on his pockmarked, small-featured face, said, "I
can't believe it, but one thing just got better already. You eased up
on the stupid no-smoking rule which is poisoning this city, good
for you."

"It seemed," I said, "a concrete way in which to demonstrate
our appreciation for the smokers among those clients we most
respect." When dealing with the cryptic gentlemen, one must not
fail to offer intervallic allusions to the spontaneous respect in
which they are held.

"Deacon," he said, employing the sobriquet he had given me
on our first meeting, "you being one of a kind at your job, the
respect you speak of is mutual, and besides that, all surprises
should be as pleasant as this." With that, he snapped his fingers at
the laden shell, and as he produced a ridged case similar to but
more capacious than Mr. Montfort d'M——'s, the man at his
shoulder whisked the impromptu ashtray from the desk, deposited
its contents in the *poubelle,* and repositioned it at a point on the

desk precisely equidistant from us. My client opened the case to expose the six cylinders contained within, removed one, and proffered the remaining five to me. "Be my guest, Deacon," he said. "Money can't buy better Havanas."

"Your gesture is much appreciated," I said. "However, with all due respect, at the moment I shall choose not to partake."

Distinct as a scar, a vertical crease of displeasure appeared on my client's forehead, and the ridged case and its five inhabitants advanced an inch toward my nose. "Deacon, you want me to smoke alone?" asked Mr. "This Building Is Condemned" C——. "This here, if you were ever lucky enough to find it at your local cigar store, which that lucky believe me you wouldn't be, is absolutely the best of the best, straight from me to you as what you could term a symbol of the cooperation and respect between us, and at the commencement of our business today it would please me greatly if you would do me the honor of joining me in a smoke."

As they say, or, more accurately, as they used to say, needs must when the devil drives, or words to that effect. "Forgive me," I said, and drew one of the fecal things from the case. "I assure you, the honor is all mine."

Mr. "This Building Is Condemned" C—— snipped the rounded end from his cigar, plugged the remainder in the center of his mouth, then subjected mine to the same operation. His henchmen proffered a lighter, Mr. "This Building Is Condemned" C—— bent forward and surrounded himself with clouds of smoke, in the manner of Bela Lugosi materializing before the brides of Dracula. The henchmen moved the flame toward me, and for the first time in my life I inserted into my mouth an object which seemed as large around as the handle of a baseball bat, brought it to the dancing flame, and drew in that burning smoke from which so many other men before me had derived pleasure.

Legend and common sense alike dictated that I should sputter and cough in an attempt to rid myself of the noxious substance. Nausea was in the cards, also dizziness. It is true that I suffered a degree of initial discomfort, as if my tongue had been lightly singed or seared, and the sheer unfamiliarity of the experience—the thickness of the tobacco tube, the texture of the smoke, as dense as chocolate—led me to fear for my well-being. Yet, despite the not altogether unpleasant tingling on the upper surface of my tongue, I expelled my first mouthful of cigar smoke with the sense of having sampled a taste every bit as delightful as the first sip of a properly made martini. The thug whisked away the flame, and I drew in another mouthful, leaned back, and released a wondrous quantity of smoke. Of a surprising smoothness, in some sense almost cool rather than hot, the delightful taste defined itself as heather, loam, morel mushrooms, venison, and some distinctive spice akin to coriander. I repeated the process, with results even more pleasurable—this time I tasted a hint of black butter sauce. "I can truthfully say," I told my client, "that never have I met a cigar as fine as this one."

"You bet you haven't," said Mr. "This Building Is Condemned" C——, and on the spot presented me with three more of the precious objects. With that, we turned to the tidal waves of cash and the interlocking corporate shells, each protecting another series of interconnected shells which concealed yet another, like Chinese boxes.

The cryptic gentlemen one and all appreciated certain ceremonies, such as the appearance of espresso coffee in thimble-sized porcelain cups and an accompanying assortment of *biscotti* at the halfway point of our meditations. Matters of business being forbidden while coffee and cookies were dispatched, the conversation generally turned to the conundrums posed by family life. Since I had no family to speak of, and, like most of his kind, Mr. "This Building Is Condemned" C—— was richly endowed with grandparents, parents, uncles, aunts, sons, daughters, nephews, nieces, and grandchildren, these remarks on the genealogical tapestry tended to be monologuic in nature, my role in them limited to nods and grunts. Required as they were more often by the business of the cryptic gentlemen than was the case in other trades or professions, funerals were another ongoing topic. Taking tiny sips of his espresso and equally maidenish nibbles from his favorite sweet-meats (Hydrox and Milano), my client favored me with the expected praises of his son, Arthur junior (Harvard graduate school, English Lit.), lamentations over his daughter, Fidelia (thrice married, never wisely), hymns to his grandchildren (Cyrus, Thor, and Hermione, respectively, the genius, the dreamer, and the despot), and then proceeded to link his two unfailing themes by recalling the unhappy behavior of Arthur junior at the funeral of my client's uncle and a principal figure in his family's rise to an imperial eminence, Mr. Vincente "Waffles" C——.

The anecdote called for the beheading and ignition of another magnificent stogie, and I greedily followed suit.

"Arthur junior's got his head screwed on right, and he's got the right kinda family values," said my client. "Straight A's all through school, married a stand-up dame with money of her own, three great kids, makes a man proud. Hard worker. Got his head in a book morning to night, human-encyclopedia-type guy, up there at Harvard, those professors, they love him. Kid knows how you're supposed to act, right?"

I nodded and filled my mouth with another fragrant draft.

"So he comes to my uncle Vincente's funeral all by himself, which troubles me. On top of it doesn't show the proper respect to old Waffles, who was one hell of a man, there's guys still pissing blood on account of they looked at him wrong forty years ago, on top a that, I don't have the good feeling I get from taking his family around to my friends and associates and saying, so look here, this here is Arthur junior, my Harvard guy, plus his wife, Hunter, whose ancestors I think got here even before that rabble on the *Mayflower*, plus his three kids—Cyrus, little bastard's even smarter than his dad, Thor, the one's got his head in the clouds, which is okay because we need people like that, too, and Hermione, who you can tell just by looking at her she's mean as a snake and is gonna wind up running the world someday. So I say, Arthur junior, what the hell happened, everybody else get killed in a train wreck or something? He says, No, Dad, they just didn't wanna come, these big family funerals, they make 'em feel funny, they don't like having their pictures taken so they show up on the six o'clock news. Didn't wanna come, I say back, what kinda shit is that, you shoulda made 'em come, and if anyone took their pictures when they didn't want, we can take care of that, no trouble at all. I go on like this, I even say, what good is Harvard and all those books if they don't make you any smarter than this, and finally Arthur junior's mother tells me, Put a cork in it, you're not exactly helping the situation here.

"So what happens then? Insteada being smart like I should, I go nuts on account of I'm the guy who pays the bills, that Harvard up there pulls in the money better than any casino I ever saw, and you want to find a real good criminal, get some Boston WASP in a bow tie, and all of a sudden nobody listens to me! I'm seeing red in a big way here, Deacon, this is my uncle Vincente's funeral, and insteada backing me up his mother is telling me I'm not *helping*. I yell, You want to help? Then go up there and bring back his wife and kids, or I'll send Carlo and Tommy to do it. All of a sudden I'm so mad I'm thinking these people are insulting me, how can they think they can get away with that, people who insult me don't do it twice—and then I hear what I'm thinking, and I do what she said and put a cork in it, but it's too late, I went way over the top and we all know it.

"Arthur junior takes off, and his mother won't talk to me for the whole rest of the day. Only thing I'm happy about is I didn't blow up where anyone else could see it. Deacon, I know you're the type guy wouldn't dream of threatening his family, but if the time ever comes, do yourself a favor and light up a Havana instead."

"I'm sure that is excellent advice," I said.

"Don't let the thought cross your mind. Anyhow, you know what they say, it only hurts for a little while, which is true as far as it goes, and I calmed down. Uncle Vincente's funeral was beautiful. You woulda thought the pope died. When the people are going out to the limousines, Arthur junior is sitting in a chair at the back of the church reading a book. Put that in your pocket, I say, wanta do homework, do it in the car. He tells me it isn't homework, but he puts it in his pocket and we go out to the cemetery. His mother looks out the window the whole time we're driving to the cemetery, and the kid starts reading again. So I ask what the hell is it, this book he can't put down? He tells me, but it's like he's speaking some foreign language, only word I understand is *the,* which happens a lot when your kid reads a lot of fancy books, half the titles make no sense to an ordinary person. Okay, we're out there in Queens, goddamn graveyard the size of Newark, FBI and reporters all over the place, and I'm thinking maybe Arthur junior wasn't wrong after all, Hunter probably hates having the FBI take her picture, and besides that little Hermione probably woulda mugged one of 'em and stole his wallet. So I tell Arthur junior I'm sorry about what happened. I didn't really think you were going to put me in the same grave as Uncle Waffles, he says, the Harvard smartass. When it's all over, we get back in the car, and out comes the book again. We get home, and he disappears. We have a lot of people over, food, wine, politicians, old-timers from Brownsville, Chicago people, Detroit people, L.A. people, movie directors, cops, actors I never heard of, priests, bishops, the guy from the Cardinal. Everybody's asking me, Where's Arthur junior? I go upstairs to find out. He's in his old room, and he's still reading that book. I say, Arthur junior, people are asking about you, I think it would be nice if you mingled with our guests. I'll be right down, he says, I just finished what I was reading. Here, take a look, you might enjoy it. He gives me the book and goes out of the room. So I'm wondering—what the hell *is* this, anyhow? I take it to the bedroom, toss it on the table. About ten-thirty, eleven, that night, everybody's gone, kid's on the shuttle back to Boston, house is cleaned up, enough food in the refrigerator to feed the whole bunch all over again, I go up to bed. Arthur junior's mother still isn't talking to me, so I get in and pick up the book. Herman Melville is the name of the guy, and I see that the story the kid was reading is called 'Bartleby the Scrivener.' So I decide I'll try it.

What the hell, right? You're an educated guy, you ever read that story?"

"A long time ago," I said. "A bit . . . *odd*, isn't it?"

"Odd? That's the most terrible story I ever read in my whole life! This dud gets a job in a law office and decides he doesn't want to work. Does he get fired? He does not. This is a story? You hire a guy who won't do the job, what do you do, pamper the asshole? At the end, the dud ups and disappears and you find out he used to work in the dead letter office. Is there a point here? The next day I call up Arthur junior, say, could he explain to me please what the hell that story is supposed to mean? Dad, he says, it means what it says. Deacon, I just about pulled the plug on Harvard right then and there. I never went to any college, but I do know that nothing means what it says, not on this planet."

This reflection was accurate when applied to the documents on my desk, for each had been encoded in a systematic fashion which rendered their literal contents deliberately misleading. Another code had informed both of my recent conversations with Marguerite. "Fiction is best left to real life," I said.

"Someone shoulda told that to Herman Melville," said Mr. Arthur "This Building Is Condemned" C——.

Mrs. Rampage buzzed me to advise that I was running behind schedule and inquire about removing the coffee things. I invited her to gather up the debris. A door behind me opened, and I assumed that my secretary had responded to my request with an alacrity remarkable even in her. The first sign of my error was the behavior of the three other men in the room, until this moment no more animated than marble statues. The thug at my client's side stepped forward to stand behind me, and his fellows moved to the front of my desk. "What the hell is this shit?" said the client, because of the man in front of him unable to see Mr. Clubb and Mr. Cuff. Holding a pad bearing one of his many lists, Mr. Clubb gazed in mild surprise at the giants flanking my desk and said, "I apologize for the intrusion, sir, but our understanding was that your appointment would be over in an hour, and by my simple way of reckoning you should be free to answer a query as to steam irons."

"What the hell *is* this shit?" said my client, repeating his original question with a slight tonal variation expressive of gathering dismay.

I attempted to salvage matters by saying, "Please allow me to explain the interruption. I have employed these men as consultants, and as they prefer to work in my office, a condition I, of course, could not permit during our business meeting, I temporarily relocated them in my washroom, outfitted with a library adequate to their needs."

"Fit for a king, in my opinion," said Mr. Clubb.

At that moment the other door into my office, to the left of my desk, opened to admit Mrs. Rampage, and my client's guardians inserted their hands into their suit jackets and separated with the speed and precision of a dance team.

"Oh, my," said Mrs. Rampage. "*Excuse* me. Should I come back later?"

"Not on your life, my darling," said Mr. Clubb. "Temporary misunderstanding of the false-alarm sort. Please allow us to enjoy the delightful spectacle of your feminine charms."

Before my wondering eyes, Mrs. Rampage curtseyed and hastened to my desk to gather up the wreckage.

I looked toward my client and observed a detail of striking peculiarity, that although his half-consumed cigar remained between his lips, four inches of cylindrical ash had deposited a gray smear on his necktie before coming to rest on the shelf of his belly. He was staring straight ahead with eyes grown to the size of quarters. His face had become the color of raw pie crust.

Mr. Clubb said, "Respectful greetings, sir."

The client gargled and turned upon me a look of unvarnished horror.

Mr. Clubb said, "Apologies to all." Mrs. Rampage had already bolted. From unseen regions came the sound of a closing door.

Mr. "This Building Is Condemned" C—— blinked twice, bringing his eyes to something like their normal dimensions. With an uncertain hand but gently, as if it were a tiny but much-loved baby, he placed his cigar in the crystal shell. He cleared his throat; he looked at the ceiling. "Deacon," he said, gazing upward. "Gotta run. My next appointment musta slipped my mind. What happens when you start to gab. I'll be in touch about this stuff." He stood, dislodging the ashen cylinder to the carpet, and motioned his gangsters to the outer office.

4

Of course at the earliest opportunity I interrogated both of my detectives about this turn of events, and while they moved their mountains of paper, bottles, buckets, glasses, hand-drawn maps, and other impedimenta back behind the screen, I continued the questioning. No, they averred, the gentleman at my desk was not a gentleman whom previously they had been privileged to look upon, acquaint themselves with, or encounter in any way whatsoever. They had never been employed in any capacity by the gentleman. Mr. Clubb observed that the unknown gentleman had been wearing a conspicuously handsome and well-tailored suit.

"That is his custom," I said.

"And I believe he smokes, sir, a noble high order of cigar," said Mr. Clubb with a glance at my breast pocket. "Which would be the sort of item unfairly beyond the dreams of honest laborers such as ourselves."

"I trust that you will permit me," I said with a sigh, "to offer you the pleasure of two of the same." No sooner had the offer been accepted, the barnies back behind their screen, than I buzzed Mrs. Rampage with the request to summon by instant delivery from the most distinguished cigar merchant in the city a box of his finest. "Good for you, boss!" whooped the new Mrs. Rampage.

I spent the remainder of the afternoon brooding upon the reaction of Mr. Arthur "This Building Is Condemned" C—— to my "consultants." I could not but imagine that his hasty departure boded ill for our relationship. I had seen terror on his face, and he knew that *I* knew what I had seen. An understanding of this sort is fatal to that nuance-play critical alike to high-level churchmen and their outlaw counterparts, and I had to confront the possibility that my client's departure had been of a permanent nature. Where Mr. "This Building Is Condemned" C—— went, his colleagues of lesser rank, Mr. Tommy "I Believe in Rainbows" B——, Mr. Anthony "Moonlight Becomes You" M——, Mr. Bobby "Total Eclipse" G——, and their fellow archbishops, cardinals, and papal nuncios would assuredly follow. Before the close of the day, I would send a comforting fax informing Mr. "This Building Is Condemned" C—— that the consultants had been summarily released from employment. I would be telling only a "white" or provisional untruth, for Mr. Clubb and Mr. Cuff's task would surely be completed long before my client's return. All was in order, all was in train and, as if to put the seal upon the matter, Mrs. Rampage buzzed to inquire if she might come through with the box of cigars. Speaking in a breathy timbre I had never before heard from anyone save Marguerite in the earliest, most blissful days of our marriage, Mrs. Rampage added that she had some surprises for me too. "By this point," I said, "I expect no less." Mrs. Rampage *giggled*.

The surprises, in the event, were of a satisfying practicality. The good woman had wisely sought the advice of Mr. Montfort d'M——, who, after recommending a suitably aristocratic cigar emporium and a favorite cigar, had purchased for me a rosewood humidor, a double-bladed cigar cutter, and a lighter of antique design. As soon as Mrs. Rampage had been instructed to compose a note of gratitude embellished in whatever fashion she saw fit, I arrayed all but one of the cigars in the humidor, decapitated that one, and set it alight. Beneath a faint touch of fruitiness like the aroma of a blossoming pear tree, I met in successive layers the tastes of black olives, aged Gouda cheese, pine needles, new leather, miso soup, either sorghum or brown sugar, burning peat, library paste, and myrtle leaves. The long finish intriguingly combined Bible paper and sunflower seeds. Mr. Montfort d'M—— had chosen well, though I regretted the absence of black butter sauce.

Feeling comradely, I strolled across my office towards the merriment emanating from the far side of the screen. A superior cigar, even if devoid of black butter sauce, should be complemented by a worthy liquor, and in the light of what was to transpire during the evening I considered a snifter of Mr. Clubb's Bombay gin not inappropriate. "Fellows," I said, tactfully announcing my presence, "are preparations nearly completed?"

"That, sir, they are," said one or another of the pair.

"Welcome news," I said, and stepped around the screen. "But I must be assured—"

I had expected disorder, but nothing approaching the chaos before me. It was as if the detritus of New York City's half-dozen filthiest living quarters had been scooped up, shaken, and dumped into my office. Heaps of ash, bottles, shoals of papers, books with stained covers and broken spines, battered furniture, broken glass, refuse I could not identify, refuse I could not even *see*, undulated from the base of the screen, around and over the table, heaping itself into landfill-like piles here and there, and washed against the plate-glass windows. A jagged five-foot opening gaped in a smashed pane. Their derbies perched on their heads, islanded in their chairs, Mr. Clubb and Mr. Cuff leaned back, feet up on what must have been the table.

"You'll join us in a drink, sir," said Mr. Clubb, "by way of wishing us success and adding to the pleasure of that handsome smoke." He extended a stout leg and kicked rubble from a chair. I sat down. Mr. Clubb plucked an unclean glass from the morass and filled it with Dutch gin or genever from one of the minaret-shaped stone flagons I had observed upon my infrequent layovers in Amsterdam, the Netherlands. Mrs. Rampage had been variously employed during the barnies' sequestration. Then I wondered if Mrs. Rampage might not have shown signs of intoxication during our last encounter.

"I thought you drank Bombay," I said.

"Variety is, as they say, life's condiment," said Mr. Clubb, and handed me the glass.

I said, "You have made yourselves quite at home."

"I thank you for your restraint," said Mr. Clubb. "In which sentiment my partner agrees, am I correct, Mr. Cuff?"

"Entirely," said Mr. Cuff. "But I wager you a C-note to a see-gar that a word or two of reassurance is in order."

"How right that man is," said Mr. Clubb. "He has a genius for the truth I have never known to fail him. Sir, you enter our work space to come upon the slovenly, the careless, the unseemly, and your response, which we comprehend in every particular, is to recoil. My wish is that you take a moment to remember these two essentials: one, we have, as aforesaid, our methods which are ours alone, and two, having appeared fresh on the scene, you see it worse than it is. By morning tomorrow, the cleaning staff shall have done its work."

"I suppose you have been Visualizing," I said, and quaffed genever.

"Mr. Cuff and I," he said, "prefer to minimize the risk of accidents, surprises, and such by the method of rehearsing our, as you might say, performances. These poor sticks, sir, are easily replaced, but our work, once under way, demands completion and cannot be duplicated, redone, or undone."

I recalled the all-important guarantee. "I remember your words," I said, "and I must be assured that you remember mine. I did not request termination. During the course of the day my feelings on the matter have intensified. Termination, if by that term you meant—"

"Termination is termination," said Mr. Clubb.

"*Ex*termination," I said. "Cessation of life due to external forces. It is not my wish, it is unacceptable, and I have even been thinking that I overstated the degree of physical punishment appropriate in this matter."

" 'Appropriate?' " said Mr. Clubb. "When it comes to desire, *appropriate* is a concept without meaning. In the sacred realm of desire, *appropriate,* being meaningless, does not exist. We speak of your inmost wishes, sir, and desire is an extremely *thingy* sort of thing."

I looked at the hole in the window, the broken bits of furniture and ruined books. "I think," I said, "that permanent injury is all I wish. Something on the order of blindness or the loss of a hand."

Mr. Clubb favored me with a glance of humorous irony. "It goes, sir, as it goes, which brings to mind that we have but an hour more, a period of time to be splendidly improved by a superior Double Corona such as the fine example in your hand."

"Forgive me," I said. "And might I then request . . . ?" I extended the nearly empty glass, and Mr. Clubb refilled it. Each received a cigar, and I lingered at my desk for the required term, sipping genever and pretending to work until I heard sounds of movement. Mr. Clubb and Mr. Cuff approached. "So you are off," I said.

"It is, sir, to be a long and busy night," said Mr. Clubb. "If you take my meaning."

With a sigh I opened the humidor. They reached in, snatched a handful of cigars apiece, and deployed them into various pockets. "Details at eleven," said Mr. Clubb.

A few seconds after their departure, Mrs. Rampage informed me that she would be bringing through a fax communication just received.

The fax had been sent me by Chartwell, Munster, and Stout, a legal firm with but a single client, Mr. Arthur "This Building Is Condemned" C——. Chartwell, Munster, and Stout regretted the necessity to inform me that their client wished to seek advice other than my own in his financial affairs. A sheaf of documents binding me to silence as to all matters concerning the client would arrive for my signature the following day. All records, papers, computer discs, and other data were to be referred posthaste to their offices. I had forgotten to send my intended note of client-saving reassurance.

5

What an abyss of shame I must now describe, at every turn what humiliation. It was at most five minutes past six P.M. when I learned of the desertion of my most valuable client, a turn of events certain to lead to the loss of his cryptic fellows and some forty percent of our annual business. Gloomily I consumed my glass of Dutch gin without noticing that I had already far exceeded my tolerance. I ventured behind the screen and succeeded in unearthing another stone flagon, poured another measure, and gulped it down while attempting to demonstrate numerically that (a) the anticipated drop in annual profit could not be as severe as feared, and (b) if it were, the business could continue as before, without reductions in salary, staff, and benefits. Despite ingenious feats of juggling, the numbers denied (a) and mocked (b), suggesting that I should be fortunate to retain, not lose, forty percent of present business. I lowered my head to the desk and tried to regulate my breathing. When I heard myself rendering an off-key version of "Abide With Me," I acknowledged that it was time to go home, got to my feet, and made the unfortunate decision to exit through the general offices on the theory that a survey of my presumably empty realm might suggest the sites of pending amputations.

I tucked the flagon under my elbow, pocketed the five or six cigars remaining in the humidor, and passed through Mrs. Rampage's chamber. Hearing the abrasive music of the cleaners' radios, I moved with exaggerated care down the corridor, darkened but for the light spilling from an open door thirty feet before me. Now and again, finding myself unable to avoid striking my shoulder against the wall, I took a medicinal swallow of genever. I drew up to the open door and realized that I had come to Gilligan's quarters. The abrasive music emanated from his sound system. *We'll get rid of that, for starters,* I said to myself, and straightened up for a dignified navigation past his doorway. At the crucial moment I glanced within to observe my jacketless junior partner sprawled, tie undone, on his sofa beside a scrawny ruffian with a quiff of lime-green hair and attired for some reason in a skintight costume involving zebra stripes and many chains and zippers. Disreputable creatures male and female occupied themselves in the background. Gilligan shifted his head, began to smile, and at the sight of me turned to stone.

"Calm down, Gilligan," I said, striving for an impression of sober paternal authority. I had recalled that my junior had scheduled a late appointment with his most successful musician, a singer whose band sold millions of records year in and year out despite the absurdity of their name, the Dog Turds or the Rectal Valves, something of that sort. My calculations had indicated that Gilligan's client, whose name I recalled as Cyril Futch, would soon become crucial to the maintenance of my firm, and as the beaky little rooster coldly took me in I thought to impress upon him the regard in which he was held by his chosen financial planning institution. "There is, I assure you, no need for alarm, no, certainly not, and in fact, Gilligan, you know, I should be honored to seize this opportunity of making the acquaintance of your guest, whom it is our pleasure to assist and advise and whatever."

Gilligan reverted to flesh and blood during the course of this utterance, which I delivered gravely, taking care to enunciate each syllable clearly in spite of the difficulty I was having with my tongue. He noted the bottle nestled into my elbow and the lighted cigar in the fingers of my right hand, a matter of which until that moment I had been imperfectly aware. "Hey, I guess the smoking lamp is lit," I said. "Stupid rule anyhow. How about a little drink on the boss?"

Gilligan lurched to his feet and came reeling toward me.

All that followed is a montage of discontinuous imagery. I recall Cyril Futch propping me up as I communicated our devotion to the safeguarding of his wealth, also his dogged insistence that his name was actually Simon Gulch or Sidney Much or something similar before he sent me toppling onto the sofa; I see an odd little fellow with a tattooed head and a name like Pus (there was a person named Pus in attendance, though he may not have been the one) accepting one of my cigars and eating it; I remember inhaling from smirking Gilligan's cigarette and drinking from a bottle with a small white worm lying dead at its bottom and snuffling up a white powder recommended by a female Turd or Valve; I remember singing "The Old Rugged Cross" in a state of partial undress. I told a face brilliantly lacquered with makeup that I was "getting a feel" for "this music." A female Turd or Valve, not the one who had recommended the powder but one in a permanent state of hilarity I found endearing, assisted me into my limousine and on the homeward journey experimented with its many buttons and controls. Atop the town-house steps, she removed the key from my fumbling hand gleefully to insert it into the lock. The rest is welcome darkness.

6

A form of consciousness returned with a slap to my face, the muffled screams of the woman beside me, a bowler-hatted head thrusting into view and growling, "The shower for you, you damned idiot." As a second assailant whisked her away, the woman, whom I thought to be Marguerite, wailed. I struggled against the man gripping my shoulders, and he squeezed the nape of my neck.

When next I opened my eyes, I was naked and quivering beneath an onslaught of cold water within the marble confines of my shower cabinet. Charlie-Charlie Rackett leaned against the open door of the cabinet and regarded me with ill-disguised impatience. "I'm freezing, Charlie-Charlie," I said. "Turn off the water."

Charlie-Charlie thrust an arm into the cabinet and became Mr. Clubb. "I'll warm it up, but I want you sober," he said. I drew myself up into a ball.

Then I was on my feet and moaning while I massaged my forehead. "Bath time all done now," called Mr. Clubb. "Turn off the wa-wa." I did as instructed. The door opened, and a bath towel unfurled over my left shoulder.

Side by side on the bedroom sofa dimly illuminated by the lamp, Mr. Clubb and Mr. Cuff observed my progress toward the bed. A black leather satchel stood on the floor between them. "Gentlemen," I said, "although I cannot presently find words to account for the condition in which you found me, I trust that your good nature will enable you to overlook . . . or ignore . . . whatever it was that I must have done . . . I cannot quite recall the circumstances."

"The young woman has been sent away," said Mr. Clubb, "and you need never fear any trouble from that direction, sir."

"The young woman?" I asked, and remembered a hyperactive figure playing with the controls in the back of the limousine. This opened up a fragmentary memory of the scene in Gilligan's office, and I moaned aloud.

"None too clean, but pretty enough in a ragamuffin way," said Mr. Clubb. "The type denied a proper education in social graces. Rough about the edges. Intemperate in language. A stranger to discipline."

I groaned—to have introduced such a creature to my house!

"A stranger to honesty, too, sir, if you'll permit me," said Mr. Cuff. "It's addiction turns them into thieves. Give them half a chance, they'll steal the brass handles off their mothers' coffins."

"Addiction?" I said. "Addiction to what?"

"Everything, from the look of the bint," said Mr. Cuff. "Before Mr. Clubb and I sent her on her way, we retrieved these items doubtless belonging to you, sir." While walking toward me he removed from his pockets the following articles: my wristwatch, gold cuff links, wallet, the lighter of antique design given me by Mr. Montfort d'M——, likewise the cigar cutter, and the last of the cigars I had purchased that day. "I thank you most gratefully," I said, slipping the watch on my wrist and all else save the cigar into the pockets of my robe. It was, I noted, just past four o'clock in the morning. The cigar I handed back to him with the words "Please accept this as a token of my gratitude."

"Gratefully accepted," he said. Mr. Cuff bit off the end, spat it onto the carpet, and set the cigar alight, producing a nauseating quantity of fumes.

"Perhaps," I said, "we might postpone our discussion until I have had time to recover from my ill-advised behavior. Let us reconvene at . . ." A short period was spent pressing my hands to my eyes while rocking back and forth. "Four this afternoon?"

"Everything in its own time is a principle we hold dear," said Mr. Clubb. "And this is the time for you to down aspirin and Alka-Seltzer, and for your loyal assistants to relish the hearty breakfasts the thought of which sets our stomachs to growling. A man of stature and accomplishment like yourself ought to be able to over-come the effects of too much booze and attend to business, on top of the simple matter of getting his flunkies out of bed so they can whip up the bacon and eggs."

"Because a man such as that, sir, keeps ever in mind that business faces the task at hand, no matter how lousy it may be," said Mr. Cuff.

"The old world is in flames," said Mr. Clubb, "and the new one is just being born. Pick up the phone."

"All right," I said, "but Mr. Moncrieff is going to *hate* this. He worked for the duke of Denbigh, and he's a terrible snob."

"All butlers are snobs," said Mr. Clubb. "Three fried eggs apiece, likewise six rashers of bacon, home fries, toast, hot coffee, and for the sake of digestion a bottle of your best cognac."

Mr. Moncrieff picked up his telephone, listened to my orders, and informed me in a small, cold voice that he would speak to the cook. "Would this repast be for the young lady and yourself, sir?" he asked.

With a wave of guilty shame which intensified my nausea, I realized that Mr. Moncrieff had observed my unsuitable young companion accompanying me upstairs to the bedroom. "No, it would not," I said. "The young lady, a client of mine, was kind enough to assist me when I was taken ill. The meal is for two male guests." Unwelcome memory returned the spectacle of a scrawny girl pulling my ears and screeching that a useless old fart like me didn't deserve her band's business.

"The phone," said Mr. Clubb. Dazedly I extended the receiver.

"Moncrieff, old man," he said, "amazing good luck, running into you again. Do you remember that trouble the duke had with Colonel Fletcher and the diary? . . . Yes, this is Mr. Clubb, and it's delightful to hear your voice again. . . . He's here, too, couldn't do anything without him. . . . I'll tell him. . . . Much the way things went with the duke, yes, and we'll need the usual supplies. . . . Glad to hear it. . . . The dining room in half an hour." He handed the telephone back to me and said to Mr. Cuff, "He's looking forward to the pinochle, and there's a first-rate Pétrus in the cellar he knows you're going to enjoy."

I had purchased six cases of 1928 Château Pétrus at an auction some years before and was holding it while its already immense value doubled, then tripled, until perhaps a decade hence, when I would sell it for ten times its original cost.

"A good drop of wine sets a man right up," said Mr. Cuff. "Stuff was meant to be drunk, wasn't it?"

"You know Mr. Moncrieff?" I asked. "You worked for the duke?"

"We ply our humble trade irrespective of nationality and borders," said Mr. Clubb. "Go where we are needed, is our motto. We have fond memories of the good old duke, who showed himself to be quite a fun-loving, spirited fellow, sir, once you got past the crust, as it were. Generous too."

"He gave until it hurt," said Mr. Cuff. "The old gentleman cried like a baby when we left."

"Cried a good deal before that too," said Mr. Clubb. "In our experience, high-spirited fellows spend a deal more tears than your gloomy customers."

"I do not suppose you shall see any tears from me," I said. The brief look which passed between them reminded me of the complicitous glance I had once seen fly like a live spark between two of their New Covenant forebears, one gripping the hind legs of a pig, the other its front legs and a knife, in the moment before the knife opened the pig's throat and an arc of blood threw itself high into the air. "I shall heed your advice," I said, "and locate my analgesics." I got on my feet and moved slowly to the bathroom. "As a matter of curiosity," I said, "might I ask if you have classified me into the high-spirited category, or into the other?"

"You are a man of middling spirit," said Mr. Clubb. I opened my mouth to protest, and he went on. "But something may be made of you yet."

I disappeared into the bathroom. *I have endured these moon-faced yokels long enough,* I told myself, *hear their story, feed the bastards, then kick them out.*

In a condition more nearly approaching my usual self, I brushed my teeth and splashed water on my face before returning to the bedroom. I placed myself with a reasonable degree of executive command in a wing chair, folded my pinstriped robe about me, inserted my feet into velvet slippers, and said, "Things got a bit out of hand, and I thank you for dealing with my young client, a person with whom, in spite of appearances, I have a professional relationship only. Now we may turn to our real business. I trust you found my wife and Leeson at Green Chimneys. Please give me an account of what followed. I await your report."

"Things got a bit out of hand," said Mr. Clubb. "Which is a way of describing something that can happen to us all, and for which no one can be blamed. Especially Mr. Cuff and myself, who are always careful to say right smack at the beginning, as we did with you, sir, what ought to be so obvious as not need saying at all, that our work brings about permanent changes which can never be undone. Especially in the cases when we specify a time to make our initial report and the client disappoints us at the said time. When we are let down by our client, we must go forward and complete the job to our highest standards with no rancor or ill-will, knowing that there are many reasonable explanations of a man's inability to get to a telephone."

"I don't know what you mean by this self-serving double-talk," I said. "We had no arrangement of that sort, and your effrontery forces me to conclude that you failed in your task."

Mr. Clubb gave me the grimmest possible suggestion of a smile. "One of the reasons for a man's failure to get to a telephone is a lapse of memory. You have forgotten my informing you that I would give you my initial report at eleven. At precisely eleven o'clock I called, to no avail. I waited through twenty rings, sir, before I abandoned the effort. If I had waited through a hundred, sir, the result would have been the same, on account of your decision to put yourself into a state where you would have had trouble remembering your own name."

"That is a blatant lie," I said, then remembered. The fellow had in fact mentioned in passing something about reporting to me at that hour, which must have been approximately the time when I was regaling the Turds or Valves with "The Old Rugged Cross." My face grew pink. "Forgive me," I said. "I am in error, it is just as you say."

"A manly admission, sir, but as for forgiveness, we extended that quantity from the git-go," said Mr. Clubb. "We are your servants, and your wishes are our sacred charge."

"That's the whole ball of wax in a nutshell," said Mr. Cuff, giving a fond glance to the final inch of his cigar. He dropped the stub onto my carpet and ground it beneath his shoe. "Food and drink to the fibers, sir," he said.

"Speaking of which," said Mr. Clubb. "We will continue our report in the dining room, so as to dig into the feast ordered up by that wondrous villain, Reggie Moncrieff."

Until that moment I believe that it had never quite occurred to me that my butler possessed, like other men, a Christian name.

7

"A great design directs us," said Mr. Clubb, expelling morsels of his cud. "We poor wanderers, you and me and Mr. Cuff and the milkman, too, only see the little portion right in front of us. Half the time we don't even see that in the right way. For sure we don't have a Chinaman's chance of understanding it. But the design is ever present, sir, a truth I bring to your attention for the sake of the comfort in it. Toast, Mr. Cuff."

"Comfort is a matter cherished by all parts of a man," said Mr. Cuff, handing his partner the rack of toasted bread. "Most particularly that part known as his soul, which feeds upon the nutrient adversity."

I was seated at the head of the table and flanked by Mr. Clubb and Mr. Cuff. The salvers and tureens before us overflowed, for Mr. Moncrieff, who after embracing each barnie in turn and then entering into a kind of conference or huddle, had summoned from the kitchen a meal far surpassing their requests. Besides several dozen eggs and perhaps two packages of bacon, he had arranged a mixed grill of kidneys, lamb's livers and lamb chops, and strip steaks, as well as vats of oatmeal and a pasty concoction he described as "kedgeree—as the old duke fancied it."

Sickened by the odors of the food, also by the mush visible in my companions' mouths, I tried once more to extract their report. "I don't believe in the grand design," I said, "and I already face more adversity than my soul could find useful. Tell me what happened at the house."

"No mere house, sir," said Mr. Clubb. "Even as we approached along —— Lane, Mr. Cuff and I could not fail to respond to its magnificence."

"Were my drawings of use?" I asked.

"They were invaluable." Mr. Cuff speared a lamb chop and raised it to his mouth. "We proceeded through the rear door into your spacious kitchen or scullery. Wherein we observed evidence of two persons having enjoyed a dinner enhanced by a fine wine and finished with a noble champagne."

"Aha," I said.

"By means of your guidance, Mr. Cuff and I located the lovely staircase and made our way to the lady's chamber. We effected an entry of the most praiseworthy silence, if I may say so."

"That entry was worth a medal," said Mr. Cuff.

"Two figures lay slumbering upon the bed. In a blamelessly professional manner we approached, Mr. Cuff on one side, I on the other. In the fashion your client of this morning called the whopbopaloobop, we rendered the parties in question even more unconscious than previous, thereby giving ourselves a good fifteen minutes for the disposition of instruments. We take pride in being careful workers, sir, and like all honest craftsmen we respect our tools. We bound and gagged both parties in timely fashion. Is the male party distinguished by an athletic past?" Suddenly alight with barnieish glee, Mr. Clubb raised his eyebrows and washed down the last of his chop with a mouthful of cognac.

"Not to my knowledge," I said. "I believe he plays a little racquetball and squash, that kind of thing."

He and Mr. Cuff experienced a moment of mirth. "More like weight lifting or football, is my guess," he said. "Strength and stamina. To a remarkable degree."

"Not to mention considerable speed," said Mr. Cuff with the air of one indulging a tender reminisence.

"Are you telling me that he got away?" I asked.

"No one gets away," said Mr. Clubb. "That, sir, is Gospel. But you may imagine our surprise when for the first time in the

history of our *consultancy*"—and here he chuckled—"a gentleman
of the civilian persuasion managed to break his bonds and free
himself of his ropes whilst Mr. Cuff and I were engaged in the
preliminaries."

"Naked as jaybirds," said Mr. Cuff, wiping with a greasy
hand a tear of amusement from one eye. "Bare as newborn lambie-
pies. There I was, heating up the steam iron I'd just fetched from
the kitchen, sir, along with a selection of knives I came across in
exactly the spot you described, most grateful I was, too, squatting
on my haunches without a care in the world and feeling the first
merry tingle of excitement in my little soldier—"

"What?" I said. "You were naked? And what's this about
your little soldier?"

"Hush," said Mr. Clubb, his eyes glittering. "Nakedness is a
precaution against fouling our clothing with blood and other
bodily products, and men like Mr. Cuff and myself take pleasure in
the exercise of our skills. In us, the inner and the outer man are
one and the same."

"Are they, now?" I said, marveling at the irrelevance of this
last remark. It then occurred to me that the remark might have
been relevant after all—most unhappily so.

"At all times," said Mr. Cuff, amused by my having missed
the point. "If you wish to hear our report, sir, reticence will be
helpful."

I gestured for him to go on with the story.

"As said before, I was squatting in my birthday suit by the
knives and the steam iron, not a care in the world, when I heard
from behind me the patter of little feet. *Hello*, I say to myself,
what's this? and when I look over my shoulder here is your man,
bearing down on me like a steam engine. Being as he is one of your
big, strapping fellows, sir, it was a sight to behold, not to mention
the unexpected circumstances. I took a moment to glance in the
direction of Mr. Clubb, who was busily occupied in another quarter, which was, to put it plain and simple, the bed."

Mr. Clubb chortled and said, "By way of being in the line of duty."

"So in a way of speaking I was in the position of having to settle this fellow before he became a trial to us in the performance of our duties. He was getting ready to tackle me, sir, which was what put us in mind of football being in his previous life, tackle the life out of me before he rescued the lady, and I got hold of one of the knives. Then, you see, when he came flying at me that way all I had to do was give him a good jab in at the bottom of the throat, a matter which puts the fear of God into the bravest fellow. It concentrates all their attention, and after that they might as well be little puppies for all the harm they're likely to do. Well, this boy was one for the books, because for the first time in I don't know how many similar efforts, a hundred—"

"I'd say double at least, to be accurate," said Mr. Clubb.

"—in at least a hundred, anyhow, avoiding immodesty, I underestimated the speed and agility of the lad and, instead of planting my weapon at the base of his neck, stuck him in the side, a manner of wound which in the case of your really *aggressive* attacker, who you come across in about one out of twenty, is about as effective as a slap with a powder puff. Still, I put him off his stride, a welcome sign to me that he had gone a bit loosey-goosey over the years. Then, sir, the advantage was mine, and I seized it with a grateful heart. I spun him over, dumped him on the floor, and straddled his chest. At which point I thought to settle him down for the evening by taking hold of a cleaver and cutting off his right hand with one good blow.

"Ninety-nine times out of a hundred, sir, chopping off a hand will take the starch right out of a man. He settled down pretty well. It's the shock, you see, shock takes the mind that way, and because the stump was bleeding like a bastard, excuse the language, I did him the favor of cauterizing the wound with the steam iron because it was good and hot, and if you sear a wound there's no way that bugger can bleed anymore. I mean, the *problem is solved,* and that's a fact."

"It has been proved a thousand times over," said Mr. Clubb.

"Shock being a healer," said Mr. Cuff. "Shock being a balm like salt water to the human body, yet if you have too much of either, the body gives up the ghost. After I seared the wound, it looked to me like he and his body got together and voted to take the next bus to what is generally considered a better world." He held up an index finger and stared into my eyes while forking kidneys into his mouth. "This, sir, is a *process*. A *process* can't happen all at once, and every reasonable precaution was taken. Mr. Clubb and I do not have, nor ever have had, the reputation for carelessness in our undertakings."

"And never shall," said Mr. Clubb. He washed down whatever was in his mouth with half a glass of cognac.

"Despite the *process* under way," said Mr. Cuff, "the gentleman's left wrist was bound tightly to the stump. Rope was again attached to the areas of the chest and legs, a gag went back into his mouth, and besides all that I had the pleasure of whapping my hammer once and once only on the region of his temple, for the purpose of keeping him out of action until we were ready for him in case he was not boarding the bus. I took a moment to turn him over and gratify my little soldier, which I trust was in no way exceeding our agreement, sir." He granted me a look of the purest innocence.

"Continue," I said, "although you must grant that your tale is utterly without verification."

"Sir," said Mr. Clubb, "we know one another better than that." He bent over so far that his head disappeared beneath the table, and I heard the undoing of a clasp. Resurfacing, he placed between us on the table an object wrapped in one of the towels Marguerite had purchased for Green Chimneys. "If verification is your desire, and I intend no reflection, sir, for a man in your line of business has grown out of the habit of taking a fellow at his word, here you have wrapped up like a birthday present the finest verification of this portion of our tale to be found in all the world."

"And yours to keep, if you're taken that way," said Mr. Cuff.

I had no doubts whatsoever concerning the nature of the trophy set before me, and therefore I deliberately composed myself before pulling away the folds of toweling. Yet for all my preparations the spectacle of the actual trophy itself affected me more greatly than I would have thought possible, and at the very center of the nausea rising within me I experienced the first faint stirrings of my enlightenment. *Poor man,* I thought, *poor mankind.*

I refolded the material over the crablike thing and said, "Thank you. I meant to imply no reservations concerning your veracity."

"Beautifully said, sir, and much appreciated. Men like ourselves, honest at every point, have found that persons in the habit of duplicity often cannot understand the truth. Liars are the bane of our existence. And yet, such is the nature of this funny old world, we'd be out of business without them."

Mr. Cuff smiled up at the chandelier in rueful appreciation of the world's contradictions. "When I replaced him on the bed, Mr. Clubb went hither and yon, collecting the remainder of the tools for the job at hand—"

"When you say you replaced him on the bed," I broke in, "is it your meaning—"

"Your meaning might differ from mine, sir, and mine, being that of a fellow raised without the benefits of a literary education, may be simpler than yours. But bear in mind that every guild has its legacy of customs and traditions which no serious practitioner can ignore without thumbing his nose at all he holds dear. For those brought up into our trade, physical punishment of a female subject invariably begins with the act most associated in the feminine mind with humiliation of the most rigorous sort. With males the same is generally true. Neglect this step, and you lose an advantage which can never be regained. It is the foundation without which the structure cannot stand, and the foundation must be set in place even when conditions make the job distasteful, which is no picnic, take my word for it." He shook his head and fell silent.

"We could tell you stories to curl your hair," said Mr. Clubb.

"Matter for another day. It was on the order of nine-thirty when our materials had been assembled, the preliminaries taken care of, and business could begin in earnest. This is a moment, sir, ever cherished by professionals such as ourselves. It is of an eternal freshness. You are on the brink of testing yourself against your past achievements and those of masters gone before. Your skill, your imagination, your timing and resolve, will be called upon to work together with your hard-earned knowledge of the human body, because it is a question of being able to sense when to press on and when to hold back, of, I can say, having that instinct for the right technique at the right time you can build up only through experience. During this moment you hope that the subject, your partner in the most intimate relationship which can exist between two people, owns the spiritual resolve and physical capacity to inspire your best work. The subject is our instrument, and the nature of the instrument is vital. Faced with an out-of-tune, broken-down piano, even the greatest virtuoso is up shit creek without a paddle. Sometimes, sir, our work has left us tasting ashes for weeks on end, and when you're tasting ashes in your mouth you have trouble remembering the grand design and your wee part in that majestical pattern."

As if to supplant the taste in question and without benefit of knife and fork, Mr. Clubb bit off a generous portion of steak and moistened it with a gulp of cognac. Chewing with loud smacks of the lips and tongue, he thrust a spoon into the kedgeree and began moodily slapping it onto his plate while seeming for the first time to notice the Canalettos on the walls.

"We started off, sir, as well as we ever have," said Mr. Cuff, "and better than most times. The fingernails was a thing of rare beauty, sir, the fingernails was prime. And the hair was on the same transcendant level."

"The fingernails?" I asked. "The hair?"

"Prime," said Mr. Clubb with a melancholy spray of food. "If they could be done better, which they could not, I should like to be there as to applaud with my own hands."

I looked at Mr. Cuff, and he said, "The fingernails and the hair might appear to be your traditional steps two and three, but they are in actual fact steps one and two, the first procedure being more like basic groundwork than part of the performance work itself. Doing the fingernails and the hair tells you an immense quantity about the subject's pain level, style of resistance, and aggression/passivity balance, and that information, sir, is your virtual Bible once you go past step four or five."

"How many steps are there?" I asked.

"A novice would tell you fifteen," said Mr. Cuff. "A competent journeyman would say twenty. Men such as us know there to be at least a hundred, but in their various combinations and refinements they come out into the thousands. At the basic or kindergarten level, they are, after the first two: foot soles; teeth; fingers and toes; tongue; nipples; rectum; genital area; electrification; general piercing; specific piercing; small amputation; damage to inner organs; eyes, minor; eyes, major; large amputation; local flaying; and so forth."

At mention of *tongue,* Mr. Clubb had shoved a spoonful of kedgeree into his mouth and scowled at the two paintings directly across from him. At *electrification,* he had thrust himself out of his chair and crossed behind me to scrutinize them more closely. While Mr. Cuff continued my education, he twisted in his chair to observe his partner's actions, and I did the same.

After *and so forth,* Mr. Cuff fell silent. The two of us watched Mr. Clubb moving back and forth in evident agitation between the two large paintings. He settled at last before a depiction of a regatta on the Grand Canal and took two deep breaths. Then he raised his spoon like a dagger and drove it into the painting to slice beneath a handsome ship, come up at its bow, and continue cutting until he had deleted the ship from the painting. "Now that, sir, is local flaying," he said. He moved to the next picture, which gave a view of the Piazetta. In seconds he had sliced all the canvas from the frame. "And that, sir, is what is meant by general flaying." He crumpled the canvas in his hands, threw it to the ground, and stamped on it.

"He is not quite himself," said Mr. Cuff.

"Oh, but I am, I am myself to an alarming degree, I am," said Mr. Clubb. He tromped back to the table and bent beneath it. Instead of the second folded towel I had anticipated, he produced his satchel and used it to sweep away the plates and serving dishes in front of him. He reached within and slapped down beside me the towel I had expected. "Open it," he said. I unfolded the towel. "Are these not, to the last particular, what you requested, sir?"

It was, to the last particular, what I had requested. Marguerite had not thought to remove her wedding band before her assignation, and her . . . I cannot describe the other but to say that it lay like the egg perhaps of some small sandbird in the familiar palm. Another portion of my eventual enlightenment moved into place within me, and I thought: *Here we are, this is all of us, this crab and this egg.* I bent over and vomited beside my chair. When I had finished, I grabbed the cognac bottle and swallowed greedily, twice. The liquor burned down my throat, struck my stomach like a branding iron, and rebounded. I leaned sideways and, with a dizzied spasm of throat and guts, expelled another reeking contribution to the mess on the carpet.

"It is a Roman conclusion to a meal, sir," said Mr. Cuff.

Mr. Moncrieff opened the kitchen door and peeked in. He observed the mutilated paintings and the two objects nested in the striped towel and watched me wipe a string of vomit from my mouth. He withdrew for a moment and reappeared holding a tall can of ground coffee, wordlessly sprinkled its contents over the evidence of my distress, and vanished back into the kitchen. From even the depths of my wretchedness I marveled at the perfection of this display of butler decorum.

I draped the toweling over the crab and the egg. "You are conscientious fellows," I said.

"Conscientious to a fault, sir," said Mr. Cuff, not without a touch of kindness. "For a person in the normal way of living cannot begin to comprehend the actual meaning of that term, nor is he liable to understand the fierce requirements it puts on a man's head. And so it comes about that persons in the normal way of living try to back out long after backing out is possible, even though we explain exactly what is going to happen at the very beginning. They listen, but they do not hear, and it's the rare civilian who has the common sense to know that if you stand in a fire you must be burned. And if you turn the world upside down, you're standing on your head with everybody else."

"Or," said Mr. Clubb, calming his own fires with another deep draught of cognac, "as the Golden Rule has it, what you do is sooner or later done back to you."

Although I was still one who listened but could not hear, a tingle of premonition went up my spine. "Please go on with your report," I said.

"The responses of the subject were all one could wish," said Mr. Clubb. "I could go so far as to say that her responses were a thing of beauty. A subject who can render you one magnificent scream after another while maintaining a basic self-possession and not breaking down is a subject highly attuned to her own pain, sir, and one to be cherished. You see, there comes a moment when they understand that they are changed for good, they have passed over the border into another realm from which there is no return, and some of them can't handle it and turn, you might say, to mush. With some it happens right at the foundation stage, a sad disappointment because thereafter all the rest of the work could be done by the crudest apprentice. It takes some at the nipples stage, and at the genital stage quite a few more. Most of them comprehend irreversibility during the piercings, and by the stage of small amputation ninety percent have shown you what they are made of. The lady did not come to the point until we had begun the eye work, and she passed with flying colors, sir. But it was then the male upped and put his foot in it."

"And eye work is delicate going," said Mr. Cuff. "Requiring two men, if you want it done even close to right. But I couldn't have turned my back on the fellow for more than a minute and a half."

"Less," said Mr. Clubb. "And him lying there in the corner meek as a baby. No fight left in him at all, you would have said. You would have said, that fellow there is not going to risk so much as opening his eyes until he's made to do it."

"But up he gets, without a rope on him, sir," said Mr. Cuff, "which you would have said was far beyond the powers of a fellow who had recently lost a hand."

"Up he gets and on he comes," said Mr. Clubb. "In defiance of all of Nature's mighty laws. Before I know what's what, he has his good arm around Mr. Cuff's neck and is earnestly trying to snap that neck while beating Mr. Cuff about the head with his stump, a situation which compels me to set aside the task at hand and take up a knife and ram it into his back and sides a fair old number of times. The next thing I know, he's on *me,* and it's up to Mr. Cuff to peel him off and set him on the floor."

"And then, you see, your concentration is gone," said Mr. Cuff. "After something like that, you might as well be starting all over again at the beginning. Imagine if you are playing a piano about as well as ever you did in your life, and along comes another piano with blood in its eye and jumps on your back. It was pitiful, that's all I can say about it. But I got the fellow down and jabbed him here and there until he was still, and then I got the one item we count on as a surefire last resort for incapacitation."

"What is that item?" I asked.

"Dental floss," said Mr. Clubb. "Dental floss cannot be overestimated as a particular in our line of work. It is the razor wire of everyday life, and fishing line cannot hold a candle to it, for fishing line is dull, but dental floss is both *dull* and *sharp.* It has a hundred uses, and a book should be written on the subject."

"What do you do with it?" I asked.

"It is applied to a male subject," he said. "Applied artfully and in a manner perfected only over years of experience. The application is of a lovely *subtlety.* During the process, the subject must be in a helpless, preferably an unconscious, position. When the subject regains the first fuzzy inklings of consciousness, he is aware of no more than a vague discomfort like unto a form of numb tingling, similar to when a foot has gone asleep. In a wonderfully short period of time, that discomfort builds up itself, ascending to mild pain, real pain, *severe* pain, and then outright agony. And then it goes past agony. The final stage is a mystical condition I don't think there is a word for which, but it close resembles ecstasy. Hallucinations are common. Out-of-body experiences are common. We have seen men speak in tongues, even when tongues were strictly speaking organs they no longer possessed. We have seen wonders, Mr. Cuff and I."

"That we have," said Mr. Cuff. "The ordinary civilian sort of fellow can be a miracle, sir."

"Of which the person in question was one, to be sure," said Mr. Clubb. "But he has to be said to be in a category all by himself, a man in a million, you could put it, which is the cause of my mentioning the grand design ever a mystery to us who glimpse but a part of the whole. You see, the fellow refused to play by the time-honored rules. He was in an awesome degree of suffering and torment, sir, but he would not do us the favor to lie down and quit."

"The mind was not right," said Mr. Cuff. "Where the proper mind goes to the spiritual, sir, as just described, this was that one mind in *ten* million, I'd estimate, which moves to the animal at the reptile level. If you cut off the head of a venomous reptile and detach it from the body, that head will still attempt to strike. So it was with our boy. Bleeding from a dozen wounds. Minus one hand. Seriously concussed. The dental floss murdering all possibility of thought. Every nerve in his body howling like a banshee. Yet up he comes with his eyes red and the foam dripping from his mouth. We put him down again, and I did what I hate, because it takes all feeling away from the body along with the motor capacity, and cracked his spine right at the base of the head. Or would have, if his spine had been a normal thing instead of solid steel in a thick india-rubber case. Which is what put us in mind of weight lifting, sir, an activity resulting in such development about the top of the spine you need a hacksaw to get even close to it."

"We were already behind schedule," said Mr. Clubb, "and with the time required to get back into the proper frame of mind, we had at least seven or eight hours of work ahead of us. And you had to double that, because while we could knock the fellow out, he wouldn't have the decency to stay out more than a few minutes at a time. The natural thing, him being only the secondary subject, would have been to kill him outright so we could get on with the real job, but improving our working conditions by that fashion would require an amendment to our contract. Which comes under the heading of Instructions from the Client."

"And it was eleven o'clock," said Mr. Cuff.

"The exact time scheduled for our conference," said Mr. Clubb. "My partner was forced to clobber the fellow into sense-lessness, how many times was it, Mr. Cuff, while I prayed for our client to do us the grace of answering his phone during twenty rings?"

"Three times, Mr. Clubb, three times exactly," said Mr. Cuff. "The blow each time more powerful than the last, which combining with his having a skull made of granite led to a painful swelling of my hand."

"The dilemma stared us in the face," said Mr. Clubb. "Client unreachable. Impeded in the performance of our duties. State of mind, very foul. In such a pickle, we could do naught but obey the instructions given us by our hearts. *Remove the gentleman's head,* I told my partner, *and take care not to be bitten once it's off.* Mr. Cuff took up an ax. Some haste was called for, the fellow just beginning to stir again. Mr. Cuff moved into position. Then from the bed, where all had been lovely silence but for soft moans and whimpers, we hear a god-awful yowling ruckus of the most desperate and importunate protest. It was a sort to melt the heart, sir. Were we not experienced professionals who enjoy pride in our work, I believe we might have been persuaded almost to grant the fellow mercy, despite his being a pest of the first water. But now those heart-melting screeches reach the ears of the pest and rouse him into movement just at the moment Mr. Cuff lowers the boom, so to speak."

"Which was an unfortunate bit of business," said Mr. Cuff. "Causing me to catch him in the shoulder, causing him to rear up, causing me to lose my footing what with all the blood on the floor, then causing a tussle for possession of the ax and myself suffering several kicks to the breadbasket. I'll tell you, sir, we did a good piece of work when we took off his hand, for without the nuisance of a stump really being useful only for leverage, there's no telling what that fellow might have done. As it was, I had the devil's own time getting the ax free and clear, and once I had done, any chance of making a neat, clean job of it was long gone. It was a slaughter and an act of butchery with not a bit of finesse or sophistication to it, and I have to tell you, such a thing is both an embarrassment and an outrage to men like ourselves. Turning a subject into hamburger by means of an ax is a violation of all our training, and it is not why we went into this business."

"No, of course not, you are more like artists than I had imagined," I said. "But in spite of your embarrassment, I suppose you went back to work on . . . on the female subject."

"We are not *like* artists," said Mr. Clubb, "we *are* artists, and we know how to set our feelings aside and address our chosen medium of expression with a pure and patient attention. In spite of which we discovered the final and insurmountable frustration of the evening, and that discovery put paid to all our hopes."

"If you discovered that Marguerite had escaped," I said, "I believe I might almost, after all you have said, be—"

Glowering, Mr. Clubb held up his hand. "I beg you not to insult us, sir, as we have endured enough misery for one day. The subject had escaped, all right, but not in the simple sense of your meaning. She had escaped for all eternity, in the sense that her soul had taken leave of her body, and flown to those realms at whose nature we can only make our poor, ignorant guesses."

"She died?" I asked. "In other words, in direct contradiction of my instructions, you two fools killed her. You love to talk about your expertise, but you went too far, and she died at your hands. I want you incompetents to leave my house immediately. Begone. Depart. This minute."

Mr. Clubb and Mr. Cuff looked into each other's eyes, and in that moment of private communication I saw an encompassing and universal sorrow which utterly turned the tables on me: before I was made to understand how it was possible, I saw that the only fool present was myself. And yet the sorrow included all three of us, and more besides.

"The subject died, but we did not kill her," said Mr. Clubb. "We did not go, nor have we ever gone, too far. The subject chose to die. The subject's death was an act of suicidal will. Can you hear me? While you are listening, sir, is it possible, sir, for you to open your ears and hear what I am saying? She who might have been in all of our long experience the noblest, most courageous subject we ever will have the good fortune to be given witnessed the clumsy murder of her lover and decided to surrender her life."

"Quick as a shot," said Mr. Cuff. "The simple truth, sir, is that otherwise we could have kept her alive for about a year."

"And it would have been a rare privilege to do so," said Mr. Clubb. "It is time for you to face facts, sir."

"I am facing them about as well as one could," I said. "Please tell me where you disposed of the bodies."

"Within the house," said Mr. Clubb. Before I could protest, he said, "Under the wretched circumstances, sir, including the continuing unavailability of the client and the enormity of the personal and professional letdown felt by my partner and myself, we saw no choice but to dispose of the house along with the telltale remains."

"Dispose of Green Chimneys?" I said, aghast. "How could you dispose of Green Chimneys?"

"Reluctantly, sir," said Mr. Clubb. "With heavy hearts and an equal anger. With also the same degree of professional unhappiness experienced previous. In workaday terms, by means of combustion. Fire, sir, is a substance like shock and salt water, a healer and a cleanser, though more drastic."

"But Green Chimneys has not been healed," I said. "Nor has my wife."

"You are a man of wit, sir, and have provided Mr. Cuff and myself many moments of precious amusement. True, Green Chimneys has not been healed, but cleansed it has been, root and branch. And you hired us to punish your wife, not heal her, and punish her we did, as well as possible under very trying circumstances indeed."

"Which circumstances include our feeling that the job ended before its time," said Mr. Cuff. "Which circumstances is one we cannot bear."

"I regret your disappointment," I said, "but I cannot accept that it was necessary to burn down my magnificent house."

"Twenty, even fifteen years ago, it would not have been," said Mr. Clubb. "Nowadays, however, that contemptible alchemy known as Police Science has fattened itself up into such a gross and distorted breed of sorcery that a single drop of blood can be detected even after you scrub and scour until your arms hurt. It has reached the hideous point that if a constable without a thing in his head but the desire to imprison honest fellows employed in an ancient trade finds two hairs at what is supposed to be a crime scene, he waddles along to the laboratory and instantly a loathsome sort of wizard is popping out to tell him that those same two hairs are from the heads of Mr. Clubb and Mr. Cuff, and I exaggerate, I know, sir, but not by much."

"And if they do not have our names, sir," said Mr. Cuff, "which they do not and I pray never will, they ever after have our particulars, to be placed in a great universal file against the day when they *might* have our names, so as to look back into that cruel file and commit the monstrosity of unfairly increasing the charges against us. It is a malignant business, and all sensible precautions must be taken."

"A thousand times I have expressed the conviction," said Mr. Clubb, "that an ancient art ought not be against the law, nor its practitioners described as criminals. Is there even a name for our so-called crime? There is not. GBH they call it, sir, for Grievous Bodily Harm, or, even worse, Assault. We do not Assault. We induce, we instruct, we instill. Properly speaking, these cannot be crimes, and those who do them cannot be criminals. Now I have said it a thousand times and one."

"All right," I said, attempting to speed this appalling conference to its end, "you have described the evening's unhappy events. I appreciate your reasons for burning down my splendid property. You have enjoyed a lavish meal. All remaining is the matter of your remuneration, which demands considerable thought. This night has left me exhausted, and after all your efforts, you, too, must be in need of rest. Communicate with me, please, in a day or two, gentlemen, by whatever means you choose. I wish to be alone with my thoughts. Mr. Moncrieff will show you out."

The maddening barnies met this plea with impassive stares and stoic silence, and I renewed my silent vow to give them nothing—not a penny. For all their pretensions, they had accomplished naught but the death of my wife and the destruction of my country house. Rising to my feet with more difficulty than anticipated, I said, "Thank you for your efforts on my behalf."

Once again, the glance which passed between them implied that I had failed to grasp the essentials of our situation.

"Your thanks are gratefully accepted," said Mr. Cuff, "though, dispute it as you may, they are premature, as you know in your soul. This morning we embarked upon a journey of which we have yet more miles to go. In consequence, we prefer not to leave. Also, setting aside the question of your continuing education, which if we do not address will haunt us all forever, residing here with you for a sensible period out of sight is the best protection from law enforcement we three could ask for."

"No," I said, "I have had enough of your education, and I need no protection from officers of the law. Please, gentlemen, allow me to return to my bed. You may take the rest of the cognac with you as a token of my regard."

"Give it a moment's reflection, sir," said Mr. Clubb. "You have announced the presence of high-grade consultants and introduced these same to staff and clients both. Hours later, your spouse meets her tragic end in a conflagration destroying your upstate manor. On the very same night also occurs the disappearance of your greatest competitor, a person certain to be identified before long by a hotel employee as a fellow not unknown to the late spouse. Can you think it wise to have the high-grade consultants vanish right away?"

I did reflect, then said, "You have a point. It will be best if you continue to make an appearance in the office for a time. However, the proposal that you stay here is ridiculous." A wild hope, utterly irrational in the face of the grisly evidence, came to me in the guise of doubt. "If Green Chimneys has been destroyed by fire, I should have been informed long ago. I am a respected figure in the town of ———, personally acquainted with its chief of police, Wendall Nash. Why has he not called me?"

"Oh, sir, my goodness," said Mr. Clubb, shaking his head and smiling inwardly at my folly, "for many reasons. A small town is a beast slow to move. The available men have been struggling throughout the night to rescue even a jot or tittle portion of your house. They will fail, they have failed already, but the effort will keep them busy past dawn. Wendall Nash will not wish to ruin your night's sleep until he can make a full report." He glanced at his wristwatch. "In fact, if I am not mistaken . . ." He tilted his head, closed his eyes, and raised an index finger. The telephone in the kitchen began to trill.

"He has done it a thousand times, sir," said Mr. Cuff, "and I have yet to see him strike out."

Mr. Moncrieff brought the instrument through from the kitchen, said, "For you, sir," and placed the receiver in my waiting hand. I uttered the conventional greeting, longing to hear the voice of anyone but . . .

"Wendall Nash, sir," came the chief's raspy, high-pitched drawl. "Calling from up here in ———. I hate to tell you this, but I have some awful bad news. Your place Green Chimneys started burning sometime around midnight last night, and every man jack we had got put on the job and the boys worked like dogs to save what they could, but sometimes you can't win no matter what you do. Me personally, I feel terrible about this, but, tell you the truth, I never saw a fire like it. We nearly lost two men, but it looks like they're going to come out of it okay. The rest of our boys are still out there trying to save the few trees you got left."

"Dreadful," I said. "Please permit me to speak to my wife."

A speaking silence followed. "The missus is not with you, sir? You're saying she was inside there?"

"My wife left for Green Chimneys this morning. I spoke to her there in the afternoon. She intended to work in her studio, a separate building at some distance from the house, and it is her custom to sleep in the studio when working late." Saying these things to Wendall Nash, I felt almost as though I were creating an alternative world, another town of ——— and another Green Chimneys, where another Marguerite had busied herself in the studio, and there gone to bed to sleep through the commotion. "Have you checked the studio? You are certain to find her there."

"Well, I have to say we didn't, sir," he said. "The fire took that little building pretty good, too, but the walls are still standing and you can tell what used to be what, furnishing-wise and equipment-wise. If she was inside it, we'd of found her."

"Then she got out in time," I said, and instantly it was the truth: the other Marguerite had escaped the blaze and now stood, numb with shock and wrapped in a blanket, unrecognized amidst the voyeuristic crowd always drawn to disasters.

"It's possible, but she hasn't turned up yet, and we've been talking to everybody at the site. Could she have left with one of the staff?"

"All the help is on vacation," I said. "She was alone."

"Uh-huh," he said. "Can you think of anyone with a serious

grudge against you? Any enemies? Because this was not a natural-type fire, sir. Someone set it, and he knew what he was doing. Anyone come to mind?"

"No," I said. "I have rivals, but no enemies. Check the hospitals and anything else you can think of, Wendall, and I'll be there as soon as I can."

"You can take your time, sir," he said. "I sure hope we find her, and by late this afternoon we'll be able to go through the ashes." He said he would give me a call if anything turned up in the meantime.

"Please, Wendall," I said, and began to cry. Muttering a consolation I did not quite catch, Mr. Moncrieff vanished with the telephone in another matchless display of butler politesse.

"The practice of hoping for what you know you cannot have is a worthy spiritual exercise," said Mr. Clubb. "It brings home the vanity of vanity."

"I beg you, leave me," I said, still crying. "In all decency."

"Decency lays heavy obligations on us all," said Mr. Clubb. "And no job is decently done until it is done completely. Would you care for help in getting back to the bedroom? We are ready to proceed."

I extended a shaky arm, and he assisted me through the corridors. Two cots had been set up in my room, and a neat array of instruments—"staples"—formed two rows across the bottom of the bed. Mr. Clubb and Mr. Cuff positioned my head on the pillows and began to disrobe.

8

Ten hours later, the silent chauffeur aided me in my exit from the limousine and clasped my left arm as I limped toward the uniformed men and official vehicles on the far side of the open gate. Blackened sticks which had been trees protruded from the blasted earth, and the stench of wet ash saturated the air. Wendall Nash separated from the other men, approached, and noted without comment my garb of gray Homburg hat, pearl-gray cashmere topcoat, heavy gloves, woolen charcoal-gray pinstriped suit, sunglasses, and Malacca walking stick. It was the afternoon of a midsummer day in the upper eighties. Then he looked more closely at my face. "Are you, uh, are you sure you're all right, sir?"

"In a manner of speaking," I said, and saw him blink at the oozing gap left in the wake of an incisor. "I slipped at the top of a marble staircase and tumbled down all forty-six steps, resulting in massive bangs and bruises, considerable physical weakness, and the persistent sensation of being uncomfortably cold. No broken bones, at least nothing major." Over his shoulder I stared at four isolated brick towers rising from an immense black hole in the ground, all that remained of Green Chimneys. "Is there news of my wife?"

"I'm afraid, sir, that—" Nash placed a hand on my shoulder, causing me to stifle a sharp outcry. "I'm sorry, sir. Shouldn't you be in the hospital? Did your doctors say you could come all this way?"

"Knowing my feelings in this matter, the doctors insisted I make the journey." Deep within the black cavity, men in bulky orange spacesuits and space helmets were sifting through the sodden ashes, now and then dropping unrecognizable nuggets into heavy bags of the same color. "I gather that you have news for me, Wendall," I said.

"Unhappy news, sir," he said. "The garage went up with the rest of the house, but we found some bits and pieces of your wife's little car. This here was one incredible hot fire, sir, and by hot I mean *hot,* and whoever set it was no garden-variety firebug."

"You found evidence of the automobile," I said. "I assume you also found evidence of the woman who owned it."

"They came across some bone fragments, plus a small portion of a skeleton," he said. "This whole big house came down on her, sir. These boys are experts at their job, and they don't hold out hope for coming across a whole lot more. So if your wife was the only person inside . . ."

"I see, yes, I understand," I said, staying on my feet only with the support of the Malacca cane. "How horrid, how hideous, that it should all be true, that our lives should prove such a *littleness*. . . ."

"I'm sure that's true, sir, and that wife of yours was a, was what I have to call a special kind of person who gave pleasure to us all, and I hope you know that we all wish things could of turned out different, the same as you."

For a moment I imagined that he was talking about her recordings. And then, immediately, I understood that he was laboring to express the pleasure he and the others had taken in what they, no less than Mr. Clubb and Mr. Cuff but much, much more than I, had perceived as her essential character.

"Oh, Wendall," I said into the teeth of my sorrow, "it is not possible, not ever, for things to turn out different."

He refrained from patting my shoulder and sent me back to the rigors of my education.

9

A month—four weeks—thirty days—seven hundred and twenty hours—forty-three thousand, two hundred minutes—two million, five hundred and ninety-two thousand seconds—did I spend under the care of Mr. Clubb and Mr. Cuff, and I believe I proved in the end to be a modestly, moderately, middlingly satisfying subject, a matter in which I take an immodest and immoderate pride. "You are little in comparison to the lady, sir," Mr. Clubb once told me while deep in his ministrations, "but no one could say that you are nothing." I, who had countless times put the lie to the declaration that they should never see me cry, wept tears of gratitude. We ascended through the fifteen stages known to the novice, the journeyman's further five, and passed, with the frequent repetitions and backward glances appropriate for the slower pupil, into the artist's upper eighty, infinitely expandable by grace of the refinements of his art. We had the little soldiers. We had *dental floss.* During each of those forty-three thousand, two hundred minutes, throughout all two million and nearly six hundred thousand seconds, it was always deepest night. We made our way through perpetual darkness, and the utmost darkness of the utmost night yielded an infinity of textural variation, cold, slick dampness to velvety softness to leaping flame, for it was true that no one could say I was nothing.

Because I was not nothing, I glimpsed the Meaning of Tragedy.

Each Tuesday and Friday of these four sunless weeks, my consultants and guides lovingly bathed and dressed my wounds, arrayed me in my warmest clothes (for I never after ceased to feel the blast of arctic wind against my flesh), and escorted me to my office, where I was presumed much reduced by grief as well as certain household accidents attributed to grief.

On the first of these Tuesdays, a flushed-looking Mrs. Rampage offered her consolations and presented me with the morning newspapers, an inch-thick pile of faxes, two inches of legal documents, and a tray filled with official-looking letters. The newspapers described the fire and eulogized Marguerite; the increasingly threatening faxes declared Chartwell, Munster, and Stout's intention to ruin me professionally and personally in the face of my continuing refusal to return the accompanying documents along with all records having reference to their client; the documents were those in question; the letters, produced by the various legal firms representing all my other cryptic gentlemen, deplored the (unspecified) circumstances necessitating their clients' universal desire for change in re financial management. These lawyers also desired all relevant records, discs, et cetera, et cetera, urgently. Mr. Clubb and Mr. Cuff roistered behind their screen. I signed the documents in a shaky hand and requested Mrs. Rampage to have these delivered with the desired records to Chartwell, Munster, and Stout. "And dispatch all these other records too," I said, handing her the letters. "I am now going in for my lunch."

Tottering toward the executive dining room, now and then I glanced into smoke-filled offices to observe my much-altered underlings. Some of them appeared, after a fashion, to be working. Several were reading paperback novels, which might be construed as work of a kind. One of the Captain's assistants was unsuccessfully lofting paper airplanes toward his wastepaper basket. Gilligan's secretary lay asleep on her office couch, and a records clerk lay sleeping on the file-room floor. In the dining room, Charlie-Charlie Rackett hurried forward to assist me to my accustomed chair. Gilligan and the Captain gave me sullen looks from their usual lunchtime station, an unaccustomed bottle of Scotch whiskey between them. Charlie-Charlie lowered me into my seat and said, "Terrible news about your wife, sir."

"More terrible than you know," I said.

Gilligan took a gulp of whiskey and displayed his middle finger, I gathered to me rather than Charlie-Charlie.

"Afternoonish," I said.

"Very much so, sir," said Charlie-Charlie, and bent closer to the brim of the Homburg and my ear. "About that little request you made the other day. The right men aren't nearly so easy to find as they used to be, sir, but I'm still on the job."

My laughter startled him. "No squab today, Charlie-Charlie. Just bring me a bowl of tomato soup."

I had partaken of no more than two or three delicious mouthfuls when Gilligan lurched up beside me. "Look here," he said, "it's too bad about your wife and everything, I really mean it, honest, but that drunken act you put on in my office cost me my biggest client, not to forget that you took his girlfriend home with you."

"In that case," I said, "I have no further need of your services. Pack your things and be out of here by three o'clock."

He listed to one side and straightened himself up. "You can't mean that."

"I can and do," I said. "Your part in the grand design at work in the universe no longer has any connection with my own."

"You must be as crazy as you look," he said, and unsteadily departed.

I returned to my office and gently lowered myself into my seat. After I had removed my gloves and accomplished some minor repair work to the tips of my fingers with the tape and gauze pads thoughtfully inserted by the detectives into the pockets of my coat, I slowly drew the left glove over my fingers and became aware of feminine giggles amidst the coarser sounds of male amusement behind the screen. I coughed into the glove and heard a tiny shriek. Soon, though not immediately, a blushing Mrs. Rampage emerged from cover, patting her hair and adjusting her skirt. "Sir, I'm so sorry, I didn't expect . . ." She was staring at my right hand, which had not as yet been inserted into its glove.

"Lawn-mower accident," I said. "Mr. Gilligan has been released, and I should like you to prepare the necessary papers. Also, I want to see all of our operating figures for the past year, as significant changes have been dictated by the grand design at work in the universe."

Mrs. Rampage flew from the room, and for the next several hours, as for nearly every remaining hour I spent at my desk on the Tuesdays and Thursdays thereafter, I addressed with a carefree spirit the details involved in shrinking the staff to the smallest number possible and turning the entire business over to the Captain. Graham Leeson's abrupt disappearance greatly occupied the newspapers, and when not occupied as described I read that my archrival and competitor had been a notorious Don Juan, i.e., a compulsive womanizer, a flaw in his otherwise immaculate character held by some to have played a substantive role in his sudden absence. As Mr. Clubb had predicted, a clerk at the ———— Hotel revealed Leeson's sessions with my late wife, and for a time professional and amateur gossipmongers alike speculated that he had caused the disastrous fire. This came to nothing. Before the month had ended, Leeson sightings were reported in Monaco, the Swiss Alps, and Argentina, locations accommodating to sportsmen—after four years of varsity football at the University of Southern California, Leeson had won an Olympic silver medal in weight lifting while earning his MBA at Wharton.

In the limousine at the end of each day, Mr. Clubb and Mr. Cuff braced me in happy anticipation of the lessons to come as we sped back through illusory sunlight toward the real darkness.

10   The Meaning of Tragedy

Everything, from the designs of the laughing gods down to the lowliest cells in the human digestive tract, is changing all the time, every particle of being large and small is eternally in motion, but this simple truism, so transparent on its surface, evokes immediate headache and stupefaction when applied to itself, not unlike the sentence "Every word that comes out of my mouth is a bald-faced lie." The gods are ever laughing while we are always clutching our heads and looking for a soft place to lie down, and what I glimpsed in my momentary glimpses of the meaning of tragedy preceding, during, and after the experience of *dental floss* was so composed of paradox that I can state it only in cloud or vapor form, as:

The meaning of tragedy is: *All is in order, all is in train.*
The meaning of tragedy is: *It only hurts for a little while.*
The meaning of tragedy is: *Change is the first law of life.*

11

So it took place that one day their task was done, their lives and mine were to move forward into separate areas of the grand design, and all that was left before preparing my own departure was to stand, bundled up against the nonexistent arctic wind, on the bottom step and wave farewell with my remaining hand while shedding buckets and bathtubs of tears with my remaining eye. Chaplinesque in their black suits and bowlers, Mr. Clubb and Mr. Cuff ambled cheerily toward the glittering avenue and my bank, where arrangements had been made for the transfer into their hands of all but a small portion of my private fortune by my private banker, virtually his final act in that capacity. At the distant corner, Mr. Clubb and Mr. Cuff, by then only tiny figures blurred by my tears, turned, ostensibly to bid farewell, actually, as I knew, to watch as I mounted my steps and went back within the house, and with a salute I honored this last painful agreement between us.

A more pronounced version of the office's metamorphosis had taken place inside my town house, but with the relative ease practice gives even to one whose step is halting, whose progress is interrupted by frequent pauses for breath and the passing of certain shooting pains, I skirted the mounds of rubble, the dangerous loose tiles and more dangerous open holes in the floor, the regions submerged underwater, and toiled up the resilient staircase, moved with infinite care across the boards bridging the former landing, and made my way into the former kitchen, where broken pipes and limp wires protruding from the lathe marked the sites of those appliances rendered pointless by the gradual disappearance of the household staff. (In a voice choked with feeling, Mr. Moncrieff, Reggie Moncrieff, Reggie, the last to go, had informed me that his last month in my service had been "as fine as my days with the duke, sir, every bit as noble as ever it was with that excellent old gentleman.") The remaining cupboard yielded a flagon of genever, a tumbler, and a Montecristo torpedo, and with the tumbler filled and the cigar alight I hobbled through the devastated corridors toward my bed, there to gather my strength for the ardors of the coming day.

In good time, I arose to observe the final appointments of the life soon to be abandoned. It is possible to do up one's shoelaces and knot one's necktie as neatly with a single hand as with two, and shirt buttons eventually become a breeze. Into my traveling bag I folded a few modest essentials atop the flagon and the cigar box, and into a pad of shirts nestled the black Lucite cube prepared at my request by my instructor-guides and containing, mingled with the ashes of the satchel and its contents, the few bony nuggets rescued from Green Chimneys. The traveling bag accompanied me first to my lawyer's office, where I signed papers making over the wreckage of the town house to the European gentleman who had purchased it sight unseen as a "fixer-upper" for a fraction of its (considerably reduced) value. Next I visited the melancholy banker and withdrew the pittance remaining in my accounts. And then, glad of heart and free of all unnecessary encumbrance, I took my place in the sidewalk queue to await transportation by means of a kindly kneeling bus to the great terminus where I should employ the ticket reassuringly lodged within my breast pocket.

Long before the arrival of the bus, a handsome limousine crawled past in the traffic, and glancing idly within, I observed Mr. Chester Montfort d'M—— smoothing the air with a languid gesture while in conversation with the two stout, bowler-hatted men on his either side. Soon, doubtless, he would begin his instructions in the whopbopaloobop.

12

What is a pittance in a great city may be a modest fortune in a hamlet, and a returned prodigal might be welcomed far in excess of his true deserts. I entered New Covenant quietly, unobtrusively, with the humility of a new convert uncertain of his station, inwardly rejoicing to see all unchanged from the days of my youth. When I purchased a dignified but unshowy house on Scripture Street, I announced only that I had known the village in my childhood, had traveled far, and now in my retirement wished no more than to immerse myself in the life of the community, exercising my skills only inasmuch as they might be requested of an elderly invalid. How well the aged invalid had known the village, how far and to what end had he traveled, and the nature of his skills remained unspecified. Had I not attended daily services at the Temple, the rest of my days might have passed in pleasant anonymity and frequent perusals of a little book I had obtained at the terminus, for while my surname was so deeply of New Covenant that it could be read on a dozen headstones in the Temple graveyard, I had fled so early in life and so long ago that my individual identity had been entirely forgotten. New Covenant is curious—intensely curious—but it does not wish to pry. One fact and one only led to the metaphoric slaughter of the fatted calf and the prodigal's elevation. On the day when, some five or six months after his installation on Scripture Street, the afflicted newcomer's faithful Temple attendance was rewarded with an invitation to read the Lesson for the Day, Matthew 5:43–48, seated amidst numerous offspring and offspring's offspring in the barnie-pews for the first time since an unhappy tumble from a hayloft was Delbert Mudge.

My old classmate had weathered into a white-haired, sturdy replica of his own grandfather, and although his hips still gave him considerable difficulty his mind had suffered no comparable stiffening. Delbert knew my name as well as his own, and though he could not connect it to the wizened old party counseling him from the lectern to embrace his enemies, the old party's face and voice so clearly evoked the deceased lawyer who had been my father that he recognized me before I had spoken the whole of the initial verse. The grand design once again could be seen at its mysterious work: unknown to me, my entirely selfish efforts on behalf of Charlie-Charlie Rackett, my representation to his parole board and his subsequent hiring as my spy, had been noted by all of the barnie-world. I, a child of Scripture Street, had become a hero to generations of barnies! After hugging me at the conclusion of the fateful service, Delbert Mudge implored my assistance in the resolution of a fiscal imbroglio which threatened his family's cohesion. I, of course, assented, with the condition that my services should be free of charge. The Mudge imbroglio proved elementary, and soon I was performing similar services for other barnie clans. After listening to a half-dozen accounts of my miracles while setting broken barnie-bones, New Covenant's physician visited my Scripture Street habitation under cover of night, was prescribed the solution to his uncomplicated problem, and sang my praises to his fellow townies. Within a year, by which time all New Covenant had become aware of my "tragedy" and consequent "reawakening," I was managing the Temple's funds as well as those of barn and town. Three years later, our reverend having in his ninety-first year, as the Racketts and Mudges put it, "woke up dead," I submitted by popular acclaim to appointment in his place.

Daily, I assume the honored place assigned me. Ceremonious vestments assure that my patchwork scars remain unseen. The Lucite box and its relics are interred deep within the sacred ground beneath the Temple where I must one day join my predecessors— some bony fragments of Graham Leeson reside there, too, mingled with Marguerite's more numerous specks and nuggets. Eye patch elegantly in place, I lean forward upon the Malacca cane, and while flourishing the stump of my right hand as if in demonstration, with my ruined tongue whisper what I know none shall understand, the homily beginning, *It only* . . . To this I append in silent exhalation the two words concluding that little book brought to my attention by an agreeable murderer and purchased at the great grand station long ago, these: *Ah, humanity!*